BROKEN DREAMS

LINDSAY MCKENNA

Blue Turtle Publishing

Praise for Lindsay McKenna

"A treasure of a book . . . highly recommended reading that everyone will enjoy and learn from."

—Chief Michael Jaco, US Navy SEAL, retired, on Breaking Point

"Readers will root for this complex heroine, scarred both inside and out, and hope she finds peace with her steadfast and loving hero. Rife with realistic conflict and spiced with danger, this is a worthy page-turner."

—BookPage.com on Taking Fire
March 2015 Top Pick in Romance

". . . is fast-paced romantic suspense that renders a beautiful love story, start to finish. McKenna's writing is flawless, and her story line fully absorbing. More, please."

—Annalisa Pesek, Library Journal on Taking Fire

"Ms. McKenna masterfully blends the two different paces to convey a beautiful saga about love, trust, patience and having faith in each other."

—Fresh Fiction on Never Surrender

"Genuine and moving, this romantic story set in the complex world of military ops grabs at the heart."

—RT Book Reviews on Risk Taker

"McKenna does a beautiful job of illustrating difficult topics through the development of well-formed, sympathetic characters."

—Publisher's Weekly (starred review) on Wolf Haven
One of the Best Books of 2014, Publisher's Weekly

"McKenna delivers a story that is raw and heartfelt. The relationship between Kell and Leah is both passionate and tender. Kell is the hero every woman wants, and McKenna employs skill and s empathy to craft a physically and emotionally abused character in Leah. Using tension and steady pacing, McKenna is adept at expressing growing, tender love in the midst of high stakes danger."

—RT Book Reviews on Taking Fire

"Her military background lends authenticity to this outstanding tale, and readers will fall in love with the upstanding hero and his fierce determination to save the woman he loves.

—Publishers Weekly (starred review) on Never Surrender
One of the Best Books of 2014, Publisher's Weekly

"Readers will find this addition to the Shadow Warriors series full of intensity and action-packed romance. There is great chemistry between the characters and tremendous realism, making Breaking Point a great read."

—RT Book Reviews

"This sequel to Risk Taker is an action-packed, compelling story, and the sizzling chemistry between Ethan and Sarah makes this a good read."

—RT Book Reviews on Degree of Risk

"McKenna elicits tears, laughter, fist-pumping triumph, and most all, a desire for the next tale in this powerful series."

—Publishers Weekly (starred review) on Running Fire

"McKenna's military experience shines through i this moving tail . . . McKenna (High Country Rebel) skillfully takes readers on an emotional journey into modern warfare and two people's hearts."

—Publisher's Weekly on Down Range

Also available from Lindsay McKenna

Blue Turtle Publishing

DELOS

Last Chance, prologue novella to Nowhere to Hide
Nowhere To Hide, Book 1
Tangled Pursuit, Book 2
Forged in Fire, Book 3

2016

Broken Dreams, Book 4
Cowboy Justice Bundle/Blind Sided, Bundle 2, novella
Secret Dream, 1B novella, epilogue to Nowhere to Hide
Unbound Pursuit, 2B novella, epilogue to Tangled Pursuit
Dog Tags for Christmas Bundle/Snowflake's Gift, Bundle 3, novella

2017

Never Enough, 3B, novella, epilogue to Forged in Fire
Dream of Me novella, epilogue to Broken Dreams
Hold On, Book 5

Harlequin/HQN/Harlequin Romantic Suspense

SHADOW WARRIORS

Danger Close
Down Range
Risk Taker
Degree of Risk
Breaking Point
Never Surrender
Zone of Fire
Taking Fire
On Fire
Running Fire

THE WYOMING SERIES

Shadows From The Past

Deadly Identity

Deadly Silence

The Last Cowboy

The Wrangler

The Defender

The Loner

High Country Rebel

Wolf Haven

Night Hawk

Out Rider

WIND RIVER VALLEY SERIES, Kensington

2016

Wind River Wrangler

2017

Wind River Rancher

Wind River Cowboy

This edition published by arrangement with Blue Turtle Publishing

www.lindsaymckenna.com

Dear Reader,

Welcome to the Delos Series! Broken Dreams is Book 4 of the series. I spent five years creating this saga-series. Readers who are familiar with Morgan's Mercenaries (45 books strong) know that I wrote about a military family. This started back in the 1990's. You and I fell in love with the Trayhern Family. It was the right tone for the tenor of the times.

Today, we're global. Those who have Internet can be halfway around the world in the blink of an eye. There are no longer the boundaries we've known before. We are a huge melting pot of humanity, warts and all. I wanted to create a global family this time that reflects the world we live in. With this in mind, I created three families from three different parts of the world who hold all life sacred and important.

The Culver family is from Alexandria, Virginia. The Kemel family is from Kusadasi, Turkey. The Mykonos family is from Athens, Greece. And like today, family members meet, fall in love and marry a partner from another country. There is a mixing of blood, experience, knowledge, philosophies and an emphasis on what is important to each of them.

The three families have grown children who are a combination of American, Turkish and Greek bloodlines. And although their lineage is far flung, all three families believe in giving back to those who have less. The Kemel family formed the Delos charities in 1950. In 1990, Dilara Kemel-Badem met and married U.S. Air Force Major Robert Culver. She moved to Alexandria, Virginia and became the president of Delos charities. They raised three children: Talia (Tal), the oldest daughter and twins, Matt and Alexa.

In Book 1, Nowhere to Hide, is the story of Lia Cassidy, a volunteer to the school in La Fortuna. You will be on the ground floor of seeing how Artemis came into being. And how ex-SEAL, Cav Jordan, assigned to protect Lia as they rebuild the burned down school, falls in love with this valiant, brave young woman.

Book 2, Tangled Pursuit, you will meet Captain Tal Culver, U.S. Marine Corps. She has nearly nine years in the Corps. A natural leader, she is the assistant commanding officer for one of two sniper units out of Bagram, Afghanistan. She will become CEO of Artemis. U.S. Navy SEAL Chief Wyatt Lockwood, a brazen Texan who has had his eye on Tal for three years, decides it's time to get this woman of his (even though Tal doesn't know it yet), to give him a chance to catch and keep her.

Book 3, Forged in Fire, you will meet Delta Force Army Sergeant Matt Culver. He's been in the Army since eighteen and is a kidnapping and ransom (KNR) specialist out of Bagram, Afghanistan. Matt's enlistment is up in four months. During a holiday program over Thanksgiving at the base, he meets Dr. Dara McKinley, a pediatrician who volunteers her time at a charity in Kabul.

They are on a collision course with one another. Matt will later become the director of KNR at Artemis.

Book 4, Broken Dreams, you will meet U.S. Air Force Captain Alexa Culver. She's an A-10 combat jet pilot, risking her life over six tours in Afghanistan. Unexpectedly she meets Gage Hunter, a quiet Marine Corps sniper who is a good friend of her brother, Matt. She finds herself helplessly drawn to the West Virginian with a soft drawl. Little do they realize when they go out to an Afghan village to give medical help to children, their lives will change forever.

FREE EBOOK!

Good news for my readers! *Last Chance* is a free eBook available to all of you that begins the Delos Series! Lia Cassidy, the heroine is an employee of the Delos charities and this book is the prologue to *Nowhere to Hide.* The free novella is 14,000 words long and sets up the premise of the saga-series for the reader. Last Chance is available at Amazon, iBooks, Kobo or my bookstore at lindsaymckenna.selz.com.

After you meet the Culver family and get to know them, their stories, and the people they fall deeply in love with, I will then be writing about the missions. These ops will come out of Delos charities that have need of protection from some faction in their country. Tal, Matt and Alexa, with a team of two hundred of the best security people in the world, will take the info and create a mission plan. One security contractor might be needed. It could be a man or a woman. Or two might be needed. The stories are fresh, intensely romantic, and heart pounding. You won't be able to stop reading!

Let me hear from you about the Culver Family and the Delos series. Happy reading!

Dedication

To J.M. Madden, my Indie author-sister who has more than helped me get grounded into my new career as an Indie author. Thank you. Check out J.M.'s books at her website jmmadden.com.

CHAPTER 1

GAGE HUNTER HAD to admit it—he was exhausted. Sitting on a bench in the Marine Corps's Force Recon unit locker room, he put a little more oil on the cloth and finished cleaning his rifle. After completing a successful HVT—high-value target—mission, he'd been picked up last night by a Night Stalker MH-47 on the side of a mountain. Once back at the base, he'd fallen into bed at the Recon HQ barracks for his first night's sleep in three weeks.

Usually, Gage bounced back after a mission, but for some reason he felt wiped out this time. He should have been celebrating his kill—after all, it was the twentieth HVT he'd taken out in Afghanistan during his five rotations here.

He rose and carried the rifle over to the nearby weapon's locker, carefully stowing it away. It was now 1400 and his stomach growled, reminding him that he hadn't eaten since breakfast at the chow hall, when he'd hungrily shoveled down a real meal of ham and eggs. While on assignment, he usually lost between ten and twenty pounds, depending on the length of the mission. Unfortunately, HVTs didn't exactly come over the border whenever he wanted them to.

His spotter, Sergeant Craig Wilson, was gone for a month. He'd earned himself a thirty-day leave, and he'd headed home to his wife and family. Gage envied him. It was mid-January, and here in Afghanistan, snow was falling in the Hindu Kush mountains. Gage knew his life as a sniper was now pretty much curtailed, except for special ops missions with the SEALs or Delta Force. Those guys moved all the time, even in winter, ignoring the ass-freezing cold and deep snows that usually attacked this beleaguered country. Gage liked working with black ops groups, and reciprocally, Marine snipers were heartily welcomed on SEAL DAs—direct action missions—regardless of the weather.

Pushing his hand through his unruly black hair, he closed the door to his weapons locker and locked it. Yeah, he knew he needed to get his hair cut soon and neatly trim the scraggly three weeks' growth of beard. He knew he'd soon have to listen to his captain growl, "Look like a Marine, damn it, not like an Afghan."

Gage had four weeks of downtime here at Bagram, and now he had to fit into the drawdown and start wearing his Marine Corps gear again. When he was on an op, he looked more like a sun-darkened Afghan than a Marine, and he hated returning to the base to become a spit-polished Marine once more.

On the plus side, his captain, Troy Donner, tended to give him some leeway. Snipers were force multipliers. A single man could go out with his rifle and disrupt ten to twenty times the enemy, scattering them, causing confusion, and breaking down authority in the ranks. In a firefight, snipers were *always* desired just for that reason. They were the cream of the crop, and Gage was often given an exception to the Corps' rules because of his status and importance as a sniper. They were the rock gods of the ground forces—looked up to, respected, and always a welcomed addition to a squad, platoon, or company operating in the badlands of this country.

Rubbing his beard, Gage decided to go over to the base barber after a late lunch of cold beer and pizza. Sure, it was the dead of winter, but cold beer tasted great anytime, and after being out on a three-week op, he looked forward to drinking a mug or two. Besides, he was sure his fellow snipers were hanging out in one of the many canteens on Bagram, making up for lost time.

He grinned as he thought of his group. They were all close to each other, like brothers who got along really well. Only Gage kept himself on the perimeter of their fraternity, and some of his friends called him a loner. Well, he was—sort of.

Leaning down, he opened his clothes locker and came face-to-face with the three photos he'd taped to the inside of the door. As he took in his family staring back at him, he again felt the emptiness of loss.

The first photo showed him and his younger sister, Jen standing together on the front porch of their Chicago row house. A surge of love overwhelmed him as he stood staring at his blond sister with her huge blue eyes, her arm around his waist, looking as if she were having the time of her life. Gage had thrown his arm around his sister's small shoulders, and they were both grinning up at their ex-Marine father, Gib, who'd taken the photo.

Jenny had been eleven then, and he'd been thirteen. It was the first day of school on that hot, humid late-August morning. Both of them were eager to check it out, but neither suspected this would count as one of the happiest days of their lives.

God, it hurt to look at these photos now. Gage had lost so much since they were taken that he stubbornly clung to them. How could he not? They were all he had left of his original family.

In the second photo, his mother, Cynthia, whose black hair and blue eyes he had inherited, stood beneath his other arm. She was partially blind but tough and strong. Despite her visual impairment, she still worked from home as a customer service assistant for a national company. She had enough energy to be a loving, caring mom to her kids.

His father, his idol, had just left the Marine Corps a year earlier and was still struggling to adjust to civilian life.

Now Gage regarded the last photo, of him and his dad. Gib Hunter had been a sniper in Iraq, a Marine Corps hero who had earned a Silver Star. At six feet four inches, he was two inches taller than his son, but Gage had inherited his dad's oval face, high-cheek bones, wide-spaced eyes, and strong, well-muscled body, along with his mother's cheerful disposition. At least, he'd always been upbeat . . . until it all came crashing down.

Gage scowled, tearing his gaze from the photos. It would do no good to rehash what had happened. Death was final. He couldn't go back and replay that scenario. His family was gone. Just acknowledging it brought a lump to his throat, and he lowered his eyes, unable to look at their faces another minute.

Closing the locker door gently, he grabbed a pair of jeans, a long-sleeved, dark green shirt bearing the gold Marine Corps symbol, a pair of thick black winter socks, and his motorcycle boots. Dropping down onto the bench, he pulled off his green Marine T-shirt, unlaced his desert combat boots, and pushed them aside. In no time, he was in his civilian clothes.

He grabbed his dark brown, beat-up leather bombardier jacket, his Marine Corps baseball cap, and a green and yellow *shemagh* that he wrapped around his neck and shoulders.

Who would he see over at the local canteen? He was hoping some of his sniper friends would be there, but you never knew. Gage was just fine sitting by himself sipping a beer in a dark corner, his watchful eyes surveying the rest of the men and the few women in it.

Glancing at the leather watch on his wrist, he saw it was 1420. Time to eat, and hopefully, to put back on some of the weight he'd lost.

★

"HEY! HUNTER! OVER here, buddy."

Gage halted just inside the loud, bustling canteen. In the far corner he saw his friend Matt Culver, a Delta Force operator, waving in his direction. His mood lifted a bit, and he nodded and made his way over. Matt was sitting by himself at a round table with three chairs.

"Hey yourself, Aslan," he greeted his friend, shaking Matt's hand and sitting down opposite him. That was Matt's middle name, and it was Turkish, meaning "lion." In his team, he was known by that name, and it suited him well.

"When did you get in?" Matt asked, waving for a server to come his way.

"Last night."

"Did you freeze your ass off?" Matt grinned as he hefted a glass of beer to his lips.

"Yeah, this time of year, it's a done deal," Gage agreed.

A server came over and Gage ordered a beer.

Matt wiped his lips and set the heavy, cold glass mug down in front of him. "We just got off ours this morning."

"You smell like it, too," Gage observed dryly. Chuckling, Matt looked down at his filthy uniform. There was mud smeared across his trousers and up across his blouse. He'd left his level-four Kevlar vest back at the weapons locker room. "Yeah, I was dying for a beer before I hit the showers." He looked Gage up and down. "You're looking a little on the lean side, my friend."

"Three-week op. Got the bastard, though," Gage replied.

"Good. Are you in for a rest?"

"Yeah, my spotter has a thirty-day leave." He shrugged. "Unless you guys or the SEALs decide to rock it out with a mission, I'm pretty much slumming for the next month until he gets back."

Matt leaned back in his chair, tipping the two front legs off the plywood floor. Music was blaring in the background. The men's voices were nearly as loud as the noise they called music.

"I'm meeting my sister Alexa. She should be showing up any time now," Matt said, looking at his watch. "She was coming off a mission about an hour ago, and her first request was for a pizza. She's a lot like me." He grinned.

The server brought over a mug of beer and Gage paid him. He'd never met Alexa, but he knew their sister, Tal, pretty well. She had run the other sniper unit at Bagram until she turned in her commission last July and left the Corps. Gage had liked Tal. She was a no-nonsense sniper unit CO. He hadn't been in her unit, but he knew everyone respected her. She was deadly behind a sniper rifle.

"I've never met your other sister," Gage said after taking a huge gulp, feeling the cold brew hit his belly.

"You'll know when she comes in," Matt promised, gesturing lazily toward the closed door.

"Oh?"

"Wait and see," he said, gloating. "She's my twin, but I was born five minutes before her, so she's considered the youngest of the family."

Family. Gage felt a twinge of sadness, then nodded. "I didn't know you were twins. Has she got brown and gold streaked hair like you?"

"Nah, she takes after my mother, Dilara, who has red hair. She's got hazel eyes, and I got the gold-brown eyes of my uncle Ihsan."

Gage knew Matt was part Turkish and part American, with a dollop of Greek thrown in. And with Matt's dark brown hair streaked with gold, along with his warm brown eyes, Gage figured his mother must have had a premonition about him before he was born. He did, indeed, resemble a golden lion, if Gage stretched his imagination a little.

"I heard you were home for Christmas," Gage said.

Matt smiled a little. "Yeah. I got engaged to an incredible woman, Dara McKinley. She's a medical doctor. You know her? Last Thanksgiving she and her sister, Callie, did a belly dance here at the USO show for everyone on base."

"Sure, I remember that dance," Gage said. "How could I forget?" He grinned. "Congratulations." He liked Matt a lot but fought back feelings of envy. "You set a date yet?"

"We're working on it. My enlistment is up in March and I'm turning in my Delta Force papers. I'm going home to work with my family at Artemis Security."

"I heard Tal talking about that before she got wounded last June," Gage said, sipping the beer and enjoying the bubbles bursting on his tongue. "You still heading up the Kidnapping and Ransom division once that place comes online?"

"Yeah," Matt said, finishing off the beer. "Ah, here comes our pizza."

Gage turned to see the bartender carrying an aluminum pan with an extra-large steaming pizza on it. His stomach growled. "Were you ordering that for you and your twin?"

"Sure did," Matt said, clearing a place on the table for the pizza. "But jump in. Alexa isn't going to eat that much." His eyes gleamed. "You and I will do some major damage to it by the time she gets here."

Chuckling, Gage nodded. "Let me pick up the cost of the pizza, then."

"Fair enough," Matt said, asking the bartender for a third plate.

The smell was intoxicating. Gage ordered two more beers and paid the bartender for everything. It was the least he could do for Matt. He'd been a good friend for years.

Gage's mouth watered as he looked at the pizza. It was a triple cheese and pepperoni, and Matt was placing a big wedge on his plate. The two men began wolfing down the slices, nearly burning their mouths, but they couldn't have cared less. Gage lost himself in the spicy-sweet taste and aroma of the salt and cheese and saw that Matt was busily attacking the rest, gulping it down as fast as he could.

Suddenly, Gage was aware of a faint, feminine fragrance. As a sniper, his senses were acute, and he picked up the subtle scent of almonds. Where was that coming from?

He lifted his head just in time to see a young woman stop beside their table and put her hands on her hips, grinning at Matt.

"Well! I'd better hurry up and grab some pizza, or it'll be all gone before I can sit down!" She greeted her brother and aimed a warm smile at them both. Gage instantly put down his pizza and stood up, giving her a slight nod of hello.

Matt did the same and then pulled out the chair between himself and Gage. "Hey, Alexa, you got here just in time! Gage and I were taking no prisoners with this pizza. Have a seat."

Gage was mute, however. All he could do was stare. Damn! Alexa Culver was drop-dead gorgeous! Never mind that she wore a shapeless desert-colored flight suit. Her red hair was almost auburn, with gold and burgundy strands mixed into the single braid between her shoulder blades. She was probably around five feet seven inches and maybe one hundred thirty-five pounds. And she was curvy in all the right places. She took off her Air Force garrison cap and stuffed it in a large pocket in the thigh of her flight suit.

Gage's heart started a slow pound of appreciation, and he sat down, surprised. Meanwhile, Alexa sat down and scooted up to the table, grabbing a wedge of pizza.

"Gage," Matt said, "meet my sister Alexa Culver. Alexa, meet one of the best Marine snipers I have the privilege to work with, Gage Hunter."

Alexa turned, smiled, and said, "Nice to meet you, Gage. I'd shake your hand but I've got pizza in both of mine." She laughed, holding his dark gaze.

"Nice to meet you, ma'am," Gage said, drowning in her gold-flecked hazel eyes.

"Oh, please, drop the 'ma'am.'" She smiled and held his gaze. "I'm Matt's sister, so any friend of his is a friend of mine."

Gage liked that idea. "Then it's nice to know you, Alexa."

She gave him a dazzling, genuine smile. "Same here."

Although he'd picked up on the heightened male interest in the room when Alexa arrived, she seemed totally unaware of it. Her full lips closed around the pizza, her eyes blissfully shutting as she savored it.

Gage felt like a shy teenager again, awkward and out of his league, as he stared at her. And then he caught himself, snapped out of it, and resumed eating, but with less gusto. This woman fascinated him. Everything she did, everything she said.

He found he was enjoying watching Alexa eat. The woman ate like she meant it, not like a lot of women who picked through their food, leaving half of it on the plate. At the same time, there was a delicacy to her, from her long, slender fingers to the clean line of her neck. He wondered if it extended to the rest of Alexa's body that was hidden beneath the frumpy flight suit.

He was mesmerized by her mouth, those lips of hers; she didn't wear any lipstick, but she didn't need any. Gage's lower body stirred, reminding him how long it had been since he'd had a relationship. This woman, though, was off-limits. She was his friend's sister, and that was taboo among military men. One did not go after a buddy's sister.

Gage tried to tamp down his interest in Alexa, who was clearly the object of longing, lust, and hunger for the other guys in the room. And why wouldn't she be? She was like a beam of sunlight in the darker places of his soul. He noted with some satisfaction the stabbing looks of jealousy thrown his way by soldiers at the bar, who were staring like wolves at Alexa, the lamb.

But she was no lamb. Gage recalled she was an A-10 Warthog driver—an Air Force combat pilot who took a lot of risks at close range, protecting the ground-pounders below. There was a fifty-caliber machine gun in the nose of her fighter, and Gage had seen A-10 pilots risk their lives time and again with low passes, throwing back Taliban attacks on Marines or Army soldiers who had been trapped.

No, Alexa might have looked like a fresh, beautiful flower, but despite her wholesome appearance, he knew she was a fearless, competitive combat pilot.

This woman was, no doubt about it. She wasn't arrogant or surly or pushing the fact that she was a captain in the Air Force. Nor was she squeamish about marching into a canteen that was 99 percent testosterone.

So what moved her? How could she have this confidence and still not strut around or think she was better than her enlisted counterparts? If anything, Alexa seemed to be humble, like her brother. Maybe it was a family trait.

Gage suddenly had a lot of questions about this gorgeous woman who was joyfully chowing down on her pizza between him and Matt. He could see the resemblance in their faces: the high cheekbones; the wide-set, intelligent eyes; the shape of their mouths and strong chins.

There were tendrils of red hair across her broad brow and around her temples. Her hair was straight and lay on her shoulders. Matt's hair was a little of both. Gage saw her finish the wedge and hold up her greasy fingers, realizing she didn't have a napkin. He quickly pulled his from his plate, handing it to her.

"Here you go," he said. Their fingertips met, and he silently enjoyed the brief touch. It was her eyes, however, that took hold of his heart. She lifted her chin, meeting his gaze, that glistening mouth of hers curving into a sweet smile of thank you.

Gage didn't see a player in her, or a woman who enjoyed manipulating others. He'd run across far too many of them in the past. Finding himself spun into her green and gold eyes, touches of sienna deep within them, he felt his heart widening. It was the most bizarre sensation, and for a moment, he couldn't think of a word to say.

"Thanks, Gage. My own brother is too busy chowing down." She gave Matt a playful look as she wiped off her fingers with the paper napkin.

"Hey," Matt sputtered between bites, "I was paying attention to my pizza! Gimme a break, will you, Alexa?"

"I want the last slice," she told them firmly, giving both of them a warning look. "You guys have already consumed five pieces each."

Gage had the good grace to blush; something he hadn't done in so long, it took him off guard. This woman was making a pretzel out of his mind *and* his body. Even now, he could feel himself straining against his jeans, and he groaned inwardly. That was *not* what he wanted now. Not here. Not with Matt's sister present. If Matt saw it, all hell would rain down. Gage pushed the aluminum tray away from himself. "You got it."

She smiled, gloating at Matt. "Where did you find this guy? He's much more of a gentleman than you are."

Matt grunted and pushed his greasy fingers down his dried-mud-covered trousers. "You know," he told her lazily, "there's a reason why his last name is Hunter, Alexa. He's just being nice because you're a girl."

Alexa burst into laughter and leaned forward, gripping a strand of Matt's hair and tweaking it a bit before releasing it. "You're *such* a bad boy, Culver." She turned to Gage. "How do you put up with this hombre?"

Gage felt the blast of sunlight from Alexa's full attention on him. His whole body reacted. Badly. Groaning, he tried to control his physical reactions to this winsome woman who was smiling at him. He had her full attention, felt it in every cell of his body. "Actually," Gage deadpanned, "he usually puts up with me. I'm not as nice when I'm out on an op."

Matt chuckled. "He got that right, sis. You gotta watch men like Hunter. He's a sniper. He might say very little, but he lets his actions speak for him." Matt shook his finger toward her. "He's a woman-killer."

Alexa's eyes widened and she gave him a thoughtful look. "Really, Gage? Are you?" She hooked her thumb over her shoulder. "My brother here is the devil's advocate in our family. He'll say things that aren't true, just to stir the pot."

A grin edged Gage's mouth as he considered Matt for a moment. "Well, if there's a lady-killer around here, it's him. But I hear he's off the market now. He just told me a pretty doctor's got him hog-tied."

Smirking, Alexa shot her brother a look. "Yes, Dara McKinley is an incredibly beautiful person. Not to mention that she's smart and she's a pediatrician. Matt got very lucky."

"I did," Matt agreed, giving them a serene smile.

Alexa turned her attention to Gage. "Are you always this quiet?"

His brows went up. "Well—"

"He's an introvert, Alexa. Give him a break, will you? Not everyone is Miss Extrovert Sunshine like you, okay?" Matt razzed her.

Laughing, Alexa gave Gage an apologetic look. "Sorry, I didn't mean to embarrass you."

"You like him." Matt gloated, giving her a brotherly nudge on the shoulder. "That's why you're picking on him." He pointed his chin in his sister's direction. "Gage, you need to know how Alexa operates. If she likes you, she picks on you unmercifully. If she's not interested, she'll ignore you."

Gage watched their byplay, both amused and nostalgic. He forced himself to stay in the present.

"Oh, Matt, that isn't true!" Alexa huffed, glaring at him. "You are really full of yourself this afternoon!"

Matt grinned broadly. "I only do it because I love you."

"Phooey." Alexa turned, reaching out, touching Gage's arm for a moment. "Don't listen to him, Gage. Please. I don't ignore anyone. I like people."

Gage felt as if he were caught in a firefight. Both brother and sister were strong personalities, and, frankly, he liked them separately as well as together. He replied, "Matt and I have known one another for over five years. I think I've got his MO down; no worries."

He saw instant relief come to her eyes. "Good," she breathed, then gave her brother a chastening look. "I wouldn't want you to think ill of me, Gage."

His chiseled mouth curved faintly. "Oh, you don't need to worry about that."

"You know, Gage," Matt drawled, leaning back in his chair, "Alexa's not in a relationship right now . . ."

The twins, from Gage's perspective, were loving, feisty, and had a solid, playful connection between them. It was something to behold. Matt clearly enjoyed pinpricking Alexa. But Alexa didn't take any prisoners, either. He didn't know how he knew it, but he'd have put all his money on that.

CHAPTER 2

ALEXA FELT AS if she were on one end of a north-south magnet and Gage Hunter was at the opposite end. The moment she'd walked up to Matt's table and looked down into Gage's deep blue eyes, her whole world had shifted. She couldn't tear her gaze from his when he looked up and saw her standing there with her hands on her hips. She didn't know this friend of her brother's—at least she presumed they were friends. He had an oval-shaped face with high cheekbones; a coal-black, scruffy beard; longish hair; and serious, straight brows.

And Alexa was intrigued, to say the least. In fact, impressions were slamming through her at Mach three with her hair on fire. Gage was tall with broad shoulders and an air of brooding intensity. He could well be a sniper, she decided, and as her gaze moved from his face downward, she saw the hog's-tooth necklace he wore, indicating that he was indeed a graduate of the highly respected Marine Corps sniper school.

No one could wear a hog's tooth unless they got it upon graduation from that tough, world-class military school. She recognized it because her older sister, Tal Culver, had earned one, too.

And then she wondered why she hadn't ever met this guy before, since Tal had run one of the two sniper units at Bagram. Alexa had met all her sister's snipers off and on through those years. Vaguely, she remembered there was a second sniper unit based at Bagram; maybe this guy was a part of that unit.

The look in his eyes was that of a born hunter, for sure, with that intensity all snipers possessed, but there was more, much more to this quiet man, who studied her just as openly as she studied him.

Alexa had always prided herself on being vulnerable, absorbing a lot of energy when she was around people. She knew a lot about astrology, and she knew her moon was in Pisces, an oceangoing pair of fish, which made her super sensitive to her immediate environment. She was always picking up information, hits, on other people if she opened herself up to them. And with this Marine, her internal radar was wide open and receiving so much about him that she almost couldn't keep up with all the information her intuition was sending her.

More than anything, she felt his deep sense of loneliness, coupled with a whole lot of grief. The loneliness actually made her wince, because she felt it like a knife cutting into her fully alive senses. He was not "pretty boy" handsome, but he was so very male and rugged, with such weary eyes that she knew Gage had hit a wall in his life.

And in the midst of all these feelings, Alexa was struck by something else—he had a yearning for her! His expression hadn't changed one iota, but when she connected with his gaze, she also connected with him on a whole other nonverbal level. Alexa was well acquainted with what went on beyond words, and she took seriously her ability to ferret out how another person truly felt toward her, whether good or bad.

In this Marine's case, there was no question that he wanted to learn more about her. In his deep gaze, Alexa found warmth, caring, and something so profound, she had no words to describe it. How crazy was that?

While Matt was right, she was between relationships, Alexa had no intention of starting another one. The timing was all wrong. In March, she would be turning in her officer's commission and leaving the Air Force to work at Artemis Security with Tal and Matt.

Beneath that shaggy hair and unkempt beard, Alexa sensed Gage was a very attractive man. She'd never been drawn to hunks, preferring men with interesting faces that revealed the story of their lives. But she liked Gage's sensual mouth, although his lower lip, slightly tucked inward, showed her that he wasn't happy. There was something about him that made her want to open her arms, slide them around his shoulders, and simply hold him. The desire to do just that was so powerful, that Alexa had to steel herself against actually doing it.

God knew, she was an open book, a toucher, a hugger, someone who lived through her senses. This man's face hid a lot, Alexa could feel that deep down, he'd never want to open up and share his troubles.

Until now, maybe? When Gage looked over at her, she felt her face flush and perceived his attention as a light, tender touch. That was different! Men looked at her with interest, even lust, and she sensed that Gage might feel those things, too, but there was so much more to it than that. And as his eyes lingered for a moment on her parted lips, Alexa swore she could feel him reach out and run his thumb across the lower one.

Funny, the skimming look he gave her was quiet, gentle, and noninvasive. He might have been lusting for her, but he wasn't like the morons at the canteen bar who were literally drooling over her when she walked in. Alexa hated that kind of schoolboy behavior and patently ignored it.

But this man's look? Alexa could feel care, respect, and tenderness each time he connected with her, and that alone made her pulse pound. As a female combat pilot, she was a rarity, and she was on a base where men outnumbered women a hundred to one. Alexa was unimpressed with men staring at her, wanting to screw her and then walk away. She disliked men who couldn't keep their brains above their belt and their balls separate.

But Alexa knew that this man could, and how refreshing that was! She'd found very few like that in her twenty-eight years.

Snapping out of it, Alexa felt momentarily dizzied and blamed stress for her reaction. She'd had a tough morning with her squadron, going out and flying low, keeping a platoon of Army soldiers from being overrun by the Taliban. Her A-10 had taken a number of bullets in the fuselage, and once she'd landed and done a walk-around with her chief mechanic, she'd been shaken. The plane could have crashed if the right bullet had gone into the wrong place on her Warthog. And she could have died in the crash; she had been flying far too low to pull the ejection seat soon enough.

Alexa thought that perhaps her strong response to Gage might be associated to her earlier scare, but this wasn't the first time she'd come close to cashing it all in. Not in her line of business.

But every time it happened, it scared her. She was too young to die. She had a whole lifetime ahead of her. It wasn't that she was afraid of flying. Indeed, she had her Boeing Stearman biplane waiting for her at an airport hanger back in Virginia that she loved to fly when she was home. She had a job at Artemis she could hardly wait to step into so she could work with Tal and Matt.

When Matt had introduced Gage Hunter to her, she'd liked his name, thinking that he did, indeed, gauge people with that scalpel-like gaze of his that missed nothing. And, check, he was a Marine sniper, just like her big sister. Alexa liked his courtly behavior toward her. When he called her "ma'am," she appreciated his respectful address, but it wasn't formality she wanted between them.

Yes, she was an officer. Yes, she knew her responsibilities as an officer. But really, Alexa treated all her enlisted people as a team, not below her in rate or rank. She had always embraced all of humanity as her equals. But Gage had thought he should respect that line in the sand, and she'd wiped it away without a second thought.

As Alexa sat there with the men, she wanted to devote her attention to Gage, because she had a lot of questions for him. She wanted to know everything about him so she could understand her powerful reaction to him. No doubt, he was an alpha male, just a quiet one. Alexa knew what it took for someone to be a Marine Corps sniper. There was a certain kind of personality that fit that career slot. They were quietly competitive, much like Matt and his men in Delta Force.

Snipers were not necessarily considered black ops, but rather were force multipliers used throughout all branches of the military. The fact that Matt not only knew Gage but considered him a friend and had gone on missions with him told her plenty. Her brother was a straight shooter when it came to knowing people and chose his friends carefully. Matt didn't suffer fools, nor did he put up with the assholes on the base, either.

Matt's friends were like him—men of strong moral fiber, values, and tons of courage. Her twin was much like Gage, deceptively quiet. While most would not pin him as type A, he damned well was. Matt's competitiveness showed up in the field and on missions. Otherwise, he tucked it away so no one would guess the depth of his power and drive.

She looked quickly through her lashes toward Gage as she ate her pizza, thinking that he was exactly the same as Matt. Probably a clone, she thought, grinning a little. Where they weren't alike, from what her internal radar was picking up, was that heavy cloak of loneliness and grief that Gage wore around him.

Matt, in comparison, felt light, happy, and whole. Gage did not. Alexa felt a strong communion with anyone who was suffering. It was her nature to reach out and touch them, give them something positive, compared to whatever silent load they carried. She always wanted to bring out a smile in another person. It was just the way she was built, and people loved her for it.

Gage hadn't smiled once. The corners of his mouth were always tucked inward, and he was quiet, rarely speaking but listening a lot. He would say little unless she jabbed him with a question that required an answer. He was like a ghost at the table.

While Alexa rarely opened up to other people, she was completely open with her own family. That was different. She loved them, cared for them, and wanted to always know and be in touch with them in every possible way.

She sensed that Gage Hunter had no close family ties, and intuitively, she felt him standing behind walls of his own making to keep others from knowing . . . something.

Matt had said Gage was an introvert. Well, Alexa was an extrovert, his exact opposite. Matt was an introvert, too, and she began to understand why he and Gage were friends—Birds of a feather and all that.

And when Gage had offered her his napkin to wipe off her greasy fingers, he'd won big points from Alexa. She wasn't surprised, though, because he reminded her of a knight from the era of King Arthur. When Matt had teased her, she'd sensed Gage's desire to help her, and when she'd touched his long, well-shaped fingers and saw his eyes widen slightly—well, that was all the dessert she needed!

Matt's radio beeped, and he grimaced. "Great," he muttered, wiping his hands on his trousers, "HQ wants something."

"Oh, no," Alexa murmured, frowning. She stopped eating her second wedge of pizza, listening to Matt, but couldn't hear the conversation due to the noise in the canteen.

Gage watched his friend's face and knew something was up. Matt had just come in off a mission, so they couldn't be throwing him back out on another one. He glanced over and saw Alexa's profile, her fine, thin brows drawn down, her mouth tight. She was worried, too.

"It's probably a detail on his mission report," he told her, trying to ease her concern.

Alexa turned, confused. "What?"

Gage motioned toward Matt. "He just came off a mission. HQ is probably comparing reports and has questions they need Matt to answer, that's all. I don't think he's going to get called back out on another op, if that's what's worrying you."

Alexa gave him a warm look. "I hope you're right, Gage. Thanks for telling me that."

He nodded, wanting to reach out and graze the soft velvet of her cheek. Instead, he focused on Matt's one-sided conversation. When Matt finally signed off, he shoved the radio back into place on his epaulet on his left shoulder.

"Sorry, boys and girls," he said, rising. "HQ needs some more intel that I didn't put down in my report." He leaned over and kissed Alexa's hair. "See you later, baby girl." Lifting his head, he looked at Gage. "Make sure she gets to her B-hut safely?"

"Sure," Gage agreed with a nod. He could see how many men in this canteen would more than likely follow her, trying to engage her, trying to get her into their beds. Worse, some women walking alone in the evening hours or at night had been mugged and raped. And someone like Alexa, who was so beautiful? Gage thought she needed a bodyguard around the clock. And he was just the man to be one for her right now. Matt was like a brother to him, and he wasn't about to allow Matt's sister to be put in the crosshairs of a rapist.

Matt gripped Alexa's shoulder as he moved past her. "Gage will take good care of you. I don't like you walking around here by yourself."

"Oh, gee, Matt," Alexa protested. "I've only been at this base the last five years. Nothing's happened."

Patting her shoulder, Matt said, "Gage is a good friend. He'll walk you back to your B-hut."

Alexa gripped her brother's hand and squeezed it. "See you later?"

"Yeah, I'll try to make it to the supply depot and help you get those clothes and shoes in boxes tomorrow morning. I haven't forgotten about it."

"Good, don't," she said, giving him a stern look.

Gage nodded good-bye to his friend. He turned, seeing Alexa stand and pull out her dark blue garrison cap and settle it on her head. Immediately, he stood and saw several men moving in her direction.

Alexa saw three soldiers ease from the bar, their eyes on her. She was going to say something when Gage put himself right in front of her, standing there like the bristling, quiet alpha he was.

She stood near his right side and behind him. This wasn't the first time she'd been hit on in a canteen. As an officer, she had the rank, and Alexa was more than prepared to use it, but Gage, as if reading her mind, lifted his hand, opening it toward her.

"Let me handle this?" he asked, giving her a sideward glance.

There was something deadly about his demeanor. Alexa gave a brisk nod and watched him turn away, facing the three enlisted soldiers, who were so drunk they bumped into one another as they approached.

The canteen suddenly quieted, and Alexa felt anger stirring in her. She hated this kind of shit. Always had. And in the past, she'd handled it just fine on her own. But there was something reassuring about Gage as he stood there loosely, his large hands hanging relaxed at his sides, his piercing gaze on the three soldiers.

There would be no fight here today if Alexa had anything to say about it.

"That's close enough," Gage said in a quiet but firm voice.

The three soldiers halted. The red-haired one snorted.

"Get the fuck out of the way, dude. We want to talk to the lady."

"She doesn't want to talk to you," Gage said, his voice low, almost friendly. "Why don't you three go back to the bar and finish off your beers? The lady and I are leaving."

Alexa silently cheered Gage on for his diplomacy. She liked that he didn't get threatening, all huff and puff. The confusion in two of the three soldiers' expressions told her Gage had made contact. The red-haired one, however, wasn't having it. He was drunk enough, stupid enough, to push harder. And Gage stood about five inches taller than the soldier. Alexa knew that when someone was drunk, details like that failed to register.

"You can leave, dude," the red-haired soldier said with a broad wave of his hand. "But she stays. She's *ours*," he sneered, glaring up at Gage.

One corner of Gage's mouth twitched. "What do you say we take this outside and settle it, then, because the lady is with me."

The gauntlet had been thrown down so quietly that Alexa barely heard the veiled threat in Gage's tone. She looked at the rest of the men in the canteen.

They were all leaning forward, straining to hear him speak. Someone behind the bar shut off the music.

Silence.

Dead silence.

Alexa gulped, her gaze shooting from Gage's harsh profile to the soldier, who was barely able to stand, six feet away from him. Before she could step in and say anything, Gage turned, cupped her right elbow, and guided her around where the soldiers stood. His gaze never left the red-haired one until they were past him.

The rest of the men in the canteen stepped aside, allowing them passage to the door. Gage pushed it open, guiding Alexa outside, his hand still firm on her elbow.

Sunlight, bright and blinding, hit Alexa. Gage continued down the wet sidewalk, which had earlier been shoveled clear of snow on both sides. Now, in midafternoon, it was melting on the desert base. The wind was breezy, and Alexa was glad to be near Gage. He was like a mountain preventing the cold air from reaching her.

"I like your style," she told him, looking up at him as she pulled on her aviator sunglasses.

"He was too damned drunk to know up from down," Gage said, shaking his head in disgust.

"I saw him latch on to the hog's tooth you're wearing."

"I was hoping he would."

Once they reached the broad sidewalk that curved along the wet asphalt two-lane street, Gage released her elbow. He didn't want to, but knew he should. Even though he wore civilian clothes, Alexa was in uniform, and her captain's bars were clearly visible on the shoulders of her flight suit. He checked his stride for her sake, keeping her on the inside of the street. He kept watching Humvees move slowly up and down it.

"I could have handled that confrontation, Gage."

"I know you could." He shot a glance down at her. "And I can just hear you asking why I didn't let you do it."

Her lips curved. "You're good, I'll give you that."

A slow grin appeared. "Hey, I promised your brother that I'd take care of you after he left. My word is my bond."

A good, clean feeling flowed through Alexa. He'd put on a pair of wraparound sunglasses, his baseball cap low on his brow. Gage Hunter was a badass in disguise, and she suddenly grinned.

"Just another thing to like about you." She saw him cock his head in her direction, knowing his gaze was locked on her even if she couldn't see it. "You're a badass," Alexa said, watching his lips twitch. This man did not give a thing away. Why? What made him close up like that?

"The enemy thinks so."

"So did those three idiots in the canteen."

"You had to feel pity for 'em."

Alexa watched white clouds scuttling quickly by. She was cold and wrapped her arms around herself, chiding herself for not bringing along her warm, thick aviator's jacket. Having been in such a hurry, she'd gotten a lift from a Humvee driver directly to the canteen from the fixed-wing terminal, leaving her jacket with her other gear in a locker.

Gage suddenly stopped, and she almost ran into him. He pulled off his leather jacket. "Here," he said, putting it around her shoulders and pulling it almost closed. "You're cold."

Stunned by his kindness, she felt her face heating up. "Thanks," she whispered. "How did you know?"

A quick smile hooked one corner of his mouth. "You put your arms around yourself. You're only wearing a flight suit." He straightened and touched her elbow. "You'll be okay now."

Alexa gratefully pulled together the edges of his huge, warm jacket. She could smell his male scent, dragging it deeply into herself, feeling her whole body respond pleasantly to it.

"But now you'll be cold," she protested.

"I'll be okay."

Snorting, Alexa said, "You're as bad as Matt is."

"How's that?" He reluctantly dropped his fingers from Alexa's elbow. Damn! He liked touching her way too much.

"He always thinks he has to take care of me."

"Isn't that what big brothers are supposed to do?" he teased, catching her pouty expression. He would have loved to kiss that lower lip of hers.

Just a pipe dream, he told himself. Alexa was an officer. Okay, she was free at the moment, with no man in her life, but Gage knew that would change pretty damn fast. A bright, intelligent, beautiful woman like her wouldn't stay off the market long.

"You're so much like Matt it isn't even funny," she grumped, giving him a good-natured look.

"We work together," Gage said. "I really respect your brother. He's solid gold."

"So are you." Alexa wanted to slap her hand against her lips as she blurted out the words and Gage hesitated briefly midstride, then continued walking. But she felt his response, and it was warm with promise. "You could be his twin brother," she teased.

"Unlike you, who *are* his twin?" He studied her for a moment, fighting to keep his hands off her.

"No," she muttered with a laugh, "this is a guy thing. Testosterone. You know?"

"No, I don't. Spell it out for me?" Because Gage did not want to assume a single blessed thing with Alexa, the beautiful redhead who was like a dream come true.

And dreams died on him. Always. The need to kiss Alexa, explore her body, damn near overrode his control. He could smell the enticing scent of almonds on her, and he would have bet that she used almond oil on her hair.

Gage could see how fiery and gleaming her red hair was beneath the sunlight. Alexa had a light sprinkling of freckles across her nose and cheeks, which he now saw since they were outdoors in the light. Her freckles just made her look that much younger.

"My brother, Matt, sees himself as a knight from King Arthur's court. Compared to today's men, he's a throwback. He opens doors for women and actually stands when a woman gets up from a table."

Shrugging, Gage said, "Nothing wrong with that, is there?"

"No, but . . . it's just odd. No other guy does it. Well, except you, now."

"Matt and I were on an op," Gage told her, "and we had some time on our hands. Matt was telling me how much he liked the King Arthur tales. I asked him who his favorite knight was."

"That was Sir Gawain," Alexa said.

"Yeah. We had a good laugh on that one because that's the one I saw myself as."

"I believe that," she said, giving him a soft smile.

"Why do you say that? You barely know me."

If he only knew how much she sensed about him, but Alexa's love of astrology never went over well with a man. She'd learned that from hard experience—a lost relationship many years ago when her boyfriend, Brad, laughed at her ability to pick up energy from other people. It had hurt Alexa's feelings deeply, and she separated from him, because she knew he would never respect her for who she really was.

"It's just a feeling around you," she answered, not providing any more information than that to Gage.

"Oh, women's intuition?"

"I guess that's one way to put it." She saw a faint smile for a moment and liked how it highlighted his strong, sensual mouth.

They came to a crosswalk; there, on the other side, was the women's B-hut area. Navy Seabees had built the four-room plywood houses ten years earlier. Now, four women in four small, cramped bedrooms were all that was left. It was Alexa's home away from home. As they crossed the wet, gleaming street where the snow was continuing to melt away, Alexa said, "What are you doing tomorrow, Gage?"

"Nothing. Just resting up from this last op. Why?"

Alexa moved down the sidewalk to the second row of B-huts. It was so narrow that Gage walked behind her. Five huts down was her hut. Turning at the porch steps, she looked up at him, handing back his leather jacket. "You probably know our mother runs the Delos charity?"

"Yes, Matt's told me a lot about it." Gage pulled on his coat, zipping it up, putting his hands into the pockets so he wouldn't reach out and touch her. She was standing so close now, her head tipped upward toward his.

She took off her aviator glasses, and he enjoyed the green, gold, and sienna in her large, warm eyes. He took off his sunglasses, too, holding them loosely between his fingers.

"I'd love to meet you for breakfast tomorrow morning, Gage. Meet me here at 0700?" She gestured to her B-hut. "Then walk with me over to the Navy supply. My mother sent a huge pallet of winter clothing, boots, and shoes for the kids of a Shinwari village nearby. Matt was going to help me separate everything out in boxes, mark what was in each one, and then get them set up for another pallet to be loaded on a CH-47 helicopter the day after. We're going out to that village day after tomorrow. It's a safe village. Well, as safe as it gets. It's a pro-American village, and I've delivered plenty of food, medicine, and clothing to those folks over the years." She gave him a pleading look. "Would you like to do that? Help us out?"

Gage saw the sincerity burning in Alexa's eyes. What man could tell this woman no? He sure as hell couldn't.

"I'd like that," he said. "I'll drop by here at 0700 tomorrow morning and pick you up."

He saw her face flush, a radiant glow in her eyes, and he swallowed hard, keeping his hands where they were, despite the urge—no, the need—to reach out and touch her. He noticed that her freckles became more pronounced when she flushed.

"Great!" Alexa laughed and stepped forward, throwing her arms around his shoulders, giving him a spontaneous squeeze of thanks. Stepping back, she said, "You really are like Sir Gawain. I'll see you tomorrow morning, Gage . . ."

CHAPTER 3

GAGE TOSSED AND turned all night long in his bunk at the barracks reserved for the sniper units. Alexa had surprised the hell out of him by suddenly throwing her arms around his neck, hugging him tightly, and just as quickly releasing him. And for a sniper who could move at lightning speed, he'd stood still, shell-shocked by her unexpected action. Looking into her hazel eyes, so full of life and hope in their depths, he was deeply moved. It was the first time in a long time.

God, she triggered things buried so deep inside him that he ached, but he had no way of stopping it. His heart was wide open. Wanting. Needing. Dreaming. Everything Gage had ever wanted had been killed, and no longer did he dream, although some nights he had PTSD flashbacks. Everyone on the base got them.

Now Alexa made him want to dream again . . . of falling in love . . . of finding the right woman. Fear rose in Gage, as it always did. He'd learned early on that loving others could get them killed.

Why the hell had Alexa done that? Why did she have to have such a positive view of life? And of him? He was no knight from the Round Table. He took lives in the line of duty and would never be thought of as a savior. After his father was slain, Gage had spun out of control. Gage was supposed to walk Jen home from school to their home. One of his teachers had flagged him down to speak to him as he was leaving to meet his sister. Gage tried to tell his teacher he had to meet Jen, but she said it would only take a minute. When he didn't show up on time, Jen started to walk their Chicago neighborhood streets alone. A gang attacked Jen on the way home from school and killed her. Gage had gone crazy with guilt, grief, and rage. When he found Jen dead in the alley, he'd called his father and then the police. His father had gone berserk, hunting down the gang members, killing two of them before they killed him. In the span of two hours, Gage had lost all but his mother. Two years in juvenile detention had tamed him but not extinguished the murderous desire that simmered inside him. He'd had dreams at least once a month of killing those who had coldly murdered Jen and his father. Two of the killers had survived, and he'd gone to court and had them put away for twenty-five years. That had satisfied some of his need for revenge, but not all of it. Gage had turned to the Marine Corps to somehow make peace with his heartbreaking past, and Marine Corps sniper school was a perfect outlet for all his losses.

Hey, at least here he was killing bad guys who made life hell for the innocent Afghans. That gave him some sense of closure, a small island of peace.

But Alexa. Damn! Being around her made him feel peace, something he'd not felt since he'd lost his family. He lay there in his bunk, his hands behind his head, staring up into the darkness, hearing the snores of his other three roommates nearby. The walls did not keep out any sounds, and normally he could sleep through it but not tonight. Closing his eyes, he envisioned Alexa's soft, open face. He still didn't see the combat pilot in her, although he knew it was there. She doubtless had many layers to her, and Gage was intrigued by her fearlessness as she had pressed against him.

Why had she hugged him? She was so damned beautiful, curvy, all woman. There wasn't a man who didn't want someone like her in his life. People just didn't go out of their way to hug someone else. His heart stirred with pain as he recalled how his mother had always hugged him and Jen.

But hell, she was an officer, and he was enlisted. The two were oil and water in the military—they didn't mix. Alexa had known better, yet disregarded the UCMJ, Uniform Code of Military Justice, curving her arms around his shoulders.

The memory of her sweet body imprinted briefly against his had sent a sheet of fire roaring through him. It had been so long since he'd been in a woman's arms. And she smelled so damned good as she held him tightly for that one moment in time. The light fragrance of almond oil, he had instantly confirmed, was in her red hair as the strands tickled the side of his beard as she embraced him.

Gage suddenly thought of her older sister, Tal, who was completely unlike spontaneous Alexa. Tal was grounded, serious, conservative, and would never be seen doing what her little sister had just done to him. He wondered, did Alexa hug everyone? Or was what she'd done with him special? How Gage wanted it to be special.

But to what end? He knew damn well if he even contemplated a relationship with Alexa, prying eyes would see them together, and male jealousy would probably rear its head. Gage was sure that he'd be turned in to his CO for fraternizing with an officer and then get his ass hung on a court-martial.

And what would it do to Alexa's career? Gage knew she was leaving the Air Force in less than three months, but he was sure she didn't want to leave with a blot on her record.

For him, it would be even worse. If he was found out and court-martialed, he'd be busted in rating and demoted. He'd worked too hard to become a staff sergeant to lose it.

Yes, he was truly fucked now, because he was desperately drawn to Alexa Culver, right or wrong. His body couldn't have cared less that she was an officer, but his head wanted to keep him on the straight and narrow. Unfortunately, his heart weighed in on the side of his brainless lower body. *Two against one. Hell.* Gage wanted Alexa. He wanted to explore what was sizzling between them. And with his body and heart in charge, who knew how long he could hold out?

★

ALEXA TRIED TO still her anticipation at seeing Gage Hunter in a few more minutes. She'd slept deeply last night, dreaming of him, and tried to imagine what he would be like without that shaggy hair and black beard. It had been an enjoyable dream, because despite how he looked, she had undressed him, splayed her hands across his powerful chest, tangled her fingertips in the dusting of hair across it, heard him groan, and felt him respond. She'd awakened this morning with dampness between her thighs.

In all her years of relationships, that had never happened before. As she sat on her bed, quickly putting her long hair into a single braid, she felt excitement over this morning jolt throughout her body. Today she was off duty and could wear civilian clothes, thank goodness. She had sent most of her items home already, prior to leaving the Air Force in another two and a half months. Her winter clothes were all that was left. She chose a dark green turtleneck sweater, which matched the color of her eyes, and jeans. They wore well in the base's dusty and dirty environment.

Normally, Alexa didn't bother with makeup, because she never wore any while flying. But this morning, she'd pulled out her small cosmetic bag and added a touch of moisturizer to her skin, which the desert liked to dry out, and put on some foundation to cover her telltale freckles. Then she'd topped it off with pink lipstick.

Alexa knew it wasn't much, but for her, it was a lot. Getting dressed up at Bagram wasn't high on her list, but she'd do it for Gage Hunter. Wanting to feel feminine because he made her feel that way, she had woven a gold and green satin ribbon into her braid as well. Then she added a pair of small gold hoop earrings her mother had given her for her fourteenth birthday. They were made in Kuşadası, Turkey, where she'd been born.

Her mother, the epitome of fashionable, had taught Alexa how to dress with "quiet elegance," as she called it. A true lady, she had taught Alexa, never boldly flaunts her beauty. Rather, she captures it like a beautiful painting that others can admire and enjoy.

Well, jeans and a turtleneck sweater certainly weren't bold. Alexa stood, holding up her small, round mirror, checking out her face, her braid, and her earrings. She didn't need any blusher because her cheeks were already pinked up with anticipation over seeing Gage again. The man certainly stirred her. Yesterday, he'd handled that scene in the canteen just like the knight she knew he was. He didn't threaten or push his weight or height around. That had impressed Alexa, because she'd had relationships in the past with men who embarrassed her with their Neanderthal tactics. Gage appealed to her womanly senses: her mind, because he was highly intelligent, and her heart, because she felt a living, invisible connection between them.

She grabbed her dark brown nylon winter jacket and shrugged it on. She'd worn her ankle-high, sheepskin-lined boots, because the supply area was cold and unheated. Adding an Afghan *shemagh* of cream and green checks that she'd bought from one of the Shinwari village women, Alexa wrapped it warmly around her neck and shoulders. Last, she pulled a dark green knit cap over her head. Alexa knew that didn't look very sexy, but where they would be working, she'd be glad to be wearing it.

Tucking her military ID into her pocket, she picked up her dark brown leather gloves. Alexa didn't look too closely at why she'd suddenly thrown her arms around Gage yesterday afternoon. He'd looked shocked by her behavior, and she'd briefly considered explaining herself. But hadn't Matt already filled him in on her? Alexa wasn't sure.

She'd see how Gage treated her this morning and where their conversation went with one another. Her heart did a funny flip-flop in her chest, and her pulse ratcheted up as she glanced at her brown leather wristwatch. It was time. Would Gage be out there waiting for her?

Alexa walked quietly out of her tiny bedroom into a hall separating the other women on either side of the unit. She tiptoed down the passage. The B-hut door had no window in it, so she couldn't see if Gage was out there. Pushing it open, she saw him standing down below the steps, hands stuffed in the pockets of his beat-up bomber jacket. He lifted his chin, staring directly at her.

Feeling as if someone had stolen the air from her lungs, Alexa halted, one hand on the door. Gage Hunter was clean-shaven, his black hair now military short beneath his green baseball cap. And God, he was impossibly handsome! Her heart pounded as she gently closed the door so it locked behind her. Turning, she gave him a radiant smile.

"Wow, Gage, you clean up nicely!" She gestured toward his face. And his mouth was to die for! Alexa had known it was well shaped, but now it was a work of art—from a kissing perspective. And he wasn't as rugged looking as she thought he might be. It was his jawline that spoke of his steadiness. His blue eyes were clear, and she saw the corners of his mouth pull up briefly over her whispered words. Alexa didn't want to wake up her friends who were still sleeping.

She moved off the porch and gestured for him to follow her down the walk. Literally, Alexa could feel Gage behind her, shadowing her like the silent ghost he was. She tried to hear him walking in those black leather boots he wore with his jeans, but heard no sound at all. No surprise—snipers were taught how to walk silently so no one could hear them approach. She halted where the small sidewalk flowed into the much wider one along the street. Turning, she smiled up at him.

"Good morning! I didn't want to say much back at the B-hut." She gestured toward the row behind them.

"I understood," he said, nodding. "You look a whole lot different this morning," he added, lifting his hand, touching the green knit cap on her head. "No one would ever guess you're a combat pilot."

She felt her heart lift as she fell beneath his spell. That sizzling, yearning energy throbbed wildly between them, just as it had yesterday when they'd first met. "I like keeping people guessing," she said with a chuckle.

Alexa liked his casual attire today; he wore a bright-red, long-sleeved shirt beneath his leather jacket, his *shemagh* loose around his neck and shoulders.

"You do like keeping people off-balance," he agreed, sliding his hand beneath her elbow, guiding her beside him. "Like yesterday. You took me by surprise when you jumped me and hugged me." He slanted her a warm look, not wanting her to take his words the wrong way. What he saw was a flush coming to her cheeks. Alexa was blushing!

For a moment, she looked away, and then met his gaze. "Didn't Matt warn you?"

"About what? You?" he chuckled. He forced himself to release her elbow and stuffed his hand into his pocket.

"Funny, Hunter."

"Do you jump men you don't really know all the time?" Gage saw the redness in her cheeks deepen, and he felt a little mean pushing her about it.

"You weren't exactly unfamiliar," she said archly. "Matt has known you for five years. Could I help that I didn't meet you until yesterday? I generally know all the guys on his team, as well as his friends here at Bagram." She shook her gloved finger in his face. "You're the one who got away." Her lips curved, her teeth white and even.

Snorting, Gage managed a partial grin as he absorbed her beauty, her lively spirit and soft heart. And she did have one, for sure. "I s'pose that's a fair assessment," he drawled. "But let's go back to jumping on me."

Alexa made a sound of protest in her throat, frowning. "Now, listen, Gage, I don't 'jump' guys, okay? Matt will tell you I'm a hugger and a toucher. Tomorrow at the village you'll see me hugging and kissing those kids all the time."

A kiss would be ideal, Gage thought, keeping it to himself. "So? Why did you do it then, Alexa? Why jump me out on your porch yesterday?"

"Because," she began, opening her hands, "I felt like you needed it. A little TLC, maybe?" She stole a quick look up at him, unsure of how Gage would take the admission. It was the truth, after all.

Gage moved them across the two-lane highway to a chow hall about a quarter of a mile away. He pondered her words. "Was that an 'I feel sorry for you' kind of hug, then?"

"Heck, no! I don't believe in pitying someone. My mother taught us compassion in action. We weren't to feel sorry for someone if we could give them a hug, a hand up, or support of some kind." She held his serious gaze. "We're human, Gage. We're social animals by nature. We all can use a hug from time to time. Don't you think?"

He gave a shrug. "I think you're right. It just caught me unawares, was all."

"I could tell by the look on your face," she said wryly. "If you're going to hang around me, you'll have to get used to the fact that I'm that way. People need hugs. They need to be touched. Held. It's in our nature."

Slowing his stride, he cupped her elbow, guiding her up the long, slightly sloped walk that led to the two-story chow hall. This one could hold two-thousand people, but at this time of morning, there were no lines. Gage dropped his hand, and as they neared the double doors, he opened one for Alexa.

He allowed the door to shut, taking in the fairly quiet chow hall. They got in line after picking up aluminum trays. Gage liked the quiet, preferring that to its usual noise level.

"I don't see Matt here," Alexa said as they stood in line.

"Was he supposed to meet us here?"

Nodding, she slid her tray in front of the cook with all the eggs. "Yes, but he was really tired from coming off that op. He'll probably show up at Supply later this morning."

Gage noted the male cooks giving longing looks in Alexa's direction. She'd taken off her knit cap, stuffing it in the pocket of her jacket, and her hair was mussed, giving her a young, girlish look. He felt protective of Alexa, although he knew she could take care of herself. All it took was a few black glares at the cooks and they quickly got the message that she belonged to him. Let them think what they wanted. Gage led her over to a corner with no windows behind it, finding a vacated area where they could sit together, looking out over the entire place.

"You're just like Matt," Alexa said, smiling, as she sat down with her tray. "Back to the wall, a position where you can see all the entrance/exit points."

Taking off his jacket, he laid it next to where he sat. There was about a foot between himself and Alexa with no one else at the table to overhear their conversation.

"It becomes second nature," Gage agreed. He saw that Alexa was eating heartily two eggs over medium, corned beef hash, and a cup of fruit.

"You're eating for two," Alexa said, grinning.

True enough. He had his tray piled high with scrambled eggs, a dozen pieces of bacon, and four biscuits slathered in gravy, along with a couple of oranges on the side. "I need to gain the weight I lost," he said, digging in.

"Matt always loses weight on long ops too," she said, frowning. "It's a hard life. I'm glad he's leaving Delta Force. We'll have him home, where it's safe."

"He told me he's looking forward to it," Gage agreed. "Are you? Or are you going to miss flying?"

Wrinkling her nose, Alexa said, "I don't think I'll ever give up flying. I own a Boeing Stearman biplane, and I fly it all the time when I'm home. I'm sure I'll be sitting in the cockpit at least a couple times a week when I'm working at Artemis. I need to keep my wings."

"Why?" Gage enjoyed how easy it was to delve into Alexa. He saw no evasiveness, no manipulation. What you saw was what you got. It was so refreshing.

"I've always loved flying. Up there"—she pointed toward the ceiling—"I feel free . . . really free. I love the silence that surrounds me . . . the clouds . . . the changing weather. Everything is on the move around me; nothing is still."

"And that sorta says something about you?" Gage asked, holding her pensive look.

"Yes, I guess it does." She reached out, squeezing his lower arm. "Sure you aren't a psychiatrist in disguise?"

He liked her teasing and shook his head. "High school education is all, Alexa."

"Could have fooled me. You know, schools are terrible. They only set up their lesson plans for one kind of learner, the visual learner. There are actually six different types. There's auditory, visual, tactile, analytic, global, and kinesthetic learners. So the other five types, when they go to school, never learn the way they need to learn, and they get dropped between the slats. If you aren't a visual learner, you're not going to be taught effectively. It usually affects your grades, too. Kids who get left out are often made to think they're stupid or slow or just can't learn, and that's just not true."

Gage nodded. "I'm best at hands-on stuff. I need to hold it, take it apart, and put it back together again. My dad bought me an Erector Set, Lincoln logs, and Legos as a kid, and I played with them for hours every day. I didn't do well with a computer, and I'm not that skilled at using them to this day."

"Then you're what they call a tactile learner. You learn by touch, by drawing, playing board games, making models like with your Erector set and Legos. You'll never learn a lot out of a manual or what's written on a whiteboard."

He quickly finished off his heap of scrambled eggs. "That's right. What kind of learner are you?"

She rolled her eyes. "I'm the visual learner. I do best with a manual or book. Which is why you're a hands-on sniper, and I fly a Warthog. Give me a manual and I can learn anything. But if you threw your sniper rifle down and told me to strip and field-clean it, I'd be lost."

Her smile and the sincerity in her sparkling hazel eyes went straight to his heart. "I like how humble you are," he admitted.

"You're the same," she said, shrugging, eating heartily. "Maybe we're more alike than we first thought?"

Gage doubted that but said nothing. "Maybe opposite bookends on a shelf?" he teased.

She gave him a studied look. "I don't think so. I think in many ways, we may be very similar."

"Give me an example." He finished the biscuits and gravy in short order.

"My mom, Dilara, says people are vegetables or a legume."

Gage grinned, brows raising. "Oh?"

"Yes," Alexa said pertly, finishing her plate of food and pulling over the cup of fruit. "You have to understand, she's from Turkey, so she uses veggies from her country to describe people. She said they fall into one of several categories. There are chickpeas, a legume, which means what you see is what you get—they're simple and straightforward." She held up two fingers. "Then there are eggplants."

Gage couldn't hold back a chuckle. "I hate eggplant!"

"I love it, but I have that Turkish gene and you don't," Alexa laughed. "If you cut an eggplant open, what do you see?"

"Rows upon rows of nonstop seeds," he said. "Which is why I don't like to eat it, because all those small seeds get caught between your teeth."

"Well," she said soothingly, patting his hand, which rested near his tray, "if I made you something with eggplant in it, you would not have that happen. It's all in how it's prepared."

"What's the eggplant personality like, then?" Gage asked, unable to stop from smiling.

"These are people who are always busy, always active either mentally or physically. They generally are very curious people, usually higher-educated multitaskers found in the sciences."

"I think I'm a chickpea, then."

"Oh, no," Alexa protested with a laugh. "I've saved the best for last! You're an onion, Gage. Just like me."

Raising a brow, he muttered, "A lowly onion?"

She held up her hands. "Well, wait till I tell you what it means, okay? Onion personalities are people who are highly complex. They have many layers to them, and they usually don't give them up easily. And because an onion doesn't have a shell, it has no way to protect itself. So onion people hide a lot of themselves from the rest of the world. Sometimes it's because they feel too vulnerable, as they lack a wall to protect them. Sometimes they just need to get to know the other person longer before they'll show other layers of themselves."

Gage picked up one of the oranges and began to put the peels on his emptied tray. "Complexity usually is an indicator of higher intelligence."

"Well"—she hesitated—"it can be, yes. But it can also mean, according to my mom, who is a brilliant onion herself that you've been shaped very strongly by family circumstances. And depending upon whether or not the family was happy or dysfunctional or if trauma occurred in it, the layers develop."

Mulling over the explanation, he slanted a glance in her direction. "So circumstances create the onion's layers of complexity during childhood?"

"Yes. For example, I come out of a very strong, loving family. But I wasn't overprotected, and I didn't have helicopter parents. Our mom and dad were very clear about Tal, Matt, and me learning independence at an early age. Not only that, they really imbued us with self-confidence. We lived in a strict household where we were expected to work and be responsible. We washed dishes, put them away, did sweeping or ran the vacuum or washed windows. In other words, they made us realize at a very early age that hard work and responsibility were expected of us. And then we spent our summer vacations either in Kuşadası, Turkey, with my mother's brothers and their wives, or with her Greek cousin over in Athens. We learned to travel when we were very young. We were taught English, Turkish and Greek in our household. I know how lucky we are, because I have friends who come from broken families."

"Interesting concept," Gage said, feeling his way through it. "You strike me as a highly complex person."

"You're an onion," Alexa said quietly, becoming serious as she spooned the fruit into her mouth.

Gage felt a shift in energy around her, could feel her probing the walls he'd had in place nearly all his life. For whatever reason, he didn't feel threatened.

Instead, he saw compassion shining in her eyes, as if she were sensing or picking something up about him on another unknown level. It was just a sense, but damned if he didn't feel like she had some kind of X-ray vision and she saw him—warts and all.

He'd hidden, all right. And he was sure that if Alexa knew the whole story about him, she'd run screaming. He was no white knight. He was tarnished. Wounded. A part of him was no damn good. Gage wished he were someone else, a man Alexa could really look up to, admire, and respect.

"Is Matt an onion?" he asked her.

"Yep, and so is Tal. We're all complex. My mother's an onion. My dad is an eggplant." She smiled fondly.

"No chickpeas, huh?" he teased, wanting to divert her from asking him anything personal about his family.

Alexa laughed and wiped her mouth with a paper napkin. "None. We're a family of three onions and one eggplant, for better or for worse."

CHAPTER 4

"HOME SWEET HOME," Alexa said, turning to Gage as he stood in the middle of a cavernous supply warehouse. She pointed to the left. "The Delos pallet is over there in the corner. Time to roll up our sleeves and get to work."

The entire place was nothing but pallets as Gage followed her over to the brightly lit corner. It was cold inside, but the lights above were warming. There was a lot going on within the warehouse, with equipment shuttling the pallets in and out at various exits, probably to be loaded on helicopters for transit and distribution.

Gage enjoyed watching Alexa walk just ahead of him as she eagerly hurried toward the Delos pallet.

He tried to tamp down his growing need to be around her. For the first time in a long time, Gage felt light. He was actually enjoying himself.

He'd had women before, and none of them had made him feel like this. So what was happening here? Alexa was warm, effervescent, outgoing, and personal with him. But she wasn't flirting. Gage knew the difference. And when they'd entered the warehouse, and Alexa talked to the sentry, showing him her security card, she'd hugged him, too. The Army soldier had blushed, but Gage could see he truly enjoyed Alexa's motherly warmth. And that was what it was. Alexa had told him she was like her mother, Dilara. She'd said enough about her mother that Gage had a pretty good picture of the woman. After all, pulling together scraps of observations was part of a sniper's skill set. And the puzzle pieces seemed to create a caring picture of Dilara Culver. For sure, her youngest daughter Alexa was a carbon copy of her in every way.

He sauntered over to a pallet that was stacked ten boxes high. They all displayed the word "Delos" on the outside. Gage was beginning to get a taste of the Culver family passion to help others as he put his hands on his hips, his gaze ranging across the huge stack of goods.

Alexa went over to the pallet, turned, and said, "Help me here, Gage? Mom has had her people at the warehouse back in Alexandria, stuff folded cardboard boxes between the rows." She smiled and leaned over, tugging out a group of them and dropping them at her feet. "Before the Army will deliver these goods to the Shinwari village tomorrow, we have to separate, identify, and code these cartons for shoe and clothing sizes." She quickly crouched down and assembled the first box.

Gage stood over her, watching her hands move quickly. Alexa had done this a time or two, he realized, smiling to himself. "Got a marker of some sort to put the intel on the outside of the box?"

Giving him a triumphant look, Alexa stood and dug into her pocket. "Yep, two black felt-tip pens. One for you and one for me."

Gage took the pen from her gloved hand. "Okay, you must have a system here, Alexa. Where do we start?" He wanted to stare into her upturned face, her eyes sparkling with excitement, her cheeks flushed. His hands itched to undo that long, red braid of hers that gleamed with the green and gold ribbons twisted within it.

"Oh, I have a system," she assured him. Standing, she gestured at the many boxes. "When they are packed at the Delos warehouse in the U.S., they are not sorted by size. For example, a box of children's shoes will hold all different sizes."

She pointed to the stack of flattened cardboard boxes near her feet. "I'm going to mark on the side whether it's girl or boy shoes and then put a size on it. When you're out in the field, you can go to that box that has that child's size in it and fit her or him. It's a lot faster than digging through twenty pair of shoes in ten different boxes, trying to find a size for the child."

Gage nodded. "That's a slowdown," he agreed.

"Once we get our boxes set up, marked, and put along the wall over there, then we can begin to open the ones on the pallet and distribute their contents to the correct box. Once that's done, we repack the filled boxes back onto this pallet. The cargo guys will come by and throw heavy netting over it and anchor it such that they can pick it up with their front-end loader and take it out to the helo."

"And how often do you do this?" he asked her, impressed. He liked seeing the commitment and care in her eyes and voice.

"Oh," Alexa laughed, shaking her head as she leaned over, drawing more boxes from between the rows. "Ever since I was about eight years old. We grew up helping Mom and our charities."

Gage gently snagged her arm and drew her back. "Let me do that. You start writing on the sides of the boxes as I get them to you, okay?"

Breathless, Alexa stared up into his warm blue eyes. His hand on hers, and she felt a stir beneath the layers of clothing she wore. "Sure . . ."

Gage released her arm as she stepped aside. "When Matt is here, what does he usually do to help you out?" he asked.

"What you're doing." She smiled. "See? I told you that you're very much alike. He doesn't like me climbing around and putting boxes together, either."

"Women are good at organizing," he said, agreeing with Matt. He carried several boxes over to the wall, and Alexa followed him.

Gage tried to stop feeling so damn happy as they labored for a solid hour getting the boxes labeled and organized. They worked in silence like a well-oiled machine, and at the end of the hour, there were thirty boxes, all labeled and waiting to be filled near the wall. Alexa had taken off her coat and gloves, and Gage enjoyed seeing how graceful she was. Even more important, she truly cared about others. It was more than just words—she backed them up with her actions. He looked around the busy, noisy warehouse and wondered how many other women would be down on their hands and knees on these dusty concrete floors, moving boxes around. Not many. It spoke of her commitment and her work ethic. She didn't mind getting dirty, either. So far, Gage could find nothing to dislike about Alexa Culver—hard as he might try, because he knew they could never have a relationship as long as she was an officer and he was enlisted.

★

"TIME FOR A break," Gage told her, holding out a bottle of water. "You've been working nonstop and need to hydrate."

Getting off her knees, Alex tucked the pen away in her pocket, taking the proffered plastic bottle. "Thanks. I can't help it, Gage. I get lost in what I'm doing, and I don't think to stop to get some water or eat."

He tipped his water bottle to his lips, drinking deeply. Wiping his mouth afterward, he watched her sip the liquid and marveled at her delicacy. Oh, he knew she was a tough combat pilot, but here, he suspected, she was just being her self.

"Let's take a ten-minute break," Alexa suggested, gesturing toward the pallet. She sat down on the wooden slats, Gage sitting next to her, but with enough room that she wouldn't feel crowded.

Alexa was glad Gage wasn't wearing his gloves or jacket anymore. Work like this was sweaty. Besides, she liked the way the material of his shirt stretched across his broad shoulders and deeply muscled chest. He looked strong and fit, but he was no bodybuilder—not as a sniper. They all ran on the lean side, like her sister, Tal.

Alex smiled as he sat down and offered her a protein bar. "You think of everything," she said, thanking him. They'd rarely chatted while they worked, each with their area of duty to perform. She'd noticed that Gage worked at a good speed and was consistent.

"You know," she said, opening up the wrapper, "you really remind me of my big sister, Tal."

He smiled a little. "Really? In what way?"

Gesturing, Alexa said, "The way you work. The way you think. Your focus. You're like a laser, Gage. Once you have your job figured out, it's in your sights and you go for it."

"I've been that way all my life, I guess."

"What's your family like? Your parents?" she asked, taking him by surprise. She looked up at him and suddenly felt a chill as he stopped chewing on the protein bar. What had she stepped into? Whatever it was, she felt a wall spring up between them. *Uh-oh.*

"My family is gone," he said abruptly.

While she felt rebuffed by his sharp tone, she also felt the pain accompanying it, and blinked back sudden tears. Looking away from Gage, she swallowed a couple of times, getting them under control.

Alexa's moon in Pisces made her an easy target for others' feelings, and she was impacted deeply and swiftly when she was really open. And she was certainly vulnerable toward Gage Hunter. She hadn't put up her protective mental shield against his powerful emotions, and now she was being hit full force by them. His pain was so raw and overwhelming that Alexa had to take a couple of breaths to tamp down her instinctive reaction.

She turned to him, holding his hooded gaze. "I'm so sorry," she whispered, reaching out, her fingers resting on his lower arm. She saw no change in Gage's expression or the haunted look in his darkening eyes. Instead, he just sat there, almost immobile, as if the question had stunned him.

Feeling bad, Alexa offered in a whisper, "Just tell me to mind my own business, Gage. I'm really sorry . . ."

Her touch was so comforting, he willed her to keep her hand on his lower arm just a little bit longer. And the truth was, as soon as she made contact with him, a lot of that grief began to dull.

He shook his head. "Knowing you a little, I was expecting you to ask. You're a deeply family-oriented person, Alexa. It's okay."

Her fingers tightened a little around his arm. "I didn't mean to stir up so much pain in you."

"It's always there," he told her with a shrug. "Never goes away. Over time, it's gotten less intense." He held her gaze, which now glistened with tears, and saw another layer of Alexa reveal itself. "Are you always this touched by others' tragedies?" he asked, watching her struggle to keep the tears back.

Making a muffled sound in her throat, Alexa nodded. "Do you know anything about astrology, Gage? It's a hobby of mine."

"Not a whole lot," he admitted. "I know I'm a Capricorn." He forced a slight smile. "Why?"

"My sister, Tal, is a Capricorn." She released his arm and sighed. "You two are more alike than I ever thought."

"That's nice to know," Gage said, trying to push away memories that demanded to rise. Inside, he was melting from Alexa's sympathetic expression. He did know how important family was to her. Now he saw her commiserate in a way some people could not. Hers was a tight family, working together, loving one another, just like his had been.

Alexa wanted to share how close in nature her sister was with Gage, and she explained, "Tal's always solid, a strong, reliable player out there on an op. You could always count on her to do the job and do it right. And you're the same way."

She had so many questions for him, but she read the wariness in his gaze, as if he were trying to steel himself against whatever she might ask him next.

"I'm still a work in progress," Gage muttered. "Nothing special."

Alexa was about to protest when she spotted Matt trotting across the huge warehouse toward them. "Oh, here's Matt!" She quickly stood, brushing off her pants. Having uninterrupted personal time with Gage wasn't going to happen today, and he was upset anyway. There was nothing she could say or do right now as her brother slowed to a walk, grinning as he came toward her. She gave Gage an apologetic look.

"Hey, everything's fine," he assured her. "Go hug your brother."

The hurt was in his eyes, and Alexa felt a sob stick in her throat. He was so brave when she could feel he wanted to weep. Reaching out, she touched his shoulder. "Thanks . . .," She turned, hurrying toward her brother.

"Sorry I'm late," Matt said, giving Alexa a quick hug. He turned, nodding to Gage, who slowly stood up. "Good to see you here, bro."

"Yeah," Gage said. "Your little sister is beating the pants off me. I can't keep up with her."

Alexa snorted. "That's not true, Matt. Gage is working as hard as you do when a charity pallet like this one comes into Bagram."

"I've never seen a Marine shirk his duty," Matt told her, serious. "So, where are we at in the process, Alexa? And where do you want me to work?"

Gage went back to his job and let brother and sister work out a schedule. He felt bad that Alexa's unexpected question had caught him off guard. And he hated that his emotions had boiled to the surface.

He also saw that he'd hurt Alexa with his gruff response. Gage wanted to apologize, but it wasn't going to happen right now. They still had a good six hours of work ahead of them, even with three people working at max speed.

★

THEIR COMBINED TEAMWORK paid off. By the time Gage shrugged into his leather bomber jacket at 1700, all the clothes, coats, winter gear, and shoes were appropriately organized and back on the pallet, ready for transport the next morning to the Shinwari village. He had always kept one ear keyed to the banter between Matt and Alexa, and by midafternoon, it had become abundantly clear that Alexa was the sunshine in everyone's life. When it looked like they'd be working until late tonight, Alexa had taken the helm and recruited two more Army soldiers who weren't doing anything. Gage smiled to himself, convinced that no one ever turned down a request from Alexa. Not with her beauty, sweet smile and earnest expression.

The Army dudes came over and fit right in, helping them get done by 1700. When Alexa gave the two soldiers a hug of thanks, Gage fought a twinge of jealousy. Both men blushed a deep red, not expecting it from an Air Force officer.

But Alexa was on her own time, on a personal mission, and she was revealing her real self, Gage thought, not playing the role of a military officer unless she had to. He saw how much a woman hugging them meant. Hell, it meant the same to him!

Alexa was warm and she smelled so damned good that Gage could easily recall the scent of that almond oil in her hair. Matt went over and shook the men's hands, thanking them sincerely for donating their time.

Pain moved in Gage's heart as he saw Matt tuck his little sister under his arm and hug her, thanking her for all her work on this project. He watched Alexa's face, the sweet smile she shared with her brother, her love for him shining from her eyes.

Gage remembered that same look from Jen. He had once had a similar relationship with his little sister. In one way, it warmed his heart. In another, he wanted to be the one who walked over and hugged the hell out of Alexa, not Matt.

Wearily, he turned away, the scene dredging up so many bittersweet memories and emotions. Unconsciously, Gage rubbed his chest where his heart lay, scowling.

"Hey, Gage," Alexa called softly.

He turned to find her standing there in front of him. Matt was talking to a loadmaster sergeant and his two crew chiefs from the helicopter where the charity goods would be taken. He helped them haul a nylon cargo net over the pallet. There was a smudge of dust on her left cheek, and, without thinking, Gage lifted his hand and brushed it away with his thumb. Alexa's eyes widened, and her lips parted slightly, he let his hand fall to his side. "You had some dirt on your cheek," he explained, rocked by what he felt from her.

"Oh!" Alexa laughed a little, touching her cheek. "I'm not surprised. Look at our jeans! They're filthy. I'm sure we'll all be certified dust balls."

"Most likely," he agreed wryly, an unwitting smile on Gage's mouth as she dusted off her jeans. She had been on the floor a lot more than the guys were, taking the divided sizes and items to the correct boxes. She looked winsome—no, *beautiful*, he corrected himself. He ached everywhere in his body for her. That mouth of hers, those almost pouty lips, beckoned to Gage, but he resisted.

"Matt has a lot going on over at Delta, and he can't make dinner with us tonight."

A pleasant shock ran through Gage. "Dinner?" He sounded confused. Alexa hadn't mentioned going out to dinner with anyone tonight. Her smile melted some of that ice in his heart.

"Absolutely, you've earned it! I'm buying. What would you like to eat tonight?"

Stunned, Gage couldn't think for a moment. "Matt was going with us, right?"

"'Was' is the operative word here," Alexa explained. "I guess there are some Taliban in the area no one knew about, hiding out in caves. Matt's CO is on it, and there's probably going to be a mission created to go after them. He's not sure if he'll get ordered to go on it or not."

Grimly, he nodded. "Yes, Matt's one of their top mission planners over there. Of course they'd call him in on something like this." He could tell Alexa was disappointed. The love between her and her brother was there for anyone with a set of eyes to see.

Gage also knew that just because they were at the same base didn't mean they got to see one another often. He felt her disappointment.

"So? It's you and me. Are you okay with that? Or do you have something else you'd rather do, Gage?" She tilted her head, peering up at him.

"No, I'd like dinner with you." He put his hand on her shoulder. "But I'm buying. In my world, a lady doesn't buy the meal. The man does."

Wrinkling her nose, Alexa laughed, reaching out, touching the upper arm of his jacket. "Okay, I surrender. I swear, were you and Matt separated at the hip when you were born?"

★

ALEXA REALIZED SHE was at a crossroads with quiet Gage Hunter. She changed after a quick shower, shimmying into a pair of dark green corduroy trousers and an apricot mock turtleneck sweater, mulling over their few personal conversations.

She'd seen the instant devastation in his eyes when she'd asked about his family and was blasted by his chaotic emotions. Pisces-moon people were such sponges. They absorbed everything in their immediate environment, good and bad.

Gage's reactions weren't bad, but they had caught her off guard. Matt had said Gage always kept his personal life personal, and now she knew why. She tried to put herself in his place. What if she had lost her family? Just thinking about it almost made her nauseous. Alexa couldn't imagine life without her family behind her. They were there for her to call. To get help from, to give her a shoulder to cry on, to celebrate who she was.

How did a person get through life without that?

She unbraided her hair, took out the ribbons, and laid them aside. Picking up her brush, she quickly created a shining russet cape around her shoulders. Tonight she wanted to look beautiful for Gage. Maybe that was one way to cheer him up. Alexa had, at odd times, seen him studying her earlier in the warehouse. It wasn't a glare and it wasn't intrusive, just interest. And along with that look came warm, fuzzy feelings, enclosing Alexa within them.

Gage would probably die a thousand deaths if he were aware of just how sensitive she really was. She knew Gage was fascinated with her and wanted her in every way. It didn't show in how he behaved with her. He was so courtly and such a throwback to the past. Where had he gotten those manners? That way of seeing women? From his father? His mother? Both?

The sad truth was, Alexa didn't know and wasn't about to be insensitive and bring up such a conversation with him again. She'd seen him wrestle with the grief her original question brought him, and then there was a shift, and the turmoil was no longer in his eyes. But she could still feel remnants of it around him, just holding less power over him.

Why did she care so much about him? Was it that terrible loneliness she felt around him—or the fact he was a hunk? Alexa knew herself. Gage had a hard, lean body, and being completely honest with herself, she knew she wanted to know how it felt to run her hands over him or take a shower with him to see the water run in rivulets down his lean form, carving out his muscle.

It wasn't just about sex. Alexa had never been able to separate her heart from sex. Both had to be there for a man to interest her. Which is what had gotten her into so much trouble in the past. She'd had six relationships in six years, and every one of them had broken up because she idealized something about her partner that wasn't true. She'd wanted it to be true, but it wasn't. And Alexa was tired of wearing rose-colored glasses. Now she was trying to look at Gage through new, more realistic eyes. For her, that was tough to do, but she had to turn the corner on her romantic idealism toward men.

What would it take for Gage to let her behind that shield he held up and protected himself with? Was it a trust issue? Secrets known only to him? Alexa grabbed a colorful silk scarf, tucking it in around her neck to ward off the cold of the desert after the sun had set. She pulled on her other jacket, a gray tailored wool one that hung halfway down her hips. It was heavy and warm, just as Alexa imagined Gage's arms would feel around her.

Picking up her black leather purse, Alexa pulled it over her left shoulder. Last, she put on her nicer set of leather gloves. Tonight, she wanted to look especially lovely for Gage. He deserved no less.

CHAPTER 5

GAGE DIDN'T TRY to hide his reaction to Alexa when she met him on the porch of her B-hut. "You look beautiful," he said, smiling down at her. He inhaled her scent, carried on a slight breeze. Her hair shone like a crimson cape about her shoulders. He'd had no idea her hair was halfway down her back, as he'd only seen it in a braid. "Your hair is so shiny," he said, marveling.

Gage knew he wasn't Mr. Suave, nor was he particularly adept at flirting. It just wasn't something he ever wanted to do; he figured honesty was always the best policy. And judging from Alexa's reaction, the delight in her wide hazel eyes, he was right.

"Thank you," she murmured. And then she said, "Well, hey"—reaching out, touching his leather bomber jacket—"you clean up pretty well yourself, Gage."

Now it was his turn to feel heat tunneling into his neck and face. He kept his hands jammed in the pockets of his jacket; then, giving her a slight smile, he said, "I only have one set of what I call 'good clothes' in my locker." He pulled at the collar of his red polo shirt beneath the jacket. "What you see is what you get."

Gage saw her lips, those wonderfully shaped lips, draw into a smile.

"You look like a model for a book jacket," she assured him, slipping her hand around his arm. "I'm starving! Are you ready to go?"

Gage appreciated her assertiveness and automatically crooked his elbow, enjoying the way her fingers wrapped around his upper arm. "We put in a good, hard day's work today, so yes, I'm hungry."

It was somewhat windy, the sky a muddled, dark color above them as night surrounded the base. Gage led her to a Humvee that he'd borrowed from his unit. He opened the door for her as she slid in, noting that her gray wool jacket fit her to perfection. He climbed in and drove them toward the restaurant.

Then, turning toward her, he admitted, "I don't know how you can be upbeat all the time. How do you do it?"

Her face was shadowy in the vehicle, as there were no lights on the base at night to prevent the enemy from sending over mortars.

Placing her gloved hands over her black purse, she said, "I've always been like this, Gage. It's not something conscious that I do."

"How do you see the world, then?" he asked. Making a stop, he turned left down another asphalt road that was much busier.

Alexa knew he was trying to understand her, and that thought alone made her giddy with hope that he'd open up to her at some point. He seemed awkward, stumbling over the questions. He probably wasn't used to getting personal with a woman.

Taking a deep breath, she dove in. "I always use astrology to explain myself," she said with a grin. "I'm a Sagittarius with a moon in Pisces. Sagittarian people are very spontaneous. We're a fire sign, so we're always out front, leading the way. I also sometimes put my mouth ahead of my brain. When I was a kid, I used to just blurt out whatever I felt, but I soon found out that I needed to develop some diplomacy as I got older. That, and thinking before I speak. There are fewer foot-in-mouth, embarrassing incidents that way," she said with a chuckle.

"I think you need to bring me up to speed on astrology, then." He smiled. "It's never been on my radar."

"It isn't on most people's," Alexa agreed. "My mom loves astrology, but then, the women in her family have always had a very metaphysical or spiritual orientation. She's very intuitive, and at times, as a kid growing up, I swore she was reading our minds. Of course, she doesn't admit to doing that, but for some reason we kids were usually caught before we were going to do something that was a no-no."

Gage chuckled. He made another turn down a street known as Restaurant Row. "Sounds like we have more in common, then. My mother was like that, too."

Alexa's heart leaped to underscore Gage's admission. It was personal. Her mind rapidly put it together. If she were forthcoming about her life, maybe he would volunteer small pieces of his own personal background.

"Maybe all mothers have that ability," she said wryly.

"Could be," Gage said, pulling into the parking lot. He'd chosen a steak house because Alexa had said earlier in the warehouse that she was ready to eat a two-pound steak after all the hard work she'd done.

He parked and shut off the Humvee, turning to her. "Is this place all right? Did I read you right? You do want a steak tonight, don't you?"

"Perfect," she assured him, reaching out to touch his arm. "I'm ready to eat a *lot*. We'll have plenty of hard work ahead of us tomorrow when we fly to that Shinwari village."

Nodding, he opened his hand and slid her gloved fingers into his. It was an intimate move, and Gage knew it, watching her expression carefully. "Then," he said, "let's go get those steaks."

He gently squeezed her fingers and released her. Instantly, he saw an emotion in her darkened eyes, but damned if he could translate it. Climbing out, he walked around the Humvee and opened the door for Alexa. When he held out his hand to her, she quickly took it. It felt good that she could reach out and allow him to help her. Gage knew it was a little thing, but it meant a lot to him that she'd allow him this privilege. Most women would have thrown open the door and climbed out on their own before he could get around to open it.

"Thanks," Alexa said, straightening and momentarily releasing his hand. She saw pleasure deep in Gage's narrowing eyes, felt his attraction to her, his want, his growing need. Her whole body went on alert, and she yearned to kiss him, but the parking lot was full of vehicles, and she knew this was a popular place for many officers.

Gage shut the door and turned, placing his hand lightly against the small of her back. He cut his stride for her sake as he led her to the restaurant's entrance. Earlier, he'd called to reserve a booth for them. The steak house was pretty upscale and a lot quieter than the pizza restaurants down the street. He opened the door and led Alexa up to the waitress, who was waiting with menus in hand, then told the girl about their reservation.

"Right this way," she said with a smile, turning and quickly walking between all the square tables draped with white linens.

"Nice place," Alexa told him as he walked at her side. The patrons were all in civilian clothes. "I usually come here about once a year when I'm deployed. I always like being here because it's quiet, and you can actually hold a decent conversation with your dinner partner."

"I don't usually come to this place," Gage admitted. "It's pretty fancy."

Alexa gave him a soft look. "That's sweet of you to put yourself out for me, then." The lighting was low, but she could see his shy response, his gaze moving away from hers for a moment. This was a man who didn't get many compliments. Gage was an alpha male, no question, but he hid it well with his quiet demeanor. "But you look just fine with the clothes you're wearing tonight." Alexa wanted to put him at ease. Yes, there were some men in here wearing suits or sports jackets, some with ties. Others, like Gage, were dressed casually, and she actually preferred that to getting dressed up.

"I don't like suits and ties," he admitted. "Never did. Of course, in the Corps, when you have to get into your uniform, there is always a tie. I put up with it because in my line of work, ties aren't required on a sniper op."

Alexa grinned and nodded. "Well said!" She was delighted that they had an intimate booth at the back away from the kitchen. The height of the booth made it even more private, which pleased her immensely. She scooted in and

Gage sat opposite her, removing his jacket and laying it down on the seat beside him. The waitress handed them the menus and took their drink orders, then left.

Gage thought the lamplight on the wall of their booth made Alexa's hair shine, showing off the burgundy, gold, and copper strands. "You look so different when your hair is down," he said.

"Versus my hair in one long braid down my back?"

He saw her lips curve. "Yes. This way"—he gestured toward her hair, which lay thickly upon her shoulders—"you don't look like a combat pilot hauling an A-10 around in the sky. You look like a beautiful young woman."

"Thank you," she said, holding his shadowed gaze. "It's nice to get dressed up and be a civilian from time to time—far better than wearing a shapeless flight suit. I really love being a girl and being girly. My mother is the same way. She loves to have her nails done, wear makeup, and be feminine."

The waitress brought back a glass of white wine for Alexa and a bottle of cold beer for Gage. They gave her their orders, and he drank some beer. Then he said, "My mother would have fallen into your girly-girl category, too. My dad was in the Marine Corps, and we didn't have a whole lot of money, but she had a part-time job. It gave her 'pin money' to get her nails done and her hair fixed up."

Alexa sipped her wine, studying him in the low light, his rugged face relaxed and tension-free. She realized he was opening up to her, and a thrill moved through her. That meant he trusted her, at least up to a point.

"She sounds like someone I would have loved to meet."

"I'd show you a photo of her, but as you know, we can't carry anything personal on us. I have her photo taped on the inside of my locker door, though."

"Right," Alexa agreed. "Nothing personal on us." Because if they were captured by the Taliban, they would look for items just like that and use them to exploit the person in captivity. Or use it on an Internet video.

"Can you describe her for me? If you want." Alexa wasn't sure how much he wanted to talk about his family.

"She had brown hair with red highlights in it, blue eyes, and was a little taller than you."

"She gave you her blue eyes, then."

"Yes. I got my dad's black hair and his build."

"You said he was a Marine?"

"Yes. He was my hero. Always will be." Gage frowned, moving the chilled bottle with beads of condensation on its surface around slowly in his hand. Looking up, he said, "He was in the Corps from the time I was born. He was deployed four times to Iraq with only six months between them. The last time, he got badly wounded and earned a Silver Star for his bravery in a firefight."

"He's a real hero, then," Alexa said softly, seeing different emotions play across his face. Tonight, Gage did not wear his guarded expression she'd seen off and on. He was more relaxed, spreading out his long legs beneath the table on either side of hers. She liked his ability to "slum it," as she called it. And snipers had a tendency to be very laid-back, casual, patient, and easygoing when not on a sniper op. If they were on one, all bets were off. They became intense, controlled, and focused. Gage personified those traits like her big sister Tal did.

Nodding, Gage said, "He'll always be my hero and my role model." He hoped Alexa would not ask about the loss of his family. He wanted to take the opportunity to open up more to her, but he realized that family meant everything to her, so he was being forced out of his comfort zone.

He found that he was willing to share with Alexa because she was a loving, highly sympathetic person. And if he looked at his reasons more closely, he saw he needed the TLC she easily gave to everyone, including him. Alexa nurtured him in ways he'd never experienced before, and he was lapping it up like a stray dog.

He hoped, in some small way, he could somehow give back to her, but he wasn't clear on exactly how. Alexa seemed to have everything, so he was mystified as to how he could contribute in some positive way.

"And you wanted to become a Marine because your dad had been one, right?"

"Yes. He was a sniper."

Alexa sat back, her fingers around the stem of her wineglass. "Like father, like son."

"Very much."

"I'm sorry you lost them, Gage. I can tell just how much they each gave you. It just breaks my heart."

Her words were a balm spreading across his soul, filling in the hole that their deaths had left in him. Shrugging, he couldn't meet Alexa's eyes for fear he'd start to cry. He'd never cried for the loss of his family, stuffing it so deep inside it would never see the light of day. They were dead. His tears would not bring them back. Marines didn't cry, pure and simple. He'd never even seen his dad cry except for one time, when Jen had been murdered by those gang members. Frowning, he lifted his gaze and held hers. "They're still alive in my heart and my memory," he rasped, fighting emotions.

Alexa reached across the table, her fingers curving around his lower arm. "You're a very brave person, Gage. I don't think I could be as put together as you if my family was taken away from me." Her fingers tightened momentarily. "I'm so sorry you lost them . . ." She choked up a little, giving him a sympathetic look.

Her fingers felt soothing to him, touching his past with warmth and caring. Gage fought down his need to haul this woman into his arms and simply kiss her into oblivion. He knew how to please a woman and reveled in it when it happened. Because of his sniper trade, he was gone on deployments far longer than he'd been stateside and couldn't maintain a relationship for as long as he wanted. And he didn't like one-night stands, either.

Nor did he like to have women come on to him at an EM, Enlisted Man's, club, draping themselves all over him when they found out he was a sniper. He never told anyone what he did in the Marines, but his buddies did, causing him a lot of embarrassment. He didn't want a woman glorifying him for killing other human beings. That wasn't the kind of woman he wanted in his life.

"I am, too," he croaked. "I used to dream, but I don't any more. Any dreams I had? They died with them." He let go of the bottle of beer in his hand and made a bold move by enclosing her fingers in his. "If anyone could understand, Alexa, it would be you." His voice shook a bit, surprising them both. She just naturally made him want to open up and spill his guts to her. He squeezed her hand and then released it, even though he didn't want to.

"I'm a natural dreamer," Alexa whispered, deeply touched by his hoarse admittance.

"Listen," he said gruffly, "this is supposed to be a happy time for us tonight. Let's talk about something else. I don't want our dinner ruined with my past."

"Sure," she said. Alexa saw Gage struggling to put his losses away. Her acute senses told her that he rarely, if ever, talked about his family. But he had with her. "It's a gift, Gage, to hear about someone's journey," she whispered, giving him a tender look. "And any journey has good and bad in it. That's the way it is in life. I'd be very honored to hear about your parents—if or when you want to tell me more, I'd love to sit and listen."

Gage felt her sincerity and saw it banked in her eyes. "I'll keep that in mind. Why don't you tell me something about yourself—preferably a happy moment."

She could feel his worry that she'd ask other important questions about his family, like, "What happened to them?" It was eating Alexa alive not to push or ask directly, but she knew Gage would slam shut on her.

She was just grateful that he'd opened the door on his family to her; it showed her that he wanted to know her better. And that he already trusted her.

People didn't start a relationship without becoming personal with one another. Her heart spun with hope, because she knew without a doubt that she wanted to know Gage on a serious level. Alexa didn't care if he was enlisted and she was an officer. She was getting out in less than three months, anyway.

What she did want to do was to protect Gage so he wouldn't get into trouble by having an illegal relationship with an officer.

And frankly, she wasn't sure what Gage wanted from her. It could be something as simple as lust or it could be deeper and more profound, a real relationship that was sexual but held important elements that would feed their hearts and souls. That was the type of relationship she wanted.

She realized that her track record was abysmal at best, and her idealistic outlook hadn't helped. Now, with Gage, she was trying to be realistic about him, not idolize him or put him on a pedestal.

On the other hand, he was heroic by nature, now confirmed by his father having been a Marine and a Silver Star recipient. Bravery ran in Gage's psyche, but that had been obvious to her from the moment she'd met him. She was drawn to his quiet confidence, which radiated like a powerful beacon from around him to her. No man had made her feel as protected as Gage did. And that had her full, undivided attention. She wasn't one to need protection, always confident and, at times, as a combat pilot, brazen as hell. She was the protector of those men and women on the ground, and she took her job seriously. Gage's kind of protection toward her felt good to Alexa. It wasn't suffocating or stifling, rather, giving her a sense of safety in their unsafe careers.

The waitress interrupted them bringing their meals. Alexa's mouth watered as she placed a plate with a thick T-bone steak, medium, down in front of her, along with a steaming baked potato with butter and sour cream on the side. She didn't want a salad tonight, instead wanting to go straight to the meat because her body craved the protein it would provide. Gage had a similar look on his face as the waitress placed his steak before him.

"I don't know about you," Alexa said with a smile, "but I'm starving!"

"That makes two of us." The words slipped out before he could stop them, and in that moment, when their eyes met and held, she was swept up in a powerful wave of happiness coming straight from Gage. His pale blue eyes shone with quiet joy.

Alexa already knew that Gage rarely smiled, and she promised herself that she would get him to smile more often. Gage was locked up tightly by his past, she realized that, but the past could be opened and the wounds drained of their toxicity. Then real healing could take place. And if Alexa had anything to say about it, she was going to help Gage, whether he knew it or not. She had a knack for sensing other people's hurts and injuries. And though he hid his well, she could sense how much this pain put him into a shield like mode where he hid his vulnerability from others and the world at large.

Alexa was going to dream for him. She'd done it for others and it worked, and she'd never wanted to do it for anyone more than she did for Gage

Hunter. He had nothing but broken dreams. She could help him create new dreams, breathe life and hope back into him. Feeling driven to do this for him felt right and good to her.

★

ALEXA DIDN'T WANT the night to end as Gage parked the Humvee and turned off the engine. They sat quietly in the vehicle, neither speaking. For two hours, they'd eaten, stuffed themselves, and talked intimately about her family. She kept plying him with stories that made him smile. One time, he'd actually laughed, and it had made her heart beat fast, because Gage's entire expression changed, taking her breath away.

It was then that Alexa realized how much the ghosts from his past still had a stranglehold on him. She saw his quiet reserve melt away as the evening wore on, and maybe, Alexa thought, she'd begun to wear down his resistance to sharing.

She'd pulled down that dark family mask he wore like a good friend, and when it slipped, she'd actually seen the real Gage. What she saw made her heart race with excitement, and with it her need to be close to him grew.

The darkness surrounded them in the Humvee. It was 2100, and most people were in bed by now. Alexa studied his profile. Gage silently regarded her, the moment rich with promise, with yearning. Alexa didn't try to think with this man; instead, she leaned over the large console and lifted her hand against his jaw, coaxing him to lean toward her. Stretching, she brushed his lips with hers. It was something she'd wanted to do all night. At first, she felt a split second of reaction in Gage, a momentary tension. But then, as her lips brushed against his, she heard him groan, his hand moving around to her nape, drawing her hard against him.

Her breath came faster as his lips took hers, and she felt the tenderness with which he slid across her mouth, engaging her, inviting her. Her fingers tightened against his jaw, an involuntary sound of deep pleasure escaped her, telling him how much she enjoyed his kiss.

Gage certainly wasn't shy in that respect, but he was a man who monitored himself with his partner. His mouth was seeking, caring, and he sipped from her lips, tasting her, placing small kisses at each corner of her mouth. He flowed into her, and she inhaled his rich, masculine scent, sending fire streaking straight down through her body. She felt him controlling his reaction to her, monitoring her. How like a sniper.

Almost smiling beneath his mouth, she opened up to his nudge and felt herself losing herself in him. Gage knew how to kiss a woman and instill fever in her blood. There was a decided art to kissing, and he knew it well. She thrilled to his touch as he slowly deepened his exploration of her.

His fingers moved lightly across her nape, her flesh skittered with heat and promise. Her breasts tightened, her nipples hardened, and he'd barely touched her. But Gage knew a woman's erogenous areas, and her nape was particularly sensitive. She spiraled into the heat and strength of his mouth taking hers. Small explosions fired off within her, and she hummed, wanting so much more from Gage.

Gradually, Alexa eased from his mouth, drowning in those narrowed, shadowed eyes that studied her with such intensity. Gage removed his hand from her nape, allowing her to sit down. They were both breathing erratically. Alexa could see the bulge of his erection against his chinos, had felt that he'd wanted to do a helluva lot more than just kiss her into oblivion. She tasted him on her lips and boldly held his gaze.

"Where are we going with this?" he asked in a low voice, searching her eyes.

"I don't know," Alexa whispered, clasping her gloved hands in her lap, "but I'm not sorry I kissed you, Gage. Are you?" She might as well find out right now if he was as interested in her as she was in him. Alexa was determined, this time, to be a realist. And instead of assuming he was, she would ask. That way, her rose-colored glasses would not interfere.

Studying his expression, she saw he was torn. "As much as I'd like to entertain something long-term and serious with you, we have a few firewalls in the way. You're an officer, Alexa. I'm enlisted."

Her mouth flattened and she nodded. "I know."

"You're getting out in March, but until then"—he picked up her hand, holding it—"the UCMJ is going to run your life. We can't have a personal relationship or you could get into trouble, Alexa. I don't want that."

"I know." Alexa held his concerned gaze. "What if I told you that I think we can be careful, Gage? That out in public we won't fraternize, but behind closed doors where no one can see or hear us, there are no barriers? Would that make a difference in how you feel about me right now?"

"Alexa, I'm so damned drawn to you I can't think two thoughts without you being one of them. Since I met you, I feel like I've been in free fall. I don't know what is happening, but I'm not afraid to take it on." And then his eyes glittered with amusement. "And obviously, you aren't either."

She grinned. "Guilty as charged. I kissed you. Not the other way around. Guess it's my personality, huh?"

"I like you that way. I like a woman who's confident and isn't afraid to go after what she wants."

Alexa studied him, her fingers wrapping around his. "I wasn't planning on meeting someone like you, Gage. I wasn't looking."

"I wasn't, either." He scowled and checked down the street, seeing an MP Humvee slowly moving toward them. The roads were patrolled regularly by security.

Then, turning his attention to Alexa, he saw her eyes burning with arousal. "I'm not the kind of man to chase a woman down just for sex, Alexa. You have to know that about me. I know a lot of men do, but it doesn't feel good to me to be like that."

"I kind of figured that out," she admitted. "I'm like that myself." She knew that the mind of a sniper was like a vast computer, weighing, measuring, sensing, and evaluating current conditions before they took a shot. Alexa realized she wasn't a target, at least not like that, but she filled his world just as he filled hers. Anxiety moved through her, because she wasn't certain about anything anymore.

"It's too soon to try to figure out what we have or where it's going," Gage told her somberly. "From my perspective, you're quitting the Air Force in less than three months, Alexa. You're leaving for home and for a great job you can hardly wait to fill. I'm over here for the next five months before I rotate stateside and finish my enlistment." Gage didn't try to fool himself. There would be a two-month separation between them, and his enlistment didn't end until this coming June. That was a long time to wait for each other.

"I know," she whispered painfully. "I know I'm leaving soon . . ."

Gage stared down at her gloved hand in his. "We're like two ships that have met in the night, crossed, but our paths aren't the same. We're going in different directions after that initial meeting."

Alexa knew what he was asking. Giving him a stubborn look, she said, "I can only speak for myself, Gage, but I *want* the right to get to know you, explore you, be with you when we can make it happen. I have no idea where this is going or what it might be for us. But I'm willing to give it a try. I've always been a risk-taker, and I want whatever time we have left to us. Maybe I'm selfish, but I can't think of anything I want to do more in the time I have left here. That is, of course, if you want it, too." She smiled gamely and waited for his answer.

CHAPTER 6

"YOU'RE A TRUE risk-taker," Gage agreed, sitting back in the seat, his hands draped over the wheel. "You're a take-no-prisoners kinda woman."

"I scare a lot of guys off," Alexa admitted, folding her hands in her lap. Because if she didn't, she was going to be all over Gage. The man was such a gentleman, with the emphasis on "gentle." Tal had been a Marine Corps sniper, but she was far more assertive than Gage was.

But he couldn't do his job if he didn't have that same kind of personality. Alexa could feel him holding back a lot with her.

"Well," he drawled, "that's their loss. You don't scare me, Alexa." On the contrary, she was like a flame, and he was the helpless moth blinded by her beauty and her generous heart.

"Phew, that's good to know, Gage. What else is bothering you about us, or about what might be?"

His lips curved ruefully as he held her intense gaze. She was totally focused, and he thought she might look that way when she was preparing for a bombing or strafing run. There was no question that Alexa was a hunter of the first order, and he reveled in her confidence and positive spirit.

"Now you're giving me the third degree," he teased, a chuckle rising in his throat. Opening his hands on the wheel, he said, "Look, I'm not the type of man who moves into any kind of relationship in a hurry. It's not in my nature, Alexa. I learned the hard way about that when I was younger. I'd like to think I learned from my mistakes."

"I'm fine with slow, Gage." She saw amusement in his eyes, but he wasn't laughing at her. "What? You don't believe me?"

"No, I believe you. But I also know that you go where angels fear to tread."

She opened her hand. "Guilty. Gage, I've learned from my past mistakes, too. At least," she said with a grimace, "I'm trying to learn. Before, I was a wishful-thinking girl. I always saw men through rose-colored glasses." She pointed to her eyes. "I made the mistake of putting them up on pedestals, and then I'd idolize them. I ignored warning signs and red flags about their personalities and then had to deep-six them."

She searched his hooded gaze. "I'm not doing that with you. I realize you're enlisted and I'm an officer. I know I'll be leaving the military in less than three months. I know you'll be stuck here. I hate all of that, but that's reality, and I've got to stay real, not dreamy or wistful."

"You're an idealist through and through," he pointed out quietly, looking out the window as an MP's Humvee passed them. He raised a finger as a sign of acknowledgment to the driver, who did the same. "There's nothing wrong with being that way, Alexa. I find idealists dream for the rest of us clodhopper realists." He slid her an amused glance. "On the other hand, I'm a pragmatic realist. In my trade, you have to be, or you'll get killed real quick out there." He pointed a finger toward the window. "I hope you don't change that part of you, because I like you just the way you are."

Alexa's heart pulsed as she sat there, absorbing his low, sexy, slight drawl. She loved his deep voice. It calmed and soothed her.

"Oh, fear not. My idealism is a fundamental part of me," she murmured. "I just need to see men more realistically, that's all."

"Well," he said with some regret, "while you're getting real about the man in your life, you need to keep in mind that I'm not anywhere near your class, Alexa. I only have a high school education. You have a college degree. I come from a lower-middle-class family at best. I know your parents are worth more money than God. You're from high society compared to me. That's another reality that sits between us."

Her brow furrowed. "Okay, so what?" She could feel the sadness in him about the fact that they came from very different backgrounds. Alexa could see Gage wrestling with all of it. "And before you say anything," she said, shaking her finger at him, "don't you dare think you aren't as smart or smarter than I am. You have a very keen intelligence, Gage. I don't give a damn if you have a college degree or not. You sure got one from the hard knocks life has given you, and in my book, that counts even more." Frustration tinged her husky voice. "I have never judged a person by their educational background. Many of the world's most creative thinkers never went to college. That's been shown throughout history so don't put that hurdle between us. Okay?" She dug into his liquid gaze.

It was then that she saw the corners of his mouth lift briefly. "Anyone ever tell you that when you get riled, you're a force of nature, Alexa?"

Bursting out laughing, Alexa nodded. "Guilty, again, as charged."

He grinned and shook his head. "I think you missed your calling. You're like a lawyer fighting for her client in front of a jury, trying to persuade them to see the case your way." He lost his smile and reached out, grazing her cheek, which was warm and firm beneath his fingertips. "And I appreciate that about you, your passion for how you see the world. That's something you never want to lose."

Her skin tingled with pleasure beneath his grazing exploration, and Alexa wanted him to touch her everywhere. Sure, it was lust. But it was so much more with this man, who was thoughtful, reserved, and conservative by nature. Just like a sniper.

"My whole family calls me a firebrand," she admitted, smiling sourly. "Tal is like you. Matt is like my dad, who's very practical and realistic."

"Then," Gage told her gently, "you're the dreamer for your family. Nothing wrong with that." He sighed and his voice dropped with pain. "My little sister, Jen, was like that for our family. She had this burning idealism in her, and she was a dreamer, too. She saw good in everything and everybody. I guess, looking at the two of you, you are a lot alike. Even though there was two years' difference between us, and I was her big brother, she was never a pest. Jen had this approach to life"—he gestured toward the windshield—"that the world was her oyster. She saw beauty everywhere. She'd bring home a baby bird that fell out of its nest, begging my mom to keep it, feed it, and help it survive." His mouth curved faintly. "Or Jen would find this pretty rock, pick it up, and bring it home to show everyone. Did we see the pictures in it? Didn't we love its colors?" He turned toward her. "Were you like that, too?"

There was such heaviness around him right now that Alexa could barely speak. So much grief. So much loss. Wanting to reach out, she kept her hands clasped in her lap instead. "Yes, I was the little gadabout in the family. I was out adventuring when Tal and Matt were doing things that were more traditional. I would drive my Turkish relatives crazy when we visited them in the summertime. I'd take off behind one of their villas and explore, and I'd lose track of time. I'd find beautiful rocks, or pick wildflowers or find a bird feather, and then bring them all back with me. I was so excited about my finds." She smiled warmly. "Of course, my poor aunts and uncles would lose track of me, not know where I was, and send their servants to locate me. They were always relieved when I walked in with my pockets bulging with the treasures I'd found. And God love 'em, they never got upset with me. Instead, they'd ask me what I found, and I'd put all the things I'd found out on the table, so excited about each one of them."

"And they were excited for you."

She took in a deep breath, meeting his watchful, dark gaze. "Yes."

"We were that way with Jen. Mom would be frantic to find her on some days. We lived in an urban area, and she would go wander the alleys and open lots, just exploring. When either Mom or I found her, she'd be chattering like a blue jay about her treasures. Her pockets were full, like yours."

Alexa ached for the loss of his little sister, and she felt his pain cutting through her. "When was her birthday?" she asked quietly.

"March first. Why?"

"She was a Pisces. She really was a dreamer, too."

Nodding, his mouth tight, he said nothing. His hands became firmer on the steering wheel. "Well," he croaked, "Jen was like sunlight to all of us. When she came in, she lit up the whole place. It wasn't anything she said or did, it was just her." He sent her a tender look. "Alexa, you're the same way."

It hurt to breathe for a moment as Alexa wrestled with all the intensity of that last comment. She realized that Gage was opening up to her, and it was a gift she didn't take lightly. "My family has always said I was like the sun god, Apollo." She shrugged a little. "My Turkish family through my mother is very deeply rooted in mythology. My uncle Ihsan once took me on his knee and told me that I was the female equivalent to Apollo. That I not only brought sunshine, warmth, and light to all of them, but that they loved me even more for having that quality. Of course, I was only eight at the time," she said, giving him a slight smile. "I honestly didn't know what he meant. I doted upon Uncle Ihsan, and he loves us kids so much, even to this day. I never forgot him telling me that. I just didn't have that awareness of how I affected people."

"It's a special quality," Gage said, his voice thick with emotion. "Yep, I sure see a lot of Jen in you . . ."

"Well, I'm sure there is. I have a moon in Pisces and she had a sun in Pisces. In a way, we're zodiac sisters sharing much the same traits.

"Being around you brings back the good things about Jen I've missed so much. There wasn't anything she touched with her smile, her laughter, or her hugs that wasn't better off for it." His voice deepened. "You're the same way, Alexa. And I appreciate those things about you so much. It brings back fond memories of Jen, of the affection we had for one another and how much I loved having her in my life."

"She sounds so wonderful," Alexa whispered, her voice choked with emotion. "Someday will you show me the photo you have of her?"

Swallowing convulsively, Gage gave a jerky nod and rasped, "Yes, I can do that . . . someday . . ."

She felt the tension rise between them, felt how fragile he'd suddenly become in her presence. "Well," she said, reaching out, brushing her hand on his shoulder, "I need to get in and get some sleep. I'll meet you over at Ops at 0700. Okay?" The struggle she saw suddenly in his expression dove down deeply through her, gripping her heart. Gage looked as if he could barely handle the emotions that had come up in their discussion. The torture in his eyes combined with his grief made Alexa want to hold him, because that's what he needed right now. And she wanted to comfort him, no question.

Nope. Wrong place and time. She allowed her fingers to ease from his shoulder, patting him awkwardly, wishing she could do so much more for him.

Gage's mouth thinned and he nodded brusquely, climbing out of the vehicle. Alexa waited for him to open the door to the Humvee. She breathed a little sigh of relief as he extended his hand to her. Taking it, she allowed him to pull her out to the curb. Tugging her jacket back into place, she sensed the tension in him, but now that they were out in the open, there wasn't a single thing she could do about it. There were eyes everywhere, and Alexa wasn't willing to open Gage up to UCMJ charges of fraternizing with an officer if someone did see them being cozy with one another.

She began to put distance between them and saw the expression in Gage's eyes as he shut the door to the Humvee. Giving her a cursory nod, he walked her down the sidewalk to her B-hut porch. He remained at the bottom of the steps as she climbed them to the building's locked entrance.

"I'll see you at 0700," she called softly, not wanting to wake anyone inside.

"See you then," Gage agreed, giving her a nod good night and forcing himself to walk away. Halfway down the sidewalk, he turned back again, making sure that Alexa had gotten safely inside her B-hut. She had. Gage knew that sometimes, drunk soldiers would come over to the female area of the base and bang on their doors, scaring the hell out of the women inside. *Drunk, disorderly, and stupid*, he thought. He was glad when the MPs were called on them and they were thrown into the brig. He wasn't about to leave Alexa standing alone and unprotected on that porch.

Two years earlier, there had been a serial rapist who prowled the women's area; five women were brutally raped and nearly killed before he was caught. Alexa was too important to Gage, and every protective gene he owned wanted to ensure her safety. As he shoved his hands into his leather jacket and slowly walked to the Humvee parked at the curb, his mind and heart were still on the past—and on Alexa. Until just now, before he'd given it words, Gage hadn't realized the connection between Jen and Alexa. But now that he was conscious of it, the similarity between them was remarkable.

Jen might have had bright, sun-gold blond hair and huge blue eyes, while Alexa had that dark burgundy hair with hazel eyes, but inwardly, they were identical in the most important ways. His heart warmed as he opened the Humvee door and slid in.

Rubbing his hands together, he started the vehicle and slowly drove away from the curb, his feelings writhing violently through him. How like Alexa to have the same magic that Jen possessed. Gage remembered some of the many hours he and his little sister went out to explore empty fields or areas where there weren't houses and yards. She was always so excited to get out into nature, always hugging trees, smelling flowers, closing her eyes and making a humming sound in her throat from the pleasure the fragrance brought her.

Tonight, as he'd kissed Alexa, that same soft hum of appreciation came from her slender throat. *It must have triggered all of this*, Gage thought as he slowly drove down one street to another.

What were the chances he'd meet someone so much like Jen? Gage was still staggered by the possibility; he hadn't believed it could ever happen. His fingers tightened around the steering wheel as he contemplated the many ways Jen and Alexa were like one another. He couldn't believe there was someone else in the world even remotely as sweet as Jen. And Alexa had the same idealism, that optimistic view that the world was full of people with good, well-meaning hearts. She was a dreamer, too.

Dark rage tunneled through him as he relived the horror of the gang of teens capturing innocent Jen, tearing at her clothes, her screams and her desperate fight for survival as he ran toward her to save her. They'd shot at him and missed. And then, the leader turned and shot Jen, killing her. She fell dead in the alley. The gang took off, disappearing down another street, leaving him to pick up her lifeless body.

Only . . . he hadn't saved her. Gage had gone over his actions that day thousands upon thousands of times. And every time, the guilt damn near ate him alive. If only he hadn't been late meeting Jen at her school. If only he'd told the teacher who wanted to speak to him after class that he'd see her tomorrow morning. If only . . .

Tears burned in his eyes and he made a muffled sound, part curse, part surprise. Angrily, he wiped them away, forcing them back where they belonged. He wasn't going to dishonor Jen by sobbing like a child who had lost everything. Reminding himself that he was his family's only survivor, he counted himself lucky to be alive.

His heart oriented gently back to Alexa, and he visualized her radiant expression, the liveliness in her hazel eyes, the innocence he felt around her. Oh, he knew Alexa wasn't an innocent. She was a fully grown woman and who had relationships before he'd walked into her life. But the kind of innocence Alexa possessed was something intrinsic to her. She would always see the goodness in life. She would always defer to hope, not hell or pragmatism.

As he parked the vehicle in the motor pool and handed over the keys to an Army private, Gage's mind remained on Alexa. He had to walk two blocks to his barracks, the chill of the night biting at his exposed ears. He hunkered down in his jacket, drawing the collar up, hands jammed in the pockets.

Damn, but Alexa's boldness made him smile! Jen wasn't like that at all. She was very shy instead. And Alexa's honesty was raw and startling to him. He'd never met a woman who came clean and asked the serious questions that every relationship eventually brought up. One kiss had opened up many doorways between them, he realized, not sorry that it had happened.

And damn it, he was so drawn to Alexa that in some ways, Gage felt helpless to combat it. His mind yammered at him that she was far out of his reach, that she wouldn't really be interested in the likes of him. Yet she clearly was, and that confounded the hell out of Gage. He was nothing special. He held terrible, heartbreaking secrets, and he wasn't the hero that Alexa thought he was. He couldn't even save his own sister.

And he knew how Alexa saw him as a hero.

No way. Not ever. It was his father who'd been a real hero. He'd loved Gage and Jen's mother, loved them. He'd done everything he could on his meager pay to see that they were cared for, fed, and had a roof over their heads.

Sometimes, Gage could feel his father yearning for more for his family. He had often talked of Jen and Gage going to college and wondered how he could ensure they'd get there. His father had wanted the best for both of them. Until that day when his whole world was shredded by the most hideous deed imaginable, the day the sun stopped shining for them all.

Gage had stopped dreaming the day his family was murdered, and he could hardly dare to imagine that someone like Alexa Culver would be seriously drawn to him.

Gage told himself it was sex and lust. That was it. He'd never had a woman tell him so bluntly that she was interested in him. Yet, he knew Alexa was not the type that hopped from one man's bed to another. He knew that for the man she loved, she would go through hell and back. His unerring sniper sense, that invisible radar he used, told him that. She was a woman who played for keeps. And if she got into a relationship, she would work hard to make it last.

God, he was in such a confusing web of events with her. He stopped at his barracks, took out the key, and opened the door. Entering the hall, he quietly shut and locked the door, assaulted by the snoring of his Marine friends as he padded silently down to the door on the left. He decided to shower early tomorrow morning before meeting Alexa. His mind was churning over so many things, his emotions in utter disarray. Now all Gage wanted was to lie down and hope like hell he'd fall asleep immediately to escape it all.

He did fall asleep, but his dreams, which were usually dark and torturous, turned to a rich canvas of his sister. He saw Jen's smiles as they enjoyed the many adventures they'd had as children. His father had deployed out of Camp Pendleton, the huge Marine Corps base in Southern California. They'd explored together the yellow, baked, cactus-strewn hills.

Jen was born when he was two. Later, as they grew up, he remembered helping his mother with Jen when she was young. His mother had a part-time job and balanced it with taking care of all of them.

Fortunately, Jen was what his mother called a "good baby," and Gage adored holding her, rocking her. She was his sister, and she and her sunlit hair always made him smile. His father had asked him to help his mother while he was gone on deployment, and Gage took that request with seriousness.

In the dream he saw his father when he'd just returned from Iraq, just in time to see Jen take her first steps. Gage had sat on the floor watching his mother ease Jen out toward her father, who had his hands outstretched to catch her in case she fell. The moment was forever etched on Gage's heart. After Jen had taken those faltering, unsure steps toward her father at his coaxing, there was a huge celebration. Even more heartwarming, Gage recalled his dad pulling him over, his arm around his shoulders, telling him about the time he'd made his own first steps. Gage heard the awe, joy, and pride in his dad's voice as he recounted that monumental event that his parents never forgot.

The dream continued, and Gage remembered that his dad, when home, was a fierce and protective parent. But he was also loving, and came into his room two or three times a week to read to Gage before he went to sleep. Gage would pick the book out, and his dad would come in, sit near his bed, and read a chapter or two until Gage fell asleep. A few nights later, they would pick up where they'd left off. This experience alone fostered in Gage a great love of books.

At thirteen, Gage had been taken aside by his father, who had been seriously wounded and had left the Marine Corps, planning to move his family to the Chicago urban area. His mother's eye condition was worsening, and she was distraught. Gage saw the strain on his father's face as well. He could feel his father's intense love for his mother—there was no question that he loved her with a fierceness that Gage had never seen between two people. Gage's dad had sat him down in the garage, where they could be alone, and had drawn up a second chair opposite him. He could remember the somber, serious tone in his dad's voice as he told him that he was going to have to grow up in a hurry. Although most kids his age still had a lot of years without responsibility left, his life was now going to be different.

Gage could feel his father's heavy heart and his concern, saw it in his dark blue eyes. His father had rested his elbows on his thighs, hands clasped between his legs. In a low voice, he told Gage that he was needed, because he could no longer do certain things due to his serious back injuries from the war. He was now in constant pain, unable to make certain movements, and Gage knew that his dad had spent nearly a year in the hospital and then in rehab, learning to walk again.

A piece of shrapnel from an RPG, a rocket propelled grenade, had struck the Humvee he was riding in down an Iraqi street. The shrapnel had lodged in his lower spine, paralyzing him for a while, but his father's fighting spirit had triumphed and he was able to walk again, as well as do most of the things he had always been able to do.

Now his father told Gage that he was tall for his age, stronger than most thirteen-year-olds, and that he was going to need Gage's help. Gage was more than ready to assist in whatever way he could. There wasn't a day that went by that he didn't see the pain in his father's face. And he knew his mother worried about the amount of pain drugs he had to take just to keep going. Even at thirteen, Gage was dealing with parent-level issues every day. His mother's eyes were so bad that she could no longer walk to her grade school to pick up Jen every morning and afternoon. Now that was his job.

Gage awoke suddenly, sitting up in bed, wiping the sweat off his brow. It was dark and he could hear the wind blowing outside the barracks. Pressing the heels of his palms against his eyes, a guttural sound escaped him. The dream was still with him—the memories of that move from California to Chicago. He remembered his father's pain from that shrapnel and how he had sat in the backseat of their car, only thirteen, but feeling strong and capable. He felt good about himself because he'd helped his father, and they'd gotten all the furniture and boxes loaded into the trailer. He was looking forward to walking Jen to and from her grade school every day once they arrived at the small row house his parents had bought.

With a soft curse, Gage pulled his hands away from his face and threw the covers off his legs, sitting up, his feet touching the cold floor. He gripped the mattress on either side of him, eyes tightly shut. Everyone had so been looking forward to that move. His dad loved Chicago, had told him so many funny stories about the city, about where they would live. He knew his dad was over the moon that they had been able to buy a small house in his old neighborhood.

Sadness swam through Gage, and he shook his head as his heartache deepened, feeling like he was about to drown in a riptide of sorrow.

Who would ever imagine that the place where his dad grew up happy would end their lives? Who would guess that after they moved there, Jen and his dad would be murdered by a street gang, leaving him and his mother in shock?

And yet, Gage had stepped into his father's shoes and done the best he could to help his mother survive the unbearable. He had held her, but no one had held him.

CHAPTER 7

GAGE WAS ON edge as the CH-47 helicopter landed outside the Shinwari village. It was 0800, the sky a pale blue, the temperature below freezing, snow covering the area around the walled village. There was a contingent of ten Marines who acted as protection for the dental and optical team that had flown in with them. Much to his disappointment, Matt Culver couldn't make it, and he'd been counting on being there for his sister.

Unfortunately, he had been called out on an op in the middle of the night, and this morning at 0700, when he'd met Alexa at her B-hut, he couldn't tell her where he'd gone. Delta Force was black ops, and everything they did was top secret.

Gage was glad the Marine squad went down the ramp first, establishing a perimeter, their M14s up and ready. This was a safe, pro-American village, but Gage knew that even the safest village was a crapshoot these days. There could always be villagers who hid their pro-Taliban stance and then came out of nowhere, attacking Americans with the intent to kill them.

Gripping Alexa's arm, he sensed her excitement. She was in the air war, not the ground war, and didn't grasp how dangerous these outings could be. Of course, she knew that Matt's fiancée had found out the hard way. Dr. Dara McKenzie had been in a van going to a safe Shinwari village when it was ambushed and attacked by Taliban. The driver had been instantly killed, and Dara escaped with Matt, while Callie, her younger sister, was taken by another Delta Force operator, Beau Gardner, in a different direction. Both couples were trying to split their pursuers, hide, and get the hell away from the firefight.

Gage wished Alexa wasn't so bubbly and excited this morning. Instead, she should have been focusing, looking around, watching the villagers' body language, and keeping alert. But that was his job. Today, he was her shadow, whether she wanted him to be or not. As they stepped off the ramp into the half-foot-deep snow, Gage was glad he'd decided to wear his sniper gear. Although he didn't carry a sniper rifle on him, he did have an M4 in a chest harness, the barrel pointed down. There was also a .45 in his holster and a Ka-

Bar knife in a sheath strapped to his lower left calf. And of course he'd brought his sixty-five-pound rucksack, fully packed with things he needed on a sniper op. No one, with the exception of the medical teams and Alexa, came to this village unarmed.

The buffeting of the blades hit them full force. The CH-47 had two blades, one front and one rear. Snow was flying up as the two loadmasters quickly released the pallet of goods, allowing it to slide down into the muddy earth. Gage pulled Alexa aside, keeping her near him to protect her as much as he could. He lifted his chin, his gaze slowly panning along the line of hills that ended where the walled village began. He saw why the village had been built there in the first place. There was a nice stream giving the area water from high up in the Hindu Kush, more than fourteen thousand feet tall ten kilometers to the east of them. The mountains looked like guardians, but Gage knew better.

These mountains held thousands of limestone caves where the Taliban hid and made plans, and stuck the innocent who had been kidnapped and were going to be taken over the Pakistan border to be sold as slaves. They used the caves to hide and then assault an unarmed village. Then the bastards would melt back into the mountains, hiding once again from the eyes of the drones.

He moved Alexa from the roar of the CH-47 and the blasts of wind tearing at them, almost knocking her down. Keeping his hand firmly around her upper arm, he saw the chief and his wife waiting at the village's opened gates. Gage had never been to this village, so he didn't know the lay of the land. As a sniper, he sure as hell didn't like the look of that heavily treed wadi, or ravine, moving vertically from the wall of the village straight up into the hills above them. It was a good place for Taliban to sit and hide and strike from. Damn!

Yes, it was winter, and yes, the Taliban had supposedly slunk back to their villages or across the border to wait until spring to make their next offensive into this war-torn country.

The back of his neck prickled—a warning that not all was what it seemed. Gage never disregarded the hair rising on his nape. Not ever. His fingers tightened around Alexa's arm and he drew her a little closer to him. She looked up, suddenly worried.

"What?" she mouthed.

It was impossible to talk with the helo's blades turning at nearly takeoff speed. The bird was a target, and the pilots wanted to offload all the supplies as fast as they could and get the hell out of there.

Gage's mouth tightened. Looking down, he thought how out of place Alexa looked here. She was like a bright, beautiful flower. Her red hair plaited in a single braid peaked out from beneath the hood of her black nylon down parka. A soft forest green turtleneck, jeans, and hiking boots completed her ensemble.

Shaking his head, he nudged her toward the village, wanting to get as far away from that helo as possible. The medical teams were hurrying toward the gate, and the people waiting for them were peering out of it. Gage put himself behind her, his hand on her shoulder, guiding her as quickly as she could get through the snow. Alexa intuitively knew that something wasn't right—he could see it by the sudden tension in her body. And that was good, Gage thought, because survival was instinctive.

Did she feel the danger? He sure as hell did. His gaze whipped from one place to another, trying to ferret out where it was lurking.

The villagers waved and smiled as the medical teams, seven female medical assistants and two male doctors in total, met with the chief. Gage pulled Alexa away from them, keeping his eyes on the ground, looking for snow or mud that had been disturbed, signs that IEDs had been planted. He searched thoroughly before he let her move a foot in any direction.

Alexa seemed oblivious to the threat, and his protectiveness amped up as he brought her near the heavy wooden gate, then waited. Placing her between the mud-and-stone wall that rose six feet high and was two feet thick, Gage turned, bringing up the barrel of his M4, a sign he was on guard.

Where the hell was the danger coming from? His nostrils flared, and he tried to pick up a scent that might tell him. With the churning of the wind from the blades' turning, it was almost impossible to smell anything.

Those hills. He knew someone was hiding in those hills. There were groves of evergreens in the wadi. A whole army could hide in there and not be seen. Gage wished he had a combat assault dog and handler with them, because the dog sure as hell would have alerted his handler of any sign of danger. Combat dogs were trained to quietly signal if they detected enemy fighters or ambushes. Also, generally two Apache gunships flew with an unarmed helicopter such as this one. But none had been available, and the colonel on duty at the ops desk approved the flight to go without them since it was a short trip and a pro-American village they were to visit. Gage had almost argued against it but kept his mouth shut. He should have opened it, damn it.

As a sniper, Gage knew patience was the key to finding the Taliban. It was possible that attacks would occur, even during the winter.

He wished like hell a drone could have at least been sent with them. He'd demanded that from the Air Force colonel. The officer had been pissed but agreed there should be some level of protection for the medical mission. One was on the way, he knew, and it was due to arrive in about five minutes. It was too damned bad that the spooks hadn't sent one ahead to check for body heat, because that would quickly have pinpointed any hidden Taliban.

Frustration thrummed through Gage as he watched the two medical groups, mostly composed of young women in their twenties. They were smiling, laughing, and chatting, as if they were on a lark.

This was not a lark. Gage knew from prior experience that these health teams, as they were referred to, were used to working in a nice, safe office on Bagram, not out in the wilds of this chaotic country. His teeth clenched as the two groups gathered around the chief and his wife. They should have gone inside the village walls. It would have been a safer place to meet. But no one was asking him to handle security for this medical team. The civilian doctors waved off the Marine sergeant's suggestions to move inside the walls. The Marines could suggest, but it was the doctors who were in charge and made final decisions.

Meanwhile, the ramp was quickly lifted and closed. The CH-47 powered up, the engines roaring, shaking the air, the vibrations rippled through Gage's tense body. He felt Alexa's hand on his arm as she peeked out from behind him. She was concerned, but he couldn't tell her anything because the noise was deafening as the helo rose straight up in the air, clawing for altitude.

His gaze cut sharply to the Marine detachment. He had complete faith in them. They were well-trained marksmen, and great guards for this group, which was clearly oblivious to the dangers that surrounded them. But they weren't snipers and could easily miss small details that stood out and screamed at him.

Alexa gripped Gage's arm, waiting for the helicopter to be far enough away so that they could talk and hear one another. His face was stony and his eyes were narrowed, his gaze never still. What was wrong? She was uneasy, and yet she felt safe because he was standing in front of her.

If she'd ever doubted his type A status, she could now put that to rest after seeing him with the Air Force colonel, forcing him to get a drone for their flight out here. She licked her lips nervously, trying to see what he was seeing.

"What's wrong, Gage? Something isn't right?"

He barely turned his head, keeping his gaze briefly on the wadi, his finger just above the trigger of his M4. "Got company. I feel a threat but I can't see it yet, but I will . . ."

"W-what does that mean?" She quickly looked at the medical teams talking through an interpreter with the smiling chief.

"I don't know," he answered slowly. "Just stay where you are. If I tell you to drop, you do it. If I tell you to run, you run with me as hard and fast as you can for that village entrance. All right?"

"Oh, God," she breathed. "Yes . . . yes, I will." Alexa stretched her neck, looking to his left. "Can't we tell someone?"

"I did. I radioed the sergeant who's heading up that squad of Marines. He feels it, too."

Hearing the frustration in her tone, Gage watched the boughs of the evergreens move slightly beneath the breeze coming off the slopes of the mountains. "Do you feel anything?"

Alexa closed her eyes, trying to keep her heart from pounding. They were at seventy-five hundred feet, and she was used to sea level. She opened her eyes and said, "No . . . I'm sorry, I don't."

"That's all right." Gage knew she was highly distracted, like everyone else except the Marines. He was the opposite: laser-focused.

Gage looked to his right and saw the Marines spreading out, always wary of IEDs planted below the surface of the snow from the night before. Sergeant Brian Jameson was a five-year Iraq War vet, and he'd spent two years in this sorry-ass country after that. So he knew the lay of the land, and Gage had confidence in him and his leadership. He, too, was on guard. His facial expression showed that he was clearly pissed at the two doctors who nixed getting their medical teams into the safety behind the walls of the village.

"That's okay," he murmured, trying not to sound so hard and gruff.

"What do you think is in there?" Alexa asked, pointing toward the wadi.

Gage quickly gripped her hand, bringing it down to his side. "First rule of warfare, don't point out the enemy. Okay?"

His voice was bemused, but she wasn't laughing.

"This is serious, Gage?"

"Very." He got on his lapel radio, talking to Jameson in a low tone that no one could hear except the man at the other end.

"This was supposed to be a safe place," Alexa muttered, worried, her gloved hand on the back of Gage's Kevlar vest. She felt the urgency bristling within him and now saw him for the warrior he was—and that was nothing like the Marine she'd met last week. This was another side of him, and right now, it made Alexa feel safer in a very unstable situation.

Snorting, Gage muttered, "There is no safe place anywhere in this godforsaken country, Alexa. You should know that by now. You've bombed and strafed the hell out of it."

Raising an eyebrow, she sighed. "The air war is very different from the ground war."

"Tell me about it." Gage lowered his voice, turning toward her for a moment. "Do me a favor?"

"Sure."

"Take off your dog tags. Give them to me."

Shocked, she stared at him. "But . . . why?"

"Because if you are captured and they find those tags on you, it won't be pleasant. They hate women in the military worse than they do the men."

Gulping, Alexa saw he was dead serious.

"Turn your back opposite that wadi and take them off. Slip them into my hand as quietly as possible. The enemy has binoculars like we do. They'll be looking for that chain around everyone's neck. They like to target military personnel first, and then NGO civilians like that cluster around the chief and his wife."

Shaken, Alexa did as he asked, pushing them into his awaiting hand. Her heart pulsed with adrenaline. "What should we do?"

"I'd like to call in some Apaches with their infrared on board, but Sergeant Jameson said none are available. We're sitting ducks out here, and I don't like it one bit."

"Should we go inside the village, then? It has a high, thick wall."

Gage couldn't keep the derision out of his low tone. "No. The medical doctors made the decision to stay out here even though Sergeant Jameson told them to get everyone inside the walls."

"What can we do?" Alexa tried to steady her voice. When she was in the heavily armored cockpit of her A-10, she felt protected. Even if she made low, slow passes to strafe and destroy Taliban trying to overrun an American position, she still felt safe.

Here? She felt like a target was on her back. Gage was placing himself between her and the world around them, shielding her. A fierce sense of gratitude rose in her chest.

She wasn't wearing a protective vest. In fact, her only weapon was a .45 pistol in a holster on her right hip. Alexa hadn't been expecting this at all.

She heard a hollow *thunk* from the area around the wadi.

"*Incoming!*" Gage suddenly yelled into his radio, alerting the other Marines. Instantly, he turned, savagely shoving Alexa down onto the muddy soil and dropping, trying to cover her. It was an RPG, fired from a launcher by their enemy.

Alexa screamed and slammed against the wall, her knees buried in mud, her hands covering her head. Gage landed hard on top of her, his arms gathering her beneath his wide, long body. She opened her mouth, knowing if an RPG was fired and it landed close, her lungs had to equalize with the pressure from the blast. If she didn't, they would turn to jelly in an instant.

She heard Gage curse, and he embraced her, tucking her head against his chest. *Oh, God!*

An RPG landed just inside the front gate of the village, the resounding pressure waves from the blast tearing the gates off their hinges and sending them flying outward. A second RPG was launched, landing inside the village near the first one fired. Alexa felt the blasts like fists punching her body, and the sounds were so loud, it felt as if thunder had literally landed upon her as the ground shook all around her. It felt like an earthquake.

She heard Gage groan, and suddenly, he went limp above her, his arms loosening around her head and shoulders. *No!* Had he been hit? Alexa squirmed, her ears in such pain she couldn't hear anything except the roar inside them.

"Gage!" she cried, trying to wriggle out from beneath him. He was so heavy! She wallowed in the mud and snow, trying to get out from under him to see what had happened.

But before Alexa could wriggle free, Gage was suddenly hauled off her. Her eyes widened as she looked upward. A man dressed in black Afghan clothing with a brown beard and hatred in his eyes stared down at her. He grinned savagely, reaching out and yanking Alexa to her feet.

Alexa got her first look at the aftermath of the attack and, to her horror, saw the chief and his wife lying at the entrance, unmoving, blood around their bodies. The young women of the medical teams had run screaming, utterly panicked, and there were men on horseback thundering after them. The male medical professionals with them had been shot. Chaos ensued.

Alexa yelped as the Taliban soldier slammed her against the wall, knocking the wind out of her. He grabbed her hands, quickly wrapping her wrists in tight ropes. Alexa fought, and he cursed in Urdu, the main language of Pakistan. He grabbed her .45 and tossed it away.

She heard screams and saw Taliban soldiers on horseback grabbing all of the female medical personnel. They each dismounted, jerking a woman to them, tying her hands, and then throwing her on their horse and mounting up behind them.

NO!

She was dragged past Gage, who lay unconscious on the ground. To her horror, she saw blood on the side of his temple. *Oh, no!* The blast had injured him! She dug in her boots, screaming and fighting back as the soldier dragged her toward his waiting horse, but he was wiry and much stronger than she was.

Alexa kicked out, trying to make him release her. He turned and raised his hand, as if to strike her, but she dodged his wide-open hand, falling to her knees on the ground. Behind her, she heard the other women's shrieks and wails. Several riders galloped by, each with a woman in the saddle, her hands tied, the soldiers whipping their animals to go faster.

"Gage!" Alexa cried, scrambling to her feet. She dodged the soldier's next slap, yanking him around. She wasn't a small woman—maybe an inch shorter than her captor. Anger leaped to his eyes as he grabbed the reins of his horse with his other hand. The animal danced around, rolling its eyes in terror.

"Gage, help me!" she sobbed, hauling back.

The soldier suddenly released her, and Alexa fell to the ground as he came at her, slamming his boot down into her chest.

An *ooofff* of air ruptured from her lungs as he put all his weight upon her chest, glaring down at her. Alexa couldn't move, the air knocked out of her. She tried to rise, but it was impossible to breathe.

The soldier was cursing angrily now, grabbing her by the hair, his fist wrapped solidly within it, and hauling her upright. The pain spread like hot needles across her scalp as she cried out, throwing her tied hands upward. Now he had full control of her. Pushing her to the horse, he forced her to mount. Once on it, he kept her head back against him, her throat exposed, putting her off balance. Kicking his bay horse, he whipped it around to leave.

Alexa nearly fell off, but the soldier had a strong hold on her hair and wrenched her upright as the horse galloped down the length of the wall. Tears jammed into her eyes, and all she could do was reach for the horse's mane and try to hold on. What was happening? Where were the other Marines? There were gunshots being fired all around the wall at different points. Her hearing came and went.

Ahead of her were Taliban on horseback, racing down the valley. They raced past the wadi they'd been hiding in and swiftly left it behind. Gage had been right! She cried out, the pain so bad that she was crying, unable to make her captor release her hair.

They galloped out of sight of the village, and to Alexa's shock, she saw three white Toyota Hilux pickups waiting around the bend. There were other Taliban soldiers with AK-47s standing by the beds, their faces grim, their fingers on the triggers of their rifles. She was stunned and didn't know what to think. Soon enough, the horses and soldiers ahead of her were stopping by each pickup. They each dumped the woman they'd captured into the bed of a truck, and another soldier in the bed shoved the women down on their hands and knees. They were slapped, kicked, and threatened with being shot if they didn't remain down on the bed. By the time Alexa arrived, she was the fifth woman in the lead truck. The soldier released her hair, bringing his horse up alongside the bed. With a shove, the soldier pushed her off the horse, and she crashed into the truck with a cry of pain.

The other four women were already hunkered down on hands and knees, cowed and terrified. Alexa heard a snarl as struggled to get up. Blackbeard leaned down, yanking her by her shoulder, spinning her onto her knees. Savagely, he shoved his hand down on the back of her neck, forcing Alexa's face into the cold metal of the bed. He kept her there, leaning down, snarling in Urdu. Alexa knew it meant "Stay down!" and she did, sobbing for breath, her scalp aching with unrelenting pain. She heard shouts and the movement of horses but didn't dare look up. *Gage!* He'd been hurt. Was he dead? *No! NO!*

The pickups were fired up, and soon they were racing through the snow, heading somewhere. Alexa and the others were bounced around, still forced to keep their heads down and remain crouched on their knees. The two soldiers with them would jam their muddy boots into their backs if they tried to lift their heads.

Alexa quickly learned to stay where she was. Her mind spun—she was shocked by the ferocity of the attack. The jolting and bumping tossed them around on the floor of the bed, and every time a woman's head came up as she was wrenched against the panel of the truck, a soldier would kick at her, forcing her head down on the floor of the truck.

Alexa heard the women crying sometimes, her hearing coming and going. She couldn't reach out to them, but their bodies were jammed against one another as the trucks roared and climbed out of the valley. She had no idea where they were, but they seemed to be moving up a slope. The wheels were spinning, mud flying everywhere. Oh, God, where were they taking them? And what were they going to do with them? Alexa bit down on her lower lip, tasting blood. Gage had looked as if he were dead! Dead!

Her heart shredded, and she couldn't stop a little cry of grief. His face had been leached white, with blood running freely down his cheek.

The world closed in on Alexa. She was slid around and bumped by the truck racing along a flatter area of the road. Fear consumed her. Her mind spun with the fact that she'd heard of Afghan women and little girls and boys being kidnapped by the Taliban and then sold in Pakistan to sick sexual monsters who would pay for a sex toy or slave to do their bidding. Trying not to heave, her stomach wanting to revolt, Alexa curled into a fetal knot.

She reminded herself that she was a military officer—the only one in this group of women. A momentary relief sped through her, and she was eternally grateful that Gage had told her to remove her dog tags. The Taliban would not know who she was because she carried no identification on her. She didn't know about the civilian women, however. Alexa's mind rolled from shock to grief and then her will to survive kicked in. Above all, she could not allow them to know who she really was. As she was bounced around in the bed, the ropes tight, cutting off circulation to her hands, Alexa focused now on creating a name and story about herself. Luckily, she'd never met these other women, and they didn't know who she was. She certainly wasn't about to let on that she was an Air Force officer.

She shut her eyes tightly, her knees bloodied, scraped, and bruised by the truck's racing at high speed, sloughing over the road, almost sliding sideways at times. Alexa knew that if anyone had been left alive in that Marine contingent, they would be calling Bagram for help. They would get Apaches up. This village was only twenty miles from the base, a hop, skip, and a jump for those combat helicopters.

They could stop these men from stealing these women and potentially stealing their lives. Alexa uttered a little cry as she again pictured Gage lying unconscious or dead on the muddy ground. He had been so vital, so full of life, so protective of her seconds before. And he'd shielded her with his own body and taken the blows and the pressure concussion from those RPGs that had been fired. He'd saved her life, at a very heavy price. If he wasn't dead, he was seriously injured. Now, teetering between sheer panic and steely calm, Alexa knew she had to be brave in a way she'd never been before.

Yes, she'd taken SERE—survival, evasion, resistance, and escape—training for two weeks. Yes, she'd been tortured and had seen other pilots flying combat aircraft tortured in the school, to show them what they could expect. And it wasn't going to be pretty, Alexa knew. What if the Taliban had captured all these women to rape them? To keep them as sex slaves for themselves, rather than selling them in Pakistan? Either way, it was a horrible nightmare. These soldiers stank of goat, of not washing for weeks, their sour smell made her stomach clench.

What else could they do with them? She had no idea. The worst possible scenario was to be tortured to death or waterboarded. She had experienced it at SERE to find out what it was like, and like everyone else, she'd failed, thinking she was dying and screaming and passing out from the experience.

Perhaps these men would behead them, a curved scimitar slicing her throat open from one ear to another. Or the women might be put on video and shown to the world. The Taliban was capable of all these things. Alexa knew what was coming, and however she looked at it, all these women, including herself, had been herded up, forced by men who hated them into these trucks, and there was a plan behind all this.

They were wanted for something. Anxiety sheared through her. Alexa felt death stalking them all.

The air icy-cold, the wind rushing past her, Alexa began shaking, her teeth chattering. She had on a heavy down parka, but the other women wore nothing nearly this warm. Yet her hands were now numb, her face as well, and she knew hypothermia was setting in. Where were they taking them?

Alexa suspected the other women were faring far worse than she. Sometimes, when her hearing came back, she heard some of them weeping, but she knew that tears wouldn't get them out of this. Alexa knew she was going to have to be strong—stronger than she'd ever been in her entire life.

She wasn't sure that help would come or that they'd be rescued. There had been no drone overhead for them.

Now she understood Gage's unhappiness about the fact that there had been no Apache escort available to fly with the CH-47 helicopter. If they had, their infrared sensing equipment would have immediately spotted the hidden Taliban in that wadi. And then they'd have fired their Hellfire missiles or used their .50 caliber Gatling gun to destroy them before they could attack their group. They had been left wide open to attack. And it had happened. That colonel at ops was going to regret his decision, which had put all of them in harm's way. She hoped he was brought up on charges and lost his rank and status.

CHAPTER 8

Tal Culver groaned in protest, rolling over in bed away from Wyatt Lockwood to answer the red security phone on her nightstand.

"Tal here," she mumbled, pushing off the warm covers, sitting up. She wiped at her drowsy eyes, trying to wake up, and felt Wyatt stir. When she looked up through the window, the January night was clear, the stars sparkling above, the trees below coated with snow. Glancing at the clock it read 0300.

"Ma'am, Benson here. We just got a call from Bagram that your sister and seven other women were kidnapped from an Afghan village twenty miles north of the base."

Terror slammed into Tal. She stood up, her heart hammering, but the Marine in her, the officer, kicked in. She waved at Wyatt, now awake and jerked her finger toward the light switch. "Tell me everything," she demanded, her voice rough as she grabbed the pen and paper she always kept nearby.

Wyatt moved quickly, naked, flipping the switch so light could flood their bedroom. Tal punched a button on the security phone, putting it on speaker.

". . . Captain Culver was on a charity mission to the village. According to Sergeant Gage Hunter, USMC, who was there, the Taliban hid in a nearby wadi and threw two RPGs to create chaos. Sergeant Hunter was your sister's bodyguard for the day. He threw himself over her and protected her from the blast, which was dangerously close. He lost consciousness, and when he came to, he saw that the male medical doctors had been killed and the women had been rounded up. The villagers came forward to show the Marines, who were there to guard them, where the women had been taken."

Tal nodded, rubbing her brow. "Has anyone contacted my parents about this?"

"No, ma'am. You're our first call."

"I'll do it," Tal whispered. She felt Wyatt's hand come to rest on her bare shoulder, trying to give her some comfort. Taking a deep breath, Tal asked, "What's being done to find these kidnapped women?"

"Sergeant Hunter is heading up the rescue effort, ma'am. He's a Marine sniper, and he knows Alexa personally. He's called the SEAL and Delta Force units here. He's got a drone up, and it's following three white Toyota Hilux pickups with the women bound and in the back. There are two Taliban soldiers in each bed with AK-47s. We've got a live feed. You need to get down here to Artemis ASAP."

Tal felt Wyatt's hand leave her shoulder. He pulled some clothes from the drawer for her, tossing them nearby so she could get dressed as soon as the phone call ended. She loved her fiancé fiercely and nodded in his direction with a silent thank-you for his help.

"What else is being done? Does Sergeant Hunter know who's behind this?"

"There's a regional warlord, Daud Zadgal, who's a Taliban sympathizer. He's behind it, says Sergeant Hunter."

"And what does Sergeant Hunter think is going to happen to these women?"

"Probably be sold as sex slaves across the border, ma'am."

Grimacing, Tal saw Wyatt's scowl deepen, his eyes darkening with silent rage. "Have you connected with Special Operations Command out of Tampa, Florida, yet?"

"Yes, ma'am, Trudy is on it. Everything is being coordinated as swiftly as humanly possible. They know your sister is among the captives. They won't spare any expense or manpower to find all of them and get them back to us."

"Great platitudes," Tal growled, "but I want a mission drawn up on this ASAP. I don't want words I want action. Anything else?"

"The drone following them shows the drivers are skirting one of the mountains on a back road. The snow is deep, and it's slowing them down. We're putting up top-secret maps of that area right now down in the War Room. By the time you arrive, everything will be up, and we can potentially see where they might be taking these women."

"Good," Tal breathed. "That's as good as it gets. Have you been in touch with my brother Matt yet? He's with Delta Force."

"Sergeant Culver is out on another mission, ma'am. His captain said he won't let him know because his team is taking down an important HVT."

"How soon will he be off this op?" she demanded, closing her eyes. Matt was one of the best when it came to this type of kidnapping scenario. She wanted him there, and Tal knew he'd want to be there for Alexa. They were, after all, twins, and they had a powerful, invisible connection to one another. Tal wouldn't have been surprised if Matt was picking up on Alexa's dangerous situation.

"Ma'am, I can't get that out of the captain. Maybe if you call him when you arrive, that might shake loose a little more Intel. You know how black ops people are. They hold their cards close to their chest."

Growling, Tal rose. "Yes, I know that." She grabbed her jeans, pulling them on. "All right, we'll be there in twenty minutes. Call anyone else that we might need on this mission into the firm."

"Yes, ma'am."

Tal punched the off button on the phone, grabbing the red turtleneck sweater Wyatt handed to her. "I need to call Mom and Dad."

"I know." He handed her a pair of thick socks. She sat down on the edge of the mattress and pulled them on. Wyatt looked stricken as he knelt down on one knee and slipped her boots on for her.

"Thanks," she whispered, giving him a warm, grateful look.

"Tal, sugar, take a deep breath on this one. We've hired good people for Artemis Security, all military vets. They know what they're doing, and they're as on top of this fluid situation as you can get under the circumstances."

Her lips twisted as she knotted the laces, standing up, quickly moving her fingers through her hair. "I know you're right. It's just such a shock, Wyatt." Sudden tears burned in her eyes.

"Hey," he rasped, "come here for just a sec." He hauled her into his arms, holding her, kissing her hair. Gruffly, he said, "Alexa is made of strong stuff, Tal. She'll get through this. Remember, she's a SERE-trained officer."

His strength comforted her, and, easing out of his arms, she gave him a wry look as she walked over and retrieved her red down jacket from the closet. "Well? You wanted to test your mission software on a real scenario. Here it is, Wyatt."

Giving her a sad look, he nodded. "Yeah, but I never thought Alexa would be a part of that rescue mission."

"Me either," Tal muttered, terribly worried and struggling to keep a brave face. She threw open the door, limping down the hall to the carpeted stairs. Her shattered ankle was still healing from being injured last June. And she still had to wear a special supportive boot around it. Wyatt was beside her, pulling on his leather bombardier jacket. As she carefully took the stairs, she was going to ask him to drive their black SUV down the snow-covered roads into the country surrounding Alexandria, Virginia. She would make the call to her parents on the drive over to Artemis.

Her stomach tightened, and she felt like she wanted to vomit. It was a visceral reaction to her little sister, whom everyone loved dearly, being captured. God only knew what could happen to Alexa, and with Tal's background as a Marine Corps sniper heading up her own unit at Bagram for five years, she knew Taliban torture methods weren't spared for women. In fact, they hated both genders with equal ferocity.

Alexa was truly in the worst kind of trouble. Could they get her out of it?

★

DILARA CULVER STARED in shock at her husband, Robert, after they received the phone call from their daughter Tal. She stood by the bed in her pink silk nightgown, her red hair in disarray as she saw her husband quickly get dressed. His mouth was set in a hard line, his eyes glittering and implacable. At six foot three inches tall, Robert Culver was a well-respected Air Force general, revered by every branch of the military. Now he was going to drive to Artemis to support Tal's efforts to find and save Alexa.

Fighting back tears, Dilara knew that emotional histrionics wouldn't get the job done. Her daughter, Alexa, had been captured by the enemy. She could tell by the way Robert looked that this was akin to two officers coming up to a woman's house to inform her that her husband had died in combat.

She wrapped her arms around herself, suddenly chilled. "I knew this day would come," she whispered unsteadily, catching his gaze for a moment. "I always had that premonition, but I kept telling myself it was because I feared for all our children over there in the military, in that country, and I didn't say anything to you."

Robert sat down on a chair and hauled on his hiking boots. "Don't go there, pet. This is not your fault." He stood, pulling back his broad, capable shoulders. Walking over to her, he settled his hands on her upper arms, his face becoming readable. "Listen to me, okay? We'll find Alexa, and we'll get her out of this situation. I want you to stay here. You need to call your brothers in Turkey and your cousin Angelo in Greece. Ask for their prayers." He cupped her face, placing a warm kiss on her lips. "I'll be in touch and send you hourly updates, Dilara. I don't want you worrying any more than you have to, all right? I'm going to call my brothers, Pete and John, on the way to Artemis. They may want to join us."

Pete was a general in the Marine Corps and John an admiral in the Navy. Right now, Robert wanted to bring all the military power they had to bear on this situation.

Love welled up inside Dilara, erasing momentarily her terrifying fear for her youngest daughter's life. She touched her husband's shadowed face, his beard prickly beneath her fingertips. Dilara had to be calm and centered for him, too. Robert was a wonderful, caring father to their three children and loved them as much as she did.

Putting on a brave front, she managed a broken smile, gazing directly up into his narrowed, concerned eyes. "Yes, that's more than all right. Get going, okay? I'll make the phone calls."

He kissed her again, hard this time. She could feel her husband's desperate wish to give her hope. Dilara knew all about the military. Tal, Matt, and Alexa had all joined different branches, and they all had jobs that were potentially life-threatening. She'd had to learn to live with the threat that one or more of them might be killed. Already, Tal had been injured on a sniper op last June, and she would have died if Wyatt had not found her in time. Even now, her ankle, held together with pins and screws, was not completely healed. Her once-athletic daughter had been slowed to the pace of a snail, which Tal hated.

She watched as Robert picked up his black leather jacket, shrugging it over a dark blue shirt. Even in jeans and hiking boots, Dilara thought, a military bearing exuded from her husband. "Be careful driving out there. The roads will be icy," she called as he pulled open the bedroom door.

"I will." He hesitated, turning, his voice going gruff. "I love you, pet. We'll get Alexa home. Somehow, some way, we'll make it happen. You just say your prayers and ask your family to do the same."

He left without a sound. Her husband was a giant among men, literally and figuratively speaking. Dilara couldn't give in to her roiling emotions, or her terror, or her mind, which kept drifting toward horrifying scenarios Alexa might have been facing at this very moment. She hurried to the closet, opening it, and pulled down a pair of black wool slacks. From the dresser, she took out a soft pink angora sweater with a mock turtleneck. This was Alexa's favorite color: pink.

Her heart felt as if it were breaking as she quickly dressed. She pushed her feet into a pair of black leather shoes and hurried downstairs. It seemed so quiet. As if the world were holding its breath. Waiting. Just waiting . . .

Dilara went to the kitchen and quickly made herself some strong Turkish coffee. She needed it, because when she called her brothers, they would be highly distraught. Her Greek cousin Angelo would be equally rocked by the news. After downing a second cup, Dilara picked up the phone, took a deep breath, and tried to steady her own churning emotions. Her Turkish family dearly loved Robert and Dilara's three grown children. Uncle Ihsan, as everyone called him, had special affection for Tal, Matt, and Alexa. As Dilara pressed the button that would connect to her brother's villa on the Aegean Sea, she leaned an elbow on the granite counter. She felt her knees weakening and sat down on a black leather stool, waiting for her brother's voice. Tears burned in her eyes. Oh, God in heaven, how was she going to break this news to her brothers?

They loved Alexa as if she was their daughter, and Dilara knew the fierce passion that Turks held in their DNA. This would shatter them in ways she couldn't imagine. And what if they couldn't find Alexa? What if she was killed? Tortured? Whether she wanted them to or not, tears leaked out of her tightly shut eyes as she waited for Ihsan to pick up the phone at the other end.

★

TAL DREW IN a breath of relief as her father strode into the War Room within Artemis Security. She sat with her assembled team of seven people. Among them was Wyatt at her right elbow. She'd left a place for her father on Wyatt's other side, gesturing for him to come in. The lights were low. Up on the viewing screen at the end of the room, a good six feet across and five feet vertically, they were watching a live drone feed.

Robert leaned over, placing a kiss on Tal's mussed hair. "Catch me up?" he asked gruffly, sitting down and pulling over a pad and pen from the center of the long, oval table.

"What you're seeing is a live drone feed, Dad," Tal said. "We've been able to identify every woman in those three trucks via facial ID. Alexa is in the lead truck, near the rear, next to the Taliban soldier. She seems to be okay, as are the other women. We haven't been able to see any wounds on them."

Robert learned forward, eyes squinting as he studied the color video, which was sharp and clear. "Is this a Pred?"

"I wish," Tal said, giving him a look, "No, not a Pred." A Predator drone carried weapons on it. Other drones carried cameras and infrared or other equipment, but no weapons. If it had been a Pred, Tal knew they could have used its weapons if necessary, but with the present situation, a loosed rocket would not only kill the enemy but the women hostages as well.

Robert watched without saying anything for the next five minutes. "They're trying to force those trucks up and over that slope."

"They aren't going to make it," Wyatt said quietly. "I've been in that area. I know it like the back of my hand. When things get wet, it turns to sticky, slippery clay. It's a bitch to plow through. Sooner or later, they're going to get stuck."

"And where are the Apaches? What's happening, Tal? These bastards are out in the open. It's an opportunity to get to them."

Grimacing, she said, "That's the problem, Dad. We can't loose a Hellfire missile or fifty-caliber bullets on them for fear of killing or injuring the women. They're all civilians except for Alexa."

Wyatt told Robert, "There's a SEAL team on the move. They've got eight men, plus Sergeant Hunter is going with them. He's a Marine sniper. He was there when it happened."

"And he won't admit it," Tal said, "but he probably saved Alexa's life when the first RPG hit so close that he took the shrapnel and blast wave from it, instead of her. He said Alexa is *not* wearing a Kevlar vest."

Robert rubbed his wrinkled brow. "Good man, this Hunter. So, he's the ninth operator?"

"Yes," Wyatt said. "I know the SEAL Bravo Platoon. Their shit is tight, and they are up to this kind of extraction mission. And I know Hunter. My team worked with him previously over the years. He's steady and reliable."

"I know Gage Hunter, too, Dad. He was in the other sniper unit there at Bagram with our unit. He's the right man to be in the driver's seat on this rescue mission. But they have to be careful," Tal cautioned. "If the Taliban hears SEALs flying in by helo, they might shoot all the hostages and run for it. We don't know what they'll do."

"What do you think?" Robert asked, sliding a glance at her.

Tal shrugged. "Sergeant Hunter, who's been a key player in this, says that there's a regional warlord, Daud Zadgal, who's a Taliban sympathizer. The way he makes money for his villages is to steal women and children from other villages outside his tribal boundary and sell them across the border." She wiped her lips, her voice dropping to a whisper, laden with withheld emotion. "Sex slaves. Sex trafficking. They'd all be sold off to the highest bidder. They could end up anywhere in the world."

Robert nodded, his face hardening, his eyes never leaving the feed. His youngest daughter was crouched in that truck, her hands tied in front of her. He could see the mud on her jeans and jacket, her beautiful red hair loose and wild.

He wished he could see her face, but her hair hid it. What was she thinking? Feeling? God, he couldn't go there.

Wyatt slid a photo toward the general. "Here's Zadgal, who collects these kidnapped women and children. I think you know of Zakir Sharan?" He saw Robert's hazel eyes narrow on the color photo in front of him.

"That sonofabitch," he breathed, anger leaking through his deep voice as he picked up the photo. He shot Wyatt a look. "You're sure about this?"

"Dead positive," Wyatt drawled. This regional warlord, Daud Zadgal, is a relative of Sharan. He's been dealing in the sex slave trade for a decade, because in his province, poppies don't grow well, so he has to make money another way."

"Shit."

Tal tried to throttle her emotions. It would do no good to break down and cry. Every man and woman at the table with them was just as emotionally affected by Alexa's capture as her family was. She felt Wyatt's warm, comforting hand move slowly back and forth across her tight, tense shoulders. There was no way she could tell anyone how helpless she felt. Alexa was half a world away and in the worst trouble of her life.

"So, do they know who Alexa is?" Robert demanded, his voice heavy with fear.

"No," Tal said. "That's the good news. Sergeant Hunter asked Alexa to take off her dog tags out at the village. He's got her tags. So if they search her, and I'm sure they will, they won't find dog tags to ID her as military."

"Thank God for small miracles," Robert rasped, rubbing his face. "We've dodged a bullet on this one."

"Sergeant Hunter said the other women are civilians, and they do not know Alexa is military, either. They only know her as a representative of Delos. Just another NGO to them. And I'm sure Alexa will keep her mouth shut about that and fabricate a fake name and anything else she needs to keep that intel out of their hands."

Robert grimaced. "Because if they knew, they'd single her out, torture her on video, and probably behead her on camera as well."

Tal winced and shut her eyes, knowing this to be true, but hearing her father say it brought it home in a terrible way. Wyatt's hand stilled on her shoulder, anchoring her, feeding her strength and courage.

Wyatt said, "They're stuck."

All eyes moved to the screen. Tal saw as the women were forced out of the trucks, the guards shoving the snouts of AK-47s into their backs, forcing them to hurry up a trail that another soldier was walking.

For the first time, Tal got a look at her sister's face. She breathed a sigh of relief, finding no bruising or swelling. So far, it seemed that the soldiers were not using their fists on them. So far . . .

Wyatt pointed to the info running across the bottom of the screen. "Sir? That's real-time intel on the SEAL team and where they're at."

"Are they going to try to get dropped in on the other side of that mountain to intercept them?"

"Yes, sir," Wyatt said. "They've got four snipers plus the Marine sniper. They're going to set up after we try to figure out the trail they're taking. I've been in that vicinity. There's a goat path that goes up another two thousand feet to that ridge and comes down the other side of it."

"Any caves on this side?" Robert demanded, his gaze pinned on Alexa as she slipped, fell, and was kicked at by a soldier as she scrambled back to her feet. His fist curled into a knot.

"Not where they are presently," Wyatt said, looking at his laptop, which held the mission software on it. "On the other side it's a whole different story. There's a huge limestone cave complex that's sometimes used as a hospital for wounded Taliban. I've been in those caves. There's water there in some of them—ice melt—and they're big. They've been used for decades as a main way station for Taliban."

"Have you got a drone up on that side?"

Tal shook her head. "The drone has software issues, Dad. They're racing to fix it, but it's still down at Bagram."

"Damn it!"

Her stomach clenched. Watching Alexa flounder, fall, and stagger back to her feet, Tal ached inside. If only she could reach out and pluck her out of that situation. The women ahead of her were getting along no better. They slipped and slid and fell as well, ice hidden beneath the newly fallen snow. She gnawed on her lower lip, hurting for her sister. The worst possible thing that could happen would be her captors managing to force Alexa to admit she was an Air Force officer. If they found that out, especially that she was an A-10 pilot, the Taliban would make short work of her.

Taliban hated the Warthog drivers with a lethal passion. Those low-flying combat aircraft wrought upon them hell on earth, and if they discovered that she was one of those pilots—oh, God, Tal just couldn't go there. She couldn't . . .

"Looks like they're taking them up and over that goat path," Wyatt said, his Texas drawl low. "They're taking them into those caves, I'll bet."

"To what end?" Tal demanded. She saw Wyatt's mouth purse. She could tell he didn't want to say it. "Tell me the truth."

Wyatt had been a SEAL and spent his entire career rooting out, finding, and kidnapping HVTs in Afghanistan. Tal knew he'd seen things that no one wanted to see. Now she felt him resisting her request.

"It's not gonna do any good to go over it. It has no mission importance, Tal. Let's keep focused on the mission. Not the what-ifs." He reached out, gripping her hand, giving her a gentle look that spoke volumes.

Tal choked back tears. Wyatt was right. She was starting to come unraveled because it was Alexa, not some unknown person about whom she could remain calm and objective. She turned her hand over weaving her fingers between his strong, warm ones.

"You're right," she managed to say in a strangled tone. "I don't really want to know. My imagination is making up enough shit."

"Second drone is up," Wyatt announced triumphantly. He watched his laptop screen. "It will be on station in thirty minutes, tops. We've got clear weather for once, but the winds at that altitude are going to be dicey."

Robert was riveted on a struggling Alexa. Every time she fell, the soldier was there, kicking at her to get up. God, he wanted to kill the sonofabitch. Just flat-out put a pistol to his head and pull the trigger. Violent anger swept through him and he gritted his teeth, watching his brave daughter climbing hard, obviously winded at that altitude. He saw the soldiers grinning, some of them rubbing their crotches suggestively as they herded the women up to the top of the windblown ridge.

Many of the women were staggering now, their arms tight around their bodies, with no warm clothing for this kind of climate and these conditions. At least Alexa was warmer—he recognized her black nylon down coat. Thank God for little things. His heart went out to those civilian women. He wasn't sure if they'd make it, but at least his daughter had military training.

She also had the Culver backbone and her mother's courage and strength. If anyone could survive this, it was Alexa. But Robert didn't wish any ill to befall any of these other young women, either.

"What are the ages of these women?" he asked.

Wyatt popped up the list on another screen on the wall beside the big one. "Young, between twenty and twenty-six years old. All single. They're working for NGOs and volunteered for their particular charity to help people in need."

"I feel so sorry for them," Tal murmured, shaking her head. "I can't even begin to imagine how they're feeling." But she could see it etched in their young, scrubbed faces. They were terrified, freezing to death, and afraid of the Taliban soldiers. Every once in a while, one of the soldiers would come up and squeeze one of their asses. Or run his hand up between a woman's legs to her crotch and then laugh. She hated those bastards. She wanted a piece of them. So far, they'd left Alexa alone, but that didn't mean anything.

Tal didn't want to watch the feed, but she had to. It was her sister in that video. It felt as if she were sitting in a Roman circus watching the Christians being stalked by the lions. It was a horrible feeling, and her stomach turned. She suddenly stood up, the chair scraping against the walnut floor. Without a word, she ran limping out of the room and down the hall toward the bathroom, her hand over her mouth. She hit the door, rushing in and barely making it to the first toilet.

Everything she'd eaten the night before came up. Tal gripped the porcelain with her hands, her knuckles white as she continued to heave. She didn't hear Wyatt come in, but when he leaned down to shelter her with his body, his arms going around her, holding her while she vomited, the tears came.

Tal sobbed quietly, wiping bile from her mouth.

"It's gonna be all right," Wyatt said, trying to comfort her, gently pulling her hair away from her shoulders. "She's made of stern stuff, Tal. It's gonna be okay . . ."

His soft drawl always soothed her, and as she weakly sat back on her heels, spitting the last of the saliva out of her mouth, she watched as Wyatt got up and left her. She immediately missed his warmth and his strength, because right now, Tal felt like she was shattering into a hundred little pieces.

Wyatt came back with a glass of water and crouched down beside her, one arm around her waist, handing her the glass.

"Put some in your mouth, swish it around, and then spit it out," he told her, holding her wounded, anguished gaze.

Tal did as he instructed. After her mouth was clean, she drank the rest of the water and flushed the toilet, hating the smell of vomit. "I need to stand up," she said, her voice quavering.

Nodding, Wyatt rose and then helped her stand, taking the glass from her hand. "Come on," he urged, guiding her out of the stall. He set the glass on the counter and then drew her up against him, wrapping his arms solidly around her. "It's okay, sugar. You needed to do this. It was building up inside you." He kissed her damp cheek, seeing the tears still trailing from her wounded eyes. He knew how close Tal was to Matt and Alexa. He smiled tenderly, continuing to rock her a little in his arms, wanting her to bawl her eyes out. Tears always helped.

Wyatt knew his voice tamed those fierce emotions of hers. She was usually cool, calm, and collected. But this was her sister, her only sister. And Wyatt knew how devoted Tal was to Alexa. He felt the woman he loved shaking now, the sobs starting to tear out of her as she gripped his shirtfront with her hands, her face buried against his upper chest. He loved her so damn much for her bravery, and her large, giving heart. Wyatt wished he could take away the knifelike pain he knew she was feeling since they had found out Alexa had been captured. He slid his fingers through her hair, moving the tips lightly against her scalp. It was something Tal loved and he loved doing it for her. Wyatt wished he could do more.

Little by little, her sobs diminished. His shirt was damp with her spent tears, but he didn't care. Moving her thick, black hair away from her face, pulling some stuck strands off her cheek, he looked down, meeting her reddened eyes. "Feel a tad better?"

"Y-yes. Thanks . . ." She gave him an apologetic look.

"Don't be hard on yourself, Tal. I can feel you goin' there." He saw her lips quirk, and she nodded a little bit, her cheek pressed against his chest, wanting his warmth, his quiet strength.

"I'm so sick over this, Wyatt," she whispered brokenly. "I had to take three weeks of SERE. Alexa only had two."

"Well, we black ops types all had to take three weeks. If we got caught, shit was gonna rain down on us, and the SERE teachers wanted us to realize the full scope of what we could expect." He caressed her hair, giving her a searching look, her beautiful green eyes marred with terror. "Alexa got enough, darlin'. She knows what to do. And if she can, she'll try to escape."

"I worry . . . I worry they'll rape her." Tal broke down in tears again, clinging to Wyatt.

His mouth thinned and he held her gently. Wyatt wasn't going to say anything, but it was a foregone conclusion that any military woman caught by the enemy in that country could expect to be raped. And he could hear the hurt, the raw anguish, in Tal's voice as she'd given words to the worst possible thing that could happen to her little sister.

Rape changed a person forever. It killed a part of their soul. It took a piece out of them they would never, ever get back.

"Hey, hey," he said soothingly, his hand cupping the back of her head, "we're not there yet."

Tal sniffed. "Then tell me what you wouldn't tell me in the War Room, Wyatt. You know what happens to these poor women and children who are kidnapped and sold as sex slaves."

He blew out a breath of air, holding her. "In the past, the Taliban took the hostages they managed to steal from an Afghan village to a cave. They usually had what I call 'holding tanks' for them. They would staff the caves with Taliban soldiers at certain times when they knew there was a raid in progress. There was a group of slave traders, men in the business, who would wait in those caves for the hostages." He frowned and hesitated.

"What else, Wyatt?" She gripped his shirtfront, shaking it. "Tell me *all* of it. I *have* to know. I'll go crazy not knowing. At least if I know, I'll be prepared."

His woman was no shirker and had a set of titanium balls on her. Wyatt had seen that stubborn courage come to life many times before. Tal hadn't been the head of a Marine Corps sniper unit all those years at Bagram for nothing.

"Okay," he rasped, "I'll tell you everything . . . But you may be sorry you asked."

CHAPTER 9

DILARA COULDN'T STAND it. After Robert's call an hour earlier, her stomach had become a nest of angry snakes that burned like a newly formed ulcer. Wyatt met her at the door to Artemis, which looked from the outside like a three-story 1850s farmhouse. It had new white siding and green shutters around all the windows.

Within that huge old farmhouse was the heart of Artemis Security. There was an underground parking area along with five levels of top-secret floors, two of them dug deep into the earth. The other three levels were aboveground and shielded by the latest materials that stopped any satellite or other surveillance device from penetrating the busy facility.

Although Artemis was officially going online next June, and it was only January, Dilara knew the operations center was well in place. The War Room, on the deepest level belowground, was state-of-the-art. Even the White House couldn't match their technology. The family had spent millions to get the very best and the most cutting-edge devices, electronics, communications, and computers—money well spent.

It was seven A.M., and the place was humming. Thirty people had been hired so far, all experts in their given area of military knowledge. Wyatt headed up the Mission Planning department and smiled slightly, giving Dilara a nod and placing his hand beneath her elbow.

"I'll take you to the elevator that goes to the War Room," he told her after she'd checked in through security. Retinal scanners were the only devices used for anyone entering or departing the building. He slowed his pace for her sake. "How are you holding up?" he asked her gently, punching the elevator button.

"Not well," Dilara admitted, her linen handkerchief in her hand. "What else has happened since Robert called me?"

"Well," Wyatt said, entering the elevator, "they've taken all the women into a main cave. The drones are overhead, watching, but they can't penetrate rock to see what's going on inside those caves." He saw her face crumple, her long, polished nails curving around her damp handkerchief.

Dilara was a beautiful woman at fifty-one years old, her red hair the same color as Alexa's. She also had incredible aquamarine eyes, while Alexa had inherited her father's hazel eyes. Wyatt had seen the uncanny similarity between Alexa and her mother.

"What about the SEAL team? Where are they?" Dilara asked.

Wyatt watched the brass doors close. "They're on their way to the caves. They have to land far enough away so they aren't seen and the Taliban doesn't hear the engines on the helo. They're landing five miles south of the cave position. From there, they'll get close to the cave entrance and watch, wait, and listen. They've got five snipers with them, and the plan is to take out the Taliban inside the cave. But until the SEALs can determine where the hostages are kept, they can't just jump in there and start shooting."

"No . . . of course not." Dilara blotted her eyes. She had already cried into her pillow after Robert's terse call. Her husband tried to sound as if everything were all right, but she knew it wasn't. She had married him at age twenty-one. He'd been twenty-six, a brash, confident, risk-taking Air Force jet combat pilot and officer. Robert had swept her off her feet, literally, and stolen her heart. He was a man who loved to learn, was cosmopolitan in his outlook, and was an astute political player who had respect from every military branch.

He was the youngest officer to be assigned to NATO in the Middle East, where they had met in Istanbul, Turkey, when she gave a talk to NATO officials about Delos. She remembered his intelligent questions after her talk his insights deep into people who struggled to make it in this tough world.

She needed him, more than ever. And she knew how much Alexa needed her family right now. There she was, alone. Surrounded by enemies who hated her. And she was so beautiful—that was what bothered Dilara most. She knew her daughter's beauty would single her out, and she'd be sold as a sex slave to some very rich man in Asia, Europe, South America, or the Middle East.

She pressed her hand against her stomach, not trying to stifle her emotions but to feel them and allow them to roll naturally through her. It was painful, but at least she wasn't like most men she knew, who pushed their feelings down and later fell ill because of it.

Wyatt led Dilara to the door of the War Room and placed his eye against the retinal scanner. Once inside, he released Dilara's elbow and she moved over to where her husband sat with Tal and several other mission planners. Robert quickly rose, pulling a chair over so she could sit at his left elbow.

"What is the latest?" she asked in a hushed voice. She saw that Tal looked pasty, her eyes red-rimmed. Her oldest daughter, usually so strong, resourceful, and steady, had been crying. Who hadn't? She saw the concern and care burning in Wyatt's eyes as he sat down next to Tal, his arm across the back of her chair, giving her a gentle touch to comfort her just a little.

Tal said, "The SEALs have infiltrated the landing location. No one's injured. They're heading toward the cave, and we have a drone over them. They are not picking up infrared signatures except for some small mammals on the mountainside."

Robert placed his arm around Dilara's shoulders in her black wool coat. Usually beautifully dressed and made up, today she was so damned pale that his heart ached. Robert wished he could do something for his suffering wife, but there wasn't much anyone could do at this point. "The moment we see any human activity, we'll be in touch with that SEAL team," he promised her.

"How far back do those caves go?" she asked hollowly, gripping the linen handkerchief in her lap.

"Dilara," Wyatt drawled, "they go on forever. The SEALs mapped this complex eight years ago because they found a makeshift hospital within it. The SEALs who first bumped into it went in and found empty syringes, bottles of medicine, bandages, and other medical items." He put the schematic of the cave system up on the screen for her to look at. Taking his laser pointer, he used the red dot to show her the area where the captives were led into the complex.

"Good God," Dilara whispered, her hand moving to her throat. "There must be forty different caves in that mountain! How do you know where Alexa and those other poor women are?"

Robert grimaced, his arm tightening for a moment around her shoulders. "We don't. I wish we did, Dilara, but there is no satellite, drone, or anything else that can go through hundreds of feet of solid rock to see what's on the other side of it. I'm sorry."

"Then what is the plan? Surely there is one?"

Wyatt used his laser pointer. "See this cave here, and how close it is to the surface of the mountain ridge?"

Dilara squinted. "Yes."

"There's an entrance there. It's big enough to place a team of SEALs down through it; they can get into the cave system that way. If we don't see any human activity in that major cave, they'll shift tactics and enter through that opening. They'll have to be very quiet and extremely careful. The first thing they have to do is figure out where everyone is. They'll have listening devices on them to pick up sounds."

"But," she sputtered, "it's dark in there!"

"Yes, it sure is," Wyatt said with a faint smile. "This team is wearing infrared goggles, and they can see no matter how dark it is. They're carrying M4s with silence suppressors. And they walk quietly, anyway. That's our backup plan."

"How many enemy are in there?"

Robert gave his wife a pleased look. "You missed your calling. You should have been in the military, Dilara."

That brought a small smile to her lips. "I use my keen strategic mind to run Delos. That's quite enough," she replied. She saw Robert wink at her, pride in his eyes for her astute intelligence and her ability to grasp a military tactical situation.

"We don't know how many more Taliban are in that cave complex," Wyatt admitted. "It could be none. It could be just the soldiers who drove the women into the cave. They may be waiting for another group to come and transport them across the border. We basically have to wait and see."

"But," Dilara said, her voice rising, "think of the women in there! What are they doing to them?" She choked up, looking anxiously at Robert.

Wyatt took a deep breath. He'd just told Tal the list of possibilities. There was no way he was going to tell a mother whose child was captive. He just would not.

"Mom? Don't go there," Tal said, and reached out, patting her hand, giving her a pleading look.

"What if they shoot them?" she asked, anxious.

"The SEALs are close enough," Wyatt told her, "that they'd hear any rifle fire. The sound, first of all, would echo like crazy throughout the entire complex, and so far, we've not heard any report. No pistol or rifle has been fired." And he hoped to God that none would be.

"I want to see that drone video feed on Alexa," she said to her husband quietly.

Nodding, Robert stood. "Come on, we'll go to another room and I'll show it to you."

Dilara tried to prepare herself as her husband led her to a smaller room off the War Room. One of the video technicians had quickly set up a screen about half the size of the other. Robert sat his wife down at the round table and asked the tech to take it back to the beginning. He wasn't sure Dilara could handle seeing it all, but if he cheated her of it, she would never forgive him. She sat, legs crossed, hands in her lap, gripping her handkerchief, strangling it. Robert ached inside, but there was little he could do to soften what his wife was going to see.

He sat down next to her, his arm around her shoulders. In as few words as possible, he painted a scene for her so that seeing the video would not be as shocking.

As he sat there, feeling his wife's shoulders draw up and tense as she watched Alexa and the other women struggling, climbing up that steep mountain slope in snow with ice beneath it, he saw her repeatedly dab her eyes. He knew every parent of every one of those women had, by now, been told that their daughters were missing in action. But unlike Dilara and Robert, they would not know the truth of what was happening to them.

Their big, high-tech security company showed everything possible, but Robert wondered how many parents were seriously prepared to see their child in this kind of dangerous predicament. He could see what it was doing to Dilara—tearing her up inside. She was trying so hard to sit there stoically, watching, but he'd been married to her for thirty years and they had a telepathic connection.

He could always feel when she was out of sorts, anxious, hurting, or joyous. And like their daughter, Alexa, Dilara wore every emotion on her face. Out in public or at her charity, she was a smooth, even-keeled, confident manager of people, showing only what she wanted them to see. But here, the suffering in her eyes, the anguish radiating from around her, washed powerfully through him, making him want to protect her—and he was unable to do so.

As Robert watched Alexa, he was proud of his daughter, because of all the women, she was the strongest of the group mentally, emotionally, and physically. Dilara winced when the Taliban soldier connected solidly with Alexa's hip as she slipped and fell. His daughter had been rolled onto her back, and he saw the rage in her face as she glared up at the grinning soldier. No, his daughter was a fighter, and that's what Robert had to hold on to. That is what would get her out of that hellhole.

Dilara made a mewling sound as Alexa was kicked again. She winced, turning her head aside.

"I think you've seen enough," he told her roughly, nodding to the tech to turn it off.

"Oh, God," Dilara whispered, laying her head on his shoulder, her face pressed against his hard jaw. "They're hurting her!"

"She's tough, pet. She'll get through this." It was all he could say. He couldn't promise that she'd live or even be rescued. As much as he wanted to give her those assurances, Robert knew he couldn't, and it savaged him as nothing else ever had.

Pressing the handkerchief to her eyes, she turned into him, wanting his other arm around her. "Here I am crying for her and I'm warm, no one is threatening me, I'm safe," she sobbed against him. And then she began to weep in earnest.

"Alexa came from us. She's got backbone and she's got guts. She can't be an A-10 pilot and not have those qualities, Dilara," her husband pointed out.

"Haven't you been able to get ahold of Matt yet? Does he know what's happened to Alexa?" Dilara asked.

"Not yet. I talked to his captain, but they're on a top secret op that's in motion, and he can't pull Matt out to tell him." His voice thickened. "Dilara, telling our son what's happened in the middle of his op could get him killed. You realize that, don't you? If he knew about Alexa's predicament, he couldn't have a hundred-percent focus on his mission. It's a distraction. And Delta operators have to have that kind of focus to survive what they do." He touched her cheek, wiping her tears away. "As soon as Matt's team has completed their mission, he'll be told. I promise you that."

Sniffing, she mumbled, "Will they let Matt help get to Alexa then?"

"No, they won't. He's too emotionally involved. He won't be thinking clearly. Don't forget, they're fraternal twins. They are so much alike in some ways, so attuned to one another." Shaking his head, he told her, "His CO will make him stay at Bagram and wait it out."

Jerking in a sigh, Dilara nodded. "That sounds as if it would be best."

"Listen, Matt's fiancée is coming over to see you in the afternoon. I talked to her and told her what was going on. She said she'd like to be with you for a while. To keep you company."

Giving him a wobbly smile, Dilara whispered, "Dara is so sweet that way. She puts herself out for so many."

"Would you like her company?"

"Yes, I would. I'll make us some good Turkish coffee."

Robert smiled briefly. "Dara loves your Turkish coffee." He patted her shoulder. "Come on, I'll have your driver take you home. I promise, if anything changes regarding Alexa, I'll call you immediately."

"What must the parents of those other women being going through, Robert?"

"Hell," he grunted. He stood, taking her hand, easing her from the chair. "Artemis Security is giving us the most information possible regarding this mission. But sometimes," he murmured, wrapping his arm around his wife's slender waist, "it's better not knowing anything at all."

★

GAGE KNOCKED BACK two ibuprofen to dull the throb of the headache caused by the shrapnel cutting into his skull after that RPG landed ten feet away from him. Now he sat crouched with the SEAL team, hidden behind bushes near the entrance to the cave complex. They were a good one-tenth of a mile away, close enough to hear and see but not so close that someone could suddenly come upon them.

Earlier, a drone had shown the women captives being herded into the cave. They'd arrived on scene an hour later. The men were in winter snowsuits, and they'd loaned him one for this mission. He was amazingly warm, considering that the wind was howling above them on the ridgeline and they were only about a hundred feet below the spine of the mountains. They wore camouflage white, light gray, and dark gray across their faces and necks. The white parkas and trousers had them blending into the two-to-three-foot snow.

Chief Nolan McQuade kept his men in a diamond pattern as they watched and waited. There was no way they wanted to be discovered by the enemy on any flank. It could get the women killed somewhere inside that cave complex.

Impatience gnawed at Gage. His heart felt raw, and he ached with concern for Alexa. When he'd come to, a Navy corpsman bending over him, he'd jerked into an upright position. The corpsman had gripped his shoulder, ordering him to remain sitting, but Gage pushed to his feet, wildly looking around for Alexa. When he didn't find her, he turned on the corpsman, who told him what had happened. When he realized she'd been captured, his knees went suddenly weak. Good thing he'd been leaning heavily against the mud wall of the village.

He'd seen the two doctors who had come with the medical teams sprawled out on their bellies, dead, their heads partly blown away. All the women were gone. Deep, muddy hoofprints were everywhere, the whole area chewed up, showing the charge of the Taliban on horseback, their focused attack, to capture them. Four of the Marines had taken bullets. And right now, a medevac was flying in to take them back to the Bagram hospital.

He had sat down before he fell down, rage tunneling through him as he looked at that wadi. This had been a well-planned assault, no question.

Gage had wanted to do something, anything, but Sergeant Jameson came over and told him what was going on. The best news was that the drone had them in sight and was following the three fleeing white Toyota trucks with their female cargo in the beds. Gage felt nauseous. He knew what could happen to Alexa and those other innocent women. None of it was good. He was supposed to protect her. But he hadn't been able to. He told the sergeant he wanted to stay with them, but the Marine nixed the idea, ordering him back to Bagram to be checked out in the ER. He had a concussion and needed to be examined. Gage snarled that he was fine, but the sergeant outranked him, and in the end, Gage had climbed on board the medevac.

When Gage left the medevac, he turned and walked half a mile over to SEAL HQ instead of heading to the ER at the hospital. He met with Chief Nolan McQuade, who had been chosen to take in a team of SEALs to intercept the Taliban with their captives. Gage insisted on going, and because he was a sniper and the SEALs were trying to get every sniper they had on this op, he was a welcome addition. McQuade was fine with it. SEALs often worked hurt but could continue to carry out a mission, and McQuade was more than happy to have Gage with his team, because he had been there when the attack had taken place. And there was no way Gage was going to tell him that there was a personal connection between him and Alexa. He'd have been thrown off the direct action mission in a heartbeat.

As a sniper, Gage could set his emotions aside and become a cold, efficient killing machine, if needed. And he wanted to kill those bastards who had taken Alexa and the other women. He wanted them bad. As he'd stood over the mission-planning board, the maps spread out along with a PowerPoint presentation, Gage wanted to get moving. Every minute wasted was one more minute that something horrible could happen to Alexa.

Just as the DA mission wrapped up, a sat phone call came in for him. Surprised, Gage had taken it and spoken to Tal Culver, CEO of Artemis Security in Alexandria, Virginia. He knew Tal, and she knew him. They'd had a casual friendship, because they were both snipers and were therefore members of a brotherhood. He'd filled her in on everything, in detail. Knowing Tal was Alexa's older sister, Gage hurt for her. He could hear the strain in her voice, and sometimes, her emotions came close to the surface. His were right there, too.

He was glad that Artemis was in the mix. From what Alexa had told him about this cutting-edge security firm, it had the best technical support and gadgetry in the world. Gage had never been so glad because anything that could help get Alexa and the others home safely, was all that mattered.

When he found out the warlord of the area, Daud Zadgal, was connected with Zakir Sharan, he nearly threw up. Now he knew why those women had been abducted. They were to be sold right out of those caves as sex slaves to the highest bidders from around the world. After being bought, they would be transported either by helicopter or truck across the Pakistan border and to the nearest international airport.

His mind raced over the near impossibility of finding Alexa if she were taken across the border. The sex slave trade was centered in Islamabad, the capital of Pakistan, and Gage resisted what he knew about it, because two of his HVTs in the past had been slave traders coming across to pick up girls, women, and little boys to transport them across the border.

Further, he'd worked with a SEAL team three different times undercover in that dirty city that throbbed with power and manipulation. Because he spoke Urdu and was a sniper, and had been dropped with the SEAL team of four men behind the border to find their way there, Gage knew a helluva lot more about it than he ever wanted to remember. Corporate jets from around the world sat at the international airport, waiting to have their newly purchased slaves hustled on board under cover of darkness. There was no Pakistan Customs, no security. Officials were bribed to look the other way. The unlucky woman would be placed on a jet and taken to her new life. And she might last weeks—maybe months, but not much longer—until she was dead, and then a new replacement was bought. It was a filthy, secret world, and Gage felt bile crawl into his throat.

While the SEAL team wanted to move into the cave complex, Gage knew they couldn't do a John Wayne charge. They had no idea how many Taliban were in there. His last mission involved waiting for his slave trader HVT to ride across the border in a white Toyota Hilux truck. The CIA had picked up cell phone chatter about the trader's whereabouts and his objective. It was always an Afghan village near the border. Gage had to set up his op near that village, hoping that the intel was legitimate, and then wait for the sick, perverted bastard to show up.

He had tried to wipe his mind of what he'd seen on the last mission involving a slave trader. Through his scope, thirteen hundred yards above the small, struggling Afghan village, he'd seen a truckload of Taliban drive in with their white Toyota truck. Gage hadn't seen his HVT among them. Was this a preliminary force? Would the HVT show up later? Often, people from other nearby settlements would kidnap a young girl, take her back to their own village, and keep her prisoner and wait for the slave trader to come by and inquire if there were any girls who could be bought.

Through his scope, he had seen a young girl of ten, her hands tied with a rope, screaming and crying, being dragged forward by an angry Afghan farmer. He watched as people from that village peeked out their doors after he passed with the weeping, fighting child. But no one would stop him. No one would help the innocent little girl. It had taken everything Gage had not to put a bullet into that bastard's head. But if he'd done that, then it would have tipped off the soldiers in the truck who were waiting for their boss to arrive.

It sickened him as the farmer dragged the girl, who wore a simple black gown from head to toe, up to the truck. When he grinned, four of his front teeth were missing. He grabbed the girl by her long brown hair, making her shriek, and lifted up her dress, baring her naked lower body to the guards in the truck. Gage's finger itched to take him out.

But damn it, he couldn't.

In the end, thirty minutes later, a second Toyota truck pulled up with the HVT in it. Gage watched the fat, arrogant bastard slide out of the truck. The farmer was bowing and scraping, holding on to the fighting child, who would not stand still. The farmer cuffed her several times as the slaver approached her. It was then that Gage took his shot. A head shot. One bullet, one kill. And then he had two more bullets in the cartridge for his Win-Mag. He aimed for the farmer next and killed him along with one of the soldiers. And then, as the soldiers started running, yelling, and screaming, looking for where the bullets were coming from, Gage released the mag and slapped in another one.

By the time he was done, eight Taliban lay dead, the little girl standing, crying, her hands against her mouth, unsure what to do. Gage saw a woman come warily out of the village toward her. She was clearly frightened, looking around, gesturing sharply to the girl to come to her. It did Gage's heart good to see the little girl suddenly sprint on her bare feet, arms open, running to the woman, who bent down, taking her into her embrace. As Gage got ready to vacate his hide, he was sure the woman wasn't her mother, but maybe a relative. As he shrugged into his heavy ruck after putting his Win-Mag in a nylon sheath and securing it, he hoped the woman would take the girl in. Maybe she would care for her, find out what village she came from, and somehow get the child back to her parents.

He could only hope. Because this was a country where hope rarely existed.

CHAPTER 10

ALEXA HEARD THE other women, all of whom were in individual wooden cages within the cave, sobbing or quietly weeping. A kerosene lantern near the cave entrance was all the light available. Two soldiers stood guard at the tunnel leading out of one end of the cave. The smell of urine and fecal matter and the taint of old, dried blood sickened her, and she sat on hard-packed earth in a primitively constructed cage six feet tall and five feet wide. At least her hands were untied and she felt the circulation coming back into her numbed fingers.

Next to her was Cathy, a blond twenty-year-old, frightened out of her mind. All she could do was sit with her back against the cave wall, legs scrunched up against her body, and weep. Alexa felt sorry for her.

Her gaze moved around the fairly large cave. At the other end of it was another tunnel with no soldiers guarding it. As a military officer, she had to look for an escape route. An unguarded tunnel could offer that possibility.

Her cage was the first of fifteen that she'd counted in the gloom. The rocks bit into her back where she leaned up against the dry cave wall. Each cage had a rusty padlock on it to keep them from escaping. The soldiers had blindfolded the women and herded them like cattle into the main cave. Each had been forced to put her hand on shoulder of the woman in front of her, all in a line, and a soldier with a flashlight had led them through the maze.

And it was a maze, Alexa realized. When they finally halted, they jerked the blindfolds off all of them. They had put them into the cages and thrown each of them four plastic bottles of water. She'd been so thirsty that she drank two of them right away. There was no place to urinate except in the cage itself, and the acrid stench wafted throughout the cave. It was a filthy place. Worse, Alexa saw rats scurrying in the shadows, moving stealthily here and there.

The Taliban had constructed the cages of slender saplings a hand's length apart some time ago. The poles had been buried deep into the grayish soil of the cave and then the tops were pulled into chiseled sockets out of the sloped cave. She'd already tried to loosen them a couple of times, but the limbs wouldn't budge. Her hair had come loose and she quickly refashioned it into a long, thick braid.

Having no idea what was to happen next, Alexa watched the two guards at the other tunnel entrance. She didn't want to think about Gage . . . how dead he had looked. Rubbing her face, Alexa knew she didn't dare dwell on it. After going through SERE, uppermost in an officer's mind was escape. If she didn't think, she'd be an emotional basket case like the civilian women. She was sure they didn't realize why they had been kidnapped and Alexa wasn't going to tell them. It would only cause more hysteria and renewed terror.

Why had they placed her first in the cage area? Was that significant? Had they already singled her out as different from the other captives? She curled her dirty hands into her lap, unsure. Alexa knew that her parents would move heaven and earth to locate her. She knew that black ops teams, either SEAL or Delta Force, would be coming to rescue them. But had the Taliban gotten away with their kidnapping before a drone could be set up to see where they'd been taken? Her stomach growled and she yearned for a protein bar.

Lifting her chin, she saw another soldier, taller than the other two, looking important, snapping orders to them in Urdu. Instantly, the men came to attention. Eyes narrowing, Alexa could barely make out a man with short black hair and a well-trimmed mustache glaring into the cage cavern at them with his hands settled imperiously on his hips. He wore camouflage clothing that Alexa recognized as belonging to a Pakistani officer.

What the hell? And then she snorted softly. Pakistan was a country where corruption, abuse of power, manipulation, and brute force ruled. The man wore a dark beret on his head with a gold insignia on the side. He packed a sidearm on his right hip. His bearing was pure arrogance and Alexa guessed him to be about forty-five. He wasn't built like the thin, underfed Taliban soldiers. Instead, he was at least six feet tall and broad-shouldered with a classical Middle Eastern square face. Alexa was sure a lot of women would lust for this man and tried to see his rank. Clearly, he was an officer in the Pakistan Army. In fact, the insignia on his beret indicated he was a member of ISI, Inter-Services Intelligence.

Alexa also saw a badge sewn on the upper left arm of his uniform, confirming he was ISI. And yes, he was up to his ass in the slave trade. The officer snapped another order in Urdu, and instantly both soldiers ran into the cave, their AK-47s strapped to their backs.

Alexa's heart rate soared as the men hurriedly unlocked her cell. She slowly moved into a crouch, tense, watching them warily. The taller one entered, snarling at her and grabbing her by the arm.

Jerking it away from him, Alexa glared back, and ducked out of the cage, straightening. Instantly, the soldiers clamped a restraining hand on each of her upper arms, propelling her toward the officer, who waited in the tunnel, his legs spread slightly apart, wearing combat boots.

Alexa allowed them to push her along. It would do no good to fight—yet. It was three against one. Her gaze went to his pistol. It had a safety strap over it, so she couldn't lunge and rip it out of the holster to use it. Her skin crawled as they stopped in front of the haughty officer. He stared down at her, his gaze stripping her from head to toe.

"Bring her!" he ordered in Urdu, spinning around and striding down the poorly lit tunnel.

Alexa wasn't going to let on that she knew Urdu. No way in hell. It gave her an advantage, even if it was slight. Adrenaline poured through her bloodstream as they pushed and tugged her along, almost at a trot, to keep up with the quick-striding Pakistani officer. They moved through a lot of caves and Alexa tried to remember the way. Finally, they turned left, down a brightly lit tunnel.

The blaze of overhead lights strung across the ceiling of a smaller cave hurt her eyes. Tears came then and Alexa bowed her head, trying to avoid the painfully bright lights. She saw two men sitting at a long wooden table that was chipped and had seen better days. There was a laptop computer with a satellite phone attached, a cell phone nearby, a digital camera, and a video camera. Just above them was a hole to the outer world and she saw wires strung up and out of it. To where, she didn't know. Her mind went blank with momentary shock. Was this a makeshift auction house? Were buyers calling in about the women who'd just been kidnapped? Were these men taking photos of them and sending them by sat phone to prospective buyers around the world?

To her left, as they hauled her in front of the table, she saw a pale green blanket that had been hung in one part of the cave. There were lights that she recognized as the type a photographer might use to take indoor photos. Her throat closed up as she rapidly put it all together.

The soldiers released her but were within easy reach of her should she try to escape. Breathing harshly, Alexa wrapped her arms against her chest as the men at the table studied her intently. The silence was heavy. She felt as if something awful were about to happen to her. It was the not knowing that made her nerves scream with anxiety.

The Pakistani officer took a third seat at the table. He gave a brisk nod to the other two, and one of the men, in a dark blue Pakistani wool robe that was heavily embroidered with gold thread, sneered at her. He was short and fat and had longish black hair, shining with some kind of pomade. The pencil-thin mustache only emphasized his thick lips. He reminded Alexa of a bloated toad and in her mind, that is what she dubbed him, "the Toad."

The man in the middle was thin, nervous-looking, dressed in traditional

Afghan clothes, a rolled cap on his head. He wore dark brown wool pants and a white long-sleeved shirt with a black vest over it. He had the laptop in front of him. Alexa called him "the Scribe."

Unsettled by the Pakistani officer at the end, his cinnamon brown eyes never leaving hers, Alexa mentally referred to him as "the General," because she recognized his rank on the lapels of his starched, clean uniform. Even his black boots were like polished mirrors.

She wondered if these men had been waiting for them. Rage flowed through her, because the General was part of the Pakistan Army—the corrupt part. She knew members of ISI had worked directly with the CIA and NSA and other secret branches of the U.S. government.

And this smug sonofabitch was a slave trader! Alexa was sure he was getting a cut out of any sales done here. Further, with his high rank, he could employ planes, helicopters, and ground vehicles, using them to get the captives across the border and deliver the slaves to the buyers. There was no name to indicate who he was. He'd taken off his badge.

She met his implacable stare with one of her own.

The Scribe said in broken English, "Please give us your name?"

Alexa wanted to curse at all of them, to tell them to go fuck themselves. She bit back on it and lied. "Donna Collins."

"Ah, very good," the Scribe said, quickly typing the information into his laptop.

"And your age?"

"Twenty-eight."

The Scribe duly noted it, smiling nervously at her.

"And your job? What were you doing at that village?"

"I'm an aid worker for Delos."

"I see . . ."

"Are you a virgin?"

Alexa's eyes widened with surprise over such an intimate question. Anger soared through her. "Go to hell," she told them in a snarl, her anger leaking through. The Scribe looked startled by her sudden change in demeanor.

The General's low laugh rumbled through his chest. "I see we have a fighter here."

The Toad gave her a measured look, interest glinting suddenly in his eyes. "Indeed."

The Scribe said, "She is the only one of the women who wasn't sniveling and crying when they were brought in."

The Toad looked more pleased, giving the General an approving glance. "This is more than I had hoped for." He gestured toward Alexa, rings on four of his five short, thick fingers, the diamonds, emeralds, and sapphires on them flashing beneath the light.

"I have a client who wants his slave to be a fighter. Pity she's twenty-eight though. He wants a girl around fifteen or so . . . That will lower the price I can get for her, because she's old. But I'm sure he would be interested in her if for no other reason than she won't bore him."

Alexa stood there, pretending not to understand what they were saying in Urdu. Her blood raced with outrage and she had to lower her eyes so they wouldn't see the anger in them.

The General gave a negligent shrug. "He'll overlook her age for the fight in her, that I'm sure of. I'm sure this American whore is no virgin."

Alexa's fingers curled into fists as she forced herself to try to relax.

The Toad chuckled.

The Scribe gave a horse like whinny, nodding his head vigorously as he typed more information into the laptop.

"My client who wants a fighter doesn't care if she's a virgin or not."

"Good," the General said.

The Scribe switched to English. "Do you carry any sexual diseases?"

Alexa stared at him in disbelief. "You can all go fuck yourselves. I'm not answering any of your questions. I want to be let go. You have no right—"

The soldier to the left grabbed her by her long braid and slammed his boot into the back of one of her knees. In an instant, her knee buckled from beneath her and Alexa found herself on the dirt floor of the cavern. She groaned as the soldier held her head back, exposing her throat.

The Toad gave her a haughty smile and spoke British English flawlessly. "Now, whore, you will not speak unless spoken to. Are we clear? The next time you speak without being asked, I'm afraid the General will be all too willing to show you some pain to remind you to keep your pretty mouth shut. Do we understand one another?"

Her breathing was choppy, her heart pounding. The pain in her scalp made her whimper as the soldier tightened down on the hair he had wrapped around his fist. "Y-yes," she gasped.

Instantly, the soldier released her, shoving her forward so she landed on her hands and knees.

"Get up!" the Toad snarled.

Slowly, Alexa got to her feet, rubbing her scalp, the pain still radiating across it.

"She'll be fully examined by the doctor later to ensure she's healthy sexually," the General told the Toad in Urdu. "Let's move on."

Stunned, Alexa barely kept her face straight. An examination by a doctor? What the hell was he talking about? Everything began to seem surreal to her. These men were talking about her like she was a piece of meat to be looked over.

The Scribe nodded. "Have you ever had children?"

Alexa shook her head.

The Toad made a pleased sound in his throat that was buried in layers of fat.

"Have you ever had a miscarriage? An abortion?"

She shook her head no, afraid to speak, afraid of the anger and rage they'd hear in her voice.

"Are you married?"

"No."

"Are you engaged?"

"No."

"How many men have you had sexually?"

The Scribe had to be kidding! Alexa's mouth dropped open. This was unbelievable! She'd had enough. "Fuck all of you. I'm not answering any more of these asinine questions! I'm an American citizen, and I demand to be released immediately!"

Instantly, the two soldiers grabbed her. They stripped off the black parka she wore, throwing it to the floor. Alexa started to fight, watching the General slowly get up, his irritation clear as he strode around the table. She saw him lift his shirt, unbuckling a thick, wide leather belt. His mouth was set, and his eyes held hatred for her as he hauled the belt off from around his waist.

She grunted and tried to break free of the soldiers as he approached her. Terror raced through her as the soldiers dragged her over to another part of the cave. There was a metal rod suspended on top of two metal posts. Alexa saw leather cuffs dangling from ropes above it. *NO!* She was not going to do this!

Before she could make a move, the General was upon her, grabbing her by the braid, yanking her head back to control her.

Screaming and cursing, eyes tightly shut, Alexa was cuffed by the two soldiers as the Pakistani officer held her still. Then the soldiers pulled on the thick ropes at either side of the metal rod, hauling Alexa off her feet, her toes inches off the floor of the cave.

Breathing hard, her shoulder sockets burning with pain as she hung helplessly, she saw the General lean closer to her, his lips lifting in a snarl. She could smell the odor of goat on his breath and she tried to pull her face away from his.

"Now," the General growled in her face, gripping her hair, making her wince, "you will learn that women do *not* speak like that to a man. *Ever!*" He released her head with a jerk.

Fear tunneled through her. Alexa's shoulder sockets were burning and she couldn't see the officer but felt his hatred circling around her. The soldiers stood by the posts, smiling.

"Pull her sweater down!" the General rapped out as he backed away, measuring the distance between him and Alexa.

Instantly, one of the soldiers tugged down the ends of her sweater over her hips. It had ridden halfway up her torso during her struggles.

Shutting her eyes, Alexa didn't know what would happen next. She heard a hissing sound and her back exploded with red-hot pain as the belt landed across her shoulders. A cry tore out of her, and her whole body jerked. Sobbing for breath, Alexa couldn't see it coming. The next time she heard that sound, she tried to brace herself. The belt landed savagely against the center of her back.

The third one laid into her back diagonally. The stinging heat made her cry out. It was impossible not to scream. Her fingers fisted as the weight of her body pulled her down. Her shoulders felt as if they were going to tear off her body as the belt kept coming, raining blow after blow upon her back. Her cries weakened with each strike and soon Alexa felt faint from the mounting agony exploding across her back. Her flesh felt stretched, as if it were on fire, the muscles beneath it swelling from the harsh blows, making her gasp for air.

Alexa lost count of how many times she was struck by the General's belt. All she knew was that the pain ripped through her whole body, making her jerk every time he whipped her. The leather was applied with such brutal force and intensity that she felt blackness overcoming her. Her skin felt as if it were burning up and exploding, her nerves on fire. And then, mercifully, Alexa moaned and her head fell forward onto her chest; she had fainted.

Pain throbbing throughout her back forced Alexa into consciousness. She slowly opened her eyes and felt as if she were floating. She looked up; bright lights glared overhead. She tried to look around, but something was drawn tight across her brow, not allowing her any head movement.

Where? What? The pain throbbed unremittingly throughout her back. She felt chilled. Where was she? Her mind seesawed back and forth. When she tried to lift her arm, she couldn't. Her mind wasn't working, but she suddenly realized she was strapped down to a cold metal table, legs parted, her heels in cold metal stirrups and unable to do anything except grunt and try to shut her mouth.

"She's coming around."

Mouth dry, Alexa heard the Urdu from a man with a rasping voice. She felt movement and then she saw him. He was in his fifties, balding, wearing metal-framed glasses and a white lab coat. Leaning over her, he studied her silently.

"Good, you're conscious." He reached over on a tray and brought up a digital camera. Standing back, he took a photo of her. Setting it aside, he pulled on a pair of latex gloves.

"Take this down," he ordered his young Afghan assistant. "This is Number 2507. Female. Red hair. Hazel eyes. Caucasian. American citizen. Five feet seven inches tall. Weight is sixty-one kilograms. No remarkable scars seen on her body. No birthmarks. No cancerous moles."

Alexa blinked as his large hands forced her mouth open. He leaned over, close to her, his breath fetid. She tried to protest but a strangled moan erupted from her instead.

"Still fighting, are we?" he murmured, smiling over at her as he moved his fingers into her mouth, checking her gums, and then taking a small penlight, flashing it to study all of her teeth. "Not many women are fighters after they've been whipped by the General, but you still have fight left in you. It must be your red hair. Maybe you'll last more than a month or two with the client who just bought you for two million U.S. dollars. He likes red-haired fighters like yourself." He straightened, turning to report to someone.

"Gums are healthy. She has six cavities, all filled. Teeth are strong and clean. No sign of periodontal disease."

Her chest heaved with adrenaline as Alexa realized with a start that she was naked on the table! And the doctor had just taken a picture of her! Humiliation tore through her as she slowly realized there were other men standing nearby. Her eyes wouldn't focus.

Everything blurred. Her mind refused to work.

The doctor looked into each of her ears, giving his assistant more information. He then moved another instrument up into each of her nostrils. The sensations weren't painful, but they were uncomfortable. Alexa moaned in loud protest, not wanting to be assaulted like this.

"Now, now," the doctor said, "it looks like I'll have to give you more of the drug. I can't have you this active while I try to examine you. The client doesn't want you harmed or bruised in any way. And the way you're fighting, you'll hurt yourself. I can't have that . . ."

Eyes widening, Alexa saw a young man bring over a small tray that held a glass bottle and a syringe lying next to it. What were they going to do to her? Rage erupted within her, but Alexa felt incredibly weak, her mind still foggy. She flexed her fingers weakly, trying with all her might to move, to jerk free of the leather cuffs binding her wrists to the table.

"Don't knock her out," the General growled. "I want to see her reaction when you give her your famous pelvic exam."

The doctor shrugged. He picked up a vial containing the drug, pulling a certain amount into the syringe. "Very well. You're a voyeur, so I'll let you watch. But don't try to tell me how much of a drug to give her. I know what I'm doing."

"This is one time I wish I were a physician," the General said, chuckling darkly.

Alexa heard his voice close to her. Dread grated on her raw nerves. Terrified, she saw him slowly walk around and stand beside her so she could see him, his hands on his hips. He smiled at her, eyes glittering with interest, as he slowly looked her up and down.

"Get her drugged!" the General snapped. "She's already been bought, and the owner doesn't want any damage done to her."

"Stop bothering her and I will."

He looked down at Alexa. "Now, Number 2507, you must calm down. You'll end up with bruises on every limb from trying to rip your arms and legs off this gurney as I continue my examination of you. I can't have that. This shot will settle you down and make it easier for me to do my job."

Crying out, choking, Alexa felt the bite of the needle into her upper left arm. She wanted to escape. *Run!*

"Stop frightening the merchandise, please," the doctor scolded him mildly.

The General shrugged. "I'd buy her myself, but she'd be the kind to find a knife and castrate me sooner or later." He grinned, a chuckle rumbling up through his chest. "Let's see how she likes the rest of your very thorough examination, doctor." He laughed softly, as if it were an inside joke known only to him and the doctor. "It's a good thing I brought her to heel with my belt earlier. She'd have been wild right now without the beating."

Whatever was in the needle, Alexa suddenly felt as if her body belonged to someone else. She tried to lift her fingers and curl them, but she could no longer even do that. Languor spread throughout her body, her muscles relaxing, and she was unable to move.

"Well," the doctor said primly, sitting down on a stool between her opened legs, "I'm not so sure it has helped at all. You'd better hope those bruises on her back are gone by the time you deliver her to the buyer." She felt the doctor's gloved hand on one of her thighs. Terror raced through her.

Alexa heard them talking about her as if she weren't there. Humiliation twisted through her and she kept sobbing, trying to move, but her body refused to obey. Her mind was clear, and she felt every invasion, every painful contraction of her body reacting violently to the cruel assault as he examined her.

She gasped for breath, black dots dancing in front of her eyes. The doctor was talking as if what he was doing was routine. More tears streaked down her cheeks as she saw the General smile at her, revenge in his expression. Nausea rolled through her.

"Just another minute and I'll be done," the doctor called to Alexa. He gave more information to his assistant.

"What a nice bedside manner you have, doctor," the General said wryly.

The doctor glared at him. "My examination of her is going to seem mild in comparison to what this client is going to do to her when he receives her."

He pulled off the gloves and picked up a new pair, snapping them on.

The General chuckled, nodding.

The assistant released Alexa's wrists from the leather cuffs and the doctor removed the straps from around her ankles and waist and released the tight, soft leather across her brow. Suddenly, Alexa was free, but she couldn't move! She was a puppet with no muscles. She grunted in frustration, closing her eyes, not even able to clench her teeth.

Her tears wouldn't stop. Tears of outrage leaked from her eyes from being assaulted with no way to fight back to protect herself and her body. Alexa was so drugged she couldn't put words together to curse these monsters. Instead, all she could do was moan and whimper with frustration and anguish.

The doctor was satisfied with his exam. "It's over now, you can relax. You're better than most, I'll give you that." He looked over at the men. "Lay her on her belly. I'm finished."

Dull, roiling pain drifted up into Alexa's abdomen, making her choke and sob. Her arms hung over the gurney as they laid her down on her belly, straightening out her legs. Whimpers of agony tore from her lips. She emitted a low, tortured sound as she shut her eyes tightly in a vain attempt to control her tears of rage and pain.

He gave the exam information to a young man with a clipboard who rapidly wrote down his findings.

Alexa's tears of outrage wouldn't stop spilling from her eyes. She had been sexually assaulted, with no way to fight back or protect herself. All she could do was moan and whimper as pain continued to throb throughout her lower body. She wished her mind wasn't as razor-sharp as it was, because she never, ever wanted to remember this time in her life.

"Send that information to the client," the doctor ordered. "I'll have test results on the slides for him by tomorrow morning. I will see if they come back clear and she has no sexual diseases. On a scale of one to ten, Number 2507 is a healthy female in every way. And she hasn't had sexual relations in, I would say, a year." He smiled a little. "So, on a scale of one to ten, she's an eight out of ten, which most American females never attain."

The assistant nodded, quickly filling in the chart blanks, and hurriedly left the cave.

He glanced over at the General. "I need to move to the next cave, where the next number is strapped down and drugged, so I can fully examine her. Let's give Number 2507 a brief respite, shall we? She's not going to have any peace ever again after you transport her over the border tomorrow. That drug will start wearing off in about thirty minutes. I'd advise ordering a soldier in here to keep an eye on her as she comes out of it."

"I will. I'll meet you in the next examination room. I'm enjoying this immensely, doctor."

The doctor smiled thinly. "And why wouldn't you?"

Alexa closed her eyes, her breathing raspy as she fought the drug in her bloodstream. She was finally alone in the cave. Nausea rolled through her as her entire abdomen cramped with pain.

As she lay there, the agony in her anal area began to slowly subside. But her back was hurting so much she couldn't stop a moan from tearing from her lips. Who knew a thick leather belt felt so awful? The pain, an awful stinging burning sensation, continued to lap through her.

Her mind went back to children she'd known who had been beaten by their father with a belt to punish them. At that time, Alexa couldn't relate to what they'd gone through.

She shivered. It was cold in the cave. The drug was beginning to slowly wear off Alexa closed her eyes. She could weakly flex her fingers, but that was all.

Another soldier arrived, throwing a black wool burka next to her head. "Get dressed!" he said in thick, stilted English.

Alexa felt the warmth of the wool near her shoulder where he'd thrown it. Gage flashed through her mind—his smile, the warmth in his eyes—and she tried to hold on to that. Alexa desperately needed a small corner of comfort right now, anything to feel safe.

She wanted Gage to remain, but he vanished behind her closed eyes. Then she saw her mother and father. Would she ever see any of them again? She was being sold to a monster that killed his sex slaves somewhere in Pakistan. She would be raped, beaten, and forced into subhuman submission. Terror moved through her as she saw again the General's wrathful expression as he came at her, wrapping the belt around his large fist.

He'd enjoyed hurting her.

A sob wrenched from Alexa, and she began to weep. She was alone.

Abandoned.

And there was no help coming. Tomorrow, the doctor had said, she would be leaving this cave—she was now a number, she had become nameless. She was considered someone's property, no longer a human being worthy of respect or equality. She would never be found by her family.

They'd never know what happened to her.

Oh, God . . .

CHAPTER 11

ALEXA WAS SLOWLY able to get her body to move over the next half hour. She was finally able to sit up and pull the burka of rough, scratchy wool over her body. She heard the cries and screams of other women drifting down the tunnel. The doctor was doing his examination on another helpless victim. And it didn't stop. Just as she managed to slide off the examination table, her bare feet hitting the dusty cave floor, another woman was brought into her cave between two soldiers, sobbing hysterically.

Alexa managed to stagger out of the way as they forced the woman onto the table where she'd been lying. Now she got to see what they'd done to her. The woman tried to fight, but the two men were strong and quickly cuffed her wrists, strapping her heels into the metal stirrups. Alexa was numb, feeling nothing. She managed to hug the wall of the cave, wanting to do something . . . anything . . . to protect this woman, but was unable to do so as her piteous cries continued.

No, help was not on its way. And Alexa hated herself, because she didn't have the strength to lunge at the soldiers to grab a pistol and take action. Drool was still leaking out of the corners of her mouth from the effects of the drug, and she shakily wiped it away. They placed the waist strap around the woman and then the tight one across her brow. Her cries turned to rasps and whimpers as she struggled.

The doctor returned with his assistant. He glanced at Alexa, now sagging against the wall.

"Get her back to her cage!" he snapped at the soldiers.

They grabbed Alexa's arms. Her legs refused to work, and as much as she tried to walk, they ended up dragging her most of the way. She saw that half the cages were empty. The women who were left in them had heard the others' cries and screams, their faces frozen, eyes wide with anxiety. Alexa felt sorry for them. They didn't know what was coming.

The soldiers pushed her back into her cell and she fell to her hands and knees, the thick, warm wool burka tangling around her lower legs. She had no more than sat down at the rear of her cage when another soldier came and threw her a pair of red slippers, telling her to put them on.

★

TERROR ATE AWAY at Alexa. She had no idea what time it was, but she had come out of her drugged stupor. A soldier tossed her two more bottles of water. Later, another soldier came bearing a tray of food, sliding it into her cage.

The slippers felt wonderful on her cold feet. The smell of the thick soup in a huge clay pot made her mouth water. Alexa hadn't eaten anything since being captured; her stomach was now tight and growling, demanding food.

She felt more of her strength returning and slowly eased to her hands and knees. The wooden tray held a crock of pottery that contained the soup. Huge chunks of bread sat nearby. Her hands shook as she crouched over the tray and jammed the bread into her mouth. Closing her eyes, Alexa groaned, chewing, gulping, and then tearing off another chunk from the loaf.

Oh, no! More screams. More terrified shrieks. Cries for help. The tunnel echoed with them over and over again, and Alexa felt pulverized by the torture she knew these women were undergoing. It was one continuous unfolding nightmare with no end in site.

Her mind was beginning to clear, and as she crouched, drinking the salty, hot soup filled with vegetables and thick chunks of lamb, she recalled the conversations going on around her. She had been sold for two million dollars to a rich man somewhere in Pakistan. Sold to a depraved monster. And the sex slaves he bought usually died within two months of coming under his control. She pushed hair away from her eyes, the stench of urine, fecal matter, and vomit now strong in the cave.

Two soldiers dragged an unconscious woman, who had once been naked and was now clothed in the same black burka as she was, back to her cage. They were careful with her, not just dropping her on the dirt floor. Instead, they positioned her so she lay on her side. Alexa figured that the woman had been sold and the new owner didn't want her bruised or battered, so some care was being taken with her.

Then the soldiers strode to the next woman in line to be examined. Having heard the screams and cries of agony from the tunnel, the black-haired woman shrank against the wall at the rear of her cage. She cried and tried to fight off the groping hands of the soldiers as they hauled her out of the cell. She fought with everything she had. Alexa saw the stoic look on the soldiers' faces as they dragged her forward. They didn't care what happened to any of the women, and she wondered if they were paid to do this or if they just did it for the entertainment.

Her ears hurt from hearing the women's screams of outrage echoing within the cave. There was nothing she could do to help any of them, and this sense of helplessness was something Alexa had never encountered. As she ate hungrily, finishing off the soup and bread, she felt her old strength returning. She pushed back against the wall, her arms around herself, grateful for the warmth of the thick burka. Her feet were getting warm, too.

The women down at the other end of the cave were silent. Terrified. Their turns would come, but Alexa was now in deep shock over what they'd done to her, assaulting her body, examining her as if she were a prized horse to be checked out before being bought. And that photo taken of her? The one with her lying helpless and naked on that examination table? Where was that being sent? Were they sending it to the buyer? Was it on the Internet? She closed her eyes.

Somehow, she had to escape, but how? Alexa opened her eyes and watched the two guards at the tunnel entrance leading to the caves where the women were being brutalized. She wondered what happened to a woman who *didn't* pass the physical inspection. What did they do to her?

★

ZAKIR SHARAN SAT at his massive teak table in his office, smiling as he looked at the screen of his desktop computer. A thin smile pulled at his lips as he sat back in the leather chair, rocking it a bit. The photo of the woman he'd just bought, a Donna Collins, stared back at him. She was naked and strapped to a table. But it was her face that stirred something in his memory.

Could it be? Could it be? His thin black brows drew downward as he enlarged her face, and his heart pounded with possibility. Moving the mouse, he chose a file that said "culver" on it. When he opened it, there was a photo of Matt, Talia, and Alexa Culver. Hatred stirred powerfully through Zakir. Talia Culver had murdered his son Raastagar, and Matt Culver had killed his other son, Sidiq. And he'd sworn vengeance and retribution against the Culver family. He wouldn't rest until he'd gotten his revenge on the three children of Robert and Dilara Culver for taking away his two beloved sons.

Sweat broke out on his upper lip as a thrill moved through him. The color photo of Alexa Culver showed her in her desert flight suit, in the cockpit of her A-10. Her red hair was in a long braid between her shoulder blades. Her helmet was balanced on the cockpit frame. She had turned when the person with the camera had snapped her photo with a cell phone. Zakir had managed to get this one photo of her by paying a lot of money to have it hacked and stolen from the flight sergeant's cell phone.

Thanks to having the best hackers in the world on his payroll, he had managed to get a photo of each of the Culver children.

His mouth curved triumphantly as he dragged the A-10 photo of Alexa Culver next to the photo of the woman on the gurney, naked and helpless. Yes! It was her! His heart swelled with a joy he'd rarely felt since his two sons were murdered. It had taken a year to get these photos. It was standard military policy not to allow officers, especially combatants, to have their photos available anywhere on the Internet. And now . . . Allah was on his side, clearly! Because one of the women scooped up in that raid at that Afghan village, by sheer luck, was none other than Alexa Culver!

Sitting back, he stared at the pictures, his gaze snapping from one to the other. Yes, it was her! He was unable to believe his good fortune, and his smile broadened. Finally, he had one of the murdering Culvers in his custody. Of course, it would have done his vengeful heart good if it had been the sniper, Talia, or the Delta Force brother, Matt. They had been the ones to actually murder his two sons. But who cared? He could use Alexa Culver just as easily to start exacting his revenge on that whole family.

Rubbing his hands together, Zakir grinned widely. He was going to make the Culver family pay for every bit of grief and loss he'd experienced. He sat there, rocking back and forth, his mind moving at the speed of light. Normally, General Bajar supplied him with young sex slaves every month or two. They did not know who they had now, and he chuckled. If he had let them know the woman's real name, the Pakistani general would have increased the purchase price, and he'd be spending many more millions to retain the right to own her. This would remain his secret.

His green eyes narrowed on the photos side by side on his desktop. Alexa Culver had lied about her name. He moved to another document, opening it, reading the doctor's report on her physical examination. She had lied about her name and what she did for a living. After all, she was military and trained in evasion when captured. His fingers curved into fists on the arms of the chair. She was going to pay for the sins of her brother and sister. Her parents would be torn apart, just as he had been destroyed by the murder of his sons. They would all pay.

Normally, Zakir had a set routine and schedule for a new sex slave to be brought to his villa in Punjab, which was set in a rural area, surrounded by fields of wheat, fruit orchards, and other agriculture. He was worth fifty billion dollars, the richest Pakistani in the country. He made his living in the Indus Valley, where his father had built an empire and left it to him when he was only twenty-three years old.

Zakir had an endless thirst for power and control. He had ruthlessly taken the base fortune and multiplied it tenfold. He had steel and iron plants in

Islamabad, textile mills in five major cities producing cloth. His shadowy activities, however, had increased his wealth exponentially, thanks to his sons. He was not only part of the poppy and opium cartel in Afghanistan but also prominent in the global sex slave black market. His money increased every year, thanks to the distribution of opium around the world. And sex slaves were becoming a fashionable necessity that every rich businessman, no matter from what country, was expected to have. He was good, fast friends with the world's biggest sex trafficker, Valdrin Rasari, of the small European country of Malgar. Valdrin bought many of his Afghan children, selling them to South American customers. It was a lucrative market, and Zakir had made millions, thanks to his alignment with Valdrin's global network.

Zakir chuckled. Rich, corporate American men were now flying overseas to their newly built apartments in Asian or European countries or haciendas in South America where the women they'd bought were kept. Town houses were popular with the rich in Africa. Apartments were preferred in Asia. Every country in the world had sex trafficking, and rich men the world over, the true connoisseurs of the very best sex slaves, were always interested in purchasing from Rasari. He had a breeding stable where female sex slaves were bred to specific male slaves to give a buyer a particular child or young teen. Buyers the world over had explicit demands regarding gender, personality, skin, eye, and hair color. And they would spend millions for just the right sex slave.

The sex slave trade was growing so fast that Zakir often couldn't fulfill the demand for his customers. He'd enlisted General Bajar from the Pakistsan Army to start infiltrating the border villages in Afghanistan, kidnapping women, girls, and boys. Little had he suspected that one day, his enemies, the Culvers, would be caught up in his net. His mind turned swiftly to all the things he would do with Alexa Culver. First, he had to be careful that no one ever discovered her presence at his villa. The U.S. would send black ops to storm the place to rescue her. No, he had to be careful and thoroughly think through his strategy. Above all, he had to protect his wife and his two daughters.

Rubbing his neatly trimmed black beard, he sat, rocking and thinking. More than anything, he wanted the Culver family to suffer as he had suffered. He wanted videos of their daughter being sodomized by his male stud slave. He wanted her cries of pain recorded. And then? He'd get the video sent secretly to Robert Culver's computer. He wanted to see the man's face when he saw his daughter suffering. If only he could be there to see it!

Elation swept through Zakir as he conceived of other videos of Alexa being raped and tortured. Yes, he was going to make their family wish they were in hell. They would weep and feel helpless and lost, just as he'd felt when word came that his two sons had been murdered in Afghanistan.

The Culver family would feel the agony of watching their beloved daughter being tortured right before their very eyes. Off camera, of course, she would be his personal sex slave. He'd tie her wrists to a bed, her legs held open by two of his servants, and he'd fuck her until she screamed. He'd destroy her soul. He'd make her a shadow of her former self. He would take everything away from her, because her family had taken everything away from him. She would pay every day, and he had no intention of ever killing her.

No, this was one time when he very much wanted to keep a slave alive for future sessions in his sex room. He would glory in what he would do to her every week. And she would learn to fear the rising of the sun every morning, wondering what would happen to her that day. Rubbing his long, soft hands together, he smiled darkly. All his prayers had been answered.

★

GAGE HUNTER TRIED to swallow his impatience. The SEALs had split up; he had moved with three of them to the other side of the ridge. They'd gone through the night fighting ankle to knee-deep snow. He was cold, his fingers numb, even with the protective gloves on his hands. The stars blinked above them in the night sky. It was 0400 by the time they'd gone down four thousand feet lower and onto another trail using their GPS.

Wyatt Lockwood had called the SEAL team leader, McQuade, alerting them to a little-used tunnel that was another entrance and exit for the cave complex. He'd gone over all the original drawings made by the SEAL contingent that had discovered it ten years earlier. No one knew it was there until he'd called and alerted them to the little-known tunnel.

At this altitude, the snow was negligible, and they trotted with their infrared goggles on, hurrying toward the entrance. The LPO—lead petty officer—Chase Drummond was in the lead, his M4 ready for action should they run into Taliban. It was doubtful that they would in Gage's mind, because usually Taliban hunkered down at night to eat and then sleep. They had no night-vision goggles with which to move, as U.S. and UN forces did. Still, they had to assume they could run into a group of them, especially near this cave entrance. Their breaths shot out in white vapor as they increased the tempo of their jogging down the trail.

His heart was focused on Alexa. He ached to take her into his arms and protect her. It had been the most helpless feeling in the world to sit and wait for something to happen at the main cave entrance. When Lockwood had called Chief McQuade by sat phone, Gage had silently cheered in triumph.

Yes! There was another entrance! And maybe . . . just maybe . . . they could get inside, find those women . . . find Alexa . . . and rescue them.

They slowly, silently approached the GPS coordinates where Lockwood had told them the entrance was located. They were at four thousand feet now, on a slope peppered with bushes bearing snow. The ground was muddy, part snow, part slippery clay, as they stealthily crouched and moved in a diamond pattern toward it. His heart was pounding in his chest, adrenaline leaking into his bloodstream. He saw a little-used road that curved around the entrance hidden by brush. Someone had used this opening before. As they got closer, Gage looked down at the tire tracks imprinted deeply into a muddy area.

"Hey," he called quietly on his mic, "there's wide tire treads visible here. They look to be fairly fresh, maybe two weeks at the most."

Drummond halted his men. He gave orders for them to crouch and rest while he made his way back to Gage, who was studying the tracks. As a sniper, tracking was one of Gage's other skills. He knelt down in the frozen mud, pointing to the tread as the LPO leaned over his shoulder, studying them.

"What do you make of them?" Drummond asked.

"These are Pakistani tire treads," he muttered, scowling. "It's an Army truck. It's a double-axle type and it has double tires on the rear of it."

"How big?"

Shrugging, Gage said, "I don't know." He took a photo of the double tire tread and said, "You need to get this on your laptop and send it to Artemis Security. They'll have the software to find out more about this kind of truck tread and most likely be able to identify it."

Drummond grunted and took the card from the camera that Gage handed him. "All right," he told his team, "stand down and take a break while I get this photo sent by sat phone."

Gage stood, carefully watching the area. The wind was biting but warmer compared to where they'd been earlier. He couldn't stop thinking about Alexa and his failure to protect her. Now she was somewhere in that godforsaken cave system. He couldn't think about what they might be doing to her and to the other women. He just couldn't go there.

Hearing Drummond talk quietly to McQuade, he kept alert, his gaze never still as he watched the surrounding area. McQuade, team leader, was on the other side of the ridge with the rest of the team, near the main entrance to the caves. Drummond was in command of their small contingent on this side of the mountain.

"It's been sent," Drummond muttered. "Now we wait. McQuade wants confirmation on the vehicle before we do anything else. Hydrate and eat, men."

Urgency filled Gage. He swore he was in psychic touch with Alexa. It had been like this since the beginning. He could feel her, feel her moods, and now, he was feeling terror and despair deep in his gut. Wiping his mouth, he turned, slowly looking up toward the ridge. Everything looked so damned beautiful and unspoiled, yet Gage knew it was a false beauty. Inside that cave system were eight women going through unimaginable hell.

Five minutes later, Drummond found out whom the tire tracks belonged to. He spoke into his mic. "Pakistani-owned Unimog U5000 truck, capable of carrying fifteen armed troops in the back."

Gage scowled as he moved farther down the slope. He could see where the truck had been driven on the valley floor. A cold chill came over him. He narrowed his eyes, looking in the general direction of where the road snaked along the valley below. What was he seeing? Or was he imagining it?

"Drum," he called softly, "switch to drone feed, now! I think I see something . . . can't make it out, on the valley floor to the east of where we are. It's on the same road we just discovered."

Gage heard Drummond grumble under his breath. He sat between two bushes, the Toughbook laptop open on his thighs, awkwardly trying to type on it to bring up the drone that was loitering above the area.

"Shit!"

Gage turned toward him. "What?"

"Sonofabitch," Drummond swore, his voice turning excited, "it's the same type of truck we just ID'd. And it's coming our way."

His heart raced. Gage asked, "Could that truck be coming here? To this entrance to pick up the women? Take them back across the border?"

"Yes," McQuade growled, anger in his tone. "You're right. If that truck comes your way, there are four of you. There's no way I can get the rest of us up and over that ridge to reach you in time to help you. We have no idea how many tangos are inside that cave system, and we don't know how many tangos are in that truck."

"Can we get the drone to ID the truck?" Drummond demanded.

"Roger that. I'll know in a minute," McQuade said.

Gage's heart pounded, and he felt a sense of urgency. "I've sometimes seen Pakistani trucks come over the border," he informed them. "But it was prearranged, and we were alerted to their coming across. They were legitimate crossings. Is this one of those trucks? Does someone at Bagram, somewhere on the food chain, know about this truck crossing into Afghan territory?"

McQuade grunted on the mic. "I'm finding out right now. Hold . . ."

Gage knew the chief would be calling into Bagram SEAL HQ. They would know. His hand moved restively on his M4, the butt of it sitting against his hip as they waited for word. "And what about Artemis Security? Shouldn't they be informed?"

"Getting to it," McQuade growled, sounding harried.

In another ten minutes, the picture emerged. Gage listened intently to the four-way conversation between the LPO, McQuade, Wyatt Lockwood from

Artemis Security, and Commander Ian Camden, head of the SEAL unit at Bagram. The upshot of it was that the truck now trundling their way would arrive in less than an hour. It was from Pakistan. It had been authorized into Afghanistan by an ISI Pakistan Army general named Tahir Bajar.

"Where's the paperwork on that request?" McQuade growled. "Where's it been authorized to go?"

Wyatt said, "We're tapped into SEAL intel out of Tampa, Florida. It says on the authorization that the truck is going to a village near you to lend medical aid. The truck's contents are listed as medical items."

"Yeah," McQuade snarled, "probably all lies. My bet is this General Bajar is part of the sex-trafficking ring, and he's using his high rank to get this truck over the border to pick up kidnapped women and children and take them back across the Pakistan border."

"If that truck veers off course," Lockwood said, "then your guess is probably right, Chief."

Commander Camden came on. "We need to verify this before we do anything."

Gage knew they could blow that truck out of existence if it didn't follow the authorization orders to go to the village lying somewhere below them in the same valley.

"Roger that," McQuade agreed. "But if that truck makes a left turn at that fork in the road coming up, that's the one that goes right by that third cave entrance where I have my men. And that's a fucking game-changer. We need to scramble and decide what to do if he makes that turn."

Gage compressed his lips, the urgency was eating him up. His gut burned with fear and possibilities. There were only nine of them, against how many tangos in that truck and inside the caves? There were eight women hostages in the mix. If the truck came their way, then it would be confirmed that it was coming to pick up the women captives.

And then what? Right now, Gage knew there were just four of them near the entrance. What was Commander Camden going to do? Would he have the truck bombed out of existence before it reached here or not? If the truck arrived, then they had tangos and the women coming out of that entrance to be herded into the truck.

It was tactically messy any way his mind leaped over the myriad possibilities. Gage wiped his mouth, unable to stand still any longer. He quietly walked around the brush, keeping his gaze fixed on the valley below. In another ten minutes, they'd know whether that Pakistani truck coming their way was legitimate or not.

And somehow, some way, the SEALs on station here at the complex had to come up with a game plan that would protect all those women from any crossfire!

CHAPTER 12

GAGE WAITED UNTIL the Unimog U5000 did indeed turn left at the fork and head toward the cavern entrance. They had an hour before the truck arrived. He moved to Drummond, crouching down next to him.

"I have an idea. You have those speaker nodes that pick up voice and sounds on you?"

"Yeah. Why?"

Gage said, "I want to enter that cave and set them down along it, so if the women are being pushed out in this direction, we'll know ahead of time. We can also hear others talking. I know Urdu. So do you. We'll be able to hear what's going on and be better able to prepare for when they come out." He looked over at the hard profile of the LPO. "What do you think?"

Rubbing his beard, Drummond cursed softly. "I was thinking the same thing. I was just trying to decide who to send in."

"Send me," Gage said, his voice firm, his eyes on Drummond's. "This is mine to do."

"I heard some scuttlebutt back at the base," Drummond said, "that you were sweet on Captain Alexa Culver. Is that true?"

Gage swallowed; he wasn't going to deny it. "I am."

"Okay," Drummond muttered, "let's get all fifteen of those speaker nodes set up if you can. We can use all the help and pre-warning we can get. And I want you wired up with a radio that has fresh batteries in there. We'll have the ability to talk or click back and forth once you get into that cave. Give us the layout and anything else you find."

"Got it," Gage said. Relief shot through him. He wanted—no, needed—to do something! He had instinctively known that Unimog would turn and come their way. He also knew Alexa and those other women were in deep trouble—he just didn't know how bad it was. His heart clenched in his chest as he freed his emotions for just a moment, allowing his love for Alexa to surface. He'd been fighting the feeling ever since he met her. No one fell in love at first sight. It was impossible. But he couldn't ignore the feelings in his heart for Alexa, even though he knew it was far too early to say anything to her. They had to have time. And he wasn't sure they'd ever get it.

Gage knew she would be changed by this experience in the caves, but he didn't know how. He knew slave traders all too well, and he sensed that something terrible and deeply traumatic had already happened to her and the other women. He knew he would love Alexa no matter what had happened. He'd be there for her, damn it, one way or another. He'd help her get back on her feet because he was in for the long haul—if she'd allow it.

In a matter of minutes, the nodes were gathered and Drummond showed him how they worked. They were ingenious, tiny, the outer shell made of waterproof gray plastic. There was a lithium battery inside each one, and the nodes could send a silent signal to Drummond's laptop that had software that could interpret the sounds. Then the voices and exchanges would be in every man's earpiece, and everyone would know simultaneously what was going on.

That gave them a major edge. Surprise was the only advantage they had on this mission. It was three SEALs and a Marine against an unknown force. And their job was to keep the women from getting caught in the crossfire. Gage wasn't sure it could be done, but damn it, they'd try their best.

Within another five minutes, Gage had shucked his rucksack and attached his helmet and infrared goggles, ready to use. He kept the Ka-Bar strapped in a sheath to his left calf. His .45 pistol was at his side, a round in the chamber, the strap across it, removed so he could pull and shoot. The M4 was ready, snapped into his chest harness.

Gage took some water from his canteen and soaked a rifle cloth with it, then quickly wiped off the greasepaint that would give him away. Where he was going, it was dark. He climbed out of the white snow gear, wearing only his olive green T-shirt and desert-colored Marine cammo pants. He tucked his dog tags inside his T-shirt. The temperature was below freezing, and his skin instantly goose bumped as he filled his large pockets with the nodes.

After a last radio check, Drummond slapped him on the back. "Don't play hero in there," he told Gage.

Gage hesitated. "I'm a sniper. I know how to stalk. If I see or hear something, I may detour, but I'll be in radio contact with you if I do. Right now, you know we need eyes and ears in there." He suddenly grinned, his teeth white against the blackness of the night. "Besides," Gage said, his voice wry, "there's no one better to do it than a Marine . . ." He slipped off toward the opening before Drummond could respond.

Moving silently through the brush at the entrance, Gage drew down his infrared goggles, flipped them on, and quickly dipped inside the cave complex. He crouched next to a wall, waiting and listening. He heard muted voices and cocked his head, listening keenly. Taking a node, he placed it on the ground next to the wall. No one would ever see it because it blended into the darkness perfectly.

Gage had seen the layout with its many caves and tunnels. He'd now memorized it. He was a sniper, and that's what snipers did—memorize the hell out of their hunting area. Crouching, he moved close to the wall, quickly trotting around the cavernous oval. It was easy to move because he could see everything. If there were animals or humans around, it would light up and glow. At the tunnel, he halted, dropping another node. Then, peering into it, he saw it was a long, steep curve downward. The floor was all limestone with no soil. It would be easy to get through.

Sweat was pouring off him as he estimated going half a mile downward. The tunnel was long and narrow. Not more than three people could walk up or down it shoulder to shoulder. The temperature in the cave was around sixty-five degrees, pleasant enough. Breathing easily, he dropped the third node at the end of the tunnel.

Straightening, he clicked his radio, letting Drummond know he was all right. Receiving a click back, Gage heard male voices drifting upward. He couldn't make out what they were saying, only that it was in Urdu. Where were they holding the women? The cavern he had reached was long, reminding him of a large cucumber in shape. At the other end of it was another tunnel. All he focused on was remaining a silent, black ghost drifting through the caverns, undetected.

He was desperate to find Alexa but scared, too, of what he might find. Was she dead? Had she been raped to death? His mind played the worst of possibilities.

He set another node at the other end of the cucumber cavern. Then he went into another tunnel that ran straight ahead, no longer canting downward. As the tunnel twisted and turned, the ceiling lowered and then became higher. At some points, Gage, because of his height, had to run in a crouch. It was a wicked tunnel. At the other end, breathing out of his mouth, he knelt, placing a node. He again clicked his radio.

Operators did the clicks because it told their team they were all right. In a situation like this, Gage did not dare talk unless he knew for sure that there were no tango ears around to hear him speak. And right now, he didn't know that. Tangos could have been guarding any of these entrance/exit points in any of these tunnels. He received one click back from Drummond.

Pulling the cover off his watch, Gage saw that fifteen minutes had elapsed. The truck would arrive in half an hour. Urgency thrummed through him and he pushed off, swiftly moving into the next cavern in the shape of a bloated watermelon. The sound of men talking became much clearer as he made it to the next tunnel. Setting a node in place, Gage crouched, ear cocked toward the sounds moving up the tunnel. He could pick out words. Two men talking, one giving orders and another sounding nervous in his responses. But there were no women's voices.

Where were they keeping Alexa and the women? Where? He shoved off, carrying his rifle up, ready to fire, as he ran silently through the tunnel that first curved right and then curved left. Sweat dripped into his eyes, burning them momentarily. Gage blinked several times, his focus on getting to the end of this long, long tunnel. The end came up abruptly. Skidding to a halt he went to his knees. He perched by the edge of the tunnel before it spilled into another cave.

His heart pumping furiously, he dropped a node next to where he was and noticed grayish light emanating from the next tunnel on the other side of the cavern. It looked like a deflated balloon. This was a rough cavern with a lot of wings and hiding places. Carefully, he stepped forward, making sure his boots didn't disturb any loose rock that had shaken and fallen down from the ceiling. The voices were clearer. There were tangos in that next cave where the light was coming from, and only a tunnel separated Gage from them.

He put a node next to that tunnel and then swiftly moved to the opposite side, where he found some hiding possibilities. This cave had partially collapsed in on itself, half of it in rubble. There were huge, white limestone boulders big as an Abrams tank here and there. There were also pieces of thin limestone that reminded him of a bird's wing. These were perfect hiding places, because the limestone was thick enough for a person to hide behind and not be seen.

Checking out several hidey-holes, Gage turned, wiping the sweat off his brow with the back of his arm, keying his hearing. This time, the voices were clear and understandable.

"Go get the women. Bind their hands in front of them!"

"Yes, sir."

Gage heard scurrying sounds, thinking it was a soldier carrying out the orders. His footsteps quickly died away, indicating he was walking away from where he was hidden.

"When is that Unimog arriving?"

"Twenty-five minutes. Relax, will you? Everything is under control. They just checked in with me by radio. They will arrive on time."

"You're going to have to push these women through the caves in a hurry!"

The man snickered. "Don't worry. After what they just went through, if we tell them to jump, they'll ask how high." He laughed.

Gage felt anger stir in him. Wiping his eyes free of the sweat, he leaned back against the wall, the M4 across his lap. He took out the canteen he carried and took a deep swig. Capping it, he snapped it onto his web belt. The women were in another cavern on the other side of these tangos, and Gage knew there was no way to get around to them. Slowly standing, he turned and quietly moved among the boulders and rubble, getting as far back in the collapsed cavern as he could.

Once he was hidden behind a massive rock, he knelt down on one knee. This time, he spoke in a low voice to Drummond. The SEAL responded with a click. Gage gave him the layout, gave him all the information, and told him what he'd seen and heard. His breathing was slowing, his hearing keyed to any unusual sound. The only way he could be heard was if someone came out of that tunnel, and he had a line of sight on it and would see them first.

"I'm going to hide here and wait for them to pass by me," he said. "We need to know how many tangos are here. Once they've all come through with the packages, I'll call in the number, the weapons, and what we're up against."

There was a responding click.

Gage rubbed his mouth, steadying his breathing, watching the tunnel. "If there aren't many, I'll take them out myself from behind. They'll never know what hit them. But if there are too many, I'll let them pass. I'm sure they won't have the women in front of them, but I'll let you know. Plus, you'll have the node speakers on. I can be eyes and ears down here to help you know the lineup. Only when they get into the entrance cave can they spread out. At that point, you'll need to figure out what you're going to do."

They were only three SEALs, but Gage knew that was as good as having a platoon of forty soldiers.

"We'll have to take out whoever is with that Unimog," Drummond said in a low tone. "It's about twenty minutes from arriving. We're going to intercept it now. The problem is if they radio that they're being attacked."

Nodding, Gage understood. "Roger. I'll maintain my sniper cover here and assist as things play out."

Drummond said, "If we can kill the driver and the others, I can drive the truck up here. And if someone from the caves calls in, I speak Urdu and can answer him. If we can fake them out, make them believe nothing has happened and that the truck is arriving on schedule, we'll have a better chance of getting those women out of there alive."

"Roger that. I'll call you if anything changes."

"Roger. Out."

Gage inhaled deeply, hearing men's voices once again. The node he had put at the tunnel could be activated, and he did so, linking it to his electronic ear device, sending the sounds into his earpiece. And he heard everything as clear as if the men were standing next to him. A small grin flashed across his face as he hunkered down to listen.

"Are they out of the cages?"

"Yes, sir."

"Bound?"

"Yes, sir."

"Any problems?"

"The blond woman, sir? She's very weak. She's saying she can't walk."

Gage heard the man swear.

"Put a gun to her head and tell her if she doesn't get up and walk, you'll shoot her."

"Yes, sir!"

★

ALEXA STOOD IN horror as a Taliban soldier came racing into the cage cave, his pistol drawn. Cathy, the blonde, was sobbing on the floor. The examination had somehow injured her. Alexa wasn't a doctor, but she could see that Cathy was in terrible pain. The women stood around, eyes wide, terrified as they saw the men bind Cathy's hands like theirs had been bound. They all wore the same black wool burkas and the same red slippers on their feet.

The soldier grabbed Cathy by her long, blond hair, jerking her head upward. He leaned over, his teeth bared as he shoved the pistol to her temple. "You get up right now or I'll shoot you where you are."

Alexa saw the soldier's finger become firmer on the trigger.

"No!" Alexa shouted. "Stop!" She rushed to Cathy. "I'll help her! Don't shoot her!" she pleaded as she leaned down, gathering Cathy up.

The soldier blinked, shocked at her unexpected action, and backed off, unsure what to do.

Another woman, Tracy, approached, and she and Alexa held Cathy up between them. "I'll help," she whispered to Alexa. "We'll walk her out of here."

Alexa froze, seeing the General storming into the cavern, his eyes blazing with fury. The soldier turned, quickly explaining in Urdu what had happened.

The General was breathing like an angry bull, his hands on his hips as he surveyed the three women. "It's time! We must go. Herd them out of here," he bellowed, yanking his thumb toward the tunnel. Gritting his teeth, he roared to the six soldiers surrounding the huddled group of women, "If any of them slow you down, shoot them where they stand!"

And then he advanced upon Alexa, Tracy, and Cathy. He curled his fist and then glared at the trembling hostages. In clear, concise English he repeated his command so there was no confusion about what he would do if they didn't keep up the pace.

"Do you understand?" the General bellowed, his deep voice echoing eerily around the cave.

All the women vigorously bobbed their heads, clinging to one another, crowding into a tight group for protection.

As the General turned, he nailed Alexa with a dark glare. "Do not make me shoot you, whore. You do as I command, or else. Do we understand one another?"

Alexa nodded, keeping her eyes downcast, not wanting to invite his wrath.

With a curse, the General spun around, barking more orders to his tense soldiers.

Immediately, the women took their positions in line. Two Taliban soldiers were at the rear of the line, two were in the middle, and two more led them out of the smelly cavern. Three kerosene lanterns were passed out to the men in line so that everyone could see where they were going.

Alexa transferred Cathy's left arm across her shoulders, and Tracy did the same with her right arm; they practically dragged her along.

"I-I can't," Cathy sobbed. "I can't do this. I hurt so much," she wailed piteously.

Alexa pursed her lips. The drug she'd been given had finally worn off. She'd slept miserably in her cage, exhausted, and had no idea for how long. Then soldiers had come in, yelling at them to wake up. They had given the women water and then ordered them out of their cages, where their wrists were bound. Cathy had to be dragged out of her cage, screaming and trying to stay in it. Every woman here now knew she had been sold as a sex slave to some man somewhere in the world. They now knew what was going to happen to them.

Trying not to think of Gage, of her parents, Tal, or Matt, Alexa swallowed a growing lump in her throat. No one had told them where they were going, but Alexa figured either they were going to truck them to the border or a helicopter was going to pick them up. And that would be the end of her life as she knew it.

All she could look forward to was the monster who had bought her. She would try to escape and make her way to India, where she could get help. Alexa wasn't afraid of trying to get her freedom. She knew it would take a huge toll on her in every way, but if she could get out of Pakistan, get to the Indian border, and beg for help from the border guards, she could get hold of her parents.

And then, rescue could come. That was her plan. But Alexa also knew that the great unknown yawned before her, where nothing was guaranteed.

Cathy suddenly collapsed with a cry, nearly knocking both of them together as her weight brought them down. Alexa stumbled, terrified that if they fell, it would bring the wrath of the General upon them.

She caught herself, as Tracy did, and they redoubled their efforts, continuing to drag the girl between them, but Cathy had given up. She had collapsed. She was injured and unable to go on.

How Alexa wanted to give in to those very feelings herself. Tracy shot her a look, her mouth pursed. Alexa nodded but said nothing. They were not to talk. And no one wanted to get slapped across the mouth, or worse, if they made the mistake of doing it.

Now the three of them were at the head of the line, struggling to move quickly as the Taliban behind them kept poking them with the barrels of their AK-47s. Alexa saw the General, the Scribe, the Toad, the doctor, and his assistant ahead of them. The assistant was laboring like a donkey under too heavy a load, carrying a lot of suitcases of equipment plus a huge rucksack over his slender shoulders. The General had an AK-47, wore a bulletproof vest, and was on guard. They came out of the tunnel and into another cavern that looked as if most of it had already caved in, with deep rubble everywhere.

Alexa wanted to tell Cathy to try walking, but she dared not speak. The General was clearly on edge now, looking around, his AK-47 held high, his finger on the trigger. Cathy weighed around a hundred and thirty pounds, and Alexa saw Tracy struggling to keep the girl upright. None of these women were in good, athletic shape like she was, and Alexa silently thanked the military all over again. At least her body was strong.

Her spirit? Well, it was bruised, bloodied, and spinning. Something had broken inside her and she could feel it. It was as if they had killed a part of her soul, and she'd never get it back. It was a hollow, dark sensation that made her even more fearful.

They crossed the cave, heading into another tunnel. Alexa's arms were tiring, and her shoulders were aching. Being strung up and beaten had drained her of any reserve. She felt deep rage, hated all men right now, wanting to kill all of the bastards, starting with the General, followed immediately by the doctor.

★

GAGE HUNKERED DOWN, remaining absolutely still. His heart leaped as he saw Alexa at the front, trying to carry another hostage with another woman from the group. He anxiously zeroed in on her. He saw no marks, no swelling, or anything to indicate she'd been struck. But he knew her well enough to see the black holes in her eyes, the tight set of the corners of her mouth, her hair in utter disarray. She was dirty, that black burka she wore too big for her as it dragged on the floor, making her trip sometimes.

The last of the line straggled in. Gage couldn't speak yet, so he clicked his radio once. He had no idea if Drummond or his team had apprehended the truck.

He received one click. Relief filled him. Something had happened and it must have turned out all right, or Drummond would not have clicked his radio. Gage didn't pray often, but he prayed now, because if the SEALs had command of that truck, this slaver group heading into the tunnel would be taken as prisoners—or would be dead—in about fifteen minutes. The most important thing was to ensure that the women would be safe. He knew if he yelled at Alexa and told her what to do, she would respond instantly. But what of the other women? Hell, they'd probably panic and not hear his order at all.

This wasn't going to be easy. All the women looked pale, drawn, terrified. Their hair was uncombed; they were dirty and dusty. They looked like they'd gone through hell itself, their eyes filled with terror.

Gage couldn't open up to his emotions, but he did let his heart swell fiercely with love for Alexa. Only she looked capable and strong, her eyes burning with rage. Clearly, she was their leader. Had she paid a price for that? Gage hoped not, but her long red hair in that braid shouted of her warrior abilities. Had one of these bastards taken her down? Raped her? Hurt her? His rage funneled up through him.

As soon as the last two Taliban soldiers cleared the cave and were well into the next tunnel, Gage broke radio silence. His hopes rose. Drummond's team had killed the driver and his partner in the cab. The rear of the Unimog was empty.

Drummond said he had driven the truck up to the entrance. A Pakistani speaking Urdu had radioed him, and Drummond had spoken in the same language, telling him they would arrive in five minutes.

More relief trickled through Gage. "I'll take out the two in the rear first as they enter that last tunnel before the group emerges into the entrance cave. My next step is to get close enough, with some timing and luck, to sneak up the line of women and use my pistol, taking out the two center guards. At that point, my gunfire is going to alert everyone, and your men will have to take out the tangos in front. I'm taking out that Pakistani general who's just in front of the line of women. You get the rest. Over."

"Roger. Out."

Cold fury wound through Gage as he slowly, silently rose. He unsafed his M4, the bullet in the chamber. Now all he had to do was to follow at a safe distance, like a ghost shadowing the line. The two Taliban soldiers at the rear were distracted, yelling at the women to hurry. They weren't looking around or checking out anything else.

A feral smile pulled at his tightly drawn mouth as he eased forward in a slight crouch—now, at last, the hunter closing in on his prey.

CHAPTER 13

ALEXA WAS BREATHING hard as she and Tracy half dragged, half carried Cathy up another tunnel. Her back was now on fire, pain radiating in every direction, because Cathy's arm was across her shoulders, which had taken the bulk of the General's belting. Tracy was truly brave, fighting to stay upright, not used to bearing so much weight for so long. The women stumbled and fell to their knees more than once, the bruising pain making Alexa limp. She was sure she'd cut her knees on the small rocks in the tunnel, feeling the trickle of blood down her calves from the injuries.

She felt intensely sorry for Cathy, whose eyes were vacant and glazed over with unrelenting pain. Alexa had never seen someone in this kind of catatonic state; it was as if the woman's spirit had fled her body, and all that remained was a physical shell.

It was horrible to watch human beings reduced to a hull of their former selves. Alexa didn't know Cathy, but her anger had reached a high point. No human being should ever have to endure this. At the same time, she was terrified that the General would shoot Cathy once they reached wherever they were going. *Oh, God . . .*

The last tunnel was brutal for Alexa, and her back felt as if it were on fire. The stinging, burning sensation throbbed throughout her, making her grunt with pain. Teeth clenched, nostrils flaring, she breathed hard, and all the women struggled mightily as the tunnel ascended steeply. Gasping for breath, Alexa tripped and fell, with Cathy crashing down upon her. Tracy was jerked off her feet, slamming into the other cave wall, crying out.

Oh, no! Alexa scrambled to her feet, hearing the General cursing at them. Now he was coming back down the tunnel toward them.

"Get her up!" Alexa cried out to Tracy, grabbing Cathy with superhuman strength, hauling Cathy's body against herself. God, she felt heavy!

Tracy scrambled, her head jerking to the right as the General roared a curse in Urdu at them, his pistol up in the air, his face filled with rage. She quickly helped take Cathy's weight, cowering as the Pakistani officer pushed past the soldiers and moved angrily toward them.

Alexa saw murder in the man's narrowed eyes, and she knew he was going to shoot Cathy. She could feel it in her bones. She had her hands free, and the Taliban soldier in front of her was shaken by the sudden commotion. He stepped backward, slipping on a rock in the tunnel.

Now! Alexa released Cathy, stepping forward and making a grab for the rifle in the soldier's right hand. He was falling backward as she wrenched it out of his grip, and then everything became a blur. Her entire focus was on the rifle.

Alexa had been trained in the weapons the Taliban used. She jerked a look down, unsafing the weapon and turning the selector to single shot.

As she aimed at the General, who was snarling, he lowered his weapon to shoot her. The women started to scream, scattering, running back down the tunnel to escape the General and his pistol.

Alexa jammed the AK-47 to her shoulder and fired at her mortal enemy.

The loud crash of the rifle going off deafened them all and echoed through the tunnel. Alexa heard nothing but saw with satisfaction a bloom of blood splatter across the General's left arm. She saw his face go from fury to surprise and then realization. Alexa fired a second shot to his head that wasn't protected by the bulletproof vest he wore, taking him down.

The pistol dropped out of his hand, but the Taliban soldier in front of her, who still had his weapon, turned, aiming at her. Suddenly, there were shots coming from behind her, and the tunnel became a deafening roar of explosions as bullets were fired. Alexa stood firm and shot the soldier in front of her.

She screamed as the soldier, who had fallen earlier, grabbed her ankle, hauling her off her feet, and the AK-47 flew out of her hands.

More shots were being fired. Alexa heard them coming from both ends of the tunnel. Who was firing? Was it the Taliban soldiers behind them? Slamming onto the tunnel floor, Alexa cried out as pain ripped up and down her bruised, battered back.

The Taliban soldier leaped up, grabbing at his rifle that lay nearby, but Alexa scrambled up, pushing off in her slippered feet, lunging for him. His hand curved around the weapon just as she landed on top of him, rolling him away from it.

And then Alexa heard the women scream—and men yelling in English! She had no time to think about what she'd heard, but Tracy dropped Cathy in the middle of the tunnel, racing to Alexa and leaping upon the soldier, pummeling him with her fists, screaming at him in rage.

It was enough of a diversion. Alexa crawled away, grabbing the rifle.

And then she anxiously peered down the tunnel, and her mouth fell open. Gage Hunter was coming up it, his eyes narrowed with a feral look in them, his .45 drawn, his total focus on the Taliban still on the floor. She blinked, unable to believe her eyes! He was running now, his body powerful, hurtling toward her and protecting all of them. How had he gotten in here? Where had he come from?

Her mind reeled. She turned, hearing Tracy scream. Before she could get a shot off at the Taliban, who had punched Tracy and knocked her out, Gage skidded to a halt, put her behind him, and fired his weapon. The explosion careened down through the tunnel, killing the Taliban soldier.

Breathing hard, Alexa looked up the tunnel. To her shock, she saw American-dressed black ops men racing toward them, their M4s up and ready to fire. They were saved! *Saved!*

Tears spilled down Alexa's face as she sagged against the tunnel, holding on to the AK-47 with white knuckles. She saw Gage turn, that hard, killing look in his eyes gone, replaced by compassion for the women, and especially for Alexa.

"It's over, Alexa," he growled, moving over to her, gently taking the weapon out of her hands. "These are SEALs. You're all safe . . ."

The words careened around in her head as she stood there, her knees weakening, feeling a relief so heady it was almost like a drug high sweeping through her. The other operators, three of them, came forward. Their faces were expressionless, their mouths set in a hard, single line.

"The rest are dead," Gage called, pointing down the tunnel. "We need to gather up the women."

He turned back to Alexa, cupping her jaw, looking deep into her eyes. "Just hang in there with me. We'll get you out of here. You're all going home."

Closing her eyes, tears streaming hotly down her cheeks, Alexa leaned into his rough, callused palm, never having needed Gage more than she did right now. But she knew there were seven other women here—women without military training, who were far worse off than she was.

Opening her eyes, gulping, she pulled away. "The others," she croaked, her voice breaking. "They need help, Gage . . . they've all been harmed . . . be gentle with them."

She saw his face change as sudden anguish came to his eyes, his mouth tightening. He drew his hand away from her jaw.

"I-I'll be all right. Just go to them. Let them know you're not going to hurt them and that you're here to rescue them." She was blithering like an idiot, the words raw, rushing out of her. She was shaking and wrapped her arms around herself, adrenaline crashing through her system.

"We'll take care of them," he promised her gruffly. "Stay here . . . I'll come back for you . . ."

Alexa forced herself to move. Tracy was sitting up, her nose bleeding profusely, swelling already around her left eye and cheek. Cathy was unconscious. Alexa went over to Tracy, dropping to her knees, holding her shoulders.

"A-are you okay?"

"Yeah," Tracy muttered, glaring at the two dead soldiers farther up in the tunnel. "Those bastards," she whispered, touching her bleeding nose.

"I don't even have a tissue for you," Alexa said apologetically.

"It's okay," Tracy whispered. She turned her head. "We have to help Cathy."

Nodding, Alexa got up. At first, she wondered if Cathy was dead, and turned her over on to her back to quickly examine her for bloodstains. There were none. Tracy moved over to her on her hands and knees.

"Is she dead?"

"No, I don't think so." Alexa heard a sudden commotion behind them, and then heard women shrieking. But it wasn't from terror. It was from joy. The team who had rescued them must have found them and told them they were safe. Swallowing, Alexa moved her hand over Cathy's hair, feeling so sorry for the young woman.

Tracy wiped tears from her eyes. "They saved us, Alexa. We're saved. Oh, God, we're going home. I don't believe it . . . I don't . . ." She suddenly gasped, pressing her hand against her mouth, her face wet with tears.

Alexa nodded, suddenly very aware of the overwhelming pain in her back. But Gage was here. He was alive! He'd survived the wound he sustained at the village. And helped to save her life and the lives of these other women. How had he and the SEALs gotten here?

Soon, she saw the rest of the women coming up the tunnel. Their wrists were no longer bound. They were free. The looks of relief on their faces said everything. She saw one operator move ahead of them with a concerned look on his face as he drew up to them.

"Is she wounded?" he asked Alexa, looking over at Cathy.

"I think so. Do you have a corpsman with you?"

"No. But we have four medevacs on the way here. They're landing in about twenty minutes. Can you two stay with this woman? I want to get the rest of the hostages up to the entrance and prepare them for transit."

Alexa nodded. "Yes, we'll stay with Cathy."

The women trailed by Cathy, who lay on one side of the tunnel. Alexa kept her hand on Cathy's shoulder while Tracy remained kneeling and cradled Cathy's head in her lap. There were sobs and tears of joy now. Alexa saw the gratitude in their eyes for being rescued and not forgotten. The last man to come up the tunnel was Gage. Her heart leaped, she wanted so badly to fly into his arms. How desperately Alexa needed a little comfort. But she wasn't going to leave Cathy. Not now.

Gage knelt down at Cathy's feet. "What's wrong with her?" he asked.

"She's been hurt internally, but I don't know where. I can't find any blood on her," Alexa whispered, shaking her head. She saw Gage look confused for a moment, and then he got it.

"She fainted?"

"Yes, from pain, I think."

Gage settled the strap of his M4 against his back. "Then I'll carry her. Why don't you two go ahead of me? I'll bring up the rear."

Alexa slowly stood. She was unsteady, reaching out to the tunnel wall to remain upright. Instantly, Gage stood, his hand cupping her elbow. "What's wrong?"

She gave him a sad look. "Everything. But I'll be okay. I'm just a little shaken up. Take care of Cathy, okay?" Her voice was low and strained. Gage gave her an intense look, searching her eyes. Reaching out, she gripped his arm. "Take care of Cathy? Please . . ."

Gage released her, worry deep in his gaze. He glanced over at Tracy, who stood nearby, and asked her if she could walk out of there or not. Tracy nodded and said she could.

Gage gently gathered up Cathy, her body limp. Alexa wanted to cry as Gage handled the woman so carefully, arranging her against his tall, strong body. She saw the sweat on the front and back of his T-shirt, realizing the physical demands he'd had to undertake. She had so many questions to ask him. She looked over at Tracy, who was still wiping blood away from her nose, and walked over to her.

"Let's lean on one another, okay, so we can get out of here?" Alexa said, reaching out for her.

"Good idea," Tracy said, her voice breaking, tears coming. "You helped save us, too," she whispered, giving her a grateful look. "Thank you . . ."

Alexa stared up the tunnel at the General's still body, and hatred welled up within her. "He'll never hurt another woman," she spat out, her emotions nearly getting the best of her. "Not ever again . . ."

Alexa clung to Tracy, who did the same to her. They weren't walking very well, fully exhausted from carrying Cathy between them, and the tunnel was at such a steep incline, they found themselves breathing roughly, taking tiny, mincing steps to reach the outer cave.

By the time Alexa got there, it was flooded with light from the headlamps of what looked like a truck parked just outside the opening. The brightness hurt her eyes, and she bowed her head. Outside, she could hear a lot of noise and activity. She caught the sounds of helicopters, a lot of them, flying around. There were six men, all in flight suits and helmets, entering the cave, heading for the huddled women, who clung to one another.

Alexa thought they might be air crewmen or medics from the medevacs. There was a woman Alexa was sure was a physician, dressed in a dark green flight suit, accompanying them.

As she and Tracy made their way slowly toward the group, Alexa saw the doctor moving among the women, swiftly assessing them medically. This was a triage situation, and she was dividing them into three categories. She didn't see Gage or Cathy. He had probably carried her out to the nearest medevac.

Licking her dry lips, she squeezed Tracy's arm as they halted near the group. "I can't believe it," Tracy whispered to her. "We're really saved. Saved . . ."

"Y-yes . . ."

Tracy slowly looked around the cave. Near the tunnel entrance, she saw all the men who had hurt them sitting on the floor, bound with flex cuffs, arms behind their backs and guarded by an American operator. Her voice deepened with quiet fury. "I hope like hell they kill those monsters for what they did to all of us."

Alexa watched the captured group, feeling satisfaction. "They'll get what's coming to them," she agreed grimly. Only the General was dead out of the original group, and they had passed four dead Taliban in the tunnel on the way up to the cave. She had seen two more Taliban dead near the tunnel entrance they had just passed.

She almost smiled, thinking about the captured group's fall from grace. Where were these sick bastards heading? To the CIA interrogation unit at Bagram, Alexa was sure. A vengeful part of her wanted to be there to see what would happen, to see fear and anxiety enter their eyes, and for them to know the kind of fear she and these other women had experienced. The CIA wouldn't be easy on any of these sick, predatory bastards.

"They're taking the women out," Tracy said, pointing toward the entrance.

Alexa looked up. She saw Gage reenter the cave, halting, looking for her. Instantly her heart sped up as soon as his gaze locked onto hers. More tears leaked out of her eyes. The tenderness in his glance as he walked over to Alexa nearly totaled her. She was shaking badly now, not sure she could keep standing.

A medic followed Gage and introduced himself to Tracy, asking if he could walk her out to the awaiting medevac. Touched that the man pulled a dark green handkerchief from a pocket in his uniform, handing it to Tracy, Alexa wanted to burst into sobs. They'd been tortured, threatened with death, assaulted, and invaded. And just this one bit of human kindness made her throat close up with tears once more.

Gage drew her gently against him, his arm going around her waist. "It's going to be all right, Alexa," he rasped, holding her tight. "Can you walk?"

All Alexa wanted was Gage, his body, his heat, his care, and that special gentleness that was so much a part of him. "Y-yes. My knees are wonky . . . but I can make it. Just keep your arm around me, please?"

He smiled, leaned down, and pressed a kiss on her mussed, dusty hair. "You got it. Come on, you're flying back in the fourth medevac with me."

Alexa turned, looking at the slave traders. "What about them?"

Grimly, Gage lifted his head. "Them?" His eyes glittered with barely held rage. "Don't worry, the SEAL team will take them aboard an MH-47 that's circling the area right now. They're heading straight to hell. The CIA can hardly wait to get their hands on them."

He gave her a look of satisfaction, gently urging her forward.

Alexa wearily leaned against Gage, her head resting on his chest, wanting to collapse with utter relief. The noise increased outside as he led her through some brush. Three of the medevacs had already lifted off, one after another. Above, Alexa could hear the familiar sound of Apache combat helicopters much higher, circling the area like guard dogs, protecting all of them with their special instruments that could locate an enemy and take them out.

She saw a huge truck at the entrance and noticed the Pakistan Army emblem on the door. It was then that it struck her that the General had planned to herd them into the rear of that massive truck, which would drive them across the border and into Pakistan. Alexa shivered.

Gage's arm closed around her even more firmly and he stopped, worried, looking down at her shadowed face. "All right?"

"I am now," she said, barely able to shout over the roar of the helicopters circling.

"Come on," he urged, pulling her forward.

Alexa saw the medevac, a crewman waiting outside it holding the sliding door open for them. The blasts of the whirling blades buffeted her. Gage turned, slid his arms around her, lifted her off her feet, and carried her aboard. Alexa clung to him, her arms around his strong neck, relaxing for the first time because she knew Gage would not drop her. Her back smarted where his arm rested against it, but she bore the pain in silence.

He carried her carefully toward the medevac and she buried her head against his neck, closing her eyes, beginning to sob from sheer relief. It was over. It was really over. And they'd all survived, when Alexa had given up thinking they would ever be rescued.

She felt such overwhelming gratefulness and love for Gage, and the fact he'd risked his life for all of them, that he'd never given up on finding her, made her cry even harder. And in response, she felt him hold her tighter, press a kiss to her hair, whispering words against her ear she couldn't understand due to the roar of the helo engines and the gusts of wind slapping and tearing at them.

Gage felt his heart tearing out of his chest as he transferred Alexa to a litter attached to the bulkhead of the Black Hawk helicopter. She lay there, and he had to move aside and sit in one of the two rear jump seats at the back of the medevac.

Tracy was brought in next and placed on the litter below Alexa's. Gage was grateful the pilot had allowed him to fly back with Alexa. Normally, that wouldn't have happened, but Gage was sure the pilot had recognized how much the exhausted sniper needed to be aboard and had given him a nod.

They were the last two hostage women to be flown out of that miserable place. The blades whirled faster, the engines thundering as the pilot lifted off into the grayish dawn light. The medic caring for Alexa placed a helmet on her head to protect her ears from the horrendous noise. Next, he placed one on Tracy's head. Gage pulled one on, too, and plugged into the ICS system so he could hear the crew speaking to one another, as well as hear the medic who cared for the woman he was falling in love with. His throat ached with tension, adrenaline still coursing through his body from the firefight. He worried for Alexa. She seemed in shock and disoriented. But then, who wouldn't have been?

Cathy had become conscious as he'd carried her to the first medevac that had landed. It had scared the hell out of him to look into her eyes and see that they were vacant, as if she'd left her body. Gage had never seen anything like that in his life, but it told him what these women had undergone. And as he had looked over the rest of the group still in the cave being triaged by the female physician among them, he saw terror, anguish, and unspeakable horrors reflected in their eyes and expressions.

Turning, he watched the medic pull a blanket over Alexa. He was asking her a lot of examination questions, and she kept pushing his hands away from her, as if she didn't want to be touched. Unsettled, Gage sat there, wanting to get up and intercede, but the g-force pushed him down in the seat as the Black Hawk gained altitude, turning, heading back toward Bagram.

"Don't touch me!" Alexa yelled, shoving the medic's hand off her arm.

Gage rose, coming over, hand on the pole that held the litter in place against the wall. He got the medic's attention. "She's been hurt by men. Can you back off?"

The crewman gave Gage a frustrated look. "I'm just doing my job. I need to see if she's injured."

"Listen, brother, she's been through hell. She's ambulatory. What do you say you just let her be? We'll be landing in about twenty minutes and she'll be taken into the ER," Gage told him, keeping his hand on the crewman's shoulder because he wasn't going to allow him to touch Alexa again. The fear in her eyes, the panic, told him a lot. "She's traumatized. Give her some space?"

The crewman scowled. "I was just trying to help her."

"I know," Gage said, "but she needs time. Maybe get her a bottle of water to drink?"

The crewman nodded. He pulled away from Gage's hand and walked to a nearby locker, opening it. "Here," he said, "you give it to her."

Giving the crewman a look of gratitude, Gage took the cold bottle of water. "Yeah. Thanks, brother."

Alexa struggled to sit up, her legs dangling over the litter. Gage drew near, making her feel safe. He handed her the opened bottle of water. "Th-thanks," she managed to say.

Gage stood there, his body a protective wall, his arm on the top of the bulkhead above her. He knew she needed to feel safe. It was written all over her. She took the bottle in both her dirty hands, tipping her head back, drinking all the water. When she was done, she shakily wiped her mouth with the back of her hand, giving the bottle to Gage.

"More?"

She gave a jerky nod.

"Stay put," he said, going over to the locker and opening it up.

Gage had recognized the deep-seated terror in Alexa's eyes, she couldn't stop crying. Before he gave her the second bottle, he smoothed the tears away with his thumb. He heard her utter a sound, saw her relief as he grazed her cheek. At least she wasn't telling him not to touch her, and for that, sharp consolation raced through him.

"Drink all you want," he told her, placing it into her hands. The look of gratefulness she gave him nearly broke his heart. She was like a frightened child looking for anyplace to hide. What had they done to Alexa? It ate at his gut, and he wanted to ask but knew he couldn't. Not right now. The other women had a similar expression in their eyes, too. Anger simmered in him. What had those bastards done to them? What? He was going crazy wanting to know. He also didn't want to know.

The Black Hawk began to lose altitude.

The crewman came over but remained at a respectful distance. "Ma'am? I need you to lie back down, please. We'll be landing shortly."

Alexa tensed. "Don't touch me."

"No, ma'am," he said, holding up his gloved hands. "I won't touch you."

"I'll get her tucked in," Gage told him with a look that was easy for the crewman to read.

"Yeah, fine. Thanks."

Alexa handed him the bottle and slowly moved.

"Do you want help?" Gage asked, moving in front of her, protecting her from the eyes of the crewman.

"N-no . . . I'm just slow . . ."

It was more than that and Gage knew it. He saw Alexa's mouth, those beautiful lips of hers, thin with pain. Something was going on, but he didn't know what. She seemed stiff and more than a little tense as she slowly lay down, stretching out her legs. The burka moved up, revealing her calves, and he reached to pull it back down, to cover her. She gave him a look of thank you. She lay on her right side, her head on the pillow, her back to the bulkhead. Saying nothing, he drew the heavy wool blanket up to her waist, leaned down, and caught her exhausted gaze. "You okay?"

She reached out, her fingers touching his bare arm. "I am now . . . thanks . . ." And then she gripped him tightly. "Gage?"

"Yes?"

"Don't leave me alone in ER. Don't go."

The sudden hysteria hidden in her raspy voice made his gut tighten. He reached out and gently touched her pale cheek. "I'm going nowhere. I'll be at your side every step of the way, okay?" The relief in Alexa's eyes tore at him. She gave a jerky nod and released him, tucking her hands against her body.

Grimly, Gage turned, standing guard as the helicopter hovered and began to land at the Bagram hospital. Right now, she wanted him nearby and was allowing him to touch her. His jaw tightened as he wiped his mouth. Alexa's captivity was at an end, but whatever she'd experienced at the hands of the Taliban may have imprisoned her mind, her emotions, and even her soul. Her journey back was just beginning. And so was his.

CHAPTER 14

ALEXA WANTED TO get out, now! The intense hustle-bustle of the ER was overwhelming to her raw senses. They had brought her in and transferred her to a gurney in an open cubicle surrounded on three sides by green curtains that hung floor to ceiling.

She'd briefly seen other hostages being taken to other cubicles, and the air crackled with tension. Gage remained at her side as she sat there, her legs dangling over the gurney, her muddy, wet slippered feet numb with cold.

A male doctor in his midforties entered, gripping a clipboard, all business. The name tag read: "Parlin, S., Major, U.S. Army."

Instantly, Alexa stiffened as he approached. A nurse followed him in, looking harried. Her heart began to pound, and she couldn't control the flood of adrenaline suddenly spurting into her bloodstream. Flashes of the other doctor, the one who had so painfully invaded her body, overlaid this doctor. She tried to fight the vision but was consumed by the terror leaking through her.

Reaching out, she gripped Gage's arm, shrinking back near him as the doctor approached.

Gage looked at her, confused, but he stepped in front of her, sensing her fear.

The doctor halted, scowling up at him. "You can leave, Sergeant," he snapped. "You've got no business being here. She's my patient. I need to get a rape kit done and to examine her."

Before Gage could protest, he felt Alexa's fingers dig into his arm. He didn't even have to turn to see what was in her face. Holding up his hand, he said in a low, warning tone, "Sir, you need to stand down. No man is going to touch her. I need to have her examined by a woman doctor. Can you get one in here, please?"

Parlin glared at him. "Just who the hell do you think you are?"

Alexa tried to steady her breathing, to stop the swirl of violent emotions shearing through her, but she couldn't. The doctor had on a pair of metal-framed glasses. He was tall and arrogant, and she wanted to scream, to run away. Gage must have sensed her panic because he moved closer, sliding his arm around her waist, holding her against his body.

"Sir, with all due respect, I'm her fiancé, and I'm going nowhere." It was a lie, but Gage didn't care. He knew if the patient was married or engaged, the person was allowed to stay, and hell could freeze over, but he wasn't leaving Alexa to this cold, uncaring male doctor. He drilled a warning look into Parlin's widening eyes. "She's been harmed by a man or men. You're not touching her." He snarled, "Get a woman physician down here to care for her, or I'm taking her out of here right now. She doesn't need this. She needs care, not attitude. Do we understand one another, sir?"

Alexa couldn't steady her breathing, her breasts rising and falling sharply beneath the burka. She watched the doctor's long face break into anger. Gage remained quiet, standing strong, staring him down, daring him to speak. The nurse, Angela Trumbull, slunk forward, young and unsure of herself.

"Dr. Parlin? We do have an obstetrician on duty, Dr. Pamela Griffin. I could call her down from that floor. She could see Captain Culver, possibly?"

Parlin snapped his head to the left, glaring down at the nurse. He moved his jaw, as if wanting to bite Gage. "Yes," he said abruptly, "get her down here." Glaring at Gage, he muttered, "You're in a lot of trouble, mister. I don't know who you are, but I'm going to find out."

"Don't bother," Gage said quietly. "I'm Sergeant Gage Hunter, USMC. Sniper."

Parlin's eyes narrowed on him. "I'm not finished with you, Sergeant. You'll be hearing from me. I'm filing insubordination charges against you."

With a half smile, Gage nodded. "I'll look forward to it, Major."

The doctor whirled around, striding away.

Nurse Trumbull moved quietly to the other side of Alexa. She studied her with sympathy. "You just try to relax, Captain Culver. I'll personally go find Dr. Griffin and ask her to see you right away, okay?"

Alexa nodded, closing her eyes. "I-I just want to get out of here . . . now . . . I can't handle this . . ."

Reaching out, Trumbull patted her hand. "I understand. Let me see what I can do for you, ma'am."

"Y-yes . . . thank you . . ."

Trumbull nodded and pulled the curtain across the front of the cubicle before she left. Alexa breathed a sigh of relief, shaking uncontrollably. She released Gage's arm. "I'm sorry," she whispered unsteadily. "That bastard will charge you, Gage."

He turned, opening his arms, sliding them around her hunched shoulders. "He's a pissant," he muttered, kissing her wrinkled brow. "Nothing for you to give one thought of worry to. Now, come here and let me hold you. That's what you really need right now."

Blindly, Alexa moaned his name and fell against him as he drew her in close to his body. He was resting his arms lightly across her bruised shoulders, and she tolerated the pain because she desperately needed his touch. Gage smelled of sweat and his own special male scent that calmed her, his arms encircling her, giving her his warmth, his care. She closed her eyes, resting her cheek against his chest. Gage felt so strong and steady. She felt spineless, as if the last two days of her life were avalanching down upon her with full force. Her emotions were wild, untamed, and tearing through her. All that mattered, all she wanted, was Gage, and he was here. He was here.

"Have my parents been notified I'm safe?" she asked.

"I'm pretty sure someone has already notified them, but I'll double-check for you as soon as we get you to a quieter area."

"Okay . . . thanks. They've got to be so worried . . ."

Gage gently caressed her hair. When he smoothed his hand across her shoulder, she flinched and cried out. Instantly, he lifted his hand, concerned. Pulling away, he looked down at Alexa. "What? Are you hurt there?" he demanded huskily. Pain was in her darkened hazel eyes. Her lips compressed.

"Yes . . . I got beaten with a belt," she admitted.

Air rushed out of Gage's lungs as he stood there, hearing the terror in her voice, seeing it in her eyes. "Damn," he rasped. And then he controlled his reaction. In that second, Gage wanted to kill the man who had done this to her. Wrestling with rage to keep it deep inside him, he smoothed hair away from her face. "What can I do? Just tell me."

She managed a broken half smile. "Don't touch my back. Not right now."

"Okay," Gage rasped. "Where else are you hurt, Alexa?"

"My back is all . . ."

"Then I won't hold you."

She made a sound of protest. "No, just hold me lightly. I need you, Gage."

Her soft cry ripped through him. "Okay, okay, it's all right. Come here, I'll just hold you until Dr. Griffin gets here." She buried her face against him, sliding her arms around his middle, clinging to him as if terrified that she would be torn away from him. She was trembling, and it tore him up even further. He nuzzled her ear, rasping, "I wish . . . I wish we were anywhere but here. I'd take you in my arms and take care of you, Alexa. I'd hold you for however long you wanted to be held. That's what you need right now, just some care. You've been through hell." His voice cracked with emotion.

Alexa hadn't known she had that many tears in her. They leaked out unbidden as he continued to caress her hair. How desperately she needed a kind, caring human touch. The animal inside her was howling and frightened, wanting to defend itself against anything and anyone. Gage was her island. Her anchor. The only one she wanted to protect her. She felt him being so careful, so light with his arms around her back. It felt as if the earth had been torn out from beneath her feet and she was in free fall.

Gage was her safe harbor, her security, because he intuitively understood what she'd endured—and barely survived.

Dr. Griffin quietly entered the cubicle. She smiled gently over at Gage as he looked up. "How is Alexa doing, Sergeant Hunter?"

Gage instantly liked the tall, slender woman in a white lab coat, a stethoscope around her neck. Best of all, she had a riot of carrot-red hair in a topknot. Gage guessed her to be in her early fifties. "She just needs a quiet place, ma'am. This ER is battering her."

Nodding, her blue eyes sparkling, Pamela walked over to Alexa. "I've got a room waiting for her up on my OB floor," she told Gage. "If you can just go and grab one of those wheelchairs out in the hall and bring it in here?"

Alexa pulled away from Gage, wiping her eyes with trembling fingers, finding Dr. Griffin's maternal nature exactly what she needed. "T-thank you for coming," she whispered. "I-I couldn't stand a man touching me."

Gage touched Alexa's fingers and squeezed them. "I'll be back in a minute."

She nodded, dropping her hands into the lap of her burka.

Pamela watched her for a moment, waiting until Gage left. Reaching out, she placed her hand over Alexa's. "Dr. Parlin wants you to get a rape kit examination. Is it necessary, Alexa? Were you raped?"

"N-no. Not raped," she whispered.

"Good to hear." She turned as Nurse Trumbull slipped into the cubicle. "No need for a rape kit, nurse."

"Yes, ma'am." She turned around and left.

"So," Pamela inquired, giving her a warm look, "can you tell me if you have any injuries?"

Alexa told her about her back. And then, hesitantly, told her about the other doctor's examination of her. She saw Dr. Griffin's eyes flash with anger but she kept her hand over Alexa's, giving her the compassion she so desperately needed at this moment.

"Okay," Pamela whispered, "let's take this a step at a time. What I want to do is give you a mild sedative. Nothing to knock you out, but to steady you emotionally. Are you okay with that?"

Alexa felt shamed. "I-I can't control how I'm feeling right now, doctor. I-I'm trying, but I feel like I'm flying loose inside. I've never been like this," she said, avoiding the doctor's kindly gaze.

"Listen, you've been through hell. This a normal reaction to it."

"I-I'll take the medicine. I need to calm down. I have to get myself back together."

"My dear child, that will take some time. But"—she smiled faintly—"I think that young man of yours is the best medicine you can have right now. He obviously loves you, and he's someone you trust."

If Alexa hadn't been so lost in her scattered emotions, she might have reacted more strongly to the doctor's words about Gage's loving her. They hadn't known one another very long, so she didn't know how that could have happened. And then she gave herself an internal shake. She'd already admitted to herself that she'd been falling in love with Gage Hunter from the moment she'd met him. "I want him with me, doctor. I don't know what I'd do without him being near right now. He . . ."—she stumbled, ashamed—" . . . makes me feel safe. I just don't feel safe anywhere right now . . . I'm sure it will pass . . ."

"I completely understand." She patted her hand. "I'll make it happen."

Gage entered with the wheelchair. In a few moments, Alexa was in it, and he was pushing her out of the hectic ER and down a quieter hallway toward a bank of elevators, with Dr. Griffin leading the way. Alexa was pale, her eyes darting as if she were a trapped animal with no way to escape. Gage wanted to help her, to protect her from all of this. He felt his frustration begin to build. Torn up inside, Gage saw the suffering in Alexa's face, the way the corners of her mouth were constantly tucked inward in pain. He worried about her back. What else had happened to her?

Right now, all he wanted to do was ease her return to the world she knew. Once they were in the small, private room on the obstetrics floor, he saw Alexa begin to relax, her shoulders slumping, exhaustion darkening her eyes.

He crouched down, one hand on the wheelchair, the other on her knee. "What do you need?"

Wrinkling her nose, she said, "A shower? Getting out of this horrible-smelling burka?" She warmed as she saw Gage nod.

Dr. Griffin said, "Let's get you clean first, and I can examine you after that, okay? I'll be out at the nurse's desk and Gage can come and get me."

"Yes," she said, "I'd like that." Anything to feel clean and to rid herself of that sick doctor's hands on her body, the General groping her. Shivering, Alexa wanted to wash herself with soap until her skin was scrubbed free of her experience.

"Can you take a shower by yourself? Or do you want a nurse to come in and help you?"

Shaking her head, she said, "No, I'll be okay." Just the idea of cooling water on her back, so swollen, aching, and burned, sounded heavenly to her.

"I'll be here if she needs anything," Gage added, giving Alexa a tender look that said so much.

Alexa met his eyes, feeling wrapped in that invisible warmth he kept placing around her. She absorbed it like the starving, needy person she was right now.

"Well," Griffin said, "I'll have the nurse bring in the medication and you can take it after you get out of the shower. Fair enough?"

"Yes . . ."

Gage remained crouched, watching her after Griffin left. "How are you doing?"

With Gage, she didn't have to be anything but herself. Opening her hands in her lap, she said, "Exhausted. I'm so tired, Gage . . ."

"You were in a long, forty-eight-hour nightmare," he said, stroking her hands. "Do you need any help getting undressed?"

She smiled. "You've never seen me naked."

"In my dreams I have."

A sound of laughter caught in her throat. She loved his engaging smile, that boyish glint in his eyes that clearly showed he cared deeply for her. How could she have missed this? Did love happen this quickly? Alexa had been drawn so powerfully to Gage. Her mind was too muddled to clearly think about what was happening between them right now.

She sobered and reached out, touching his heavily bearded cheek. "I haven't thanked you yet for saving our lives, Gage. You're such a hero in my eyes . . . my heart. If you hadn't been there when you were, the General would have probably killed all of us."

"No," he murmured, "you got the AK-47 away from that soldier." Pride glinted in his eyes and he said, "You're a warrior, Alexa. I saw what you did in that tunnel. It was so damned brave of you. I was so proud of you in that moment." He leaned up, placing a soft, searching kiss on her lips.

Alexa leaned into his tender kiss, which was meant to heal her, steady her. She wrapped her arms around his shoulders, desperately needing the warmth and strength he was feeding her.

Separating from her, Gage saw the exhaustion in her eyes, his mouth with the taste of her on it. "Come on, let's get you cleaned up."

"You can hardly wait, Gage."

He chuckled and eased to his full height, holding out his hand to her. "Guilty on all counts. Come on."

It felt dreamlike to Alexa, sliding her fingers into his strong, caring ones, being gently pulled upward. She was slightly dizzy and stood for a moment until it passed. "I'm so tired," she muttered, shaking her head.

"You probably didn't sleep for forty-eight hours," he said, guiding her to the bathroom. As she pushed off the ruined red slippers, shoving them aside, Gage went and turned on the large shower stall faucets.

"Make the water tepid?" she asked.

"Sure," he said.

Alexa started to raise her arms to pull the burka off and grimaced when she tried to move them above her head. Pain in the sockets of her shoulders protested loudly. Further, the tight, burning skin of her back screamed at her.

Gage frowned and walked over to her. "What's wrong?"

"Nothing. Can you help me get this thing off?" She nervously avoided his sharp, concerned gaze. Right now, Alexa was more worried about what Gage would think about her back than his seeing her naked.

"Sure," he murmured, leaning down, gathering the hem of the wool burka, slowly pulling it upward. He saw fear in Alexa's eyes as he pulled it higher and higher, revealing her long, beautiful legs. As he did so, he saw a lot of cuts and bruising, along with dried blood below her knees where she'd obviously fallen a number of times.

"Your knees have to be hurting you." He held her gaze and gave her a moment to prepare for his seeing her fully naked when he removed the burka.

"They're achy, yes."

"Ready?"

She quirked her mouth. "This isn't how I envisioned you seeing me naked for the first time, Gage."

He leaned over, brushing a kiss over her lips. "It's all right. We need to get you cleaned up."

Just his gentle teasing, the care in his eyes, made her nod. "Go ahead, I'm ready . . ." But was she? Alexa tried to gird herself for his reaction to her back. She had no idea what it looked like, only how it felt.

Gage pulled the burka up across her belly, revealing her small, perfectly formed breasts, brought it over her head, and then eased the sleeves off her arms as she shakily held them out toward him. "There," he murmured. "All done." He dropped the burka on the floor, pushing it aside. "You'll never have to wear another one. How about that?"

Gage saw how embarrassed she was and tried to ease her discomfort. Alexa rallied and gave a brief nod. "Come on, the shower's waiting on you." He walked over, pulling the glass door open for her.

Alexa moved into the white tiled shower, the tepid water just right. She turned toward Gage, not wanting him to see her back. "Do you have a washcloth? A bar of soap?"

Nodding, he moved to the counter and picked them up. The glass was frosted on the shower stall and showed the outline of her body. "Here you go." He placed them in her hands. "I'll be nearby, in the other room, if you need me. Just call?"

"Okay," she whispered. "Thanks . . ."

Gage picked up the ruined red slippers and muddy, dusty burka, stuffing them into a nearby plastic bag, knotting it. He left the bathroom, leaving the door slightly ajar. He keyed his hearing to the water in the shower, listening as he shoved the bag containing the burka down into a large wastebasket. He didn't want Alexa to get dizzy and fall and hurt herself. She was fragile. And he wanted to help her so much, but he felt useless because he didn't know fully what had happened to her.

Twenty minutes later, he heard the shower shut off. He walked in, handing a huge, thick white towel through the slight opening in the door. He understood her modesty, slipping it into her proffered hand so she wasn't standing naked in front of him once again. Gage then retrieved a smaller one for her soaking-wet hair. Alexa opened the door after wrapping the towel around her body, hand gripping the ends between her covered breasts. Her long red hair plastered around her head, a dark burgundy mantle against her flesh. He took her elbow, helping her step down to the rug on the tile floor.

"Here," he murmured. "Turn around and I'll get your hair into this towel?"

Without thinking, Alexa turned her back toward him.

Gage anchored for a split second, his breath stolen out of him as he stared at Alexa's back. The entire area was heavily bruised with vivid violet and bright purple colors. Worse, it was heavily swollen. Instantly, Gage knew if he overreacted, it could further harm her. Gently, he gathered the heavy, wet strands by lifting them off her shoulders. He could feel her tense, as if waiting for his reaction, as if trying to protect herself from it.

Biting back rage and anguish over what she'd suffered, Gage shoved it all down. Right now, Alexa needed him. She didn't need his emotional drama. God knew she'd had enough of both in the last two days being a hostage.

"Want me to gently pat your back dry for you?" Gage hoped his voice sounded normal. He heard a little intake of Alexa's breath, saw her shoulders slump, the tension leaving her. He'd been right: she had been waiting for him to make a big deal of her injuries.

"Yes . . . please?"

After wrapping her hair, he took another, smaller towel and curved his hand around her upper arm, behind her. "Let me know if this hurts." He carefully laid the soft towel against her shoulder.

"N-no . . . that's fine . . ."

She was trying so hard to be brave, to act as if nothing was wrong. He wanted nothing more than to wrap his arms around this woman, tuck her against him, and hold her safe. But he could do none of those things. He continued to slowly place the towel across her upper back. He pressed his splayed hand against the towel around her against the rest of her back to absorb any moisture.

"How bad does it look, Gage?"

Her voice was anxious. He kept his hand around her arm and straightened. "Pretty black-and-blue. It has to hurt like hell." Gage felt her release a little more tension, responding to his quiet, even tone.

"It will heal."

"Yeah, over time, it will." Gage struggled to sound calm and unaffected.

"Is—is the skin opened? Any infection that you can see?"

"No, it's closed." *Thank God.* But he didn't say it. "It looks swollen, and it's hot to my touch."

"It burns like fire," she whispered, shaking her head.

Gage moved around Alexa, facing her, placing his hands on her upper arms, holding her wavering gaze. "I'm so sorry, Alexa. So damn sorry we couldn't get there sooner . . ." He slid his hands around her face, pressing his brow to hers. "I'd give anything to have gotten there faster than we did . . . we all would . . ."

Alexa sagged against him. His tenderness took away all her fears that he'd be angry, disgusted, or God knew what else about seeing her injured back. All she saw in his stormy eyes was burning care for her. Gage held her lightly in his arms.

"Just rest," he whispered against damp strands of her hair. Gage felt her surrender completely to him, and he was so damned grateful that the trust between them was still strong and unbroken. He felt her fingers move up across his T-shirt, and his flesh leaped beneath her grazing touch.

Gage had no idea how long they stood there in one another's arms. He worried that Alexa would get chilled with the door open, and he coaxed her out of the bathroom, helping her slide into a soft, green cotton gown that fell to her knees. He tied it up in the back and then helped her into the bed. Bringing out a comb and brush, he sat down on the bed facing her, his hip against hers.

"I don't know how good I am at combing out snarls in a woman's hair, but I'm willing to give it a try," he said, smiling hesitantly, searching Alexa's eyes. Gage knew she couldn't lift her arms high enough to comb her own hair.

"You're a brave man, Hunter."

It was a weak joke, but he rallied beneath her courage. "Hey, I'm a man with a plan. If I don't do a good job, you'll let me know, right?" He smiled at her, watching her perk up a little.

"Go for it."

She sat very still as he took the towel off her head and patted the strands nearly dry before he started to pull the comb through them. Gage winced whenever he hit a snarl, slightly pulling her scalp. Alexa would cringe, purse her lips, but say nothing.

"Listen," he said as he finished, her hair shining around her shoulders, "I'm going out to talk with Dr. Griffin about examining you later. You need to sleep. What if I can get her to leave you alone until you wake up later? Or do you want something to eat or drink?"

"I just want to sleep," Alexa said, rubbing her eyes, exhaustion stealing through her.

Gage slid off the bed, placing the comb and brush on the bedside table. "Okay, you got it. Lie down."

"Could I ask a favor of you?"

"Sure, of course. What do you need?"

"Can you call my parents? Just to make sure they were notified that I'm safe?" She took the pad and pencil on the nearby tray and wrote down a phone number, handing it to him.

Gage nodded. "I will."

"Tell them as soon as I get some sleep under me, I'll call them myself, okay?"

"I know they'll look forward to that. I'm sure someone has already let them know we rescued you and that you're okay."

"That's what I thought. But"—her voice grew husky with tears—"I know they'd love to hear from you. You were there. You don't have to tell them everything, but just let them know I'm okay and I'm going to get well."

Gage wasn't sure he could tell them that, but he nodded and said, "I'll take care of it for you. Now, come on, lie down."

Alexa did, on her side. As she snuggled down into the pillow, Gage pulled a light cover up to her waist. He leaned over, kissing her cheek.

"Sleep the sleep of angels, because you are one," he rasped, grazing her damp hair with his fingers.

Those were the last words Alexa remembered before her heavy eyelids closed and she slid into a deep, healing sleep. Gage was here. He would stay with her. He would keep her safe in this new, unsafe world.

CHAPTER 15

“TAL?”

Tal raised her head from her desk at Artemis Security. Her newly hired assistant, Tamara Kirtner, buzzed her on the intercom.

“Yes?”

“There’s a Sergeant Gage Hunter on your sat phone line.”

Her black brows drew down. “Okay, thanks. I’ll take it.” Tal switched the phone on. “Gage?”

“Yes. Alexa gave me a sat phone number, and I thought it was to her parents.”

She sat up. “What do you know about Alexa?” she demanded, her heart suddenly taking off. Artemis Security was not allowed live video feed of the actual assault on the cave where the women hostages had been taken. Wyatt had raised hell. And Robert Culver, a general with a lot of influence, couldn’t budge the military on that decision, either. The higher-ups said that because Robert’s daughter was involved, the company could not take part in the video feed. Everyone was pissed as hell, and so they sat, waiting, with no word—until now. Tal knew her father was going to take this to the Joint Chiefs of Staff. Artemis, regardless of who was in jeopardy, needed full access to all mission plans, no matter who was involved. She was sure her father, who was one of the most adroit political generals, would eventually get his way. But it didn’t help her family right now, who waited without word.

“Hasn’t anyone contacted you yet about her?”

“No,” she said, tensing. “How do you know about Alexa? Is she all right?”

“Sorry,” he said apologetically. “I thought you’d been told by now that Alexa and the other women were rescued roughly an hour and a half ago. We just arrived at the ER here at Bagram with all the women hostages. They’re being tended to medically right now.”

Gasping, Tal leaned over. “Hold on one sec, Gage, I need this taped for my parents and the rest of my family.” She pressed a record button to save the conversation. “Go ahead. Is Alexa all right?” Automatically, Tal closed her fist, trying to steel herself against anything he might say. He must have been part of the team who had rescued them. She had a hundred questions, but she had to let him speak. She listened intently to his words. When he finished, she asked, "So you were part of the rescue team?"

"Yes, I was."

Tal closed her eyes, feeling grateful to the depths of her soul. "This is such great news, Gage. I don't understand why we weren't contacted earlier. Why did you have to make this call to us instead?" Tal heard his hesitation.

"Well, it could be that whoever is in charge of such things wanted an assessment of Alexa's injuries before telling you how she was. Dr. Griffin, her doctor, agreed to let Alexa sleep first, and then she'd examine her after she woke up, because her injuries weren't life-threatening."

Hearing heaviness in his tone, she pursed her lips. "Thank God you called us. I'm so glad Alexa gave you my sat phone number. This is the best news."

"I'm sure your folks will get the official call shortly after Alexa is examined. I ended up with you on the line. She's pretty much in a state of shock and hasn't slept in the last forty-eight hours since her kidnapping, so it looks like she gave me your number by mistake."

"That's completely understandable." Her hand tightened around the phone. "How is it that you're making the call? I thought an officer in charge would be doing this." Again, she felt hesitation on his part.

"It's a little complicated," he admitted. "Alexa and I were seeing one another for about two days before this happened. We . . . uh . . . well, were getting along pretty well."

"Even though she's an officer and you're enlisted?"

Gage sighed. "Yes, guilty as charged."

"It doesn't matter to me. You need to know that. Have you been with Alexa since you rescued her?"

"Ever since the assault on the cave system, a few hours ago, yes. Why?"

Tal rapidly put it together. Obviously, there was a much stronger connection between her sister and Gage than he was admitting.

"Alexa was concerned that you'd worry about her, and she said to tell you she's all right. Once she wakes up? She said she'd call you herself."

"Is she all right, Gage? Really?" Tal demanded tightly. "And damn it, I can feel there's a lot you aren't telling me. I need to know everything. Did they rape Alexa? Harm her in any way?" She felt a lot of emotions coming from Gage. It blew her away that Alexa and he had begun a relationship. Where had they met? How serious was it? From the sounds of his deep voice, the way he wrestled with the emotions she could hear behind his words, it was very serious.

"Look," he rasped. "This I something I'd want Alexa to discuss with you over the phone, Tal. Right now, she's asked me to stay with her. And I just pissed off a doctor down in the ER because he scared the shit out of her and I stopped him from touching or examining her." His voice lowered with frustration. "She got whipped with a belt on her back. That's all I know. I saw her back just now when she came out of the shower and it's pretty bruised and swollen, and she's hurting from it."

"Oh, God," Tal whispered, her voice rough with emotion. "H-has she been raped? Do you know?"

"I don't know," he sighed. "I wish I did, but, Tal, she's totaled emotionally, in deep shock over whatever happened to her. She doesn't want any strange man touching her. She's okay with me holding her, and she's okay with a woman nurse or doctor touching her. I guess that's good news. But I don't know the extent of her injuries or anything else that's happened to her. Right now, all I'm trying to do is give her a safe harbor. She's spun out, shocked, and scattered. The other seven women? They're in far worse shape than she is, from what I could tell, but they're civilians. And I need to fill you in on the mission and what happened."

Tal nodded. "Good, because the Joint Chief of Staff has cut off our live feed to the mission because it involved one of our family members. We don't know what happened after you and those three SEALs after you arrived at that other entrance, Gage. Leave nothing out on the rest of that op?"

She listened intently as he moved into the mission, her eyes closed, her heart pounding with fear and anguish for Alexa. When he was finished, she said, "As usual, you're downplaying your part in their rescue, Gage." He was always self-effacing, always giving others credit. It was one of the many qualities that Tal had always appreciated about him; above all, Gage Hunter was a team player. Her heart warmed to him, knowing that his courage to enter that cave system alone had saved Alexa and the other women, hands down. Someone should have been writing the man up for a damned medal.

"Look, all I care about . . . is Alexa."

"Okay, so what should we do here? I know when my parents hear our conversation they're going to fly over to Bagram in a heartbeat to be with Alexa. I just heard from Matt's CO, and he's coming off that op tomorrow morning. I know he'll want to see Alexa as soon as he gets back to Bagram. And God, my whole family will want to fly in and see her, too."

"My assessment, Tal, based upon what I've seen of Alexa since we rescued her, is that she doesn't want to be around people. They had to move her up to Obstetrics because she couldn't handle the ER, all the noise, the activity, the movement of people in and out of her cubicle. She's fallen apart emotionally."

"God," Tal rasped, standing up, suddenly feeling she needed to do something, anything, to help her sister.

"I'm sure she'll want to see her immediate family, though," Gage reassured her. "Family is important in something like this . . ."

"She wants to feel safe," Tal uttered, pacing the floor of her office, scowling, thinking. "Family means safety to Alexa. It would anyone in a circumstance like this."

"Well," he said wryly, "I think if Matt gets here, that will help her stabilize. I'm in a little bit of a jam right now, and I've got MPs standing by to take my statement. I'm not sure I'll be able to be with Alexa, despite what she might want. And right now, she really needs people she loves to be nearby. I think it'd help her a lot."

"MPs?" Tal muttered. "What the hell, Gage. What did you do?"

He nervously cleared his throat. "That ER doctor, the guy who busted into Alexa's cubicle and was going to force her to do a rape kit? I told him he wasn't getting near her and to find a woman doctor to treat her. He didn't take it well. He told me he was going to write me up for insubordination to an officer."

"Shit!" Tal breathed. She anchored to a halt. "Okay, you stay with her. I want you like glue next to her bed. Don't you dare leave her side until Matt arrives. I'm putting a call in to his CO right now. Further, I'll have my uncle Pete Culver call your CO ASAP." She went to her desk, grabbing a pen and paper. "Give me his name and his contact number, Gage. Because my uncle is a general in the Marine Corps, he'll make damn sure that you stay exactly where you are—with Alexa."

"Sounds good to me," Gage said, relief in his voice. "I can use all the help I can get right now. I don't want to be in the brig when Alexa needs protection until Matt or your family can be here to stand guard over her."

"Can I get you on this sat phone number, Gage? Will you have it on you?"

"Actually, I borrowed it from the nurse's station. I have to give it back to them. But you can call it, and they'll come and get me, because I'll be in Alexa's room."

"I need to get the MPs to stand down and get that ridiculous charge removed."

"Trust me, Tal, I don't want to be anywhere else." He lowered his tone. "She's very fragile . . ."

"I hear you, Gage. Thank you for being there. You're the right man to be with her. In my book, you rock, Marine."

"I'll call you once I know more about what they're going to do with Alexa."

"I'm in touch with her CO already," Tal assured him. "Right now, from what you're telling me, everyone's probably waiting on that examination and the results. That's going to determine what the Air Force will do with her.

They'll have a flight surgeon assess her to find out when she can return to duty and fly again."

"I don't see how she can go back to flying any time soon."

Tal stilled. "It's that bad, Gage?"

"I'm not a psychiatrist or a flight surgeon, Tal, but I know Alexa well enough. She's nothing like the person you knew before. This kidnapping has changed her world and changed her. I don't know for how long . . ."

★

IT WAS NEARLY dinnertime when Dr. Pamela Griffin finished with her examination of Alexa. She was a physician but had never interviewed or had to perform a physical on someone who had been kidnapped with the express purpose of making them a sex slave. As she sat down in her office off the main hallway from obstetrics, she dropped the clipboard on her desk and went to the window, looking out the venetian blinds. The night was closing in now, with no hint of a sunset across Bagram, the January weather quixotic, cold, and unpredictable. Her stomach was tight and she rubbed the area. It was important she enter her findings into the computer. She knew the flight surgeon over at the A-10 unit at Bagram was waiting for it. Tomorrow, Major Jill Donahue would have the information and would come over and assess Alexa Culver herself.

Shaking her head, Pamela sat down, wanting a shot of whiskey. It wasn't something she had often, but on a really bad day like this it helped unknot her sensitive gut. Pushing her fingers through her hair, she pulled over her laptop and opened up the patient-file program. She had to get this over with.

There was a knock on her door.

"Enter," she called, wondering who it was. There was no shift change yet. Her eyes widened as a tall man wearing an Air Force uniform with general's stars on his epaulets entered. Behind him was a woman with red hair, dressed elegantly in a black wool pantsuit, her face tense.

Instantly, Pamela shot to her feet, coming to attention.

"At ease, Captain," the general said, standing aside, allowing the woman into the large corner office. "I'm Alexa's father, Robert Culver." He shut the door they both approached her desk. "This is my wife, Dilara Culver. I'm sorry to barge in unexpectedly like this, but we just landed at Bagram. I wanted to see you first, since you examined our daughter. Do you have time to sit and talk for a moment before we go see her?"

"Of course, sir." Pamela quickly came around the desk and brought two chairs in front of it. "Can I get you anything to drink, sir? Mrs. Culver?"

Dilara gave her a weak smile and sat down, her black leather purse in her lap. "No, thank you, Dr. Griffin. Please, relax. We're here as parents, for our child. This isn't military business."

Robert removed his hat, placed it on the edge of the desk, and sat down. "Please, sit down. Relax. I'm assuming you've examined Alexa?"

"Yes, sir, I have." Pamela sat down and opened up her clipboard. She saw the somber look in their eyes, the fear, as if they were trying to prepare themselves against whatever she might say. "Please understand, your daughter requested that only her parents, brother, and sister have the privilege of seeing the results of my examination."

Robert nodded. "That's good to know."

"Sergeant Gage Hunter, who helped rescue her and the other women, has been with her almost nonstop at Alexa's specific request."

Dilara winced, biting down on her red lower lip, clutching the bag a little more tightly.

Robert slid his arm soothingly around his wife's shoulders. "Is he with her now?"

"No, sir. The MPs arrested him earlier." She grimaced. "That didn't help Alexa at all, to have them march into her room and put him custody. She was very upset."

Robert nodded. "We're working out this issue as we speak. My people are in touch with the doctor who charged Sergeant Hunter. I feel it will get straightened out shortly."

"Good," Pamela said. "Because Alexa relies heavily on him for now." She took a breath and added quietly, "Let me quickly go over my findings. And please, time your discussion on any of this with your daughter. She's on very shaky ground. I had a tough time getting her to give me what little information she shared with me. I found most of what I needed in a physical examination of her. It was very hard on her, and I feel badly that I had to do it, but she understood."

"Is she all right now?" Dilara asked.

"I just gave her a mild anti-anxiety medication, Mrs. Culver. Alexa is tired, still sleeping a lot, off and on. She's not eating much, which, when you understand what she went through, isn't surprising."

"Tell us," Robert demanded.

Pamela knew there was no way to sugarcoat her findings. If the parents didn't know the whole truth, they couldn't help their floundering daughter. She went over everything. And the more information she gave them, the more Dilara Culver tensed. "There are abrasions outside and inside her vagina, but they will heal within a week. Her anal area is similar, but there is a slight tear at the entrance. I numbed the area and put two stitches into the tear, and she should be fine in a few days. She didn't suffer any pain from the procedure."

"Oh, no." Dilara wobbled, pressing her gloved hands to her lips, looking at her husband, tears in her eyes.

"She was not raped, Mrs. Culver," Pamela said gently.

"In a sense," Robert growled, "she was."

"In the strict legal sense, she was not," Pamela said. "But that does not mean that Alexa's reaction to the violation isn't going to be similar to that of any rape survivor. I'll know more about this tomorrow when Major Donahue, the flight surgeon, interviews her. Like I said, I'm not a psychiatrist. I can only tell you what I observed from a compassionate human perspective."

Dilara blotted her eyes, her mascara running. "She was tortured," she whispered. "Oh, God . . ."

Pamela compressed her lips, watching the general try to comfort his distraught wife. His face was a mass of rage, his eyes narrowing the deeper she went into her findings on Alexa.

Robert asked, "In your opinion, Dr. Griffin, how should we behave toward our daughter? Obviously, we're not going to ask her what happened."

"No, I think right now a lot of care, a lot of love, no judgment, no questions, is what she really needs."

Dilara sniffed. "What about those other poor seven women?"

"They all received similar treatment. We have one woman who just came out of surgery because her anal cavity was compromised and torn. She could have died in three days if they hadn't been rescued. As it is, she's going to be fine. Well . . . she'll be fine physically, but the mental and emotional abuse all these women suffered is going to take years to come to grips with. It's a terrible sentence."

"Was Alexa the only one to be whipped with a belt?"

"Yes."

"Did she tell you what happened?" Robert demanded.

"No," Pamela said. "I couldn't get it out of her. She just retreated, almost went catatonic on me. Asking her questions drives her deep into herself, sir. It's as if speaking about it brings it all back, which makes sense. She breaks out into a sweat, starts shaking, crying, and doesn't want to be touched by anyone. Not even me. Well, I should amend that. Sergeant Hunter, her fiancé, can hold her. When she's like that, she wants to be in his arms and be held. He's been really good for her."

"Fiancé?" Dilara said, eyes widening. She looked to her husband and then at Pamela. "She never told us she was engaged."

"Well, Sergeant Hunter told Dr. Parlin that he was Alexa's fiancé."

Robert's mouth quirked. "That's news to us, but it's not important right now. If our daughter trusts him and is willing to let him support her, that's all I care about at this moment."

"Y-yes," Dilara whispered, blotting her eyes with the handkerchief. "We owe him so much . . . so much."

"He was part of the rescue team," Pamela told them. "He'll never tell you this, but he's the one who went into that cave system alone and found the women. I've seen the SEAL report on what he did."

"Yes, I've seen it, too," Robert said. "He's an outstanding Marine."

"Right now, your daughter absolutely relies on him, sir. She was so upset when the MPs took him away from her. I hope you can do something soon?"

"It's in process, doctor."

"C-can we see our daughter now, doctor?" Dilara asked.

Pamela gave Dilara a sympathetic look. "Of course. I'll take you down. My advice is to see where she's at. If she's sleeping, allow her to sleep and quietly leave. Or just take a chair and sit and wait for her to wake up. Obviously, she's exhausted. All the women are."

"I want to stay, no matter what," Dilara said.

"What about her back, doctor? What is her prognosis?"

"Sir, she's been badly beaten. The bruising and swelling are going to be painful for her for the next week or so. I've got her on ibuprofen for the pain, and it's reduced some swelling, so it's helping her rest better."

"Can we hug her?" Dilara asked.

"Yes, but very carefully," Pamela suggested. "Her back is very, very sensitive."

"Of course, it would be," Dilara agreed faintly, shaking her head.

Pamela gave them a compassionate look. "Your daughter survived this. I think that's what you must hold uppermost in all of this. She was rescued. And she's going to live. All eight women will heal physically from this. I think you need to have a session with Major Donahue after she gets done talking with Alexa tomorrow. She's a licensed psychiatrist, and I'm sure she could give you some pointers on how to help Alexa instead of causing her more pain than she's already in."

"But with Sergeant Hunter? She's calm around him?"

"Not calm, but stable," Pamela said. "He's like an emotional anchor to her right now."

Dilara sniffed and whispered, "Robert, you have to get him to remain with her."

Grimly, Robert nodded. "It's going to happen."

Pamela had no doubt it would, judging by the set of the general's square jaw and the hardness that came to his hazel eyes. She could see Alexa in both her parents, and certainly, Alexa's attractiveness came directly from Dilara Culver, who reminded Pamela of a beautiful, world-class model.

"Alexa is probably asleep right now, but let's go down and peek into her room. And, Mrs. Culver, we can always get another bed in there so you can remain with her and sleep nearby. I'm sure Alexa would find that a great comfort right now."

Robert rose. "That's a good idea." He put his hand on his wife's shoulder, his voice lowering. "I'm going to get my staff car and have my driver take me over to where they're holding Sergeant Hunter. And, Dilara, you stay with Alexa. I'll deal with the MPs."

Dilara rose. "Yes, of course."

Pamela felt sorry for them as she walked around her desk, leading them out of her office and down the highly polished hall. She couldn't imagine how the other seven women who were alone must have felt, their parents half a world away, unable to visit them.

Only because General Culver was in the military, and his daughter was, too, could this happen. Civilians were not allowed on the massive Army base.

It was Captain Alexa Culver who had been roughly handled, but it wasn't the worst violation. The other hostage, a woman named Cathy, had been brutalized even further. Neither of those two women, in Pamela's estimation, was going to emerge from beneath this toxic trauma easily.

All the women had suffered cruelty, and they would heal in time, but Pamela wondered just how long it was going to take each of them to emerge from the shadow of this horrific, life-changing trauma.

CHAPTER 16

Gage's eyes widened when an Air Force general came into the interrogation room where he was being held. He instantly leaped to his feet, coming to attention as the tall, husky officer entered. The officer in charge who had been taking his statement entered as well. Lieutenant Adam Huson had a sheepish look on his face, his mouth set.

"At ease," the Air Force general rumbled. He looked to the lieutenant.

Lieutenant Huson said roughly, "The doctor has dropped the charge against you. You're dismissed."

Blinking, Gage watched the officer quietly close the door, leaving him with the general, who stood sizing him up from across the table where he stood at attention.

Taking off his hat, Robert pulled out a chair. "Sit down for a moment, son, we need to talk."

"Yes, sir." Confused, Gage had no idea who this man was until his gaze settled on the name tag on the officer's dress blues: "Culver, R." He gulped, then sat down opposite him at the table. So this was Alexa's father! He folded his hands in front of himself, holding the man's hard, incisive gaze.

"I'm Alexa's father," he said. "And I understand from Dr. Griffin that you're her fiancé?"

Shit, now he was in more trouble. Wincing, Gage sat back, rubbing his hands on his trousers. "I lied to the ER doctor, sir. When I brought your daughter into the ER from the medevac, he was bullying his way into her cubicle and scaring the hell out of her. He was demanding she get the rape kit test." He scowled, his voice heavy. "I knew your daughter for three days before her kidnapping happened. We were getting along very well with one another." Gage felt his emotions surging up, and he looked away, placing tight control over them. He swiveled his head to meet the general's implacable gaze. "Alexa trusted me, sir. She was falling apart in the ER from everything that had happened in that cave. I wasn't about to let that doctor anywhere near her. He was insensitive, and she was cowering behind me, begging me not to let him get near her." His mouth thinned. "I told him to get a woman doctor to help Alexa and that he wasn't going to lay a hand on Alexa. He demanded to know who the hell I was." He shrugged. "I lied and told him I was her fiancé, because I knew that if I said that, he'd have to obey my wishes, even if he wasn't listening to your daughter."

"And he wrote you up for insubordination."

"Yes, sir, he did."

"And you were willing to still stand up for my daughter, Sergeant? Knowing that he would?"

"Yes, sir," he replied, holding the general's stare. "Alexa needed me, needed to feel safe. I wasn't about to walk away from her, even if it meant I'd take the fall."

Rubbing his jaw, Robert sized up the Marine. "My older daughter, Tal Culver, spoke highly of you. I talked to her before we left to come over here."

"I know Captain Culver well, sir. For five years now. We were in different sniper units here at Bagram, but everyone respects her. She's a good leader and has tried a number of times to get me into her unit, but my CO refused to allow the transfer to go through."

Robert placed his hands on the table. "Because you were good, that's why, Sergeant."

Gage shrugged. "I take pride in whatever my responsibilities are, sir. My father was a Marine Corps sniper. He earned a Silver Star in Iraq. I always want to make him proud of me."

"Well, son, he should be. Thank you from my wife and me, as well from our son and other daughter, for being there for Alexa." He held out his hand toward Gage.

Shocked, Gage shook it, disbelieving that a general could suddenly become emotional, that hard mask melting off his face. Instead, he saw a father who was tortured and suffering over his daughter's pain.

His own voice was none too steady, either. "I'd do it again in a heartbeat, sir."

"Okay, I need you to be honest with me, Sergeant." Robert leaned forward. "Dr. Griffin says my daughter is highly unstable emotionally. She said that Alexa relies heavily on you, that you're like an anchor to her right now."

"Well," Gage protested, "until her family arrived, sir. I was only doing what I could until Matt, or you, came here to be with Alexa."

"Tal was right," Robert growled, sitting back in the chair, giving him a stripping look. "You're damned humble and won't admit your part in anything."

Gage grinned a little. "I'm a team player, sir. I figure whatever I do will be seen and acknowledged, or not. That doesn't matter to me. What does matter is how I feel about myself taking on a mission or, in this case, shielding Alexa until her family could arrive so she could go home and be with you."

"You've known her three days?"

"Yes, sir."

"Tell me how you met."

Gage didn't know what to think of the general or where this line of questioning was going. He briefly told him, skirting around the fact that he was falling in love with her. And he wasn't even sure it was reciprocated. Too much had happened too fast, and right now, Alexa's whole world had been shattered. Gage did not expect her to know where their relationship was or where he wished it might go. He wouldn't put that burden on her. The focus had to remain on her, not what might be, or what he wished might be.

When he finished, he could feel the general thinking. It was in his narrowed eyes, the way he looked. It was more a feeling or a sense than anything obvious on the man's face.

"Right now, my daughter is still asleep, Hunter. My wife is with Alexa. When she wakes up, we'll be able to find out a little more about her condition. Further, the flight surgeon is going to interview her. I'm going to wait to see what she says because she's a psychiatrist. Dr. Griffin doesn't think Alexa will be cleared for flight duty again, at least, not soon."

"I agree with that, sir, but I'm not a shrink."

His mouth pulled into a faint smile. "None of us are, but Alexa is our child and we know her well. You have a connection with her that is personal and very important to her, as I think it is to you?"

"Yes, sir, Alexa means the world to me." That was all Gage was going to give her father. To say more would only be messy, because he hadn't ever spoken of his heart, his feelings for Alexa, to anyone, even to her.

"All right," Culver said in a rumble. "You need to go back to your CO with the papers that Lieutenant Huson will have waiting for you out at the front office. Take them back to him, Gage. You're cleared of all charges."

"Yes, sir. Thank you, sir. I know you had a lot to do with this."

"Alexa needs you."

Gage took in a deep breath, his hands clasped on the table. "I want to be there for her, sir. For as long as she wants me to."

★

DILARA HAD EASED out of Alexa's room, surprised, she saw her husband striding down the hallway toward her. She hurried to meet him, sliding her hand around his arm and leading him to the nearby visitors' lounge. He had been gone nearly three hours.

"Is Alexa awake?" Robert asked as Dilara sat down on a green plastic couch. He sat down nearby, taking off his hat.

"Yes, we had a good talk. She just went back to sleep. She's exhausted, Robert."

"Tell me everything," he urged.

"Dr. Griffin wasn't kidding when she said Alexa was rocky emotionally." Dilara rubbed her brow. "This has devastated her," she said, her voice wobbling. "It took everything I had not to break down and cry in front of her."

Reaching out, Robert rubbed her shoulder gently. "This is going to be hard on everyone, pet. I'm sorry . . ."

She sniffed and fought back her tears. "I told her you were helping Gage, and you should have seen her face. She broke down and started crying. All I could do was hold her. Later, Alexa told me what Gage did in that cave, how he'd saved all the women . . . and her . . ." Her voice strengthened. "He's a real hero in this, Robert. You need to know that."

"When I talked to him, he completely downplayed his part in the mission. He gave the credit to the SEALs he was working with."

Dilara stared and then shook her head. "Tal said he was humble by nature."

"Sure is," Robert agreed, "but a fine young man."

"Alexa asked for him. I mean, she wants to see you, of course, but I could see the desperation in her eyes, I heard it in her voice. He's her world, Robert, right now."

"I think Hunter has fallen in love with her, but he's not admitting it. He says it's only been a few days. He's got his head screwed on straight. It's too soon to say anything to anyone, even Alexa."

Shaking her head, Dilara whispered, "It doesn't take much to see the care she has for him in her eyes, Robert. There's something very strong and special between them. It might not be love yet, but something good between them has taken root. But I didn't press it with her. Now is not the right time."

Robert lifted her hands from her lap, enclosing them with his own. "What we have to do right now, is to get that flight surgeon to speak to Alexa. Listen, you must be hungry. Let's go to the officers' club here on base, eat, and settle in at the distinguished visitors' quarters here on base. Alexa will probably sleep until we return. And then we'll both go in and visit with her."

"She'd love that, darling. I know she's so grateful that you're going to help Gage."

Robert rose and held out his hand to his stressed wife. "Come on," he urged her quietly, "let's go eat. We'll leave word at the nurse's desk where we'll be in case they need to get hold of us."

★

ALEXA FELT AS if someone had bottle-brushed her from the inside out. She'd been on a high of sorts this morning when she'd finally gotten to see her parents again. She'd slept throughout the night and awakened at 0600. Just knowing her family was nearby was such a boost for her. Matt had already dropped by and he'd buoyed her. She hadn't seen Gage yet and missed him terribly. At 0800, Major Donahue had arrived. Now it was 1000. She had just finished her interview with her and told her that Gage was at his HQ right now. He'd be over to see her sometime later.

This morning, she felt more stable. Alexa worried about the other women, wondering how they were doing. She felt guilty because her parents had been able to fly in to be with her and comfort her and their families had not.

Her world was now very different, and she had found herself nervous and over reactive when a male orderly came in with her breakfast at 0700. She'd immediately gone on the defensive. Alexa tried to tell herself he wasn't a threat, but he was a man and a stranger. Hating that she couldn't control her emotions and the anxiety that was constantly savaging her, she breathed a heavy sigh of relief when he left her room.

But her heart ached for Gage. She missed him. He filled a special place within her, on every level. Her parents, who loved her so much, filled other areas of her life. Between them, she felt far more solid than she did yesterday. Today she was coming out of the shock and trauma, realizing that she really had been saved, that this wasn't some dream of hers. It was real.

What would Major Donahue put in her report? Right now, flying an A-10 felt like it was part of a dream from another place and time. It didn't feel real to Alexa. How could that be? She loved to fly. She loved doing what she did.

She had been saving the lives of men and women every time she sat in that cockpit. But now her career seemed empty, lifeless, as if it belonged to another person, which scared Alexa. It was as if the General had stripped her of part of her soul, taken something precious and ripped it out of her. Hatred welled up in her, raw and powerful. She had killed the sonofabitch, and it gave her satisfaction like she'd never known before. He would never hurt another woman the way he had hurt her.

★

"WHAT ARE YOUR decisions, Major?" Robert Culver asked the flight surgeon. He and Dilara sat in front of her desk at the A-10 squadron's HQ. It was late afternoon and he could hear the takeoffs and landings at the fixed-wing terminal nearby.

Jill Donahue sat in her desert-colored flight suit at her desk. "I'm not recommending that Alexa go back to flying, General Culver. Instead, what I'm recommending is that she be grounded for three months and seek appropriate therapy for what she's experienced. Your daughter's head, her emotions, to put it into common civilian terminology, have been shattered by this trauma." She opened her long, spare hands. "And rightfully so. She's only reacting like any normal human being would to this kind of situation."

"I see," Robert said. "And after three months?"

"I'll have another interview with her, sir. Nothing is promised here. If she isn't ready, that's how I'll call it."

Dilara moved in her chair, frowning. "Major, have you treated women who have been abused like this before?"

"Yes, ma'am, I have. I spent three years in college working at a women's shelter near the campus. I'm familiar with abuse to women and children, as well as rape survivors."

"That's good to know," Robert said quietly, nodding. "Maybe you can help us out here, Major. Under the circumstances, what do you really recommend for Alexa, knowing what you know now?"

Jill sat back, her face softening. "I asked Alexa what she'd like to do. She was ardent of wanting to go to the family cabin in the Great Smoky Mountains near Washington, D.C. It was a place where she took her leave when she could. The way this trauma has affected your daughter, in my professional opinion, I'd say she needs time alone to sort out what's happened to her. If I could authorize her to decommission, go home, and do exactly that—spend time alone in that cabin in the woods—I'd do it. But that's beyond my purview, as you well know, General Culver. All I can do is ground Alexa, give her a day job here at ops, and ensure she gets the therapy and counseling she needs."

"But if Alexa turned in her commission, Major?"

Jill smiled a little. "Then, of course, she could go home and go to her favorite cabin. Sometimes, people do better being alone. They aren't distracted. They have the time to think, to feel through their trauma. Sometimes a family can suffocate the survivor. They want to help her, they feel helpless, so they give her too much attention, and she feels pulled, like a puppet on strings. A survivor will prioritize pleasing others over what she needs personally to heal from the experience."

Dilara grimaced. "We'd suffocate her, Robert. And my family . . . they want to fly in to see her, but we told them no, that she wasn't up to company yet."

"Yes," Jill added, "this is what I'm talking about. Captain Culver needs space and alone time. We all know what's best for us to heal. Most of us don't listen to ourselves or trust ourselves to do just that. I feel strongly that your daughter truly knows what will help her get back on an even keel with herself. I think a couple of months of quiet cabin time, and a slow integration back into your lives, would be very healing for her."

"Does that mean we don't see her or talk to her on the phone?" Dilara asked, worried.

"Of course not. The first month, I'd send her emails and let her know that you love her and that if she needs anything, you're there. Keep it light. No pressure. Don't ask anything of her. Let her offer it, instead. The second month, ask if you can drop in for a visit for a couple of hours. Don't overstay. Let Alexa define the visit if she wants it at all. Everyone heals at a different rate, Mrs. Culver. No psychiatrist can sit here and predict how long that will take because every person is unique."

"So," Robert said, "what you're saying is to stand back and let her call the shots on what she needs?"

Jill nodded. "Yes. The less pressure you put on her and the less you question her about her experiences in that cave, the quicker she'll heal. And someday, when the time's right, she'll tell you what happened. Right now she's ashamed, humiliated, and guilt-ridden. This is a typical rape survivor reaction."

"But," Dilara said, stumbling over her words, "she wasn't raped."

Jill shook her head. "Mrs. Culver, I realize that different states in the U.S. define rape, and the types of rape, differently. In my book, with my three years working at a rape crisis counseling center, your daughter *was* raped. It might have been with a man's fingers, but the outcome, her reaction to it, is the same as if the man had put his penis into her vagina and anus instead. She was violated. It was against her will. She'd been drugged twice before that doctor could fully examine her because she was fighting back and trying to defend herself. When you're given a drug that renders your body unable to respond, but your mind is as clear as a bell, it's rape of the worst kind, because you remember everything. The drug didn't render her unconscious; those bastards specifically chose a drug like that because they wanted her to remember. They wanted to show her that men had control over her at all times, that they owned her body, and that they could do anything they wanted to her. In my opinion, that's rape, pure and simple. But I'm not here to argue the legality of it. My job is to see how it affected her and how deeply. And how it's going to affect her flight status."

Dilara winced at the doctor's bluntness, but she absorbed it without speaking. She pressed her hand against her lips, barely able to look over at her husband, who was suffering equally from the flight surgeon's unvarnished statements.

"Under the circumstances," Robert said gruffly, emotions coloring his words, "we need to ask our daughter what she wants to do."

Jill nodded, giving them a sympathetic look. "Yes, that would be my best suggestion. Your daughter had her control violently taken from her. You're giving her control back by asking her what she wants to do. That will help her heal. It will help her figure out her life, since this happened to her."

"What about Sergeant Gage Hunter? My daughter needs him."

Jill sighed. "In a way, Alexa is lucky to have had him in her life before this happened. Whatever their relationship, it was healthy and growing. Both, I suspect, were falling in love with one another when this trauma occurred. Sergeant Hunter has stepped up to the plate to help her. He's very unique, General, in that his feelings for Alexa transcend what was done to her. That's highly unusual, and I can tell you that most boyfriends, after their girlfriend is violated, will run the other way, unable to cope with her trauma."

"But he hasn't run," Dilara said, hope in her voice.

"No, he's run *toward* her, not away from her. That's why I feel strongly that whatever their connection, it's solid. And it's healthy, because he is able to be in her company, and she allows him to touch and hold her. He represents everything good about men to her. I don't believe he's honestly aware of all of this in psychiatric terms, but that doesn't matter."

Robert turned to Dilara. "I believe they care for one another. Three days doesn't create love. That happens over time."

"Alexa never mentioned it to us," Dilara said, nodding slowly. "But in my heart"—she pressed her hand to her chest—"I feel Alexa is deeply drawn to him. She might not be fully aware of all her feelings toward Gage yet because it's far too soon, but she relies on him."

"Well," Robert cautioned, "she's relying on us, too. We're her family."

Jill smiled faintly. "In a way, Alexa is lucky. She has a man in her life who clearly cares for her, is loyal, and will stand by her. He already faced down that doctor in the ER and protected Alexa from him. That should tell you a lot. Whether those two have proclaimed their feelings to one another yet doesn't really matter. What does matter is that Alexa trusts this man. Two men violated and injured her. Yet, she can see Sergeant Hunter in a healthy way, which gives me great hope that she will work through this if he's at her side. I know their relationship is young, but it could well develop over the coming months. They can email one another and Skype, and he is someone she will talk to openly, because she trusts him."

"That sounds like a good plan," Dilara whispered, her voice trembling. "I was so afraid . . . so afraid she'd hate all men after what happened to her."

"Sometimes, Mrs. Culver that does happen. You never know how a woman is going to respond to sexual violation."

"So you feel Sergeant Hunter is central to Alexa's healing?" Robert asked.

"I think you'd better ask Alexa that . . . I'd tread carefully, General. If you ask her what she needs, she'll tell you. Just follow it up with other questions until she can define what will make her feel as if she's in a healing environment of her choosing. Take it from there."

"Thank you, Major, you've been more help than you know," Robert said, standing, reaching across the desk, shaking her hand.

Jill stood. "You're welcome, sir." She gave Dilara a kind look as she rose from the chair. "It might be a good idea if you two received some counseling, too. Alexa may not be the same person you know for a while, as she goes through the gauntlet of healing. Do also contact your local rape crisis center. They always have psychologists and psychiatrists who volunteer and are on hand to help the partner or family of the rape survivor."

★

DILARA WALKED BESIDE her husband as they reentered the Bagram hospital by the main doors. It was nearly nightfall. She halted just inside the hospital, looking up at her husband. "What do you think, Robert?"

He grimaced. "I think we need to ask Alexa what she wants to do. If it were up to me, I'd tell her to decommission herself from the Air Force right now. That way, we could fly her to the U.S., and she could get on with her life."

"I was thinking the same thing," Dilara said. She pulled off her leather gloves, stuffing them into the pockets of her black wool coat. "And I really want to talk to a rape crisis counselor. We are obviously behind the curve on what to do to help Alexa."

"Yeah," he grunted, "no question about it. I'd give my right arm to get her home. I hope like hell she'll leave the Air Force and come home. Let's see what she thinks. We may be surprised."

CHAPTER 17

"GAGE!"

He grinned a hello in Alexa's direction, slipping inside her room. "Hey, I just got cut loose from my unit. How are you doing?"

He saw that she was sitting on top of the bed, which was made. Her parents had obviously brought her some clothes from home. Instead of wearing a green hospital gown, she was in a pair of loose, flowing black jersey pants and a soft pink long-sleeved T-shirt of the same material that brought out the natural blush in her cheeks. On her feet was a pair of thick, black wool socks and a pair of black corduroy slippers.

Her eyes looked much less murky than they had the last time he'd been with her.

Alexa slipped to the side of her bed, her legs hanging over it as Gage's smile warmed her to the depths of her heart. "A little better," she whispered, opening her arms, wanting—needing—him, his nearness, his scent, that smile that let light chase away the darkness that inhabited her. She wasn't disappointed as he halted and folded her gently into his arms, kissing her cheek, nuzzling his face into her hair, which lay around her shoulders.

"Mmm," he growled, "I've missed the hell out of you. I'm sorry I couldn't be here any sooner."

It was so easy for Alexa to sag into Gage's arms, lean against his hard, strong body, and allow him to hold her. "I missed you," she said, her voice muffled against his chest. "So much . . ."

She smelled clean this time. He picked up the sweet scent of rose soap on her skin and the light fragrance of almond oil in the strands of her shining red hair. Easing away from Alexa, he barely held back the words "I'm falling in love with you" as he framed her face with his hands, drowning in her eyes, which reflected love, he hoped, for him. Gage wanted it to be love, but wasn't sure. Hell, he'd felt it in that subtle joy emanating from her. For the first time since her capture, some of the old Alexa had returned. It made him feel humble, because he hadn't been sure he'd ever see that woman again. "You smell good," Gage muttered, smiling down at her, brushing her lips with his, hearing that sweet sound of pleasure in the back of her throat as he deepened his exploratory kiss against her soft, eager mouth. This time, for the first time since getting kidnapped, Alexa returned his kiss with such aching tenderness that his closed eyes filled with tears.

Gage didn't kid himself. He had been inwardly holding his breath since getting her out of that cave complex. He'd worried that Alexa had been forever changed, afraid that he would lose her before he had a chance to claim her heart and make her a permanent part of his life. Gage knew it was a fool's dream, knew he wasn't worthy of Alexa, but he was willing to try.

Instead, as he eased from her wet lips, tasting the hot chocolate she'd drunk earlier, the woman he was falling in love with had surfaced. He didn't know for how long, or even if it would last, but for this one magical moment, he absorbed her, never wanting to let her go.

"You know," he began, his voice roughened as he smoothed his thumbs across her warm, velvet cheeks, "I always told myself I wasn't worthy of someone like you."

He saw her brows draw down.

"How could you think that, Gage?"

He didn't want to burden her with his miserable childhood. Instead, he lifted her hand, pressing a kiss to the back of it. "To me, you're a beautiful goddess come to earth, and I've fallen at your feet, lost in your eyes, the laughter in your voice . . . and me, I'm just a mere mortal . . ."

"You're a hero in my eyes, Gage," she whispered, reaching out, touching his bearded face. He was wearing his Marine winter uniform cammos, a dark green T-shirt, and over it was a bulky, warm tan-colored jacket. He smelled of cold air and desert. "My dad told me earlier that he got those charges removed."

"Yeah," he chuckled. "I'm a free man again. My CO's glad, believe me."

She frowned. "When do you have to go out on an op again, Gage?"

"There's a blizzard coming in, so I don't think I'll be assigned to go anywhere. For now, I just have to be on call. My CO has given me orders to stay with you, which was a shock. I think your dad got to him."

She nodded, holding his hand. "My dad is pretty persuasive when he wants to be."

"He's got general's stars to back him up, too." Gage lifted his hand, smoothing her hair away from her face. "You look nice in these clothes. Not the Air Force officer, but a young lady lounging around instead."

"My mom brought these." She touched the black jersey trousers. "I love this fabric. It's comfy and warm."

"How's your back doing?" He saw Alexa's eyes grow a little cloudy, knowing the question dragged up the event for her. Maybe he shouldn't have asked. He didn't want to hurt her all over again.

"Better. It still smarts and burns, but I slept through the night and never woke up, so that's progress. Could you tell me what it looks like?"

Gage nodded and gently eased the jersey fabric about a third of the way up her back. Leaning down, he said, "It doesn't look as swollen, Alexa. It's a lot more colorful today, purple, blue, and violet." He brought the fabric down, smoothing it across her hips. Rage simmered in him. He wanted to kill the bastard who'd done this to her.

"That's good," she said, nodding. "I haven't let my mom or dad look at my back yet." She chewed on her lower lip. "I'm afraid they'll get really upset."

Gage grazed her cheek with his fingers. "Listen, you do whatever feels right and comfortable, okay?" He somberly searched her lowered gaze. He ached to hold Alexa, curl her up beside him and just hold her. "Have you eaten yet?"

"No . . ."

"Tired of hospital food yet?" he teased, giving her a slight smile. It felt like Alexa had run out of energy already and was once more cycling down into what he silently called hell, that emotional garbage pit of terror, anxiety, and God knew what else that boiled inside her. One moment, she was like her old self, bright and positive. And just as swiftly, Gage saw her lose that battle with the trauma as it swept through her once again. He cupped her jaw. "You need to eat, sweetheart. Will you try for me?"

Rallying, she sighed and looked up into his shadowed face. "I know . . . it's just been so rough . . . first, there was Dr. Griffin, which brought back so much of what happened to me in the cave, Gage. I couldn't stop crying while she examined me."

"I'm so sorry. But it's over. Dr. Griffin got what she needed for her report, so it's not happening again."

"The flight surgeon, Major Donahue, was in here this morning. That was grueling. Two hours. I was so emotionally wrung out when she was done asking me question after question."

Gage smoothed his fingers down her cheek. When Alexa laid her cheek in his open palm, he felt a lump forming in his throat. She was fragile once again, so breakable. Gently, he kissed her lips, wanting desperately to infuse her with his energy, his love.

"We'll take this an hour at a time, Alexa."

She lifted her chin, staring at him. "What will happen to you, Gage? I-I know you can't leave Bagram, and I have a feeling I'll be leaving very soon. I told the flight surgeon I couldn't fly right now." She held up her hands, and he saw a slight tremor in them. She said, in a choked voice, "I'm not fit to fly . . ."

Hearing the pain in her voice, knowing what it cost her to admit it, Gage placed his hands on her firm thighs. "No one could, Alexa. No one," he said, and captured her hands, bringing them to his chest, pressing her palms against his shirt. "Did the flight surgeon give you any help? Things that could assist you through this?"

"Yeah, some things," she said absently.

"Like?" he coaxed. Alexa was struggling not to cry again. He knew she hated crying, thinking it was a sign of weakness, but Gage knew differently. He'd cried buckets of tears after the murder of Jen and his father. He'd never wept so much in his life, and it would hit him out of the blue in the most unexpected times and places. He was seeing the same pattern in Alexa.

Grief, he realized, had its own way with each person, and Alexa had lost so much of herself in that cave that she had every right to grieve.

Alexa shakily wiped away the tears falling down her cheeks. "S-she asked me what I wanted to do. What I felt in my heart and gut that would help me heal." Her lips twisted, glistening with tears.

"And what did you tell her?" It hurt Gage so damned much to see those tears continue to well up in her large, beautiful hazel eyes. Gage remembered back to when Alexa would laugh, her eyes shining the color of spring willow leaves and the gold of sunlight. He didn't see much of either of those colors now.

Sniffing, she whispered, "My family owns a beautiful, rustic cabin in the Smoky Mountains. I love the mountains, Gage. I love their quiet, their solitude. My family would go there during July and August of every year, on weekends, because it was so miserably hot and humid in Washington, D.C."

"Sounds nice," he murmured. "Tell me about this special place." He could hear a slender thread of hope in her hoarse voice as she spoke about it. Gage knew if she could go home, go to that cabin, that it would support her healing. Alexa needed peace and quiet. She couldn't handle the daily challenges of life yet.

She reached for a tissue, blowing her nose and wiping it. Holding the crushed tissue between her hands, she said, "It sits back off a four-hundred-foot cliff, up near the top of a mountain. I guess I love it because it's so out of the way, so quiet. When I was there, I always felt like I was being pumped full of energy, I felt so alive when I was in that place. That's why it's so special to me."

"Sounds like a healing place for you," he said.

"That's what the flight surgeon said. She was really a nice woman, Gage, very understanding. She felt the woods and the mountains could work their magic on me." Alexa gave a halfhearted shrug. "I don't know what the flight surgeon is going to recommend in her report on me. If I stay here, I'll be grounded and probably run the Ops desk over at the fixed-wing terminal."

"Are there any other options? Did she suggest a woman therapist who might be able to help you through this?"

"She said she'd recommend therapy." Grimacing, Alexa said, "That's going to be a death knell to my career in the Air Force, Gage. I won't get any higher rank because of that. There's such a prejudice against a pilot seeking out counseling or therapy."

Gage knew the military system, and he knew Alexa was right. Anyone, enlisted or officer, who had psychological issues noted in their personnel file was dead in the water. They wouldn't get early rank and sometimes were overlooked for a higher rank because of the prejudice the military had against people who needed counseling. His mouth turned down, he saw the defeat in Alexa's eyes.

"You do need help," he said gently, holding her gaze. "I know I feel like I'm floundering with you, sometimes, Alexa. I want to help you. I wish I had some kind of knowledge or training about how to be there for you instead of saying or doing the wrong thing."

"You've been so good to me, Gage, so patient." Her voice shook with tears. "If you hadn't been here for me now, I-I don't know that I could have come this far. I know I have to be strong, and I have to fight to get over this, but right now I'm coming down off a cliff I thought I was going to be pushed over. I thought I was going to Pakistan for a life as a sex slave." She swallowed hard, her eyes bruised with anguish. "Do you know how scared I was? How helpless I felt?"

He shook his head, giving her an apologetic look. "I'm trying to put myself in your shoes, but as much as I want to, I can't. And that's what has me scared. Scared that I'm going to scar you more than you've already been." He moved his hands slowly up and down her arms, holding her tearful gaze. "I hurt for you so much. I want to take away your suffering, Alexa, but I don't know how."

Hearing his words, low with emotion, Alexa felt such a rush of love for Gage that she couldn't speak. He gripped her upper arms, staring at her, his mouth contorted, anguish in his eyes. She leaned forward, resting her brow against his shoulder, feeling his arms lightly embrace her, his mouth near her cheek, his breath unsteady. She could feel the rise and fall of his chest, feel him wrestling with so many barely held emotions. He was hurting as much for her as she was for herself.

The realization was poignant, strengthening Alexa deep inside, her heart opening completely to him. Gage was so unselfish, and so damned giving to her, without thought or care for himself. He'd been that way in the cave, too, putting his own life on the line for all of them. The strain in his voice shook her as little else could. If Alexa had ever questioned his care for her, she never would again.

They'd not spoken about possibly falling in love with one another. They'd not broached the subject. How could they? They'd known one another for all of four days! Tears cascaded down her drawn cheeks, and she licked her lips, tasting their salt. Resting her hand against his chest, she said, her voice quavering, "You've given me back hope, Gage. I thought I'd lost it. I never thought I'd ever have it again."

He kissed her temple. "I want to give you everything. I'm not going to let this event define us. I won't. It's something we have to get through together, one step at a time . . ."

★

THE NEXT MORNING, Alexa was grateful when her parents brought her a real breakfast from the cafeteria. She looked forward to being with them, but seeing the strain of the situation on both their faces made her feel guilty.

"Do you know where Gage is?" she asked them. Last night, the three of them had visited her and she'd loved having them with her. Gage was still uncomfortable with her father, who was in uniform. She understood how he felt. Her father had treated him not as a Marine Corps sergeant, but as if he were a friend of the family, and little by little, Gage had responded to the new relationship her father was offering him.

She hadn't told them how much Gage meant to her. The topic hadn't come up yet. But they did know the key role he had played in rescuing her and the other abducted women. He was a bona fide hero to Alexa, now and forever.

After breakfast, her father rose from the chair, took all their emptied trays, and stacked them nearby. He pulled out a paper from his briefcase and gave it to Alexa. "This is the flight surgeon's report."

Her heart dropped as she took it. "You've read it already?"

"Yes." Robert sat down. "But you need to read it, and then we'll talk."

Alexa rapidly scanned the two-page report from Major Jill Donahue. Her heart sank and her stomach clenched. The bottom line was that Alexa was grounded for three months. She would run flight scheduling at ops here at Bagram and the major would retest her after the three month period to see if she was ready for flight duty or not.

Setting the report aside, she crossed her legs on top of her bed. This morning, she wore a pair of loose jeans and a pink mock turtleneck sweater. "This is what I expected," she told her parents. She saw her father nod, his mouth set.

Dilara looked at her daughter. "What do you want to do, Alexa? We'll support you no matter what your decision is. You know that."

She rubbed her brow, trying to gather her thoughts. Since her capture, her mind had felt like it was off its tracks. Major Donahue said it was the cortisol in her bloodstream caused by anxiety, and in time, she told her, it would stop. Lifting her chin, she looked at them.

"I was going to turn in my commission to the Air Force in March anyway. It's mid-January." She opened her hands. "I think I want to turn in my commission now. I'd like to go home. I have a job waiting for me, one that I want. I know I can impact the lives of other women and children who need our help."

Robert nodded, watching his daughter. "That job will always be there, Alexa, and I agree with your decision to decommission yourself from the Air Force."

"Good, Dad, because I've given this a lot of thought."

Dilara leaned forward, reaching out, touching her daughter's knee. "We'd love to have you home, Alexa. Then we wouldn't have to worry . . ."

Grimacing, Alexa whispered, "I know, Mom. I know the three of us have really made you worry nonstop about us. None of us has a safe job."

"When you come home," Robert asked, "what would you like to do, Alexa?"

"You probably think this is silly, but I really want to go to our cabin in the Smoky Mountains. I need time to get my head wrapped around what's happened to me."

"Sweetheart, you just tell us what you need and it's yours," he said, his voice layered with emotion. "You can stay there for as long as you want. There's no rush for you to join Artemis. You need to focus on yourself first."

Relief raced through Alexa. "Really? You wouldn't mind?" She searched her parents' faces.

"Of course not," Dilara whispered, choking up. "You know what you need for your healing, Alexa. It's important that you listen to that small voice inside you."

"Anything else?" Robert asked.

Alexa sighed and wrung her fingers. "I know I haven't told you much about Gage and me . . ."

"We see how much you care for one another," Dilara said gently. "And he's been so good for you, Alexa."

"Yes," she said in a whisper, afraid, but knowing she had to ask. She turned to her father. "I know this is impossible, Dad, but if I could have one wish, it would be to have Gage with me while I'm at the cabin. He helps me so much. He listens to me, and I can talk to him." She gulped, realizing she'd said it wrong, her own feelings a morass. "I mean—"

Robert smiled a little. "We know what you mean, Alexa. We understand. That young man has been with you before, during, and after your capture. Right now, he's a lynchpin in your life and recovery."

Her shoulders sagged and she gave them a grateful look. "I'm just telling you how I feel right now. What feels right for me."

"And we want you to stay there," Dilara told her firmly. She looked at her husband. "Robert, can you help get Gage out of Bagram so he can be with Alexa?"

"First," Alexa said quickly, "I need to speak to Gage about this. I'm not even sure he'd want to do it. Okay?"

"Then speak with him. What I can do is make some inquiries and see if it's possible."

Alexa chewed on her lower lip, frowning. "I know it's impossible."

Robert shrugged. "Impossible is something I work with every day of the week." He gave her a slight smile. "But first, let's see if Gage would want to do this."

"Absolutely," Alexa agreed.

"Do you want to call Major Donahue and tell her you want to decommission?" Robert asked her.

"Yes, I'll do that."

"I'll have my staff bring over the papers for you to sign later. This might take a few days, but it should be painless."

"Then," Dilara said, "could you fly back with us? Would you like that? Or would you rather do it another way?"

Wrinkling her nose, she said, "I'd much rather fly back with you. I'm not ready for a C-5 cargo plane or a commercial flight. I feel too fragile, Mom. I feel like I don't have any skin to protect me right now."

Robert rose. "Then, baby girl, you'll come home with us."

It sounded so good to Alexa. So much weight began to dissolve from her shoulders. Tears sprang to her eyes, and she forced them away. Her voice was low and off-key. "Thanks, Dad, Mom. You have no idea how freeing this feels to me . . ."

Dilara made a soft sound as she rose, touching her shoulder, moved by her daughter's fragility. "You're made of strong stuff, Alexa. We'll help you all we can. All you need to do is ask us, and we'll be there for you. You don't have to go through this alone. You have family who loves you so much."

Alexa reached out, gripping her mother's soft hand, needing her support. "Thanks, Mom. Thanks for understanding. I was afraid . . . well . . . afraid you wouldn't . . ."

Dilara shook her head, giving her a warm, loving look. "What has happened to you is so outside your reality, Alexa. No woman ever thinks she'll be kidnapped and suddenly be thrown into a living hell. We think you're doing amazingly well, considering everything."

She closed her eyes for a moment, clinging to her mother's hand, desperately needing her love and care right now. "I just didn't want to hurt you by wanting to go to the cabin instead of staying home with you, Mom." She searched her mother's incredible aquamarine eyes, which were now filled with tears.

"You're a grown woman, Alexa. You have control over your life as you see fit. We're not hurt at all. Your dad and I want only to support you in ways that you need. That's all, okay?" She tilted her head, smiling into Alexa's clouded eyes, smoothing a few strands of hair away from her temple.

Alexa slid her arm around her mother's slender waist, hugging her. "I love you so much," she said, her voice quavering. "I don't know what I'd have done without you coming . . . being here . . ."

Lightly, Dilara placed her arm around Alexa's shoulders. "You are so loved, darling girl. Our whole family prays daily for you. They want to see you, but they understand why you need this time to yourself. When you feel like it, they'll fly over to see you, but I don't want you to feel any pressure about this, okay?"

"Tell my uncles and cousin Angelo that I love them all dearly. It's just that right now, I can't handle a lot of people, Mom."

"They completely understand," Dilara said, squeezing her just a little bit, aware of her painful back injuries. "But I think that when you go to our cabin in the Smokies, they would love to send you over some Turkish food."

Laughing a little, Alexa sat up, giving her mother an affectionate look. "I'd love that. It would be wonderful . . ." She saw her mother's expression fill with hope. Alexa knew how devastated they were over what had happened to her. "I'm sure Uncle Berk is dying to send over a banquet for me."

She chuckled. "Well, between you and me, they're waiting eagerly to hear what you'd like. They each have a chef, and they've been sending me emails about having your favorite Turkish foods made and sending them here to Bagram, but I begged them to wait just a bit longer until things were sorted out."

Smiling tentatively, Alexa whispered, "I love them so much, Mom. Maybe once I get to the cabin I'll email them."

"Don't do anything except what your heart tells you, Alexa. I can always email them myself. We want you to heal. We want to give you whatever it is that you want. All right?"

Alexa felt warmth beneath her mother's quietly spoken words. The love in her eyes for her soothed her anxiety. Alexa hated feeling apprehensive all the time, no matter who was around. The only person who calmed her and kept fears at bay was Gage. And really, she needed to talk with him. Alexa wasn't sure Gage would want to leave Bagram to be with her even if he could. Yet she saw the care for her in his eyes.

What would he say? It ratcheted up her agitation even more, because in her heart, she needed him more than anyone else. And Alexa saw no way for the Marine Corps to simply let Gage go and come home to her. It seemed like an impossible dream.

CHAPTER 18

GAGE WAS LATE seeing Alexa. He knocked lightly at her door and eased in. It was nearly 1000 and he'd overslept, something he never did, but it revealed how stressed he was. Now he saw Alexa with her laptop on her lap, sitting in a chair beside her bed.

"Hey," she called, giving him a soft smile of welcome.

Gage nodded and closed the door. "Sorry I'm late. I overslept."

Alexa patted the chair next to her. "I think we're all a little fried over this, don't you?"

He grimaced and sat down, pulling the chair around so he could face her. "You're probably right. How are you doing this morning?"

"Well," she began, closing the laptop and setting it on the rolling tray table next to her, "my parents visited me earlier. I've got a lot of decisions to make, Gage." She held his concerned gaze. He was dressed for winter, his knit cap between his long, spare hands—hands she ached to have touch her.

"Okay," he murmured. "What happened?" He could see the worry in Alexa's eyes. She had wrapped her hair up into a red mass on her head, the strands caressing her temples. Sensing change, he tried to appear relaxed. If he tensed up, he knew Alexa would get tense, too. She read him pretty well, and his job, as he saw it, was to reduce stress for her, not amp it up.

Taking a deep breath, she told him about her decision. He frowned when she then said, "But there's more, Gage, and it involves you directly."

He listened carefully, seeing hesitation, fear, and yearning in her eyes. "You know I'd do anything to help you, Alexa. Just tell me," he urged quietly.

"My dad asked me if I wanted anything else besides going to our cabin in the Smokies. I told him yes, that I wanted you there with me."

If an RPG had gone off next to Gage, he couldn't have been any more shocked. He sat up, rubbing his hands on his trousers. "Seriously?"

"Yes, seriously." Giving him a pleading look, she whispered unsteadily, "Look, I know we haven't known one another that long, but I feel such a wonderful connection with you, Gage. The cabin has three bedrooms. You could stay with me, just for a little while, couldn't you? You have no idea how much you've helped me . . ."

"I'd do it, Alexa," he offered heavily, "but my captain isn't going to let me just walk away from my deployment. I don't see how I could. It's not that I don't want to—I do." He shook his head, feeling stonewalled by the military system. His heart and soul were with her. He never wanted their connection to end. He wanted it to continue to grow and flourish.

"You'd come for a visit, then, if you could?"

"Of course." *In a heartbeat,* he thought. But he bit back the words. Gage had no idea how she'd feel about him falling in love with her. There was just too much on her plate to go there yet. He saw relief come over her. "But I don't know how it could happen, Alexa, I really don't."

"I don't either," she admitted, her lips quirking. "My dad said he'd see what he could do to make it happen if you did want to hang around me for a little while longer."

Gage realized Alexa had no idea he loved her. They'd kissed, yes. He'd held her. He'd cared for her. There was no reason for him to go there, not with the trauma she was presently wrestling with. It wasn't the right time to broach his growing feelings for her, his dream built from the shattered pieces from his past. Alexa made him want to dream again of a future—with her. Gage was so damned scared, but he had to try. She inspired him, whether she knew it or not. "If your dad can arrange a miracle, I'd come visit you, Alexa."

Never had Gage wanted anything quite this bad, but he saw no possible way to overcome the military machine to make it happen. Yet, he saw such optimism in Alexa's eyes that he didn't want to be a wet blanket and dash her hopes.

"Look," he said evenly, holding her gaze, "I think the time alone will help you. You're already starting to climb out of the cellar from your shock, Alexa. Even if I can't make it, you'll be all right."

She nodded and tucked her lower lip between her teeth, trying to be brave. She saw the desire in Gage's eyes, heard his emotions so close to the surface as he spoke to her. "When is your enlistment up?"

"June of this year." He gave a painful shrug. "And I don't have any leave coming, either. I already thought of that, but my leave is used up, so I couldn't get out of here by using it."

It seemed hopeless. And he saw her begin to accept the reality of their situation. His heart wrenched, because there was nothing more that Gage wanted than to be there to support Alexa. It didn't matter if she loved him or not. Gage was already accepting that possible reality. He knew there would never be another woman like Alexa in his life. Not ever. She was so damned special.

"Well," she offered, "let my dad see what he can find out."

"Sure," he murmured. Already, Gage could feel her being slowly torn away from him. Alexa needed a friend, someone she could talk to, someone who would listen with his heart. He was all those things to her and Gage knew it. Every kiss they'd shared was like heaven visiting him. He'd felt her warmth, tasted her sweetness, dreamed of so much more with Alexa. But it was slipping through his fingers and Gage accepted the bitter reality of it all. Her father was powerful, no question, but even he had limits on his authority.

"What will you do when you get to the cabin?" Gage wanted to detour her because he saw how crestfallen Alexa was as she realized what they had to overcome to be together.

"I want to read, to draw." She gave a small shrug. "I love to paint. I'm going to get my canvases and oil paints and take them up with me."

He smiled a little. "I didn't know you were an artist."

"Oh," Alexa protested, holding up her hands, "I'm not very good at all. I just love to put color to canvas. That's about it."

His smile widened. He ached to take Alexa in his arms and love her until she melted through him. "Do you have any of them on your cell phone?"

"No," she said, a faint smile coming to her lips. "I would never brag about them, believe me. I'm more like a third grader with poster paints."

"Well, I'd still like to see them. What else will you do while you're up there?"

"Take photos. I'm much better with a camera than I am with paints, believe me." She sat back, becoming nostalgic. "I was thinking I could go out when the winter weather wasn't too bad and take photos of nature, then bring them back to the cabin and maybe try painting some of them. I guess I need time to just be, Gage."

He knew that one too well. "I understand that. I really do." At thirteen, he'd been lost. So damned lost. And he had his mother to take care of in the aftermath. Gage had never had a time when he could do what Alexa would do—go away, escape the world for a while, and just get himself slowly back together again.

"Let's keep our fingers crossed, then," she said, holding his gaze. "If anyone can work a miracle, Dad can."

★

ALEXA TRIED NOT to cry when her father told her there was no way to break Gage free so he could go home with her. He'd already told Gage privately over at his barracks what the captain of the unit had said. She'd known he had no leave coming; it could have been granted to him if he had. It was the only legal route.

"You tried, Dad." She mustered a look that convinced him she wasn't upset with the decision.

He came over to where she stood by her hospital bed and gave her a careful embrace, kissing her temple. "I'm sorry. I know how much Gage means to you, Alexa," he said heavily, releasing her, looking deep into her eyes.

"It's okay," she managed. She saw her mother looking so sad, standing with her hands clasping her black purse. "It's all right . . . I still want to go to our cabin."

"Of course," he said. "Tomorrow morning at 0800 we'll leave Bagram. Your CO told me that the papers are ready for your signature. They're sending over someone this afternoon so you can sign them. Then"—he managed a slight smile—"you'll be a civilian again."

"And you can come home," Dilara said softly, giving her a loving look. "I know Tal can hardly wait to see you."

Her heart twisted and turned in her chest. Struggling to put on a brave face for her parents, her voice broke a little. "Yes, I'm more than ready to get out of here." Because only bad memories came with this place now, Matt had to stay behind, but his enlistment would be up shortly, and he'd be home with her, too. She'd have her family once again. The only thing she would miss would be Gage. She barely clung to what little returning strength she had, wanting to sob her heart out over his being torn out of her life at a time when she desperately needed what he gave her.

"We've got some people packing up all your clothes and other items over at your B-hut," Robert told her. "They'll be shipped home, so you don't need to worry about that."

Everything seemed heavy and gray to her, and Alexa realized it was depression or something akin to it. She felt her parents' worry because Gage couldn't be with her. "That's great, Dad. Thank you." She nervously moved her laptop to the bed. "Is it possible to see Gage one last time before I leave?"

"I'm sure it is. I'll make a call over to his captain."

"I-I'd like to have dinner with him tonight."

"I'll see that he's cut loose to come over here."

Alexa held herself together until her parents left, and then she crawled up on the hospital bed, sobbing into the pillow so no one could hear her.

★

GAGE FELT AS if there were prison bars around his heart, squeezing it until his chest was suffused with pain. He'd gotten cleaned up as best he could before coming over to have dinner with Alexa. Stopping at a shop on base, he found a few red roses that were past their prime, but that was all they had to sell. He'd bought some gold foil wrapping paper and a bright green ribbon, and put the stems in a plastic baggie so they had some water. It wasn't much, he realized with a sinking heart. Alexa deserved healthy, strong red roses, not these. Given that the base was out in the middle of godforsaken nowhere, he was lucky to have found any at all.

Taking pains, he'd trimmed his beard so it looked neat, not scruffy. He'd gone to one of the barbers on the base and had his hair trimmed, too. Tonight, he wore civilian clothes, chinos and a polo shirt. Over them, he wore his leather jacket. It was colder than hell out, and snowflakes were starting to fall. By midday tomorrow, a snowstorm would arrive. He was glad that Alexa was leaving in the morning, because when the snow hit, the base would still be operating 24/7. He tried to calm his angst about Alexa, unsure of where she would be emotionally, he knocked on her door.

He quietly entered and saw her standing by her bed. The ache in his heart increased tenfold because she looked gaunt and pale beneath the fluorescent lights above her. The look in her eyes devastated him as he closed the door behind him. Tonight, he was going to put on an act for her benefit. Alexa couldn't know how miserable he was, how badly he felt at losing her before they ever had a chance to connect solidly with one another.

"Maybe these will cheer you up?" he said, holding out the bouquet. He saw her expression soften as their fingers met. "I'm sorry these roses look so wimpy. It was all they had."

Touched, Alexa whispered, "No . . . they're beautiful . . . thank you," and she gave him a sweet look as she leaned over, inhaling them. Lifting her face from them, she said, "They smell wonderful, Gage. This was so thoughtful of you," as she delicately touched one of the red blooms.

Nervously, he moved his hands down the sides of his trousers. "I got lucky," he murmured, making a gesture toward the bouquet. "I found some gold foil and green ribbon. I wanted it to symbolize the color of your eyes, as I saw them."

Alexa shook her head and placed the roses on the tray table. "You are just too good to be true, Gage Hunter." She walked up to him as he opened his arms to her. He was a warrior, and he was tender, and she drowned in his blue eyes that told her so much. Encircling his shoulders, she leaned up on tiptoes, caressing his mouth, hearing him groan, his arms instantly folding her against him.

It was a kiss she never wanted to end. It took the last of her strength not to cry as he exquisitely reciprocated her questing lips against his, coaxing them open, tasting her, asking her to taste him—and she did. His masculine scent spiraled down through her body, sending heat and yearning suddenly exploding through it. Since her cave experience, Alexa had felt numb in some ways.

Miraculously, Gage made her traumatized body and mind want once more.

Crushing herself wantonly against him, feeling his erection pressing against her belly, she moaned, deepening the kiss, moving her tongue slowly against his, her breasts growing firm, the nipples hardening. Alexa, shocked, realized she hadn't felt anything like this since her capture.

The warmth of Gage's mouth was like magic flowing across her lips, and she couldn't get enough of being connected with him. Her heart broke as she realized this could be the last time she would see him. Would she ever see him again? Alexa didn't know, and a sob made her throat tighten as she pulled away from his mouth, breathing unsteadily, submerged in his intense, burning gaze. "I don't want to leave you," she managed to say.

He lifted his hand, smoothing her loose hair away from her cheek. "Listen," he teased her huskily, "I'm kinda like a bad cold. Once you get me, you can't get rid of me." He saw hope come to her glistening hazel eyes. Saw her lips part, begging to be taken again by him.

"You're the best cold I've ever contracted, Hunter."

He smiled a little and kept her in his light embrace over her bruised shoulders, content to have her arms wrapped around his waist, leaning against him, trusting him. And then he became serious, holding her gaze. "The best thing is for you to go home, Alexa. It's ideal under the circumstances. You'll get the time you need to sort everything out. You'll have your parents nearby, your sister, Tal. Matt will join you in March. You'll be with people who love and care for you. That's the difference between healing and an open wound, and as much as I'm going to miss you, I know this is the right thing for you to do."

"In some ways, Gage, we know each other so well. In other ways, I barely know you at all," Alexa told him shakily.

His mouth crooked. "It isn't like we've had time to explore one another, is it?"

Shaking her head, she relished his warmth, his gentle strength, even though he was a man. Blips of how she was handled in the cave kept cropping up, and Alexa kept trying to ignore them, because Gage was not like those monsters. He gave her peace. Security. A sense of caring that she would have called love, but she wasn't certain about that. "I want to know everything about you," she said, her voice strained. "Everything. My parents taught me that we are the way we are today because of our parents and the way we were raised. Your folks must have loved you so much because they've given you everything that I need right now."

Wincing internally, Gage leaned over, pressing a chaste kiss to her brow. "Alexa, I probably have no right to ask you this, but when I return home I want to come and visit you. I'd like to pick up where we left off, if you still feel the same toward me . . . toward us . . ."

Her eyes shone with more green and gold in their depths than they had recently, and Gage's heart lifted with hope.

"I'd like that, Gage. A lot."

"June's a good time, early summer. I've never been back to the Washington, D.C., area."

"It is beautiful at that time of year," she said. "I want you to come see me, Gage. We can stay in touch by email and Skype until then?" She searched his gaze, never wanting anything so much as for him to say yes to her request.

"I'd like that." Not quite believing his ears, but feeling threads of joy weaving around his heart, he said, "Alexa, I don't have much. That's what worries me about us. I'm not rich. I'm just a Marine Corps sniper. I don't have any other trade. I'm a high school graduate, that's all."

She moved her hand across his chest, feeling his flesh tighten beneath her fingers. "And you have the courage of a lion, Gage. You put your life on the line for others. You're willing to sacrifice yourself to save others." She tilted her head, gazing deep into his darkened blue eyes. "Those are far more important qualities to me than anything you've just said. Money can't buy a person's courage, or their tenderness. Or sensitivity to others." Her voice broke. "If it hadn't been for you, I wouldn't be here today." She pressed her hand against her lips, beads of tears on her thick red lashes as she stared up at him.

"You're such a softy, Ms. Culver," he teased, kissing each of her eyes and smoothing her tears away with his fingers.

Opening her eyes, sniffing, she rattled, "Don't you dare belittle yourself like that to me again, Gage. Do you think I care about any of that? I've had nearly a week with you and I like what I see. I always did."

Looking away for a moment, Gage felt a ton of heaviness dissolve within him. Cocking his head toward her, he rasped, "And I've always liked what I see in you, Alexa."

The vibration in his voice was like a song through her body, her heart opening wide to him. "Then let's see one another when you get out? Please?"

"I can't stay as long as I might want to, Alexa. I'll need a job. There's a lot I have to do when I separate from the Corps."

"Whatever you can share with me will be enough, Gage."

"We'll work it out," he promised, grazing her cheek, wanting so badly to love her, but it was the wrong place and wrong time. In the back of Gage's mind he wondered if Alexa would be well enough by June to want anything more than a friendship with him.

He knew what he wanted. He wanted Alexa forever in his bed, tucked beside him each night. His dreams had become torrid and filled with hopes he didn't dare to believe could come true.

"Okay," she said, "like you said once, we'll take it an hour at a time."

"Yeah, my dad taught me that when I was real young. He taught me patience when I was a pretty antsy kid." Gage smiled fondly in remembrance.

"When you come for a visit I want to hear about your parents and your sister. Bring your photos, your stories. I want to know them even though they're no longer here. You are who you are today because of your family."

Her sincerity damn near buckled him. "I'd like that," he murmured. With Alexa, he had a salt-of-the-earth kind of woman. No one would ever guess her family was one of the richest in the world. She could have sidestepped going into the military and fighting for her country. She could have had it so easy, but that wasn't the road she'd chosen. Gage knew it was because of her parents. General Culver had instilled a love of America into his three children. And Mrs. Culver had the world's largest charity organization. She too was giving back to those who had so much less. Alexa had been shaped by both of them to be of service to her country and to others. In Gage's eyes, that was more than commendable. It made her someone he respected. Never mind that he was falling helplessly in love with this brave redheaded woman. They had so *much* to discuss, to hammer out between them. Most of all, Gage was realizing more and more each day he spent with her and her parents that these were people who were loyal to others. There were no manipulations, no games. They were dirt honest, as he'd been raised to be.

"By then, I hope I'll be back in the saddle working at Artemis Security with Tal and Matt. Matt's coming home in March to take over the KNR division. I'm going to be the director of the Safe House division within the firm."

"I imagine," he said, catching several strands of her hair and tucking them behind her ear, "that you'll find your work very satisfying. You'll be helping an awful lot of people who need a hand up. You're just the person to do that, Alexa. You have a goodness in you that I've rarely found in anyone else." Except for his family.

Alexa pressed her hand to his heart. She could feel the slow, hard beat of it beneath her palm. "Takes one to know one, you know? You've been a wonderful surprise to me ever since I met you, Gage. My big sister, Tal, always kids me about being psychic and feeling things around other people. I've got to admit, she's right. When I met you I was so powerfully drawn to you, I didn't know what to do. It was shocking in a good way." She smiled a little, holding his gaze. "That's why I chased you." She watched his mouth curve ruefully.

"That's what you were doing?"

"Yes. I think it rattled you."

He smiled more. "I have to admit, I was surprised by your boldness."

"I didn't think snipers ever got rattled."

A chuckle rolled through his chest. "You flummoxed me, for sure." Sighing, he cupped her jaw and placed a light kiss on her smiling lips. “Here I was, a lowly Marine sergeant, and this gorgeous redheaded pilot comes after me like a laser-guided rocket. What was I to think?”

Her heart lifted with joy because, right now, Gage was vulnerable with her, open, inviting her into his world and how he saw her. A rush of pleasure blotted out all the darkness that was buried deep within her. “Well,” she said coyly, “when I leaned over to kiss you that night in the Humvee, you sure didn’t seem shocked. You were right there, Hunter, kissing me back. Weren’t you?”

He laughed for the first time since she’d been kidnapped, Alexa had that effect on him, on his heart. “I like a woman who goes after what she wants,” he said, grinning.

“Just one of my many skills.”

“Yes, I was surprised when you leaned over to kiss me.”

“Why didn’t you kiss me, then?”

He saw a spark of the old Alexa come to her eyes. It was such a gift for them to have this moment. She was in an up cycle, and Gage reveled in it and in her. “Because you were an officer and I’m enlisted, that’s why.”

“I didn’t let it stop me, did I?”

“No, you sure didn’t, and I’ve got to tell you, I was a very happy man when you dive-bombed me.”

Playfully, she hit his upper arm. “Really, Gage. Do you think I’ve ever done that before?”

Shrugging, he said, “I don’t know.” Alexa looked delicious when she pouted, those large, intelligent eyes flashing with playfulness. He was getting a glimpse of the woman he always suspected was hiding behind the officer’s uniform. And he’d been right. Gage was almost giddy with that discovery.

“Well, I’ve never been this forward with a man in my life. But it was your fault.”

“I see. It’s always the guy’s fault, right?” Now he did laugh, and rocked her a little in his arms, their hips against one another. Gage knew she must have felt his erection. He was almost in pain from it, but he wouldn’t have traded this moment with Alexa for the world. She didn’t tease him, didn’t roll her hips or make a suggestive move that told him she was comfortable with the next step in their intimacy. She made him hungry. Made him dream. Made him hope. If only . . . if only he could tell her.

CHAPTER 19

GAGE COULD BARELY contain his emotions as he swung his Harley into the hidden parking lot at Artemis Security. A week earlier, Alexa had alerted the security officers at the entrance that he would be coming to the company to see her. The June sunlight showed off the Virginia rural area to perfection. It was a far cry from the dry desert of Afghanistan. He parked his bike in the underground parking lot beneath the 1850s restored farmhouse. If he hadn't been in email and Skype contact with Alexa since she'd left Bagram, he'd have been fooled, thinking that this was a working farm.

As he walked to the elevator, he noticed the tight security. From Alexa's encrypted emails back and forth between them, he'd learned a lot more about Artemis and the role it played in trying to protect their eighteen hundred charity locations around the world. At the elevator, a guard took the pass that Alexa had sent to him. The guard took it, nodded, and allowed him into the elevator then the sentry called Alexa on his radio, letting her know that Gage was coming up to the fifth floor. The officer keyed in a code for that floor only and then stepped out, giving him a nod.

His heart beating hard in his chest, Gage wondered how Alexa was going to react when she saw him. No longer did he have his beard. His longish hair was cut military short. He wore a pair of jeans, a black T-shirt, a black leather jacket, and motorcycle boots. Pushing up his red baseball cap with the Marine Corps emblem embroidered on the front, he settled his wraparound sunglasses above the bill, as well. He wondered what her reaction would be to him today.

The months since her capture had been rough on her. There were many times Gage had wished he'd been there in person for Alexa. She was still seeing a woman therapist, Dr. Becka Courtland, once a week. Tal Culver, the CEO of Artemis, had just hired Becka as their in-house psychiatrist, and Gage was glad for both her and Alexa. The therapy had been emotionally rough on Alexa, and although she didn't say much about it, Gage had seen, during some of their Skype sessions, the stress in her face and in her eyes. Alexa couldn't hide anything from him. The months apart had only deepened his love for her, even at a distance. They never talked about such things. Instead, from Gage's perspective, they had gotten to know one another through sharing their lives with one another. Sometimes, their talks were funny, other times serious, heart-wrenching, or illuminating. He felt the time and distance was a blessing in disguise. He hoped she felt the same and he'd know pretty soon now, his stomach tight with tension.

As the elevator whooshed him upward, he ached to have quiet time with Alexa. They never talked about love, in fact, they both skirted around the topic. Gage also circumvented what had happened to his family, although he had shared with Alexa many stories of his childhood years, about his sister Jen and his parents. He just hadn't told her the rest of the sordid story. That was something, if she brought it up, he'd tell her in person. Gage wasn't looking forward to sharing it, but it was an integral part of him. If Alexa wanted to move forward with their growing relationship, then he had to come clean. She had to know.

He worried about telling her because she was actively dealing with her own trauma and Gage knew how long it had taken him to come out of the grief and shock of his family being murdered. It would be the same, in some ways, for Alexa.

When the doors opened, Gage broke into a welcoming smile as he saw Alexa waiting for him. The joy in her eyes reminded him of the old Alexa before the kidnapping. She was wearing a pink linen pantsuit with a tasteful white silk tee beneath it. Her red hair was a shining mantle around her shoulders. The Turkish gold earrings she wore fell halfway to her shoulders, giving her an exotic look.

"Gage!"

He gave her a bashful grin and opened his arms to her after he stepped off the elevator. The lobby was empty and he was glad. "Hey, you," he growled, taking her into his arms. She smelled of sweetness as she launched herself against him, her arms going around the shoulders of his black leather jacket, reaching up, smiling. Alexa was warm and happy, and if Gage had any doubt that their relationship was real, that was answered as her lips met his in a soul-stealing kiss that rocked his world.

His world was focused completely on Alexa, the warmth of her mouth against his, her feminine scent, the softness of her breasts pressed to his jacketed chest, drove him hard with need. Love welled up through him swiftly, and he eased his mouth from hers, framing her face, drowning in her sparkling hazel eyes, which danced with unfettered happiness. She was so alive, like a wriggling puppy in his arms. He smiled down at her, his heart lifting, opening. He wanted her so damn badly.

"You look beautiful." He grinned, lightly kissing her smiling mouth.

"And you look incredibly handsome! My God, Gage, you could pose as a model!"

He flushed, feeling heat rush to his face as he released her. Alexa immediately stepped back but reached out, sliding her hand into his.

"Well," he muttered, "I don't know about that," and he gave her a hesitant grin.

"Phooey! Are you tired? Do you want to rest? Or would you like a tour of our offices? Tal and Matt are here. They're down in the Bunker, the first two floors belowground, and they'd love to see you, too." And then she added, giving him a coy look, "Tal has something she needs to speak to you about. Maybe we could go there first? And then I can give you the nickel tour of Artemis."

"Sure, whatever you like. It took me three days to get back here from Camp Pendleton, where I separated from the Corps. I'm not real tired. Let's go."

"Oh, good!" Alexa pressed the button and the doors to the elevator opened. She pulled him in, leaning up, kissing his cheek. "I'm so glad you're home, Gage."

"Me too," he murmured, sliding his arm around her shoulders. "You look good." *Whole.* Almost like her old self. But Gage knew from those first days after her rescue that Alexa had cycled up and down like a roller coaster. He wondered if she was still going through that pattern of healing. He'd find out later. She leaned into him from beneath his arm, sliding hers around his waist, hugging him fiercely, giving him a look that awakened his lust-filled fantasies. He was glad he was wearing jeans, because it wouldn't show.

Alexa led him down into the Bunker. Their operations planning center was located in the subbasement, the lowest level of the five stories that comprised Artemis. Its location deep underground protected all the important electronic assets of the company. As she walked down the light gray carpeted hall, she led him to an enclosed glass area that held all their servers, electronics, and security measures, plus the backup generators, in case electricity was cut off to them. Gage was more than impressed.

Next, she led him down to the mission planning rooms on either side of another hall. The place hummed with people coming and going. Gage looked into some of the open rooms and saw at least fifteen people at work, or at a table with laptops and huge screens hung on the surrounding walls.

"Kind of reminds me of the CIA at Langley," he told her. "Similar, but your company looks like it's running with top-of-the-line equipment."

"And people," she added proudly, nodding, holding his hand as they walked down the long, wide hall. "We're hiring the best of the best, Gage. They are all veterans of the military or CIA, Mossad, the NSA, or other black ops organizations from around the world. We employ men and women from foreign military branches as well. They come from Israel, Jordan, the UK, Canada, Europe, South America, and Africa. We're still getting our security teams together, sorted out and assigned. It's a huge job and we're nowhere near up to speed," she said.

Alexa halted at a closed door, opened it, and Gage recognized Tal Culver, who was sitting at the end of a large tiger maple table that gleamed beneath the lights. She wore a pair of white cotton trousers and a white blazer, a bright red tee beneath it. Next to her was his good buddy Matt Culver, dressed in jeans and a black T-shirt, like himself.

"Gage!" Tal said, standing up, she smiled and, held out her hand to him as she came around the table. "Good to see you again."

He shook her hand, smiling. "Same here, Tal." And then he chuckled. "Seems odd not to call you 'Captain Culver' or 'ma'am.'"

Tal smiled and released his hand. "We're civilians now, Gage."

Gage nodded and reached out, shaking Matt's hand as he stopped next to Tal.

"Glad you could make it, Gage. Come on in and have a seat. We've got coffee if you're interested." Matt pointed to an espresso machine in the corner of the room.

"Hey, coffee sounds real good," Gage murmured.

"Espresso?" Matt asked.

"Naw, just plain black coffee, thanks."

Tal slid her hand around his arm. "Come on, sit down with us. We have some business to discuss."

Gage sat down at Tal's right elbow. Matt brought the coffee over to Gage as well as a cup for himself. Alexa sat opposite Gage, looking as if she knew some big secret and was barely able to keep it to herself. He loved her for her ability to be that open, that vulnerable, with him.

He picked up the coffee, thanking them.

Tal said, "Gage, you and I have known one another for five deployments. I never succeeded in drawing you over to my sniper unit because your captain knew just how good you were."

"I wanted to come over to your unit, believe me," he told her. "You had better numbers. I wanted to be on your team, Tal. But a sergeant in the ranks doesn't have any pull to do anything except follow orders. You know how it is."

"Indeed I do," she said. "Look, Matt, Alexa, and I are still building the foundation of Artemis from the ground up. We're officially online as of June first—today. But we've been in the trenches since late last year, even as this place was being built around us."

The door opened and Wyatt Lockwood entered with his laptop beneath his arm. He nodded to everyone.

"Gage, this is my fiancé, Wyatt Lockwood. He's the head of Mission Planning for Artemis."

Gage reached over, shaking Lockwood's hand from across the table. He sat down next to Alexa.

"Nice to meet you, Gage," he drawled. "Sorry I'm late. I got embroiled in a last-minute mission change on an op." He opened up his laptop.

"You're here," Tal said. "That's all that counts, cowboy."

Gage grinned at the repartee between the two of them. He knew from Alexa that Tal was going to marry Wyatt in August over in Kuşadası, Turkey. The look in the man's eyes as he held Tal's told Gage how much in love they were with each other. Glancing at Alexa, he caught her looking at him with that same look in her eyes. His heart skipped a beat. This was some kind of official meeting that he hadn't been told about. What was going on?

"Yes, ma'am, this Texas country boy aims to please his boss lady," Wyatt said, smiling absently as he fiddled with the keys on his laptop.

Gage saw the screen down at the end of the mission room light up. It was a huge panel screen, nearly the length of the wall it hung on. He'd seen similar ones at the CIA, but this one was even larger. He saw Wyatt put up a blueprint of Artemis on the screen.

"Okey dokey," Wyatt said, turning to Tal, "I think you can move on, darlin'."

"Thanks," she murmured, giving him a smile. Turning her attention to Gage, she said, "I'm looking for an ex-military sniper to run the sniper corps here at our firm. We need the best of the sniper cadre at Artemis, for obvious reasons, when we go out on an op to a country where one of our charities is being threatened. Gage, I want you to head up this department. Your name is well-known, you are highly respected, and you know the ins and outs of the sniping business." She pointed her laser at a diagram showing all the divisions and departments of Artemis. "You would work under Wyatt. He heads up all of mission planning for us. We're developing the sniper department right now. We have other ex-military snipers who want to work with us, but I wanted to wait until you got here." Her voice lowered. "There's no one more qualified than you to run that department. We will give you a salary of one hundred and eighty thousand dollars a year to run it for us. Are you interested?"

Shock rolled through Gage as he stared in disbelief over at Tal. She was serious. Dead serious. "I . . . didn't expect this, Tal."

Grimacing, Tal muttered, giving her sister a look, "Believe me, after Alexa found out, I practically had to tape her mouth shut so she wouldn't tell you before we could get you here to our office."

Laughing, Alexa raised her hand. "Oh, guilty as charged, big sis!"

Gage saw the hope, the yearning, burning in Alexa's eyes as she turned her attention back to him. He'd been worried about trying to find a job somewhere. About the only thing open to him was going into law enforcement, joining the CIA, or finding a security job with some corporation. "Well," he hedged, holding Alexa's gaze, "the kind of jobs that are out there for someone like me aren't many. And the ones that are available don't appeal to me. I don't want to become a police sniper, nor do I want to work for the spooks, because I'd be overseas more than I'd ever be home here."

Wiping his mouth, he looked at all of them. "And I sure didn't want a job running a security detail for a corporation."

"No," Wyatt drawled, "you're right. But if you come to work for Tal, she'll treat you right. You'll have full autonomy over your department. You'll answer directly to me. You've not only got five years of experience, Gage, but you also taught at the Marine Corps sniper school for two years as an instructor. Tal, Matt, Alexa, and I all agreed we need someone of your caliber to head up that department. I think you'll find our benefits package, the medical and dental plan, better than anywhere else you could go. Plus, you would be with people you know. Tal is a known person to you." He briefly gestured in her direction. "We all work for her, and you know she was a fine leader of her sniper unit at Bagram."

Nodding, Gage looked across the table at Alexa. She was barely able to sit still, so much of her old bounce was back.

"What do you think?" he asked her.

"I think you should take it, Gage."

"I guess," he told them, opening his hands, "I need to sit with this offer. I'm a sniper, and we never make a fast move. We chew on it, look at it from a lot of different perspectives and angles first."

The most important consideration—and it wasn't something Gage could speak about—was whether or not he and Alexa had a relationship that was going somewhere. He couldn't see himself working at Artemis if she didn't want the same thing he wanted—love and, at some point in the future if that went well, marriage.

Alexa became somber, giving her siblings a look. "Gage and I have a lot to talk over," she offered quietly.

"Understood," Tal said. "Gage, take your time. You're our first choice and we want you, but you need to sort other things out first."

Gage nodded. "Thanks for understanding. It's a dream-come-true kind of offer, and I am interested."

Tal rose. "That's good enough for me. Alexa? Why don't you show Gage around?"

★

"WILL YOU COME home with me tonight, Gage?" Alexa stood with him in her office after she had shown him the entire facility.

He closed the door to her office and turned, walking over to where she stood near her desk. "Is that what you want?"

She reached out, moving her fingers down his arm. Gage had taken off his leather jacket, and he looked powerful in just his black T-shirt. She felt the muscles beneath her fingertips tighten as she grazed his flesh, saw his eyes narrow upon her. "More than anything."

Hearing the tremor, the yearning, in her voice, he nodded. "I'd like that."

"I'm taking the next week off with you just as we discussed on Skype," she said, searching his eyes. "I want to drive up to our cabin in the Smokies, Gage. We have so much to talk about . . ."

He saw the anxiety in her eyes and felt it as well. The need to protect her was always simmering just beneath the surface, and he drew her into his arms. She came willingly, resting her head against his chest. "Then that's what we'll do, Alexa. I felt good about it when we discussed it last month. I feel good about it now." She nuzzled into his chest, her hands sliding slowly up and down his chest. His fierce love for her nearly made him tell her just that, but Gage was a sniper and knew timing was everything. There were some things they had to get out of the way first, things that Alexa needed to know about him no matter how painful they were for him to speak about.

She sighed softly. "Do you know how long I've waited for this moment?"

"No, but it's nice to know," he rasped, kissing her hair, inhaling the slight almond fragrance.

"There was so much I wanted to say on Skype, but I know you were monitored, and I couldn't say much at all."

"Same here," he admitted, skating his hand lightly down her back. "And what I need to tell you, Alexa, I don't want on an encrypted video chat. What I have to say to you, what I want to share—that's strictly between you and me."

Easing away, she gave him a warm look, briefly touching his clean-shaven jaw. "Then shall we stop at my condo? I've got my bags packed. All I have to do is put it in my car and water my houseplants, and then we can leave. It's only a three-hour drive west of here. Are you game?"

Was he ever! He filled himself with that radiant look in her eyes. "I'm game." He released her before he could smother her in his arms and kiss her senseless. Wrong time, wrong place, but soon that would change.

★

THEY SAT OUT on the wraparound porch of the two-story log cabin, which looked over the setting sun to the west of them. Gage pushed the toe of his boot idly on the cedar deck as the swing moved gently back and forth. They'd arrived a few hours earlier Alexa had made them a steak dinner, salad, and garlic toast. For dessert, she had brought up a cake she'd made the day before, a lemon cream. Before leaving her condo, she had climbed into a pair of jeans, hiking boots, and a pale lavender tee that outlined her small, beautiful breasts and slender body. What made Gage smile was that she placed her long hair into a set of braids, giving her such a youthful look. No longer did she look like the director of the Safe House division.

"This," she whispered, leaning her head against his shoulder, her forehead against his neck, "is perfect. I feel like I'm in one of my dreams . . ."

Hearing the elation in her low tone, his squeezed her shoulders gently. "This is better than any dream I've ever had. All I've ever had is broken dreams. Can I dream along with you?"

Alexa opened her eyes and leaned back enough to meet his downward gaze. "There was so much I wanted to talk to you about, Gage, but we couldn't any earlier than now."

"I know." He lightly kissed her. "Time hasn't been on our side, has it?"

She shook her head, smoothing his T-shirt across his chest. "Gage, you need to know something . . . something that I've been wanting to tell you from the moment I met you."

His hand stilled on her hair and he saw the turmoil in her eyes, heard the quaver in her voice. "Tell me." He held his breath because he lived in fear that Alexa would, at some time, tell him that she didn't see them in a serious, long-term relationship like he did. His stomach clenched, waiting. He saw fear in her eyes, trepidation. He allowed his hand to fall on her shoulder, smoothing the material of her shirt.

"I never got to tell you all that happened to me after we were kidnapped."

"I figured that when the time was right you'd share it with me, Alexa."

She pulled out of his arms and turned, facing him. "I've had nearly four months since it happened, Gage. And I've been lucky from the moment you and the SEALs rescued us." Reaching out, she laid her hand on his. "You were there for me and"—she swallowed, giving him a searching look—"I need you to know just how important that was to me. I know I was a basket case after we got back to Bagram."

"Anyone would have been," he said, his voice low. "All the women were reacting just like you were."

Giving a nod, Alexa whispered, "It's been rough since I got back to the U.S., Gage. But I'm sure it has been for all of us."

Her mouth tightened and she looked away for a moment. The evening was so silent, the breeze barely moved the trees around the cabin. The soft pinkish light from the sunset gave the area a beautiful radiance but it wasn't how she felt inside. Picking up his hand between her own, she began to tell Gage everything that happened to her. As she did, she saw anguish, rage, and turmoil come into his eyes. It was hard to speak the words, to say them aloud. Her fingers became clammy as she told the story, leaving nothing out. His fingers, warm and strong, curved protectively around hers.

"Physically? I've healed up just fine. If it weren't for Becka and my weekly sessions with her, I'd have been lost in all my rage, my grief, and so many tears. God, I've never cried so much in my entire life, Gage. I'm not one to cry a lot anyway. But this pushed me where I had no way to protect myself. If you hadn't been there for me afterward, I know I wouldn't be where I am today."

Gage could barely contain his reaction to her story. The harm done to Alexa was far more extensive than he'd ever realized. And it hurt him to see the terror still lurking behind her glistening eyes, to hear a tremor every once in a while in her hushed voice as she forced out the words to share with him. "I'm glad I was there, sweetheart. I wouldn't have it any other way." He squeezed her cold, damp hands. Just speaking about it sent her into a physical reaction.

"You were the key to my getting my feet under me again, Gage." Alexa dragged in a deep breath and looked around the quiet porch. There was an owl somewhere in the distance calling to its mate nearby. The sounds were soothing to her. "Becka took over where you left off. She's got training like Major Donahue had, in rape and domestic abuse situations. At first I had nightmares four or five times a week. I couldn't sleep. My mind was churning over everything that happened to me. Just being able to drop by her office at Artemis and sit down and talk to her for a few minutes was of enormous help."

"No one could get through something like this by themselves," he agreed. But inwardly, Gage was shaking with rage. The only good thing out of it was that Alexa had killed the general who had done so much damage to her psyche, to her. That gave him brutal pleasure. And he could tell that while she didn't like killing anyone, it had given her a modicum of retaliation against the sick sonofabitch. Gage could tell it bothered her, though.

"Listen," he urged her, "you were a combat pilot, Alexa. You were in the air war. You never saw what your bombs or that fifty-caliber Gatling gun did to the enemy below you."

"You're right, I didn't. I'm not sorry I killed that bastard. He would have shot me if I hadn't shot first. And worse? If I hadn't killed him, he'd have shot the rest of the women around me. I'm not sorry I did it, but I'll always pay a price for it . . . usually in my nightmares."

"And where are you at right now in your healing process?"

She smiled a little. "See? That just another thing I love about you, Gage. You see things from a positive viewpoint."

His heart leaped when she mentioned the word "love." Lifting her hand, he kissed the back of it, feeling the warmth of her flesh, the scent of her. "Bad things happen to everyone," he told her somberly. "It's what we do with what happened to us that counts."

CHAPTER 20

THE PALE PINK wash from the sunset deepened, turning the woods surrounding the cabin Alexa's favorite color. Sitting with Gage on the swing was a dream come true for her.

"Has coming home helped you?" Gage asked, absorbing her upturned face.

Anxiety riffled through her as she admitted, "Getting home, going to work at Artemis, allowed me to shift my focus from me to my job, Gage. That was good. I wasn't trying to run from my feelings; Becka said it was important to work through them and not ignore them or try to suppress them. Tal was great. She gave me immediate support, focused me, and told me what I needed to know to start working at Artemis. I've always known that the Safe House branch of Delos offered help for abused women and children, getting them back on their feet and sometimes training them to run a small business. Whatever Delos could do to help them get back their self-confidence was up for consideration, as long as it gave them hope for a future. They wouldn't ever have to rely on a man to provide income or food again."

"And those are all worthy goals," Gage agreed.

"Yes, and they're right up my alley. And I've already been able to put in place a new directive for Safe House." Her mouth flattened, anger coming to her eyes. "I had heard, off and on, about women and children being kidnapped and sent into sexual slavery, Gage. I'd read it in the newspaper or hear it on the news. But it never impacted me . . . until now."

"And of course it does." Gage nodded understandingly.

"Better believe it," she agreed hotly. "Look, I've had the experience, or close enough to it. I never want to see a child or woman treated like that. I've been in a number of international meetings with Mom, her brothers, and my cousin Angelo. I've pushed through the directive that we give sexual slavery top priority, right along with foreign fathers stealing their American children from their wives and hiding them so mother and child will never reunite. I've been working closely with Becka because she's tied into the local rape crisis center in Washington, D.C. I'm also working with women advocates across the world now, gathering all of them into one network where we can share information with one another."

Her voice deepened with emotion. "I just didn't know, Gage. I didn't know, until it happened to me, what a horrific, life-changing, awful experience a child or woman goes through when captured and forced into sexual slavery."

Gage held her anguished gaze and gently stroked her hand. "But you're doing something positive about it now, Alexa. That's as good as it gets down here. I'm really proud of you, and proud of what you're doing."

Her shoulders slumped and she nodded. "Thanks. You know, it helps me, too, Gage. I have so much anger inside it scares the hell out of me. Becka told me it's normal, but I can't live like this. I've always been a very upbeat, positive person, as you know, but this experience has slammed me to the ground, and it's changed me forever. It's made me realize something that's so ugly about men. It's hard to swallow some days. There are some major sickos out there, and they're everywhere, even here in the States."

Gage reached out, sliding his hand along her shoulders. "You're throwing yourself into this, and that's great, but I wonder if you're giving yourself enough time to heal . . ." He frowned, his concern clearly etched on his face.

She laughed abruptly. "You and Becka, you're a pair! She's been on me about that, too. In a way, Gage, I need to do this, because it fulfills me. I love focusing on this issue and getting the network up and functioning. Then I can bring together all the groups that are trying to rescue these women and children from such a terrible existence. I'm taking all the anger boiling inside me and using it proactively to make positive changes. I'm scheduled to go before a Senate hearing next month with Sarina Elstad from Oslo, Norway. Her younger sister, Kiara, was kidnapped off a street in that city at twenty years old. She ended up in the country of Malgar, a sex slave to Valdrin Rasari." Her lips flattened, her voice tight. "That son of a bitch is the most powerful sex trafficker in the world. Sarina's father is very rich, and he spent years trying to find Kiara. They finally sent in a black ops team and were able to rescue her at age twenty-four." She shook her head. "Poor Kiara. Those four years broke her, and Sarina has become a major world voice against sex traffickers as a result. When she speaks, people listen. There are other women advocates who are front and center on this issue. Because Delos is throwing its considerable weight and importance as a charity into it, it sends the Senate a message. We can't wait to get legislation started."

"It's a good first effort," he agreed, holding her pained gaze. "We can only change the world one step at a time."

"You're right." She studied him the dusk light, his face shadowed but so strong-looking. "I need to know how you became so sensitive to me and my situation, Gage. From the stories you've shared with me about your past, you had a really happy family like ours. When I was nearly hysterical after you rescued me, you seemed to know what I was experiencing. You had the right words; you were able to reach me when no one else could. I was in such chaos."

Tilting her head, Alexa studied him. "I've had enough time to look back on what you did for me, Gage. And I know something tragic happened to your family. I know they're gone, but you never told me what happened to them. Will you? Because I feel it's such a powerful part of you. No one had the words for me, the depth of understanding you had, when you got me out of that hellhole. My poor parents were floundering, unsure of what to say or do. But you didn't—because you knew! How, Gage? Please tell me."

Gage felt his gut twist and knot. He'd known this day would come. He stopped rocking the swing. "Would you like to go for a sunset walk on that trail near the cabin?" he asked her. He knew he couldn't sit still and do this, and he saw Alexa give him a small smile.

"Sure." She stood up, holding out her hand to him. "Come on . . ."

The trail was shadowed in a pink wash, winding through the trees. Gage walked with Alexa, his arm around her shoulder as they moved down the flat, wide expanse, deeper into the woodlands.

At first, the words came hard and there were a lot of silences between them. Alexa's arm was around his waist and he absorbed her warmth, her womanly strength. He left nothing out. He felt Alexa squeeze him, holding him close to her, giving him silent reassurance. Sometimes, he heard a soft moan coming from her, an expression of sympathy for him.

They entered a small clearing, the shadows gathering as the last of the pink and red sunset began to slowly dissolve on the western horizon. Gage turned and rested his arms across her shoulders, looking down into her anguished features. Alexa would always be very sensitive to the pain others experienced; it was her nature, he realized.

"I live with my guilt that I was late that afternoon to walk my sister home from school. I've often wondered whether, if I'd been there, that gang would have attacked her."

Alexa heard the heaviness in his tone and saw the raw guilt on his face. "But that was completely out of your control, Gage. You had no way of knowing. You didn't plan on that teacher wanting to talk to you at the last minute, delaying you so you couldn't meet Jen."

"I know, sweetheart, but it's not a rational thing. It still eats at my soul."

She moved forward, leaning lightly against Gage, her arms curling around his shoulders, which carried so much tension in them. "Becka has gotten me to realize that there was nothing I could have done going to that village with you that morning. Neither of us could have known what was waiting for us. We did the best we could, Gage, under horrendous circumstances."

"But I felt danger," he rasped. "I felt it when we landed, and I couldn't pinpoint it until it was too late, Alexa."

"And that's because you're a sniper, so you're attuned to everything around you. But it doesn't make you perfect and it doesn't mean you'll know what that threat is, Gage. That's asking way too much of yourself." She held his clouded gaze, felt his pain. "It's the same as not knowing that your teacher's holding you up would put Jen in jeopardy. You can't see the future, Gage. None of us can."

He made a grumbling sound, shaking his head.

"The 'if only's' of life plague both of us," she offered him, looking deep into his troubled blue eyes, which were filled now with agony. "If only I hadn't decided to go out to that village. If only I didn't believe in helping others who have less than I do." Alexa reached up, brushing a few strands of hair off his furrowed brow. "But there are positive 'if only's' too, Gage. If only I hadn't decided at the last minute to meet Matt at the canteen. I wouldn't have met you. If only I hadn't kissed you in the Humvee . . . well, you know the rest."

She gave him a sad smile, her hand grazing his face, all her love in that touch. "If only you didn't have the courage to kiss me back. We can't live our lives in that kind of tortured state. We can only do our best at the time, Gage. That's as good as it's going to get for all of us."

"I know you're right," he offered gruffly, moving his fingers along her shoulders, feeling the heat of her skin beneath the fabric. "There are better days when I can put it in that perspective. And then there are worse days when I sink down into the guilt regarding Jen. My one act got not only her murdered but my dad as well. And it broke my mother in ways I can't even begin to imagine."

She whispered his name, leaning up, her lips brushing his mouth. He'd withheld so much pain from the past. Her fingers gliding upward, framing his face, she opened her lips, feeling his hungry response to her, hearing a groan come from deep within him. For this one moment, Alexa wanted to give back to Gage. Yes, she'd had part of her soul destroyed by the captivity and torture. She knew she'd never get it back. But Gage? He had been a thirteen-year-old boy who had been snared in a circumstance no one could have foreseen.

Her heart opened wide, wanting to surround Gage with angel wings, wanting to give back to him all the love, care, and tenderness he'd always effortlessly given her. This was the man she loved. And that had never been clearer than it was right now.

She felt him give to her again as he embraced her, despite his pain. She lay fully against him, their breath now shallow, quickening as their mouths eagerly sought one another. He tasted of coffee, of lemon cream cake, his scent driving her crazy with need for Gage in every possible way. Sliding her hands through his short hair, nestling her hips against his, she felt the strength of his erection, and a low moan of desire vibrated in her throat.

Gage tensed, his mouth opening hers, his tongue coaxing her own. Her nerves heated, desire becoming an ache between her thighs, sending the signal through her that only Gage could relieve. Alexa knew he would be the consummate lover, more concerned for her pleasure than his own. Gage had always put her first, and he would when she finally surrendered herself over to him. How often had she dreamed of just this moment!

Lips tingling, she pulled away, caught in his narrow, dark gaze as he studied her. "I want to love you," she whispered unsteadily.

"Are you sure?" he rasped.

Alexa understood the nature of his question as he searched her gaze, worry beneath his yearning response. She stepped back a few inches, moving her hands down his arms, feeling the tightness of his muscles. "I'm sure I want you, Gage. I know I've got issues because of what they did to me in that cave. But you're aware of them now."

"I am," he said, catching her hands, holding them. "I want to take you to bed with me, Alexa. I want to love you, but I worry about that. You need to be in control. You need to tell me whatever it is that might make you uncomfortable."

"I will, Gage. More than anything, I trust you. I trusted you throughout the kidnapping ordeal, remember? You could hold me, kiss me, and I never felt panic or anxiety. I always felt just the opposite—I drank in all your love, your care, and your protection." She gave a small shrug. "I've talked to Becka about this. I haven't had sex in a year and a half. My job as a pilot, the demands and stresses on us and our time, never gave me an opening to have a relationship—until I met you. And then I found myself trying to figure out a way to get you alone and get you in my bed." She grinned a little sheepishly.

He smiled, moving wisps of hair away from her ear. "I was plotting and planning the same thing, believe me."

"We're always on the same wavelength, aren't we?"

He became serious, cupping her shoulders, keeping his gaze on her warm smile. "We always have been, whether we talked about what we were going through or not. I wanted to give us the time we needed, Alexa. I wasn't expecting you to be kidnapped and injured. Now, I'm concerned about how you'll react to my loving you. And I'll confess, I even visited Major Donahue, the flight surgeon, and talked to her about you. I told her I was falling in love with you, and that when I got out I was going to hunt you down and see if we could make a life together. I told her that if we could, I was worried about how you would react to having sex with me."

"And what did she say?"

"Well, she pointed out that rape survivors all react differently to a man loving them. On the plus side, though, she said that because you never saw me as the man who hurt you, it meant you still trusted me, and it was a very positive sign that you wanted me to hold you and kiss you. She said if I touched you wherever you had been hurt—it might cause a reaction, like a flashback. But most important, she told me to talk to you and get everything out front. She said you might not know your own reaction until I actually touched you in a certain area. If you flinched, froze, or tensed, I needed to stop and do as you needed at that point."

"Becka told me the same thing. She explained that my body is a minefield right now, and neither of us would know what it would or wouldn't react to. She said the mind remembers everything, for better or worse. My body has physical memories of what happened to me, and they're beneath the surface. I won't know until you do touch me, Gage." She gave him an apologetic look.

"The major said that if we were both willing to love one another, it was a positive step, because some women, after being raped, don't ever want a man to touch them again—even men they know."

"I love your touch," Alexa whispered. "So please, Gage, never stop connecting with me. When I was spiraling down into that hell, you were there, you coaxed me with your voice, your hands . . . your kisses . . . it all helped pull me back from that abyss. It allowed me to breathe, to catch my breath, to accept that my emotions were wild and raw. Your being there supported and strengthened me. There's never been a time when I didn't want your kisses, your care." She smiled up into his eyes, seeing relief enter them. "You can't hurt me," she said. "I know that, despite all that's happened to me. And I want you. Does that help?"

He released a shaky breath. "Yeah, it helps. It's not a guarantee, but we've talked honestly, and I have a much better feel for how you are now, Alexa. All I can say is, I will always put you first, whether it's in or out of bed."

She looked at him tenderly. "I know that, and I love you for it. Please, Gage, it will all be okay. I just know it will be."

"I think," he admitted wryly, "you have more trust in me than I have in myself."

"Then," she said, giving him a sweet look of yearning, "let's walk back to the cabin and find out." She curled her fingers into his. "More than anything, Gage, I've been waiting to love you from the moment I met you. Nothing's changed. It never will . . ."

★

"ARE YOU PROTECTED?" Gage asked her as she sat on the edge of the mattress of the king-size bed. He pulled off his boots, setting them aside.

"Yes." She smiled as she moved her shoes beneath the bed. "And I'm healthy."

Gage said, "So am I." What was left of the sunset, a pinkish hue, filled her bedroom. The window was open to allow in the sweet, pine-scented air. The room was rustic, with an old oak dresser, a braided rug of red, yellow, and blue beneath the large bed. There were hurricane lamps with small light bulbs in them. A large porcelain bowl with a white pitcher placed in it sat on top of the dresser. He liked the colorful quilt across the bed, matching the colors of the rug beneath it.

Gage watched the play of light across Alexa's soft features, her braids giving her the look of a schoolgirl. "Let me undo your braids? Your hair has always called to me."

Alexa moved to the center of the bed and knelt there beside him. "Come here," she whispered, "and please unbraid my hair."

Gage felt every muscle in his body screaming for her. He'd never wanted a woman like he wanted Alexa. It was that trust in her eyes that sent a powerful wave of love washing through him as he moved to her, their knees touching one another. "I've never unbraided a woman's hair before," he said almost shyly, untying the red yarn holding the first one. He watched as his touch made her eyes half close. Alexa rested against her heels, her hands on her curved thighs. "You're so damned sexy," he muttered, quickly and easily pulling the strands apart. "You're as sensual as a cat. Did you know that?"

Alexa made a soft sound in her throat as he eased the strands apart. "I'll be your cat, then," she whispered.

He opened the second braid, the strands falling into his fingers. The pleasure he felt as he slid them slowly through that thick, shining red mass made his erection tighten against his jeans.

Alexa tipped her head back as he slid his fingers across her scalp, moving those sleek strands, watching the setting sun catch the crimson, gold, and sable colors running through them.

"Mmm, that feels delicious, Gage," she whispered. "Don't stop . . . I love your touch . . . want it . . .need it . . .need you . . ." She closed her eyes, drowning in the radiating heat wherever he massaged her scalp and sent his fingers tunneling through her unbound hair.

Heartened, he leaned over, feathering light kisses against her exposed throat, hearing almost a purr catch in it, watching as her lips parted, their corners lifting as he continued to slowly nip, lick, and then kiss his way down to her slender collarbone. Moving his hands through that abundant mass, he brought it across her shoulders, allowing it to tumble down her back. Gage monitored her closely, watching as her nipples hardened beneath her tee, watched her fingers begin to open and spread on her thighs, heard her breath quicken. Gage had had his share of women in his life and was well aware of the signs that sensual hunger was beginning to escalate. Just the way her lips tilted upward told him he was giving her pleasure. Easing his fingers beneath the edge of her tee, he observed Alexa more closely.

When she was kidnapped, she had been stripped of her clothes and was naked and vulnerable to the men who had captured her. He allowed his fingertips to glide against her warm body, feeling her breath catch as he slowly lifted her T-shirt up. She barely opened her eyes, so caught up was she in his slow, deliberate exploration, their closeness. When she did open her eyes to gaze at him, they burned with desire for him.

Alexa lifted her arms so he could bring the material up and over her breasts. There was a slight flush on her cheeks, and her breath became more and more shallow. He saw she wore a lacy lavender bra that barely held in her breasts, the nipples hidden just beneath that delicate lace. How he wanted to lean down and capture one of them in his mouth as he pulled the tee off her.

The animal in him wanted to take her hard and fast, feasting upon her slender, velvet, hot flesh but his heart counseled differently, and he listened to it. He dropped her shirt on the floor, meeting her barely opened eyes. Already, she was beginning to melt at his very contact, and before Gage could ease the straps from her shoulders, she gave him a sensual smile.

"Now it's my turn," she said, her voice smoky with desire, reaching out to slide her fingers beneath his T-shirt. "You have the most beautiful chest, Gage. You have no idea how long I've wanted to touch you all over . . ."

He returned her feral smile with one of his own and let her lift up his T-shirt and pull it off. It landed next to hers on the floor. "Touch me anywhere you want, sweetheart. I'm all yours," he told her, never having wanted her more than he did that very moment.

"Lie down on your back? I want to explore you . . . ," Alexa gently instructed. "I'm in charge now." She leaned down and kissed him deeply.

Gage remembered what Major Donahue had told him about allowing Alexa to take the lead. It was important that she feel in control, not the other way around. Gage couldn't have been happier to lie down, placing his hands behind his head on the pillow. He saw Alexa's hunger and in response, his erection grew even harder.

She surprised him by straddling him after she removed her jeans and her panties. Now all she wore was that delectable scrap of bra that held her beautiful breasts. He loved her boldness as she knelt above him, her thighs against his hips. And when she spread her long fingers open, palms flat against his hard belly, slowly easing them upward, as if memorizing him, Gage groaned, closing his eyes, surrendering to her exploration of his body.

His flesh leaped and tightened beneath her exploring hands, the heat of her palms inciting a riot within him, making him tense as she began to tangle her fingertips through the dusting of dark hair across his chest.

"You feel so good to me," she crooned softly, leaning over and brushing his lips with hers. "You're so hard, so powerful, Gage."

Her words fired through him, making every nerve leap and throb wherever she smoothed her hands across his chest and neck. Then she enclosed each of his broad shoulders with her warm hands and massaged them. This woman knew how to pleasure a man, no question. And when she leaned down, her lips moving against his nipple, Gage almost came undone.

He automatically released his hands from beneath his head, gripping her shoulders, sucking air between his clenched teeth. Jesus! He hadn't expected this! And the raging fire from his nipple down to his throbbing erection damn near did him in. He felt her lips leave him and a breathless laugh followed as she pulled out of his grasp.

"Don't touch me, not yet," she whispered. "Just lie there, Gage, okay?"

Opening his eyes, his breathing harsh, he grunted, "Easy for you to say."

She sat up, nestling herself against his hard erection beneath the jeans. "I've wanted to do this for so long, Gage . . . let me keep exploring? Just a little while longer. I just love feeling you like this."

Gage automatically lifted his hips, wanting that feminine heat of hers, feeling how damp she was, the fabric of his jeans soaking up her sweet fluids. He'd have given anything to touch her there, kiss her there, love her right there, right now. The flushed look on her cheeks, the dancing arousal in her eyes, told him he had to stand down, as painful as that was going to be. Above all, Alexa's trust was center stage. Gage had no idea how far they could go or if he could even enter her, much less fully love her.

Alexa had been right: they were both walking through a minefield. And the ache in his erection tripled as she moved her body slowly from side to side, teasing him.

And then she placed her hands flat against his abs, sidling down to his long thighs. He watched through narrowed eyes as her long, graceful fingers unsnapped his jeans and slowly unzipped them. His erection was thick, heavy, and sprang upward, only to be trapped by the light blue boxer shorts he wore. He watched the pleasure in her face as she slowly moved her fingers teasingly over him. Groaning, he arched into her hand, never wanting her to let him go, feeling the burning ache intensify beneath her knowing fingers as she felt him.

"You," she whispered, releasing him, "are so beautiful," and she eased off him and tugged and pulled his jeans off him. Then she came back, asking him to lift his hips so she could pull his boxer shorts down. Gage had one hell of a time remaining on his back, doing as she asked. His erection was free. He watched as her gaze moved to it and she licked her lower lip, which sent a wave of fire through him. He had no idea what she was going to do next and at this point he didn't care. Every contact was sensual and even better she was so bold. He loved her so much; he wished these moments would never end.

Most important was that their first time be good for Alexa. If they could just cross that minefield together, if he didn't make the wrong move or in some way bring back a tortured memory, Gage was going to feel like the luckiest damned man in the world.

CHAPTER 21

ALEXA WAS OVERWHELMED by the heat, strength, and love she felt for Gage. Her initial anxiety—her fear that she would freeze or not want to be touched intimately by him—began to dissolve. She prayed he would understand and allow her to reintroduce herself sexually, because the fear that she would hate it was very real. And she'd been too afraid to tell Gage that, even though he was the most understanding man she'd ever met. He'd done nothing to make her think he wouldn't accept her fears or help her work through them, and with his help, she was becoming swept up in the heat of her fierce love for him, his groans making her wet and her thighs slick.

There were so many wild emotions loosening up within her. Fear clashed with hunger, and love with anxiety that she'd be rejected. She was afraid she couldn't respond as she had in the past, and at the same time was excited by Gage's harsh breathing, his hands gathered in the quilt, and her own knuckles whitening as she tried to topple her resistance to her need for physical intimacy.

She saw the intensity of fire in his eyes for her, felt it in his erection, which lay like hard, warm steel against her slick entrance. Saw it in the grimace on his face as he fought to give her what she wanted. He loved her so much he was willing to grant her what she needed in this blazing moment. And her entire body ached to have him within her.

"Just a little longer," she gasped, her breath harsh, her hands tight against his chest as she closed her eyes. That moment turned molten as she took him into her, a slow, rocking inch at a time, as if feeling her way, literally, through the halls of her fears, anxiety, and consuming need for Gage. She felt guilty for not telling him why she needed him this way, why she had to prove this to herself, to her body. The moment he slid into her, he growled her name, gripping her arms, arching into her. His thick, hard length opened her, stretched her, burned, and then her body accommodated him as Gage stroked her gently, firing off the nerves within her, making her cry out as they were both hurled into a white-hot cauldron of excruciating pleasure. She was so lost, tumbling, feeling her body react and tighten upon him as he surged into her, taking her, bringing forth another desperate cry from her.

"More, Gage . . . more . . . please . . ."

Her hoarse pleading broke the hold he had kept on himself. He slid his hands around her back, releasing her bra, watching her breasts tumble free, and her peaks ripe and hard. Leaning upward, he took her nipple into his mouth, suckling her. Instantly, she was galvanized, her back arching, head thrown back, more whimpers coming from her. Gage could feel her body releasing more juices, surrounding him as he thrust into her welcoming confines. Her fingers dug into his chest, her breath hitching, small cries torn from her.

He released her and moved to the other breast, and the moment he captured her peak, he felt a convulsion grip his erection. She cried out, freezing. Radiance suffused her face.

Nothing ever made him feel as good as a woman having an orgasm. He growled Alexa's name, settled his hands around her soft hips, rocking into her and increased the pace, increasing her pleasure, her whole upper body flushed from the ongoing orgasm imploding through her. He twisted his hips, moving as deeply into her as he could, reaching that secret spot within her that triggered an additional orgasm.

And then she sobbed. Tears rushed down her cheeks. As the orgasm ebbed, Gage brought her down against the length of his body, holding her. Alexa buried her face against his neck, her arms tight around him. Her body shaking, he soothed her with his hands as he stroked her back, whispering words of love to her, nuzzling into her loose, tousled red hair. He could smell her sex and ached to release within her but kept his steel control, because something else was going on here, although Gage had no idea what it was. He could feel her shaking, her sobs deep, her body shuddering.

He kissed her hair and kept talking to her quietly, rocking her a little in his arms, allowing her to cling to him.

Finally, Gage eased out of her, drawing her onto her back while he propped himself up on one elbow, beside her. Alexa spooned against him, and he held her, gentling her, listening to her sobs lessen over time. Finally, she stopped crying and he leaned down, kissing her wet cheek. More than anything, he wanted her to know that it was all right for her to cry. As she lifted her hand, pushing her hair away from her face, she barely opened her eyes.

He smiled faintly. "I've never had a woman cry after an orgasm," he teased.

Sniffing, Alexa swiped at her tears. "I-I was so scared, Gage," she managed to say, her voice strained.

The look of apology she gave him totaled Gage. "What do you mean? Did I scare you?"

"N-no . . . I was scared."

Gage lay very still, understanding for the first time. Alexa was vulnerable and fragile in his arms, her slender, warm, body molding to his. They fit well together. He caressed her cheek, looking deep into her bruised eyes. "You were worried that you might not want to make love with me?"

He saw her barely nod, licking her lips, licking the tears out of the corners of her mouth.

"Well," he said huskily, "it seemed to me everything was working fine. I thought I might have hurt you."

She reached out, tangling her fingertips through the hair on his chest. "No, you would never hurt me, Gage. It was me, my own head. I was so worried that I'd freeze, or I couldn't go through with it. I was afraid to tell you that . . ."

Easing his hand down her back, cupping her cheeks, he gave her a warm look. "There is nothing wrong with you or your body. Trust me on that one."

"But I-I used you, Gage. I didn't want you to touch me for fear I might react badly. I needed to make sure I was going to be all right and be able to enjoy sex again."

He eased his fingers through her hair, caressing her, caring for her, hearing the fear and strain in her halting, wobbling voice. "You didn't use me, Alexa. Hell, I enjoyed it."

"I'm so messed up, Gage," she choked out, shaking her head. "I've been trying so hard to put that kidnapping behind me . . ."

"It's not that easy. You're in a hurry, and you can't be. It takes time. A lot of time."

Alexa buried her head on his chest, holding him. "I just want to love you, Gage, like you really deserve."

A rumble moved through his chest as he laid her on her back, his arm beneath her neck, her red hair a shining mass. "You are my life, did you know that?" He took his thumb, moving it lightly across her lower lip. "When I saw you, I thought I was gazing at the sun, the moon, and the stars. You were so alive, Alexa, that I felt your energy filling me up." He feathered small kisses across her brow, whispering, "You lifted me out of my darkness, whether you knew it or not. I wasn't really living since my family was murdered. So much of me died that day. And then, five years later, my mother died, shortly after I joined the Marine Corps. I was hurting so much, I felt cut off from life." He raised his head, his brows knitted, his eyes looking into the darkness that now embraced them in the room.

"You fed me, Alexa. You fed my imprisoned heart, my dying soul. I had such a powerful experience when you walked into the canteen that I felt like my life changed from darkness into light." He saw her eyes widen, saw much anguish dissolve, replaced with wonder and awe as he spoke to her. His mouth curved faintly as he trailed his fingertips down the length of her neck, kissing the pulse beating at the base of it, feeling her life beneath his mouth.

Moving his tongue down her slender collarbone, he felt her arch, a low moan slipping from her parted lips. Gage was going to taste every inch of her sweet, hot body, show her just how alive she really was, help her stop listening to her worries about being only half a woman. She was *all* woman and he was going to show her right now.

Curving his hand around her breast, he felt how firm it was. Brushing his lips across that peak, he felt her quiver in his arms, gasping as he began to tease it with his lips and tongue. Gage was going to melt her mind, fuse her body with his, and feel her take flight in his arms, because he loved this incredibly brave woman.

He could easily forgive her for not telling him what she feared most, because she was still in the middle of a long recovery. It had taken him five years to deal with his initial grief and the loss of Jen and his dad. Hers wouldn't take that long, he hoped, if he had anything to do with it. He was going to love her so completely, so thoroughly, that all she felt was him. All she smelled was him. All she tasted was him. And all she saw was him, because he loved her.

Alexa felt herself drifting into fire and pleasure, the two inseparable as he teased and suckled each nipple. She writhed and bucked her hips against his hard, warm length, wanting desperately to please him, because she'd taken everything he'd given her but had given nothing in return. And Gage made it so easy to give to him, open herself to him, lavish him with her sinuous body molding to him and writhing against his powerful, quivering form. His tongue was wickedly licking her, tasting her, and he made a gruff sound of appreciation deep within his chest, his mouth moving lower and lower to her belly, to the juncture between her legs. By the time his mouth, hands, and tongue had trailed a white-hot path of fire to her aching lower body, all thoughts had been banished, burned up in the river of her need for him.

He knelt between her thighs, his callused hands easing them apart, and she opened fully to him, gripping his hunched shoulders as he came over her, his hands on either side of her head, his gaze dark and smoldering. This time, Alexa smiled with anticipation, feeling free at last of her inner darkness as he nestled himself against her thick, honeyed gate. Calling out his name, her fingers digging into his shoulders, pulling him toward her, lifting her hips and feeling him thrust into her, brought her into his world of aching need. Gage. Only Gage.

He thrust into her, claiming her, taking her, riding with her undulating hips, whispering her name roughly against her ear. He gripped her thick hair, holding her in place, plunging into her, making her cry out with pleasure, her back arching into him, meeting every thrust with equal joy and lightness. Her heart sang. Her body was singing a song of love with Gage, their rhythm strong and steady between them, their breaths coming in gasps, their bodies damp with sweat, gliding effortlessly against one another.

She felt the building pressure of another orgasm stalking her with each thrust, each harsh explosion from between his clenched teeth. He carried her with him as she lost all awareness except for that of Gage's body, his hard muscles guiding, plunging, her cries against his neck, her eyes tightly shut, riding waves of pleasure he was creating within her. And just as she screamed, her fingers clenched into his short hair at the back of his head. It felt as if her body had imploded with the force of the sun bursting within her.

She felt Gage suddenly stiffen, his hips jerking, his hands tightening into her hair, holding her very still as she felt his release flooding her. Her orgasm was a fiery torrent, bathing his erection, buried in her to the hilt. In those liquefying moments when she spun out into a galaxy of exploding stars, all she felt, all she absorbed was Gage's body fused with hers.

Gage collapsed upon her, his face inches from hers, sweat beading his drawn brow, his eyes slits, his breath coming in hard gasps as he released her hair, his hand trembling over her temple and cheek. It was that male smile tugging at the corners of his beautifully shaped mouth that made her smile in return. She touched his nose with her own, closing her eyes, drowning in the light and beauty he had spun around them with his kisses, his hands, and that wickedly delicious tongue of his.

Alexa leaned into him, her lips coming to rest upon his, their breath moist and mingling.

"I love you, Gage Hunter," she said as she opened her eyes, drowning in his glittering blue gaze. Weakly, she raised her hand, her fingers trailing against his cheek. "I love you . . ."

He caught her hand, placing a kiss in her palm. "You're mine," he growled, pinning her with a dark look. "You always were. Now we just made it official." He gave her the hungry look of a wolf claiming his mate—her.

How much younger Gage looked at that moment. Her body hummed with heat and ongoing sweet contractions of pleasure because he was still embedded within her, a part of her. And she didn't ever want him to leave her. He was a heavy, warm blanket of the most wonderful kind. Even now, he was potent, and she could feel him growing once more within her as he twisted his hips, teasing her.

"I was flying," she confided, smiling against his mouth.

"So was I. You are incredible. One of a kind." He lifted away, propping himself up on one elbow, leaning over her, studying her with a sniper's intensity. Smoothing strands of hair sticking to her temple and cheek, he leaned down, nibbling on her earlobe, nipping it, lavishing her velvet skin as she moaned.

"I love you, Alexa Culver. You're the only woman I ever want in my arms." His low, gruff words flowed through her like sunlight piercing the dark storm clouds that remained within her. She barely opened her eyes, engulfed in the love shining for her alone.

"When didn't we love one another, I wonder," she asked, meeting his liquid gaze, consumed and surrounded by the love she could feel embracing her within. She was in his arms, nestled next to his body, well loved physically and even more so emotionally. This man knew how to show his love without fear, without any thought other than filling her wounded soul with his own body, mind, and heart.

Easing out of her, he rasped, "Stay put. I'll be back in a moment."

Alexa nodded, missing him already, her body glowing, still throbbing with satiation. She closed her eyes, sinking back onto the bed. She must have dozed, because she awakened when the bed dipped. Gage came over and sat facing her, a warm cloth in his hand and a small towel. Her heart turned with love for him as he gently cleaned her up. It brought tears to her eyes as she lay there watching him care for her. Never had a man done this for her.

"You have to be sore," he murmured. "A year and a half without a partner . . . and we went at it pretty hard."

Her lips pulled upward. "Hard? Is that a pun, Hunter?"

His mouth moved into a boyish smile as he gently wiped the inside of each of her thighs. "Guess it could be, couldn't it?"

"You're unbelievable." Alexa reached out, her fingers grazing his shoulder. "You didn't have to do this . . ."

He gave her a warm look. "You need a little TLC."

Wasn't that the truth? She lay back, closing her eyes, absorbing his tender ministrations. "I think you're a figment of my imagination come to life," she murmured, reaching down, her fingers brushing his hard thigh.

"Oh? Were you dreaming of bedding a sniper before I met you?"

Alexa managed a choked laugh. "I like your dry sense of humor after making love. Don't stop. I love it." And then she lost her smile, meeting and melting beneath his smoldering look. "I love you, Gage."

"I know you do." He moved the soft towel between her thighs. "I saw it often in your eyes. I wanted to believe in what I saw, Alexa, but I talked myself into thinking I was imagining it. Pretty dumb, huh?"

"Why?"

He patted the insides of her thighs and stood up, placing the towel and cloth on a nearby chair. Coming back to bed, he put a couple of pillows against the headboard and then sat down, his back against them. "Come here," he rasped, pulling her up to her knees. "Close to me . . ."

She loved being pulled across his long, muscular thighs, cosseted beneath his right arm, her head coming to rest on his broad, capable shoulder. Sighing, she said, "I could get used to this. I like how you hold me after we make love."

"Best time is always afterward," Gage agreed, easing her hair away from her cheek, leaning down, his mouth tenderly moving against her lips, loving her all over again.

"Mmmm," she managed to say, that happy sound in her throat as she responded eagerly to his slow, molten kiss. She glided her hand across his chest, feeling the dampness of his skin, the silkiness of his hair sprinkled across it. His kiss was intimate, slowly drugging her mind, bringing her satisfied body back to life, encouraging the flames that had been reduced to glowing embers to reignite. And as he cupped her breast, her flesh prickled, her nipples tightening, wanting his attention once more.

Already, Alexa could feel his erection lengthening, thickening against her hip as she lay across him. Gage was a thorough lover, but then, he was a sniper, wasn't he? Snipers were into the details, and she moaned as he lavished her nipple with his thumb, sending bolts of heat downward through her, stoking those coals to burning life once more. She swore she could feel him saturating all his senses with her, and it made her smile beneath his mouth as it lazily explored hers.

"What are you smiling about?" he asked, pulling away just enough to engage her half-closed eyes.

"You . . . how you don't miss one inch of me, anywhere. That's the sniper in you. You're into all the details."

His mouth curved and he chuckled. "It's who I am."

"Oh," Alexa sighed, "don't ever change. I love how you just loved me. I feel so very, very spoiled."

He studied her in the darkness, a small night-light shedding just enough illumination so that he could see the soft curve of her face, the radiance in her eyes, the joy surrounding her. "I intend to spoil you every day in large and small ways. Wait and see."

"You touched my heart so deeply when you brought me that bouquet of roses when I was at Bagram. Do you remember?"

He grimaced and gave a short laugh. "Yeah, I remember hunting all over the base to find you red roses. And the only ones on that damned base were two days from wilting."

"I loved them," she said softly, holding his amused expression. "They meant so much to me, Gage. I knew it was January, and I don't know how you even found them. It blew my mind."

"Your eyes are about to close," he rasped, kissing her cheek, sliding his hand down the curve of her back. "Go to sleep. I'll hold you safe . . . forever, if you'll let me."

CHAPTER 22

ALEXA DIDN'T WANT to leave their cabin and go back to Alexandria. Gage had gone into a small nearby town as she packed her luggage. Her body glowed from their lovemaking just before lunch, and she had to admit, she couldn't get enough of what he gave her. She knew it was love—real love. Before, when she'd thought she'd fallen in love, it hadn't been even close.

Outside, the June sky was clearing, turning a light blue and cloudless. The scent of pine, of fresh, clean air, gently moved through the cabin's opened windows. It was nearly two P.M., and she heard Gage drive into the parking area in front of the cabin. She folded the last of her clothes, tucking them into her luggage, and smiled softly, looking at Gage's black nylon bag. His was one-third the size of her luggage.

"Hey," Gage greeted her, standing in the doorway

She turned, startled. He knew how to walk without ever being heard. Standing there in those jeans outlining his powerful lower body, that dark green T-shirt that showed off his deep chest and broad shoulders, she smiled. In his hand was a bouquet of red roses, gold foil wrapped with a bright emerald-green ribbon surrounding them.

"Oh, Gage!" Her heart turned to mush as she ran over to him. "Gage . . . you shouldn't have . . ." She saw him give her the smoldering look of a man who loved her with his life.

"This is to make up for those old bedraggled ones from Bagram," he said, sliding the dozen red roses into her opening hands. Leaning over, he kissed her. "For you, sweetheart."

Deeply touched, she sank her face into the healthy red roses. "Mmmm, they smell wonderful, Gage!" She lifted her face, smiling into his darkening blue eyes. Alexa knew that look. He wanted to love her one more time before they left the cabin, and so did she.

"Come sit with me on the porch swing for a moment?" he said. "I have something I need to share with you."

"Sure," she said, taking his hand. "Let me put these in a vase in the kitchen first, okay?"

"For sure," he chortled. "We don't want any more wimpy red roses for you, do we?"

She laughed with him. In no time, she'd found a glass vase and placed the roses in it. "I love the gold foil and green ribbon," she offered, turning to him as he waited for her.

"It's the color of your eyes when I hold you in my arms."

He was so romantic. Alexa melted beneath the hungry look in his smiling eyes. "It's so thoughtful of you, though," she whispered, walking with him out to the porch. A robin sang nearby, the sun peering through the trees surrounding the cabin.

Today, she wore a set of loose white shorts, a sleeveless magenta tee, and her sandals. Gage brought her to the swing and they sat down, rocking it slowly back and forth. This was her favorite place to be with him—besides the bed.

Gage sat nearby, his knee touching hers. The sunlight was scattered and danced silently across the area. "I'm going to miss this place," he told her. "The quiet. The solitude."

"Me too," she sighed. Reaching out, she slid her hand into his. "But we can come up here any weekend, Gage. The whole family uses it, and we can check with Wyatt and Tal and Matt and Dara to make sure they aren't reserving it first."

"We'll work something out," he assured her. "We always do."

She leaned back, tipping her head against the cushions. "We do, don't we? No matter what, we made it this far together."

"Do you like what we have, Alexa?"

She became somber, her hand tightening around his. "I love it. I love you, Gage. I don't want life without you in it."

"Me either," he rasped. He pulled a small box from his jeans pocket, released her hand, and offered it to her. "I want what we have to be permanent when you're ready, Alexa. Open it, please?"

She sat up. It was a small black velvet box, a little worn and old. "What's this, Gage?"

"Gotta open it to find out." He sat there, watching the confusion in her expression. And then, when she opened the lid, a gasp flew out of her. Instantly, her eyes widened and she stared at him.

"Gage!"

He held on to his trip-hammering heart and slid his hand beneath hers as she held the two rings encased in the box. "This is my mother's wedding set that my dad bought for her when he proposed to her, Alexa. It's one of the few things I have left to remember them by." His voice deepened with emotion. "I love you. I know it's too soon to marry, but I need you to know that's how I see us growing and what I see us moving toward. I wanted to give you this set as a promise from me to you that I'm serious about you, about us. That I want, more than anything, a lifetime with you, not just living together."

She blinked back tears as she delicately touched the simple ring set. There was a small solitaire diamond engagement ring and a plain gold band with it. She saw some scratches on it, and it made her heart swell with love for Gage. Words stuck in her throat, and she closed the box, holding it in one hand, and turned, cupping his recently shaven face. Looking deep into his vulnerable eyes, she whispered, "I want the very same thing, Gage. I love you, now and forever," and she leaned forward, seeking and finding his mouth.

The moment turned heated and filled with promise as he groaned, sweeping her into his arms and putting all the fierce love he felt for Alexa into a deep, long kiss. He tasted the salt of her tears as they fell, but this time, Gage knew they were tears of joy.

Sliding his fingers through her loose, thick hair, he eased gradually from her mouth, holding her gaze.

"I'm not rich, Alexa, but money can't buy the love I have for you. I can only offer you myself and my heart, and hope that it's enough."

Totaled by his humility, Alexa whispered brokenly, "You have something money could never buy, darling. Your love for me, and all the times over the past six months you proved that you loved me. You risked your own life to save me and those women. If that isn't love, I don't know what is. Do you?"

He caressed her damp cheek, kissing her eyes, with that incredible warmth burning in their depths for him alone. "No, I don't. And I'd do it again if I had to." He smiled a little. "But that's not going to happen. We're here in the States, and you're safe. My job is make you feel protected, loved, so you can heal from the past." He threaded his fingers through her hair, the strands clean and strong, reminding Gage of Alexa's inner strength. "What I'd like to do is to go see Tal tomorrow and tell her I'm taking the job to head up the sniper department at Artemis. Then I'd like us to find a place, a house maybe, out in the farm country near where we work. I don't like the city, and you don't either. You can have any house you want, because I'll be making enough money to handle the mortgage. I want you happy, Alexa."

"That sounds perfect, Gage. It doesn't have to be a fancy house. I'm not fancy by nature."

He chuckled. "Well, that hotel of a house your parents have is huge."

"That's because my mom's global family comes for a visit at least two or three times a year," she laughed. "No, I'd love to find a small farmhouse with a little bit of land where we can go for walks—maybe even a hike every now and then."

"Sounds perfect to me." Gage closed his hand over hers, which held his ring box. "Keep these. I don't want to pressure you about marriage, Alexa. We're still learning a lot about one another. We have time now. And I'm fine with whatever you need. I just want to be there to support you, help you work through what happened."

Sniffing, she wiped her eyes with the back of her hand and then opened up the ring box. She pulled out the engagement ring. Something caught her eye and she saw there was an inscription on the inside of it: *I'll love you until I die, and beyond.*

Gage nodded, his voice deep with emotion. "My dad had that inscribed for my mom."

Holding the engagement ring, Alexa felt fresh tears rush to her eyes. "He loved her so much . . . just like you love me—and I love you."

★

TAL AND WYATT were at their condo when a knock came to their door Sunday evening. Tal was sitting on the couch and Wyatt was at the kitchen table, his laptop open, working on a software program.

"I'll get it," he told her.

"Are you expecting anyone, Wyatt?"

"Nope," he said, rising from the chair. They had just eaten dinner and he'd put the dirty dishes in the dishwasher.

Opening the door, Wyatt grinned. "Well, well, look what the cat drug in," he drawled, standing aside and gesturing for Alexa and Gage to come in.

Tal twisted around. "Alexa! You two back from the cabin? Come and sit down!" She rose, dropping her magazine on the sofa and walking toward them.

Alexa hugged her big sister and then Wyatt. "We wanted you to be the first to know," she said, breathless. Gage shook Wyatt's hand and nodded hello toward Tal. He came up, sliding his arm around Alexa's waist. "Look, Tal." She held up her left hand, the engagement ring sparkling.

Gasping, Tal held her hand and then looked over at them. "This is wonderful! And not exactly unexpected by someone in this room." She grinned at Wyatt.

Her fiancé chuckled and came over, patting Gage's shoulder as he came around to look at Alexa's engagement ring. He arched an eyebrow, giving Tal an amused look. "I did tell you so, didn't I?"

Tal wrinkled her nose. "Yes, you did, cowboy." She laughed and turned to Alexa and Gage. "Last Friday, Wyatt came into my office and said that Gage was going to marry you, Alexa."

Wyatt grinned broadly, his hands on his hips.

Gasping, Alexa turned to the tall ex-SEAL. "Truly?"

"Yes, ma'am," he confirmed. Giving Gage a merry look, he added, "It was pretty obvious to everyone except our CEO here," and gestured in Tal's direction.

"He's psychic as hell," Tal muttered, giving Wyatt a dark look. "The ring's beautiful, Alexa." She hugged her sister. "I'm so happy for you!" And then Tal released her and hugged Gage. "You're going to be my brother-in-law. I hope like hell that means you're taking that job we offered you?" she asked, releasing him.

Gage had the good grace to smile. "Of course I'll take the job, Tal. It's a great opportunity, and thanks for offering it to me."

Wyatt clapped him on the shoulder. "Good man. I knew you would!" He gave Tal a smug I-told-you-so look.

"Smartass," Tal muttered, giving him a sour grin.

"Hey, SEALs are pretty locked into the energy around them," Wyatt said, gesturing for the couple to come into their living room. "Come on in, boys and girls. This calls for a celebration. Beer or wine?"

"I'll take a beer," Gage called.

"White wine for me, Wyatt," Alexa said.

"You want a shot of whiskey?" Wyatt drawled, giving Tal a triumphant look.

"No," she muttered. "You're really rubbing salt into my wounds, Lockwood."

He chuckled as he opened the fridge door. "It isn't often I get to one-up you. Want some white wine, too?"

"Yes," Tal said, sitting down opposite Alexa and Gage. "Please."

"Okay, two beers for the men and two glasses of white wine for the ladies," he murmured, grinning like a wolf that had caught his prey.

Tal smarted beneath Wyatt's typical SEAL confidence and competitiveness. She slid a leg beneath her, resting against the other sofa opposite Gage and Alexa, the coffee table in between. "So? Have you set a date?"

"No," Alexa said, giving Gage a soft smile. "We've only known each other six months. We want to buy a small farmhouse somewhere near Artemis and live together for a while."

"Mom and Dad are going to be shocked," Tal said as Wyatt brought over two glasses of wine.

"Oh," Wyatt said, "I think your mom's already ahead of the game, darlin'. She knows."

Tal took the wine. "You really think so?"

"Your mother misses nothing," Wyatt said, grinning. "But then, you two gals should already know that from growing up with her."

Tal gave him a dirty look. "I hate know-it-alls," she grumped good-naturedly, the corners of her mouth tugging upward.

Wyatt came back with two bottles of cold beer beaded with condensation, handing one to Gage. "I'm just good, is all," he said, congratulating himself, giving Tal a warm look that spoke volumes. "Hey," he said, raising his beer, "here's to you, Alexa and Gage. Congratulations. Even if you aren't Navy, Gage, you are a Marine and part of the Navy. So, welcome to the family, brother."

Gage stood and clinked Wyatt's bottle, leaned across the coffee table, and touched Tal's proffered glass. He then sat down and lightly touched Alexa's glass. "To us," he said gruffly.

"To us," Alexa agreed, her voice trembling with emotion, her love for this man flooding her heart.

★

AUGUST

"WELCOME HOME," GAGE said as he carried Alexa across the threshold of their newly purchased farmhouse. He nudged open the screen door, the woman he loved in his arms, walking into the large living room of their hundred-year-old home.

Alexa sighed, her arms around his shoulders as he easily carried her into the huge parlor. "This is wonderful," she whispered, leaning over and kissing his jaw. They had found the two-story farmhouse five miles away from Artemis.

Alexa knew Gage had issues with his being poor while she was rich, something that Gage was reconciling within himself. They had spent the last month searching for turn-of-the-century furniture, and it had been a labor of love with Gage. He bought all of it with his own money, and Alexa approved it wholeheartedly. There were some pieces of furniture that he had in storage that had belonged to his family, and Alexa wanted them to be a part of their life. There was an oak table, hewn and made by hand, that had been passed down through his mother's side of the family since the 1700s. Now it graced their dining room, along with a set of twelve chairs.

This would be a place where her family could gather for a Sunday afternoon meal. Gage had grown up with that tradition, and Alexa wanted to bring that back to him, to give him warm memories of the past, but also build upon new ones that they would create together. He'd cried for the first time when she'd sat with him in the parlor after the table had arrived via a moving company. She'd held Gage as he finally cried for the loss of his family. She knew from many long, searching talks with him over the past few months how deeply wounded he had been by their sudden loss.

And just as he had so often held her when she'd burst into tears out of the blue, the shock and horror of her capture still working its way out of her, she had been able to turn around and hold him with her woman's strength, with her love, as he held her and sobbed out his losses to her. She had even cried with him.

As Gage settled her down into the flowery couch, lying across his lap, leaning back against the arm, she sighed and nuzzled into his jaw. His arms came around her, strong and protective. Alexa could feel his love pouring out of him, melting through her, healing her. In the last two months, there had been ups and downs for her, but she was getting used to it, seeing how her psyche was slowly healing from the trauma she'd sustained within that cave.

Becka had been a wonderful therapist and was becoming a loyal friend as well. She and Gage were like bookends, holding and supporting Alexa when a memory, a flashback, would slam into her, rendering her incapable of anything but an emotional reaction. It was then that Tal or Matt would call Gage from his office.

He'd come, quietly shut the door to Alexa's office, hold her, and listen to her fears, her anxieties, her rage. It was his calm, stable demeanor and his endless patience that allowed her to work through those crises.

"Looks kinda pretty in here," Gage murmured, settling Alexa against him. He looked around at the frilly, lacy, feminine curtains at the front windows, which allowed plenty of light to cascade into the large room. The stained glass lamps were on, their blended colors glowing like out-of-season Christmas bulbs. The large maple sideboard was in the other room, along with his mother's beautiful antique oak table. It warmed Gage's heart like nothing else, because it was as if his parents were there with him, if only in spirit.

This was a dream come true for Gage. He still couldn't believe that the warm, effervescent, generous woman in his arms, who worked tirelessly at Artemis, was his. He loved her dedication to helping others, and he would support her by being the quiet shadow standing behind her. She was like Tal and Matt and their parents—all driven to serve. It was in their blood, in their family, and he'd discovered that the care they had for humanity was stunning. The family might have made its fortune from shipping around the globe, but a billion dollars each year was poured into the Delos infrastructure. And now, with Artemis online and most of the security teams hired, the assembling of a small army of men and women contractors who would serve and protect Delos's charities was becoming a reality.

As Alexa surrendered to him, her hand resting on his chest, quiet and soft within his embrace, he rested his jaw against her hair. Artemis, under Tal's capable leadership and direction, was already putting teams out in the field. The charities didn't all need help, just those in second- and third-world countries. Alexa's Safe House division, however, often needed one or two operators going in undercover, most often to seek out a foreign-national father who had stolen his child from an American mother. He hadn't realized just how pervasive this problem was until now.

Alexa threw herself into her work and had created a huge global database of domestic abuse and sex-trafficking cases. Wyatt Lockwood was working with six other software designers on special software to reveal and hunt down slavers in every country where they existed. Toward that end, he and Matt were hiring special units of men and women who would go after these predators. They even had the quiet backing of the U.S. government. In fact, Tal and Alexa were flying to a secret meeting of thirty-five countries, two days from now. They would be gathering in Paris, France, to lay down a new foundation to stop the kidnapping of children and women and keep them out of the nightmare world of sex slavery.

Gage was proud of Alexa's efforts. She was changing the face of this terrible issue because of what had happened to her. She was turning her own wounding into a proactive stance so that others could heal in turn. Or be rescued out of such an awful circumstance, returned to their families.

From today forward, they had a house to call their own. They would live here and love here together. He leaned back now, sliding his hand gently down her spine and across her hips, loving Alexa.

"Dreams do come true," he told her, a catch in his voice, barely opening his eyes to see her expression. "Broken dreams can be mended and glued back together. I never thought they could, but now, I know better."

Alexa stirred, leaning back just enough to catch his smoldering blue gaze. A tender smile pulled at her lips. Lifting her hand, she slid her fingers across the hard line of his jaw. "Yes, they do. And *you* are my dream come true . . ."

THE END

Don't miss Lindsay McKenna's next DELOS series novella and novel,

Secret Dream, 1B, novella epilogue to Nowhere to Hide

And

Hold On, Book 5

Available from Lindsay McKenna and Blue Turtle Publishing and wherever you buy eBooks!

Turn the page for a sneak peek of *Hold On*!

Excerpt from

Hold On

Book 5 Delos Series

BY THE THIRD day at the Kabul, Afghanistan orphanage, Army Sergeant Beau Gardner had been pleased to observe that Callie was less grumpy toward him. Between his rounds with Matt inside and outside the orphanage, he'd volunteered to help change diapers at the diaper station. He'd told Maggie, the owner of the charity, that he was good with babies and that if she wanted, he'd feed, bathe and diaper them if she wanted.

Well! She jumped at his offer and he found himself in what they called "the baby room" when he wasn't on his security walks. And by now, he was used to the rhythm of the busy, overcrowded orphanage.

Beau was dealing with a three-month-old baby girl as her nine-year-old sister, Aliya, stood nearby looking on. She watched as he placed her tiny sister on the soft white blanket spread across the table where diapers were changed. He was busy talking to Aliya in Pashto, drawing her out, making her feel comfortable in his presence as he unpinned the soft cotton diaper from the gurgling baby girl. He smiled down at the little one, her green eyes wide with wonder as he gently removed the dirty diaper, dropping it in a nearby bucket of water and bleach. He'd also volunteered to clean dirty diapers and put them in the aging washing machine at the back of the orphanage, afterward.

Callie McKinley peeked in through the open door, her attention caught by the low, soft conversation between Beau and nine-year-old Aliyah. It seemed impossible that a man of his height and size could move so delicately as he slipped a fresh diaper beneath the baby's bottom. She had to admit it, just watching him made her heart turn over with emotions she hadn't felt for a long time.

Beau was truly a sight, she had to admit, with his tall, broad shoulders, his Kevlar vest over his long-sleeved blue T-Shirt. His jeans fit his body to perfection and Callie could no longer ignore it. But it was Beau's low, crooning voice in that southern drawl of his that mesmerized both her and the baby. He was a Delta Force operator, a badass, yet he expertly pinned each side of the infant's diaper into place with safety pins. He made sure her little crocheted booties were snug on each of her waving feet, brushed her black hair aside from her round face with his spare, calloused fingers.

"Are you done?" she now asked, coming into the room. Callie leaned over, giving Aliya a warm hug.

"Just about," Beau murmured. He rearranged the baby's wool pullover. "Cute little thing, isn't she?" and slid one hand beneath the baby's tiny neck and the other beneath her buttocks, lifting her up and handing her over to Callie.

"She's adorable," Callie admitted, gently taking the baby. "I'm ready to bottle feed her, now."

Nodding, Beau said, "She's all yours. I've got diapers to rinse out," and he grinned, leaning down and picking up the tall plastic bucket filled to the brim with wet, dirty diapers.

Callie laid the baby against her shoulder, patting her back gently. "You've done this a time or two, haven't you?"

"Told you before," Beau said, smiling broadly, "I have two younger brothers, and my Ma put me to work as soon as I could handle a diaper, clean it, and replace it on my baby brothers. It wasn't lost on her that I was good at it," and he chuckled, moving past her and heading down the hall toward the laundry room.

Callie frowned, sliding her hand comfortingly along the baby's back. Ever since she'd snapped at him a few days ago, he'd acted as if she no longer existed. No more hungry, longing looks in her direction from him. No more flirting with her. Yet, Beau had made himself quite indispensable around here, just like Matt Culver, another Delta Force sergeant, had. They were good men and brave soldiers, and they cared about this place and the kids. It wasn't a game to them, although Callie didn't fool herself. Matt was here because he was attracted to Dara. Her sister was definitely falling for the Delta Force sergeant, too—she could see it. And Beau had showed up to court her.

And now, Callie couldn't still her curiosity about Beau Gardner. Any guy who could happily change a diaper got her attention!

He had just finished placing the diapers in the washer when Beau felt someone enter the laundry room behind him. He turned, seeing Callie standing there, frowning at him, confusion in her expression.

"What?" he teased. "Got another diaper job for me?" he asked as he straightened, turning on the machine.

"Are you doing anything tonight after we get back to Bagram?" she surprised him by asking.

At a momentary loss, Beau said, "No. Why?" He watched her move nervously from one foot to another. He stood there, hands at his sides, holding her gaze.

"Would you like to join me for some beer and pizza tonight?"

Well, hell, you could have knocked him over with a feather! Beau remained serious, trying not to let the surprise show in his face. He thought for sure after Callie had chewed him out days earlier, she wanted NOTHING to do with him. EVER. "Sure, I'd like that. Do you have a favorite place?"

The Books of Delos

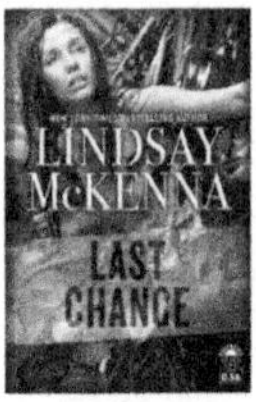

Title: ***Last Chance*** (Prologue)
Publish Date: July 15, 2015
Learn more at:
delos.lindsaymckenna.com/last-chance

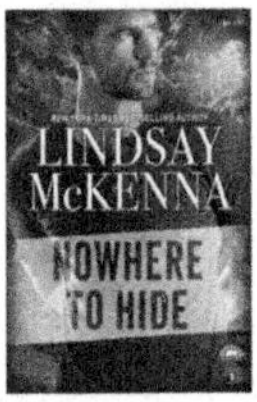

Title: ***Nowhere to Hide***
Publish Date: October 13, 2015
Learn more at:
delos.lindsaymckenna.com/nowhere-to-hide

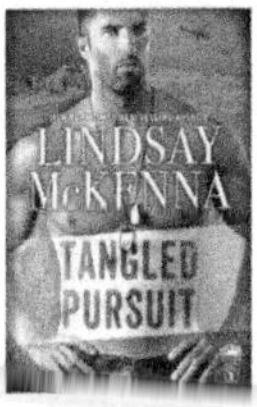

Title: ***Tangled Pursuit***
Publish Date: November 11, 2015
Learn more at:
delos.lindsaymckenna.com/tangled-pursuit

Title: ***Forged in Fire***
Publish Date: December 3, 2015
Learn more at:
delos.lindsaymckenna.com/forged-in-fire

Title: ***Broken Dreams***
Publish Date: January 2, 2016
Learn more at:
delos.lindsaymckenna.com/broken-dreams

Everything Delos!

Newsletter
Please sign up for my free quarterly newsletter on the front page of my official Lindsay McKenna website at lindsaymckenna.com. The newsletter will have exclusive information about my books, publishing schedule, giveaways, exclusive cover peeks, and more.

Delos Series Website
Be sure to drop by the website dedicated to the Delos series at delos.lindsaymckenna.com. There will be new articles on characters, publishing schedule and information about each book written by Lindsay.

Quote Books
I love how the Internet has evolved. I had great fun create "quote books with text" which reminded me of an old fashioned comic book…lots of great color photos and a little text, which forms a "book" that tells you, the reader, a story. Let me know if you like these quote books because I think it's a great way to add extra enjoyment with this series! Just go to my Delos Series website delos.lindsaymckenna.com, which features the books in the series.

The individual downloadable quote books are located on the corresponding book pages. Please share with your reader friends!

Follow the history of Delos:
The video quote book will lead you through the history of how and why Delos was formed. You can also download the quote book as a PDF.

The Culver Family History
The history of the Culver Family, featuring Robert and Dilara Culver, and their children, Tal, Matt and Alexa will be available as a downloadable video or PDF quote book.

***Nowhere to Hide*, Book 1, Delos Series, October 13, 2015**
This quote book will lead you through Lia Cassidy's challenges in Costa Rica and hunky Cav Jordan, ex-SEAL. Download the book and enjoy more of the story.

***Tangled Pursuit*, Book 2, Delos Series, November 11, 2015**
This quote book will introduce you to Tal Culver and her Texas badass SEAL warrior who doesn't take "no" for an answer.

***Forged in Fire*, Book 3, Delos Series, December 3, 2015**

This quote book will introduce you to Army Sergeant Matt Culver, Delta Force operator and Dr. Dara McKinley.

***Broken Dreams*, Book 4, Delos Series, January 2, 2016**

This quote book will introduce you to Captain Alexa Culver and Marine Sergeant Gage Hunter, sniper, USMC.